PRAISE FOR
WENDY MARKHAM'S
NOVELS

Bride Meets Groom

"Contemporary fans will love this."
—*Rendezvous*

"Romance fans will enjoy this lighthearted romp."
—*Affaire de Coeur*

"A heartfelt love story . . . sexy and funny."
—**TheRomanceReadersConnection.com**

Hello, It's Me

"A sweet romance for hopeless romantics."
—*Booklist*

"Touching and humorous . . . Markham's novel will keep you glued to the page."
—*Romantic Times BOOKclub Magazine*

more...

Once Upon a Blind Date

The Nine Month Plan

Love,
Suburban
Style

Books by Wendy Markham

The Nine Month Plan
Once Upon a Blind Date
Hello, It's Me
Bride Needs Groom
Love, Suburban Style

Love, Suburban Style

Wendy Markham

WARNER
FOREVER

NEW YORK   BOSTON

Copyright © 2007 by Wendy Corsi Staub

Cover design by Diane Luger
Cover photo by Herman Estevez
Book design by Giorgetta Bell McRee

Warner Forever is an imprint of Warner Books, Inc.

Warner Forever is a trademark of Time Warner Inc. or an affiliated company. Used under license by Hachette Book Group USA, which is not affiliated with Time Warner Inc.

Warner Forever
Hachette Book Group USA
237 Park Avenue
New York, NY 10169
Visit our Web site at www.HachetteBookGroupUSA.com

Printed in the United States of America

First Printing: July 2007

10 9 8 7 6 5 4 3 2 1

Dedicated in loving memory of our cousin,
Laurie Steinberg (June 1954–March 2006),
and her mom, Aunt Shirley Staub
(February 1926–May 2006).
And in celebration of the family they left behind:
Don, Michael, Mitchell, and Beth; Tom, Felicia,
Scott, and Suzanne.

And, as always, for my own:
Brody, Morgan, and Mark.

Acknowledgments

With gratitude to my editor, Karen Kosztolnyik, and the staff at Warner Books; my agents, Laura Blake Peterson, Holly Frederick, and the staff at Curtis Brown, Ltd; my publicists, Nancy Berland, Elizabeth Middaugh, Kim Miller, and the staff at Nancy Berland Public Relations; Pam Nelson and the staff at Levy Home Entertainment; and to Kyle Cadley, never a Fancy Mom, always a friend.

Prologue

I brought supplies." Geoffrey Lange thrusts a plastic shopping bag into Astor Hudson's hands the moment she opens the apartment door.

"What kind of supplies?"

"Let me get past this obstacle course, and I'll show you." He steps first over the threshold, then over her sleeping cat, Chita Rivera, and finally over the heaping plastic basket of unfolded clean clothes Astor carried up from the basement laundry room an hour earlier.

She dropped it just inside the door and rushed to answer the ringing telephone.

Now she really wishes she hadn't.

She was having such a great day so far—especially for a Monday—before the call came.

The June sun has finally broken out after three straight days of cold rain, pleasantly warm, but not yet hot, on her shoulders during her early-morning run in Central Park. Cosette, her fifteen-year-old daughter, actually smiled and didn't protest too vigorously when Astor insisted on kissing her good-bye before school. She then ran into her friend Melinda from 3C in the laundry room, and they grabbed a quick, gossipy latte together at the Starbucks on the corner while their washers were sudsing and spinning.

Then came the call . . .

Which she relayed tearfully, word for word, in a subsequent IM to her best friend Geoffrey, who fortuitously happened to be online when she signed on to Google Deeanna Drennan. *Once again, an upcoming young actress has usurped Astor for a lead role.* This time, it was for an upcoming Broadway revival of *Brigadoon*.

Face it. You're over the hill.

She has to remind herself of that, because Geoffrey isn't going to be the one to say it. Being a loyal, loving sort, he rushed right up Broadway from his apartment eight blocks away to lend an ear, a shoulder—and supplies, no less.

This is getting to be a regular ritual.

Geoffrey hugs her hard against his brick wall of a chest and shoulders—he's been hitting the gym religiously.

I should have been, too. Maybe then I'd still be getting cast.

Aloud, she says, "I'll live."

"But you so deserved it. You totally look the part."

"I don't know . . . Fiona is supposed to be in her early twenties."

"So? You could be in your teens."

She snorts at that. Though with Astor's petite build, long auburn ringlets, and big green eyes, her agent often assures her that she looks at least a decade younger than her age—which is thirty-four.

"And anyway, no twenty-year-old's voice has the maturity and color yours does," Geoffrey goes on. "You were robbed."

"I knew you'd say that."

"Deeanna Drennan—whoever she is—won't hold a candle to you, honey."

"I knew you'd say that, too."

"That's why I'm here."

"You're right. You're a good friend, Geoff."

"I am a good friend. Which reminds me . . . I promised my friend Andrew in L.A. that I'd try and find him a place to live."

"In L.A.?"

"No! Here in New York, of course. He's sick of getting typecast as a plus-sized, effeminate gay man—which he just so happens to be—so he's going to try auditioning here for a change. Know of anyone who wants to sublet their apartment?"

"I'll ask around." Shifting gears, she asks, "What 'supplies' did you bring?"

"Whatever I could buy at the Duane Reade on Columbus Avenue on such short notice, to help you get over this," he replies, and strides across the living room. "It's positively funereal in here. For God's sake, let there be light."

He raises the shades on the two windows to usher in the morning sun. Thanks to the apartment's southeastern exposure, the place brightens instantly.

"There, that's better, isn't it? I mean, you're not a vampire . . . though your daughter is starting to look like one if you don't mind my saying."

"I told her the same thing just yesterday. I'm sure it's just a phase."

Cosette, who until recently shared her mother's all-American wholesome beauty, dyed her brown hair jet-black—without permission—and has taken to wearing thick, dark eye makeup and a somber wardrobe utterly devoid of color.

"No offense, but she looks like she's channeling Morticia Addams," Geoffrey says.

"Which is particularly interesting because my real name was Addams. Two D's and everything."

Geoffrey's eyes widen at that news. "You're kidding. What was your first name?"

"Margaret. But I went by Meg."

"Why did I never know that after all these years?"

"You never asked."

She and Geoffrey have been friends ever since they were both in *Les Miserables* together. Astor played Cosette; Geoffrey was the understudy for Marius.

"I never thought to ask. Does that mean I'm completely self-centered?"

She grins. "Not completely."

"So Meg Addams?" Geoffrey says thoughtfully, looking her over. "That's your name?"

"*Was.*" She created the stage name "Astor Hudson" the moment she graduated from high school, and never looked back.

"Meg Addams sounds so . . . small-town."

"She was small-town."

"I thought you grew up in the New York suburbs."

"I did. But Glenhaven Park is way up there in Westchester County. It might be less than fifty miles north of Manhattan, but it's more small-town than suburbia."

"What, no strip malls? No minimarts? No eight-lane, five-way intersections?" asks Geoffrey, who grew up in Jersey.

"None at all. Big old Victorian houses, tons of tall shade trees, dirt roads, shops on Main Street where everybody knows your name . . ." Astor sighs.

"You suddenly look homesick."

"I suddenly am."

Though, perhaps not so suddenly.

Lately, she's found herself thinking a lot about her hometown. Glenhaven Park is less than an hour's ride on the Metro-North commuter line, but it might as well be in the Midwest for as often as she's been back there in the past decade. She's an only child, and her aging parents, who had her late in life, retired to a golf community on the South Carolina coast the minute she left home.

"I should take a ride up there some weekend," she tells Geoffrey a bit wistfully. "Want to come?"

"Honey, you know I'm allergic to suburbia. Charming small towns included." He gestures at the shopping bag. "Go ahead, unload the provisions."

Smiling, Astor begins removing the contents one by one and setting them on the coffee table.

The table's surface was already cluttered with three days' worth of mail and newspapers, a bag containing the toilet paper she bought on Friday, and Cosette's forgotten—or more likely hastily discarded—bag lunch: all heaped in the shadow of Astor's proudly displayed Tony Award with its comedy and tragedy masks etched on the mounted circular medallion.

"Entenmann's chocolate doughnuts, Kleenex, a DVD of . . . *Sunset Boulevard*?" she reads from the label.

"The movie with Gloria Swanson, not the Andrew Lloyd Webber musical. But I thought it was still appropriate. *All About Eve* would have been more fitting, but they didn't have it."

"It's a drugstore. I can't believe they had *Sunset Boulevard*."

"Bargain DVD bin." He shrugs.

Meg isn't sure she wants to immerse herself in the tragic tale of a faded star desperate to make a comeback, but Geoffrey means well. And anyway, it is somewhat fitting.

"Let's see what else you brought," she says, going back to the goodies. "A bag of Lays barbecue chips, yum . . . and a package of . . . stool softener?"

"Oops, that's for me," Geoffrey interjects, plucking the box from the pile and stashing it in the pocket of his vintage bowling shirt.

"And a bottle of Grey Goose vodka—you didn't get this at Duane Reade . . . and it's only half-full."

"That came from my liquor cabinet. I thought you'd need to drown your sorrows."

"It's only"—she checks her watch—"ten-forty in the morning."

"We'll make bloody Marys."

"I don't have tomato juice or horseradish or—what else goes in a bloody Mary? Celery?"

"Never mind, we'll drink it straight. Let's get a couple of glasses. You've got ice, right?"

"That's all right . . . I'm waiting for Laura to call me back about another audition, and I need to keep a clear head."

"Then I'll drink for both of us," Geoffrey decides, poised in the kitchen doorway. "Is the bag empty?"

Astor peers inside. "Just this—it's yours, too." She proffers a package of condoms.

"Oh, no, those are for you, honey."

"For what?"

"That you even have to ask that makes me sad."

Geoffrey shakes his head. "How long has it been since you—"

"Not that long." She pauses. "Unless you think six months qualifies as—"

"You poor thing." Geoffrey shakes his head. "We've got to find you a man."

"Geoffrey! *Not* finding a man is the whole point, remember? You were there when I made my New Year's resolution."

They were at a rooftop party together in Hell's Kitchen, sharing a bottle of Veuve Clicquot and their respective sorrows. Just blocks from the Times Square melee, they could hear the chaos from their perch, close but not in view. They chose not to go downstairs to the host's apartment to watch the ball drop on television with everyone else at midnight.

That was mainly because neither of them had anyone but each other to kiss.

Geoffrey's new—and destined to be short-lived—flame, Elliot, was performing in a Rodgers and Hart review on a cruise ship somewhere in the Caribbean. Astor's most recent flame, Ken, was at the party with *his* current flame, a walking cliché in a short skirt, plunging neckline, and stilettos.

Astor shouldn't have been surprised when Ken broke her heart after a seven-month, too-good-to-be-true relationship.

She's always been a passionate, impulsive soul. That comes in handy in her business; not so much in matters of the heart. Every time she's ever met someone new and promising—despite her best intention not to get involved—she eventually lets down her guard, falls hard—and gets hurt.

She's been there, done that, more times than she cares

to count, in a pattern that began with her ex-husband and ended—hopefully for good—with Ken.

That's why it's crucial to avoid the kinds of men to whom she might find herself attracted. She's getting too old and too emotionally exhausted to go through another heartbreak.

"Give it up already, Astor," Geoffrey is saying. "I mean, come on. Who keeps their New Year's resolution?"

"Not you."

Geoffrey's was to cut up all his credit cards and live within his means. It lasted almost forty-eight hours. Then he stumbled across a January White Sale, and it was all over.

"At least my resolution was reasonable in the first place," Geoffrey tells her.

"So was mine."

"Giving up men?"

"Not forever. And not all men. Just the ones I might fall in love with. I can still date."

"Isn't falling in love the point of dating?"

"No! At least, not for me. Not anymore."

"Then why don't you place an ad in the personals? Single white female seeks swarthy, neurotic, unemployed—"

The ringing telephone mercifully interrupts him.

"That's Laura."

"Good luck!" Geoffrey calls after her as she goes to answer it in the bedroom.

She's going to need more than luck, because for the second time today, Astor Hudson finds herself on the receiving end of a dreaded phone call.

When she emerges from the bedroom, Geoffrey looks up from the vodka he's pouring.

Seeing the look on her face, he lowers the bottle. "What is it, honey?"

She just shakes her head, still speechless.

"Oh my God, you're scaring me. Is someone dead?"

"Not yet," she says when she finds her voice. "But I swear, when I get my hands on my daughter . . ."

"What's wrong?"

"That was the headmistress of Cosette's school. She was just expelled for having a gun in her backpack."

Chapter

1

"Station stop: Glenhaven Park," a robotic voice announces as the words flash in red on the electronic scroll overhead.

Glancing out the window at the vaguely familiar wooded countryside, Meg tucks today's *New York Post* into her black leather tote bag and nudges her daughter in the seat beside her. "Come on, Cosette, put that away, we're almost there."

Cosette's pencil-darkened brows furrow and her liner-blackened eyes refuse to budge from the open copy of *Rolling Stone* in her hands.

Oh. She's plugged into her iPod.

Meg reaches out and plucks a tiny earphone from Cosette's right ear.

"Hey!"

"We're almost there."

Cosette shrugs. "You go. I'll just ride to the end of the line and meet you on the way back down to the city."

"You're not doing that."

"Why not?"

"Look, you can make this as difficult for me as you possibly can, or you can cooperate. Either way, we're getting off this train in two minutes, and if I have to drag you by your hair, believe me, I will."

Of course, she won't. She's never laid a hand on Cosette in her life; she won't start now.

Anyway, Cosette could—if she dared—shake her off like a pesky bug. Her daughter is a good three inches taller than Meg's five-four, and probably weighs more, too. Not that Cosette has an ounce of fat on her black-garbed frame. But Meg, normally slender, is now verging on skinny.

She hasn't eaten much of anything—including the chips and doughnuts Geoffrey brought—all week, since Monday.

The day she lost the part to Deeanna Drennan.

The day Cosette got kicked out of school.

The day Astor Hudson died, and Meg Addams was reborn.

Now it's a gorgeous Saturday morning on the cusp of summer, and the train is chugging to a stop in Glenhaven Park at last.

At last. Yes . . .

The ride up from Grand Central was only an hour; but Meg realizes now, as she glimpses the soaring white steeple of the First Presbyterian Church on the green, that she's been waiting much, much longer than that to come home.

Home?

The word catches her off guard.

Glenhaven Park hasn't been home since her parents sold the family's two-story brick Tudor on North Street.

But suddenly, this self-contained village in the northern reaches of Westchester County feels more like home than

Meg's two-bedroom, rent-controlled Upper West Side apartment has in the dozen years since she moved in.

Over at 31 Boxwood Street, a ladder is propped against a three-story home with a mansard roof, wraparound porch, and forty-six windows.

Sam Rooney knows all too well that there are forty-six of them. Not because he grew up in this house but because he counted the windows before he started scraping them back in the beginning of April.

He expected to have had that part done and the painting started by mid-May at the latest, but he was only able to work on them in sporadic weekend moments when the weather was dry and sunny. Weekdays were out entirely; even on his high school science teacher's schedule. Long gone are the days of blowing out of school on the heels of his students, arriving home shortly after the last bell.

Back then, he was teaching in Pelham, where they lived at the time. Sheryl was around to shuttle Ben and Katie from play dates to Brownies and Cub Scouts.

Those activities, which the kids retained after the move to Glenhaven Park, have long since given way to various engagements that are even more time-consuming: lessons, sports practices, tutoring, appointments with doctors, orthodontists—and, of course, child psychiatrists for both.

That's a must when you lose your mother suddenly and tragically . . . even now that it's been over four years.

Four years.

Sometimes, it feels like just yesterday that Sam was waking up next to Sheryl.

Other times, it feels as though it happened—as though *she* happened—in another lifetime, to somebody else.

But on this sun-drenched June Saturday, his thoughts aren't on his late wife or the life they used to have—they're on forty-six windows that need to be painstakingly primed before they can be painted.

The trim will be cranberry, to contrast with the varying shades of yellow on the clapboard, shingles, and gingerbread embellishment.

Last year, when Sam added to his home improvement agenda the insane task of painting the exterior of his recently inherited Queen Anne fixer-upper, he was actually amused that the color palettes read like a supermarket shopping list: from butter to lemon to mustard.

Now there's nothing amusing about anything remotely involving paint.

But today is dry and sunny and breezy, and he needs to get moving on this trim so that it's all finished before summer's humidity and afternoon thunderstorms descend.

He's halfway up the ladder with a full bucket of white primer when a bloodcurdling scream nearly causes him to topple backward.

Whoa!

It didn't come from either of his kids—he dropped twelve-year-old Katie at piano lessons ten minutes ago, and fifteen-year-old Ben couldn't emit a high-pitched scream if he tried; his voice is decidedly baritone these days.

No, it came—not surprisingly—from the house next door.

Sam maneuvers his lanky frame down the ladder, sets the bucket on the grass, and takes off running around this side of the house to the backyard.

Here we go again, he thinks as he sprints across the side

yard and crashes through the overgrown hedge on the property line—just in time to hear another screech and a loud bang.

The sound a door would make if, say, someone bolted through it, scared out of their mind, and slammed it shut behind them.

Terrific. The newest residents of the old Duckworth place—a nice young family from Brooklyn—haven't even moved in yet, and already it's starting.

"Station Stop . . . Glenhaven Park."

Snatching the magazine from Cosette's hands and ignoring her protest, Meg grabs her daughter's arm and escorts her off the train with a smattering of other riders.

The long, concrete platform looks exactly the same as it did the last time Meg was here. Only then, she was headed *to* New York . . . for good.

Or so she thought.

"This way." She leads the glowering Cosette along the platform, toward the stairs that rise to the enclosed station one story above the tracks.

From there, opposite flights of stairs descend back to ground level: the commuter parking lot and taxi stand on one side of the tracks, the main drag of the business district on the other.

"I can't believe I've never brought you here," Meg tells her daughter, as they descend to the street.

"I can't believe you're bringing me here at all—especially today, of all days," Cosette mutters.

Meg ignores her, just as for the past forty-eight hours, she ignored Cosette's pleas to let her keep her standing Saturday afternoon movie date with Jon, her boyfriend of

the past four months. Jon, who—as Meg just discovered—
is not a high school student at Fordham Prep in the Bronx,
as Cosette implied. No, he's a college sophomore at
Fordham *University* in the Bronx—and part of the reason
Cosette was expelled—just before finals, no less.

"You were *this close* to finishing the school year!" Meg
shoved her hand in her daughter's face, her thumb and
forefinger pressed together. "*This close!* Couldn't you have
hung in there for another two weeks without getting yourself into trouble?"

"It wasn't even a real gun," was Cosette's maddening
reply.

"You didn't bother to tell that to the kids you threatened
with it, did you?"

"What would have been the point of that?"

"What was the point of any of this?"

"It wasn't my fault. I'm not the one who goes around
harassing people because of how they look. *They* should
have been kicked out of school, not me."

Privately, Meg happens to agree with her daughter on
that count—at least, that the school should also have a zero
tolerance policy against bullying.

If only she had known that a group of kids have been
tormenting Cosette at school lately. Kids who used to be
Cosette's friends, back when they were all on the soccer
team together. Meg knows their parents; in fact, knowing
their parents, she isn't particularly surprised by the kids'
behavior.

She herself was frequently cold-shouldered by the
cookie-cutter women she dubbed the "Fancy Moms" from
her first encounter with them. With their moneyed husbands, spectacular Central Park West apartments, and

tasteful designer wardrobes, they did little to conceal their contempt for a single working mom. Even if she *was* an accomplished Broadway actress. Meg knew they regarded her Tony Award with as much esteem as they would a "World's Best Mom" coffee mug—not that it ever mattered to her.

Well, not much.

And she certainly never let on to Cosette that she felt ostracized by the Fancy Moms.

Just as Cosette never told Meg what their mean-spirited little brats were doing to her.

Still, there was no excuse for how her daughter chose to handle the daily abuse when it threatened to go from verbal to physical.

After a couple of girls got their boyfriends to gang up on her after school last Friday, a shaken Cosette turned to Jon.

Not to her mother, or a teacher, or the principal.

No, she turned to her much-older boyfriend, who gave her the fake gun and told her to brandish it the next time anyone dared to bother her.

Bad advice.

"What do you think I should have done, then?" Cosette demanded. "Dyed my hair into a perfect blond pageboy, gone shopping at Talbots, and run for student council?"

How was Meg supposed to answer that?

Yes, life would be easier for Cosette if she were a conformist.

But you *weren't,* Meg reminded herself then—and again now, as she lands on Main Street, where she spent her formative years.

She can't help but remember how, bitten by the acting

bug her freshman year, she quickly gave up trying to fit in with the preppy crowd at school.

But I never threatened anyone with a gun.

Her daughter's offense is so heinous that Meg wasn't even sure where to begin punishing her. Being grounded for a month is a good start. And Cosette seems to think this Saturday afternoon jaunt to suburbia is a fate worse than that.

But maybe she'll come around.

After all, Glenhaven Park is the quintessential all-American small town, and it looks particularly appealing on this beautiful summer day. Everywhere you look, flags are flapping in the slight breeze. The grass and shrubs and trees are verdant and lush. Brilliant blooms spill from window boxes and hanging pots.

"Well?" Meg asks her daughter as they pause on the sidewalk. "What do you think?"

Cosette glances around glumly.

Meg follows her gaze, taking in the broad, leafy green that stretches for three blocks. A brick path meanders the length of the park, past clusters of wrought-iron benches and tall lampposts. In the center, surrounded by a bed of pink and purple annuals, is the bronze statue dedicated to the eleven local soldiers who died on D-day.

The road on either side of the green is lined with tree-shaded sidewalks, diagonal parking spaces, and nineteenth-century architecture.

On this, the northern end: a row of mom-and-pop shops and businesses that have been there for years. The quaint pastel storefronts appear to be in surprisingly good repair for their age—better repair, in fact, than they were back when Meg lived here.

At the southern end of the green, the street becomes more residential, lined with stately nineteenth-century relics Meg recognizes from her childhood.

There's her friend Andrea's old home, a classic Victorian with multiple turrets and a wraparound gingerbread porch. It used to be white with black shutters; now it's a bona fide painted lady, clapboard and trim enhanced by complementary vintage shades of green and gold.

Next door to that is the looming stone mansion where Miss Oster, the high school Latin teacher, lived alone with a half dozen cats . . .

And across the green, the three-story monstrosity once home to the Callahans, who had sixteen redheaded freckle-faced kids and assorted pets. There's no one hanging out any of the windows or dangling from tree branches out front, and the lawn is no longer covered with bikes, scooters, and wagons. It's probably safe to assume that the Callahans have all grown up and moved on.

"I wonder if anyone I know still lives around here," Meg muses.

In the split second after she poses that mostly rhetorical question, mostly to herself since Cosette doesn't appear the least bit engaged, Meg spies a familiar figure strolling toward them along the sidewalk.

"I don't believe it!" she exclaims, clutching Cosette's sleeve—long, and black, despite the midday heat.

"I don't, either. There's not even a Starbucks around here," Cosette grumbles.

"No, that's Krissy . . . Krissy!" Meg calls and waves at the woman.

Hmm. Maybe it isn't Krissy after all; she doesn't wave

back, nor does she even look up from the cell phone or BlackBerry or whatever it is that's poised in her hand.

Is it Krissy? Krissy Rosenkrantz was Meg's first kindergarten friend, and her partner-in-crime right up through graduation. When they signed each other's yearbooks, they wrote about all the things they were going to do together, like get tattoos and travel through Europe, and they prefaced their signatures with BFA—*Best Friends Always*—and YFF—*Your Friend Forever.*

Meg's last memory of Krissy Rosenkrantz is of her standing by her father's packed Jeep on the stifling August morning she left for Bennington College, with a heartfelt promise to visit Meg in New York over Columbus Day weekend.

Columbus Day came and went, Thanksgiving came and went, the years came and went, and Meg never saw Krissy Rosenkrantz again . . .

Until now.

Or is it really her?

Most of her face is obscured by large brown sunglasses, but there's something about her that seems so familiar . . .

"Krissy?" Meg calls again, waving both her arms over her head this time to get her attention.

"Mom, shh! Stop making such a spectacle. What are you doing?"

"I could swear that's an old friend of—yes, it *is* her!" Meg recognizes the distinct motion with which the woman tosses her thick, tawny hair over her shoulder as she pockets her electronic device.

"You're Krissy Rosenkrantz," she says triumphantly, sidestepping right into the woman's path.

The woman looks up, startled, her perfectly arched

brows rising above the frame of her glasses . . . then breaks into a grin.

"Meg?"

"I knew that was you!" Meg hugs her. "Though when you didn't answer me when I kept calling you, I did wonder for a minute."

Krissy smells like expensive perfume. She's crisply dressed all in white: cool linen pantsuit, designer pocketbook, leather sandals with heels. As Meg releases her she can't help but wonder if she's left a newsprint smudge on her old friend's back.

"I'm sorry . . . I didn't even hear you! Probably because nobody's called me 'Krissy' in ages! I go by Kris, now . . . and it's not Rosenkrantz, it's Holmes."

"You're married?"

"Twice. And divorced. Twice. But I kept my first husband's name—even when I married the second. I wanted it to be the same as my son's. How about you? Are you married?"

No. But I didn't even keep my own name—first or last, Meg wants to tell her.

No need to get into the whole Astor Hudson saga here, though. Especially now that she's all but decided to give up everything about that life—not just the name, but everything that goes with it: both the stage career and the city.

It's time to open a new chapter. She'll miss the creative outlet of performing, but she hasn't craved the spotlight in years—not like she did in the early days. She's achieved what she set out to do; she is—no, *was*—a genuine star.

And now the star is aging, fading; her voice is mature, but so are her face, her body, her mind. Deeanna Drennan was a blessing in disguise once the dust settled. Losing the part—and accepting that her ingenue days are long over—allowed Meg to realize that she doesn't need a stage career to fulfill her anymore.

What she needs at this stage in her life is to move on to something new.

Perhaps *something old* is more apt.

Cosette doesn't know about any of it yet. As far as she's concerned, this jaunt up the Metro-North tracks to Westchester County is simply a pleasant—for Meg, anyway, if unpleasant for Cosette—way to spend a summer Saturday afternoon.

Meg isn't going to tell her daughter anything more until she's certain what their next move will be—and when it will happen.

All she knows at this point is that she's going to be settled in a new life, with Cosette, before the school year resumes in September.

Glenhaven Park is the natural place to commence the search for a new home . . . since it once *was* home. And still feels like it . . . at least, so far.

"I'm still Meg Addams," she replies in answer to Krissy's—rather, Kris's—question.

Cosette rolls her eyes at that, undoubtedly thinking, *Still? You haven't been Meg Addams since you left this place behind.* At least she doesn't say it.

"And who is this lovely young lady?" Kris asks, turning to look at her.

"This is my daughter, Cosette."

Who is looking like anything but a lovely young lady. Cosette's unnaturally black hair has been straightened and shorn so that it falls past her shoulders in a vaguely shaggy nonstyle. Her eye makeup is Halloween-thick and her once rosy, healthy complexion is masked beneath a layer of ivory pancake base. Any curves she possesses are camouflaged beneath a boxy, long-sleeved black T-shirt and black jeans, and she's wearing black boots—yes, *boots*—in June.

"It's nice to meet you, Cosette." With a jangling of chunky gold bracelets, Kris stretches a manicured hand toward Meg's daughter.

Meg wonders if she's remembering that she, like Meg, was also a nonconformist at Cosette's age. Though their most extreme physical deviation was to triple-pierce each other's earlobes using a threaded sewing needle, an ice cube, and a potato.

Meg still has the battle scars to show for it, though these days, she rarely wears six earrings at once. And a quick glance at Krissy's lobes reveal only a pair of tasteful gold studs.

"It's nice to meet you, too," Cosette is saying, politely extending her own black-polished fingertips to shake hands.

Meg heaves an inner sigh of relief that at least the good manners she worked so hard to instill didn't go the way of Cosette's auburn ringlets and wholesome prettiness.

Kris turns back to Meg. "So what are you doing here in town, and when did you get back?"

"About two minutes ago. We just stepped off the train."

"From the city? You're still in New York? Last I knew, you were on Broadway. Literally."

Meg raises an eyebrow, surprised, somehow, that news of her stage career has made it back to her hometown. Then again, it's not as if it's all that far away from the city—and perhaps not the cultural morass she recalls.

"How did you know that?"

"Mr. Dreyfus talks about you all the time, about you having success on Broadway," Kris tells her. "I think he takes personal credit for your success."

Meg smiles. Mr. Dreyfus is her former high school drama teacher. "He was definitely responsible for getting me started."

After all, it was Mr. Dreyfus who believed in her from the start. He even cast her, as a freshman, as the lead in the all-school musical—causing an immediate scandal, particularly among the senior divas.

"Is he still teaching at the high school?"

"Sure is. Plus he directs a drama program for teenagers through the town's recreation board. Do you realize he's only ten years older than we are? The teachers all seemed so old back then."

"Most of them really were," Meg recalls, aware of Cosette shifting her weight, bored. "Are a lot of them still there?"

"None of them, except Mr. Dreyfus."

"What about our old friends? Who else is still around?"

"Just me, really. And 'old' is right."

"Oh, come on, you look exactly the same. And so"— Meg sweeps an arm to indicate Main Street—"does this place."

"You think?" Kris shakes her head. "You haven't taken a close look yet, have you?"

"Not yet . . . why?"

"Just . . . trust me, Meg, nothing stays the same. Including me. So, are you married, or . . . ?" With an eye on Cosette, Kris tactfully trails off.

"Divorced," Meg says briefly.

No need to go into the gory details—and not just because Cosette is here. She rarely discusses her ex-husband. In fact, she had known Geoffrey a few years before she even got around to telling him the truth about her ex . . . and she did so only because it would have been awkward not to, under the circumstances.

They were standing on line at Regal Cinemas on Fourteenth Street at the time. Normally Geoffrey pooh-poohed mainstream movies, but the indie film he wanted to see was sold out, so he suggested they catch the new summer blockbuster "starring that hot action movie guy."

Who happened to be none other than Calvin.

"How could you not have told me that you were married to *him*?" Geoffrey asked when he managed to recover from his fake faint.

"Trust me, it's not something I like to think about. The only good thing that came out of that marriage was Cosette. Whom, by the way, he has never even been interested in meeting."

Geoffrey's jaw dropped. "He's never met his own daughter?"

"He walked out when I was eight months pregnant and never looked back."

That was before Calvin was a big star, but he was already on his way.

The only contact Meg has had from him in the last fifteen years is the sizeable alimony and child support check that arrives monthly like clockwork from his West Coast lawyer's office.

But without him, there would have been no Cosette, and for that, Meg is grateful. She held her breath as Cosette grew older, but her daughter embodies none of her father's less-than-admirable characteristics—except, perhaps, for his moodiness. But then, he's an actor; most actors are moody.

Cosette, for that matter, could be an actress. She's a natural onstage, and performed in a few professional musical productions when she was younger. With her father's acting talent and her mother's voice, she'll be able to go far, if she chooses to pursue that route someday. But Meg pulled her back when she realized New York is just too cutthroat when it comes to child performers. She didn't want that for her daughter; Cosette's life has always been complex enough.

But maybe, she thinks hopefully, Cosette will want to get involved in the local theater once they move. *If* they move.

"I'm sorry to hear that," Kris is saying, and Meg snaps right back to the present. Oh. She's talking about the divorce.

She can't tell her old friend that she's better off without the jerk. Not with Cosette standing right here. She's been asking more frequently about her father, and Meg is determined not to bad-mouth him. But it's pretty hard to find anything remotely positive to say about a man who chooses not to acknowledge his own child, especially when that child isn't exactly oblivious to his absence in her life.

"So are you still acting, singing, dancing . . . all that good stuff?"

"I'm on a career hiatus at the moment, actually," Meg tells Kris, and feels Cosette tense up beside her.

For as many mother-daughter clashes as they've had since Cosette hit adolescence, Meg's daughter remains a staunch, proud supporter of her mother's work. She was outraged about the lost *Brigadoon* role and assured her mother that something much bigger and better must be right around the corner.

Meg has yet to tell her that *smaller*—but infinitely better is more what she has in mind at this point.

"What about you? What are you up to these days?" she asks Kris.

For Meg, who is a big believer in cosmic coincidence, the unexpected answer is a clear sign that her tentative new life plan is meant to become a reality.

"I'm in real estate," Kris says cheerfully. "I sell houses right here in Glenhaven Park."

Rounding the corner into the front yard, Sam immediately spies the source of the scream. Lori Delgado, soon-to-be-lady-of-the-house, is standing on the unkempt lawn. She's wearing exactly the same clothing as Sam: faded Levi's, a white T-shirt, and sneakers. Ah, the Saturday-in-suburbia homeowner uniform.

Unlike Sam, who's *Been Here, Done This* more times lately than he cares to count, she's wringing her hands and staring fearfully up at the gloomy Victorian house.

"What's the matter?" Sam saunters to a stop—knowing only too well what's the matter.

"This place is haunted!"

Yup, just as he suspected. She must have heard the rumors about the place, and now the legendary Duckworth ghost has already put in an appearance, courtesy of the power of suggestion and a vivid imagination. In broad daylight, no less. Usually the new owners wait until the wee hours, and well after they've settled in a bit, before they start seeing things.

Sam wonders wearily if he should feign surprise, as he did with the last two sets of new neighbors. Or should he just come right out and admit that he's well aware of the home's reputation?

Indeed, having grown up right next door, he's known all his life that the old Duckworth place is supposedly haunted. Neighborhood kids used to dare each other to walk up the steps on Halloween night—not that deaf old Mrs. Duckworth would have heard the doorbell, much less greeted them with mini Zagnuts and tiny boxes of Chiclets.

In fact, that was the whole point.

In retrospect, there was something purely all-American about having grown up on a street like this, with a house like that. And in retrospect, Sam figured out that the "haunted" rumors stemmed from the home's ramshackle appearance and classic Victorian architecture. With its broken shutters, untidy yard, and black wrought-iron fence, the Duckworth place exudes a delicious air of foreboding.

Which is why Sam, mired in skepticism, remains utterly unfazed by the string of recent events involving the place.

Now, he mildly addresses the new homeowner: "Haunted? Why do you say that?"

"Why? Because I just saw a ghost!" Lori Delgado blesses herself and murmurs something in fervent Spanish. "I just want to go home."

Sam wants to remind her that this *is* home—it's about to be, anyway—but is pretty certain she means home as in Brooklyn.

"Where are your husband and your kids?" Sam asks, looking around and seeing no evidence of the couple's ten- and twelve-year-old daughters or their SUV, which was parked on the driveway earlier.

"We left the girls with my mother, and Joey just went down to the hardware store. We were going to start working on the kitchen today." Lori bites her lower lip.

Sam nods. This place is even more of a fixer-upper than his.

Sure, the three-story house, with its mansard roof, fish-scale shingles, and elaborate original trim, has tremendous potential. But Agnes Duckworth, the spinster who moved in circa World War II and rarely emerged, was hardly a female Bob Vila. In all the years Sam lived here as a kid, he never once saw anyone do any kind of maintenance on the house next door.

Old Agnes passed away a good two years ago, and the house has since changed hands three times. Nobody stays long enough to do anything to it.

Sam is really hoping the Delgados will, though. Not so much for the neighborhood aesthetic, but for his daughter's sake.

"They've got two girls, Dad!" she announced excitedly. "And they're around my age, and really nice!"

Poor Katie is starved for female companionship. She lives with her father and brother, their only local relatives are Sheryl's widowed dad down in Larchmont and Sam's bachelor brother in Manhattan, and the neighborhood is full of boys.

"What, exactly, happened in there?" he asks Lori Delgado.

She shudders and describes, in her thick accent, how she was removing a switchplate in the kitchen when the light started turning on and off.

"You probably just did something to the wiring," Sam informs her. "Do you want me to take a look at it?"

"No," she says sharply. "It wasn't just that. The room got really cold, and I could feel that I wasn't alone. And when I turned around, I saw . . . something."

"What was it?"

"A person. Just standing there in the doorway, watching me."

"Was it a tiny, wrinkled woman with a pitch-black bun?" Sam asks with a grin, remembering his sporadic childhood glimpses of old Agnes Duckworth—

"Are you laughing at me?"

"No, of course not." He carefully straightens his mouth.

"I have no idea what the ghost looked like. I didn't stay long enough to see."

She shudders and hugs herself.

Sam refrains from telling her that it was probably her imagination. At this point, he doubts she's capable of glibly shaking off the trepidation and going back up the sagging steps on her merry way.

She turns to him. "Um . . . Sam, is it?"

When he nods, she asks, "Do you mind if I use your telephone to call Joey on his cell? Mine is in the house, and I'm not setting foot back in there. Ever!"

"*Ever?*" Sam echoes, and adds hopefully, "But . . . what about when you move in?"

"We aren't moving into a haunted house. I told Joey that this deal was too good to be true. I knew there was a reason this house cost over a couple hundred grand less than anything else in this neighborhood."

"Well, it's a fixer-upper," he points out, and she snorts.

Sam wonders if she's aware how many owners it's had since Agnes Duckworth died. No need to mention that now.

He has a feeling it won't make a difference, anyway. Lori's mind is obviously made up.

"Sure, you can use my phone."

Sam leads the way toward his own ramshackle Victorian next door.

So much for the nice new neighbors with daughters Katie's age.

Boy, is she going to be bummed when she finds out.

Chapter 2

It just sold again for *how* much?" Meg asks, thinking she must have heard wrong.

"The asking price was one point one. It went for one point two."

"Million."

"Right."

Meg curses under her breath, knowing Cosette can't hear her anyway. She's in the backseat, plugged into her iPod and not even pretending to be interested in Krissy's impromptu tour of Glenhaven Park.

Krissy turns her silver Lexus down North Street en route to Meg's childhood home, newly occupied by a married couple with a teenaged daughter.

"Did somebody add on to the house or something?" she asks, trying to fathom who would pay that kind of money for a very nice, but certainly not lavish, suburban home.

"No, it's pretty much the same as it was when you lived there, actually. There's a new patio out back. But the kitchen really needs to be updated. I think they said they were going to gut it."

"One point two million, and it needs a new kitchen? I can't wait to call my parents and tell them."

"Are you sure you want to do that?"

"You're right. Why frustrate them?" Meg decides her parents are better off oblivious to the fact that, had they waited another decade or so to sell their house and move south, they'd have gotten five times the money for their retirement nest egg.

"So basically"—Meg casts a glance over her shoulder to make sure Cosette isn't listening—"you're saying that I can't touch a house in my own hometown for under a million dollars."

"There are a few in the high sixes and low sevens," Krissy tells her. "Why? Are you thinking of coming back?"

"Yes, but shh." Meg indicates her daughter with a nod. "I don't want to break it to her just yet."

"Oh, she'll love it here. There's so much for kids to do. We've still got a terrific recreation department."

"Really?" Meg remembers participating in some of their community theater programs when she was growing up. "Do they still put on plays and musicals?"

"Yes. And a lot of kids play soccer . . ."

"Soccer? It would be good for Cosette to get back into that."

"There's a swim team, too."

"Unfortunately, she can barely doggy paddle." Or ride a bike. Or toss a Frisbee. Or play hopscotch.

This isn't the first time Meg is realizing just how deprived her urban child has been.

Too bad we can't afford to move here, she reminds herself, as Krissy slows the car in front of the house where she grew up.

"Oh my God." A wave of nostalgia washes over Meg. She presses her knuckles against her mouth. "Can you pull over for a second? I just want to look at it."

"Sure."

"Cosette . . ." She turns to wave at her daughter in the backseat until Cosette removes one earphone, music blasting from it.

"What?" She is obviously aggravated at the interruption.

"I just want to show you where I lived with Grandma and Grandpa."

Her daughter flicks a gaze at the brick Tudor. "It's nice."

"It looks almost exactly the same, except the trees are taller and my mother always planted red geraniums in that bed out front, instead of pink . . . what are those things?"

"Impatiens." Krissy laughs. "City girls don't do much gardening, huh?"

"Not unless you count the stuff I'm growing on leftover takeout in my fridge."

"Well, for the record, geraniums need sun. This yard used to get it when the trees were younger. But now look. It's all shade. Impatiens love shade."

"I'll remember that." But Meg doubts she'll become much of a gardener even if she winds up here in suburbia. She has a fear—well, according to her daughter, it's an obsession—when it comes to bees.

Bees, wasps, yellow jackets, hornets . . . things that buzz and sting.

It stems from a childhood incident when she accidentally stepped on a hive while playing at a friend's house. She wound up in the emergency room, puffy and in terrible pain.

She hasn't walked barefoot through the grass ever

since . . . not that there's much opportunity for that in Manhattan.

Meg glances over her shoulder to see that Cosette is plugged into her iPod again, having supplied the obligatory interest in the old homestead. "Listen, Krissy . . . I need you to find me something that I can afford. I really want to come back."

"Just like that? One look at your old house, and your mind is made up?"

"I've been thinking about it for a long time." Well, that depends on how you define "long."

"What's your price range?"

She's been socking away all those alimony checks from Calvin for quite some time, so she has a good idea what she can afford without a mortgage. Financing the house is out of the question, considering that she no longer has a solid source of income.

"Five hundred is my limit." It seemed like such an astronomical number until . . . well, right this second.

"There's nothing at that price right now," Krissy says flatly. "If you can go up to six seventy-five, I might be able to—"

Hearing a car door slam, they both look over at the driveway to see a shiny red BMW now parked there. A tall, tanned blond man in tennis whites and stylish sunglasses has emerged and is looking at them.

"Hello, Brad," Krissy calls through her open window. "It's Kris Holmes—from Better Homes Realty."

"Oh! Hi." He takes a few steps closer. "I know the market is hot, but don't tell me you're here to talk me into selling already. We're not even unpacked yet."

Kris laughs. "No, this is my old friend Meg Addams,

and that's her daughter Cosette"—she waves a hand at the backseat—"and Meg grew up in your house. She wanted to see it."

"Really? Do you want to come inside?"

"I'd love to." Meg looks at Kris.

"You go ahead. I'll stay here and return a couple of calls." She pulls out her cell phone.

Meg starts to ask Cosette if she wants to come, but why bother?

Climbing out of the car, she finds the homeowner extending a handshake. "I'm Brad Flickinger. Meg, is it?"

"Yes. This is so nice of you," she says, following him up the familiar brick walkway edged with narrow mulched flower beds. "How long have you been here?"

"Six weeks. We love it. You moved away from here?"

"Yes, but I'm coming back." That decisive statement just pops out, but it sounds right. It feels right.

"That's terrific. Glenhaven Park is a great place to live. Come on in."

It feels strange to have him hold open the door for her as she steps inside—as though he lives here and she's just visiting.

Which—hello!—is exactly the case.

It's just . . .

How many times did Meg burst through that door and run through this house calling "I'm home"?

The layout is the same, but the color palette, the furniture, the art, and the rugs are not. It even smells different. Like paint, and perfume. And strangers.

Brad takes her through the house. Every room brings back a memory. There's the hearth in the living room where she used to perform show tune medleys for her tirelessly enthusiastic audience: her parents. There's the radiator window seat in the dining room where she spent a chilly January weekend reading *To Kill a Mockingbird* for eleventh-grade English. There's the crack between the kitchen countertop and the tall pantry cupboard where she lost a love letter she had impulsively written to her unrequited high school crush, Sam Rooney.

The notches her father cut into the molding beside the back door are still there. They've been painted over a few times, but she can see the marks that measure her height every year on her birthday.

Seeing her running her fingertips over the wood, Brad remarks, "It's not in great shape—it's all nicked up—but Olympia and I are about to gut this kitchen and redo everything, including stripping and refinishing the moldings and floor."

"That will be nice," Meg murmurs, turning away from the door and her memories. "So Olympia is your wife?"

He nods. "And Sophie is my daughter. She's over at the dance studio, rehearsing for her jazz recital this afternoon."

"Mrs. Heyl's dance studio?"

"No, Broadway Baby, above the sushi place on Main."

Broadway Baby? Sushi place?

Things sure have changed around here, Meg thinks.

Aloud, she says, "Broadway Baby sounds like something I would have liked when I was a kid."

"You took dance?"

"Yes, but back then, it was only ballet. They didn't offer much of anything that had anything to do with Broadway. I had to get there on my own."

"Get there? You mean Broadway?"

"Yes."

"So you perform?"

"Well . . . not anymore. But I did."

"In which show?"

As she gives him the briefest possible rundown of her stage credits, Brad's eyebrows rise toward the sunglasses now perched on his head. "And now you're moving back up here?"

She nods. "I'm going to give voice lessons, and maybe—"

"Will you teach kids?" he cuts in enthusiastically. "Because our Sophie—she's thirteen—is incredibly gifted when it comes to musical theater, and Olympia and I were just saying that we need to step it up a notch."

Meg has no idea what he means by that, but since it apparently involves her being able to earn any kind of income from the apparently well-off Flickingers, she nods in total agreement. "I'd love to meet your daughter and maybe—"

"Terrific. Do you have a card?"

"No, I . . . not yet. If you have something to write on, I'll give you my cell number."

"Great." He opens a drawer and promptly produces a pen and pad. "You're going to love it here."

Feeling oddly territorial, she wants to remind Brad that *she's* the one who grew up in Glenhaven Park . . . and *he's* the newcomer.

"I'll have Olympia call you," he promises. "And not just about Sophie's voice lessons—my wife is very plugged in. She'll introduce you to everyone."

Meg murmurs that that would be nice, but again, she's struck by the implication that she's the outsider in her own hometown. And how plugged in can someone be after only six weeks?

"Do you have any kids?" Brad is asking as he walks her to the front door.

"One. A daughter. She's fifteen."

"Terrific. Sophie can show her around."

Right. Meg can imagine how that will go over with Cosette. A thirteen-year-old would-be starlet introducing her to small-town life.

Oh, well. As soon as Meg finds a place for them to live, and she and Cosette are settled in, she's positive they'll both feel right at home here.

Outside, she finds Kris chatting through her open car window with the driver of a Hummer Alpha that's pulled up alongside. Cosette is still tuned out in the backseat, masked by sunglasses and plugged into her iPod.

"Oh, Meg, there you are. This is my friend Laurelle Gladstone." To Meg's surprise, a woman is behind the wheel of the Hummer. "Laurelle, Meg."

Laurelle is a petite blonde who might not seem as outrageously dwarfed if she weren't wearing oversized Chanel sunglasses and driving a vehicle built for military combat. She's dressed not in fatigues, but in a cute, appliquéd turquoise tank top that reveals a delicate collarbone and arms.

"Nice to meet you."

"Mmm," it sounds like Laurelle responds. It's hard to tell. Maybe she didn't say anything at all. She didn't seem to move her mouth.

"So, Meg is about to start house-hunting here in Glenhaven Park," Kris informs Laurelle.

"Mmm." Meg is convinced that's the extent of Laurelle's conversational capability until she adds, mostly to Kris, "My neighbor is about to list her place."

Kris's eyebrows shoot up. "Cari Winston?"

"Yes."

"Do you know who's getting the listing?" Kris asks hopefully.

"I think Sotheby's. Sorry."

She doesn't look it.

To Meg, Laurelle says, "If you're looking, you should come see this place before someone jumps on it. Three acres and a stable."

"A stable is right up my alley, at this point," Meg mutters wryly, mostly to herself, though Kris smirks.

"So you have horses?" Laurelle brightens.

"Uh, no."

"I thought you said—"

"Forget it. Sorry. It was a joke." Meg smiles feebly.

"Oh . . ." Laurelle rests her left hand against her cheek, clearly bewildered—yet, Meg suspects, with the presence of mind to show off the enormous diamond solitaire and studded band on her fourth finger. "What was the joke?"

Meg can't stand people who insist on making you repeat something you both know they aren't going to find funny anyway. How not surprising that Laurelle is that annoying kind of person.

"You know . . . that I need a stable . . . to live in. Because the real estate market is so out of reach here."

"Oh. I get it." Laurelle isn't amused, though she pretends to flash a smile for a fraction of a split second. "Well, I've got to get to yoga, so . . ."

"See you later." Kris waves.

"Don't forget to leave the name of your cleaning woman on my voice mail," Laurelle calls out before pulling away. "I'm desperate. I swear, it's impossible to get good help these days."

She didn't just say that, Meg thinks, *did she?*

Just to be sure, she asks Kris as she settles into the front seat beside her.

"Yeah, that's exactly what she said. Don't look at me that way."

"What way?"

"Listen, Meg, you might think she's a snob, but she's a really nice person. She's really busy, too—she used to be the CFO of the Drysdale Corporation."

Which means nothing to Meg, but Kris seems to think that it should, so she nods and asks, "What does she do now?"

"She's a stay-at-home mom. And she's the head of Sharing and Caring."

Whatever that means.

Meg can't help but think it's hard to imagine Laurelle involved in sharing, much less caring, but who is she to judge?

"*And* she's gone through three maids in the last month," Kris adds, "so she's really hyperstressed."

Again, how not surprising, Meg thinks, as she watches the Hummer roll off down the street.

Changing the subject—sort of—Meg asks, "She's actually going to yoga in that?"

"In that outfit? No, I'm sure she'll change there."

"No, I mean in that tank she's driving. I thought she might be heading off into combat in rugged terrain somewhere, but no, she's toddling off to yoga."

Kris laughs. "Actually, a lot of people around here drive them."

"So let me see if I've got this straight—a Hummer is the must-have vehicle for civilian moms to get around suburbia."

"I wouldn't say must-have."

"Good. Because I don't think that'll be in my budget anytime in the near future. Then again, they're a pretty good size . . ." She snickers. "Maybe I can just buy one and live in it."

A week later, Meg is sprawled on the floor of her living room, the *New York Times* Real Estate Section spread out before her; Chita Rivera curled up and purring on the small of her back.

Scanning the list of homes on the market in Glenhaven Park, she mutters, "Nothing, nothing, nothing . . . and more nothing."

She should probably be saying *something, something, something,* and *reeeeaaallly something.*

Each home listed is more expensive than the last, with the final coming in at a whopping eleven-million-dollar asking price.

That's right. Eleven *million* dollars.

In Glenhaven Park.

Which, she's discovering, has changed drastically since she left.

Oh, it's still a charming, beautiful, desirable place to live . . .

If you're a multimillionaire.

Which she isn't.

"Are you sure there's nothing at all available in my price range?" she asked Kris repeatedly, as they drove around town last Saturday after leaving her—or rather, Brad Flickinger's—house.

There isn't a thing.

Which is astonishing, considering that Meg's price range is half a million dollars, thanks to religiously banking most of her alimony checks all these years.

In Glenhaven Park, that won't even buy a two-bedroom condo in the new complex sprawled on the hillside above the Congregational church.

Not that Meg wants a condo, anyway.

No, she's longing for a house. A home. A place all her own, hers and Cosette's. A self-contained dwelling with only a basement beneath the floor and just a roof, maybe an attic above the ceiling—as opposed to stacks of other apartments filled with strangers. She wants four outer walls with nothing on the other side but a view in every direction and plenty of fresh air.

That's just not going to happen in Glenhaven Park, where, according to Kris, an influx of "city people" over the past decade has resulted in skyrocketing home prices.

Meg can't even afford surrounding towns like Bedford Hills or Mount Kisco, which is where Kris dropped them at the train station to go back to Manhattan.

"Don't worry, we'll find something for you," she called optimistically from the window of her Lexus.

Something. Meg doesn't like the sound of that. But if a condo is the only way she can go home again, maybe she'll have to consider it.

And she does want to go home again. Desperately.

When Meg spoke to her parents the other day, she mentioned her trip to Glenhaven Park and the old house. She told them that the old coffee shop is now a sushi restaurant, with Broadway Baby and Baby Buddha, a kids' yoga studio, occupying the floors above. The old five-and-ten is an Internet cafe; the shop where she used to buy her clothes is now a pricey boutique that sells Lucky jeans, but not Levi's.

Meg neglected to tell her parents what their house on North Street is worth now. Nor did she reveal that she's giving up on New York City after all these years.

It isn't so much that she fears the inevitable barrage of I Told You So's—though she's not looking forward to that.

No, it's more that she doesn't want to get into the whole Cosette thing with her mother and father. They've always been worried enough as it is about Meg raising her daughter single-handedly. They want her to find a nice man who's willing to marry her and be a father to her daughter. The last thing she needs is to tell them she's given up on men—much less that Cosette got kicked out of school.

Plus, the fewer people in the loop on the move, the better. She still hasn't mentioned anything about it to Cosette—though the way her daughter has been moping around the apartment this past week, Meg wonders if she might actually welcome the change.

Oh, who am I kidding?

Cosette is going to balk at moving, no matter what.

Meg has nothing to lose by keeping her plans to herself until they come to fruition. Which should be right around the twelfth of never, the way things are going.

She flips to the Westchester County Rentals section— equally dismal, according to Kris. It isn't so much that local rentals are out of Meg's price range. There just *aren't* any. Not in Glenhaven Park, anyway.

Meg supposes she could look elsewhere, but her heart isn't in it.

She's scanning down the list of locales for prospects in her hometown when the telephone rings.

Startled, Chita Rivera meows in protest and jumps off Meg's back.

"I'll get it!" Cosette streaks into the room, leaps over the departing cat, and snatches up the receiver, breathlessly asking, "Hello?"

Meg watches her face fall.

"Who?" Cosette asks. Then, "Oh . . . hang on."

"It's for Meg Addams," she says flatly. "I assume that's you."

Cosette isn't thrilled with Meg's name change and insists that she'll remain Cosette Hudson no matter what her mother's real name is. Meg respects that choice. She just wishes her daughter would respect hers. Astor Hudson needs to retire.

"If call waiting beeps in," Cosette says, handing over the phone, "will you pick up?"

"Why?"

"Because I'm waiting for a call."

"From whom?"

"From Jon. Okay?"

So that's it. Trouble in paradise, judging by Cosette's scowl and the way she skulks out of the room.

Maybe Joe College couldn't deal with Cosette being grounded. Which is fine with Meg. He's too old for her daughter anyway.

"Hello . . . Mrs. Addams?"

Meg doesn't want to be one of those "It's *Ms.*" sticklers, so she simply says, "Yes?"

"My name is Olympia Flickinger." The woman's voice is crisply efficient. "My husband said you want Sophie to attend your voice studio."

A few things about that statement aren't entirely true—sending Sophie to her was Brad Flickinger's idea, and she hardly has a studio.

But again, why be a stickler?

"Yes," she says, "Your husband told me that your daughter is a budding musical theater talent."

"Is that what he said? Brad tends to play things down. I'd say the bud is in full bloom where Sophie's concerned. We've been interviewing voice instructors, and unfortunately, we haven't found any of them to be acceptable. We'd like to set up a meeting with you at your earliest convenience."

"Actually, Mrs. Flickinger—"

"I prefer Ms."

"I'm sorry. Ms. Flickinger, my studio isn't open just yet."

Thud.

"When do you expect to open?"

"Not for another couple of months. Why don't I take down your number and give you a call then?"

"Well, Sophie is going away to camp until the end of August. I'm sure we'll have found someone by the time she gets back, but I'll give you the number anyway."

As Meg is jotting it down, call waiting beeps in.

Rather than attempt to put Olympia Flickinger on hold—she always winds up disconnecting the call and something tells her Ms. Flickinger wouldn't appreciate that—she hastily ends the call and switches to the other line.

"Meg?" It isn't Jon's voice, but an unrecognizable female. "Good, you're home. You've got to come up here right away."

"Who is this?"

"Kris Holmes!"

"Oh!" *Krissy Rosenkrantz.* Meg smiles. "What's going on?"

"A terrific house is about to come on the market, and it's in your price range. Are you interested?"

"Are you kidding? I'll take it!"

Kris laughs. "A motivated buyer. That's what I like. Don't you even want to look at it first?"

"I guess. What's it like?"

"Two-story Victorian, original woodwork inside and out, huge yard, five bedrooms, two baths, needs work, but . . ."

"I'll take it," Meg says again, only half-kidding.

Or perhaps, she realizes, not kidding at all.

Does she dare to believe that she can actually leave the city behind and reclaim her hometown? That she can get her daughter away from the bullies and the bad influences and give her the kind of idyllic childhood Meg herself had?

Well, for what's left of it, anyway.

In a few short years, Cosette will be off to college . . .

And I'll be alone in the suburbs . . . which is probably even lonelier than being alone in the city.

Unless I meet someone up there . . .

Where the heck did that thought come from?

From Geoffrey, of course, with his constant patter about how she needs a love life. A real love life, not random dates here and there with men who are more self-involved than Calvin was, even.

"Listen," Kris is saying, "catch the next train up, and we'll go look at it."

"I'm on my way." She's already on her feet, padding to the bedroom to change from her yoga pants into "real" clothes.

"Good, I'll meet you at the station."

"Where is this house, anyway?"

"How well do you remember Glenhaven Park?"

"Are you kidding? Kris, the town is tiny, and I spent the first eighteen years of my life there."

"Okay, then . . . it's on Boxwood Street. Do you remember Boxwood Street?"

"Sure do." How many times did she detour up that shady street, hoping for a glimpse of Sam Rooney, her unrequited high school crush, who lived at Number 31?

"Which house is it?" she asks, thinking it would be a kick if it were the Rooneys' old house.

"Number 33. Remember the old Duckworth place?"

"The haunted house?" She knows it well; it's right next door to the Rooneys'.

"Uh, right."

"That's the house?"

"Does it bother you?"

"Does what bother me?" Meg asks, pulling a pair of khakis from her drawer and wondering how badly they need ironing.

"That it's supposed to be haunted?"

"Are you kidding? The only thing that bothers me at this point is that I can't touch real estate in my own hometown." She opens the linen closet to find the iron.

"Well, you'd better get up here if you want it, because people will come out in droves at this price."

"I want it," Meg tells her firmly.

Glenhaven Park, here we come.

Chapter
3

"Whose idea was it to move in August?" Meg groans, stepping out of the air-conditioned U-Haul truck into the soupy, eerily still early-evening air.

"Everything about this stupid move was your idea," Cosette informs her, slumped in the passenger's seat with an equally sullen Chita Rivera on her lap. "You didn't even ask me what I wanted."

"Sorry," Meg informs her daughter, "but you lost your vote when you got kicked out of school. This is my decision—and it's already made. Welcome home."

Cosette scowls harder, if that's possible.

"Come on, let's go."

"No. It's too hot. You can see the heat radiating off the asphalt. I'm not setting foot out there."

"It wouldn't be so hot if you weren't draped in all that black," Meg retorts, shoving wisps of hair off her already-sticky forehead.

"At least my clothes match, and these were bought in the past few months, instead of the past five years," Cosette replies, casting a disdainful eye at Meg's orange tank top and red shorts.

Meg opens her mouth to reprimand her daughter's blatant disrespect but thinks better of it. Cosette is right about her outfit—which she wouldn't be wearing in the first place if she hadn't, while loading the van in concrete-radiated city heat, sweated right through her original shorts and top—no more current than this getup, but at least not clashing.

She was forced to change into the first items she'd found in the first suitcase she could locate in the full van.

They've just spent an entire weekend packing all of their worldly belongings—aside from the furniture, and her prized piano, which she hired a professional company to move. No, not just packing, but also scrubbing the apartment for Geoffrey's friend Andrew, who's arriving from L.A. to sublet it tomorrow.

They followed up that rigorous forty-eight hours with three more in this rented rattletrap, which is how long it took to make the mere fifty-mile trip up from the city. Traffic was miserable, thanks to the timing—late Sunday afternoon in summer, which meant a barrage of upstaters returning from the Jersey Shore and the Hamptons.

So who wouldn't be cranky at this point?

Geoffrey wouldn't be cranky, that's who.

He parks his shiny red Prius at the curb behind them, checks his hair in the rearview mirror, then climbs out and stretches lazily, like a cat awakening from an afternoon nap. "Well, that was fun."

"You actually sound like you mean that." Meg strides around to the back of the U-Haul and tries to figure out how to unlatch the doors.

"I *do* mean it. There's nothing like a Sunday afternoon drive in the summer."

"That was no Sunday drive, it was a nightmare, and it's no longer afternoon."

Geoffrey checks his watch. "You're right! Who's ready to go get dinner?"

"I am!"

"I thought you weren't getting out of the van," Meg says to her daughter, who has materialized at her side.

"I think Chita Rivera needs to go to the bathroom. Here." Cosette thrusts the squirming cat into Meg's arms and tells Geoffrey, "Let's go find a diner."

"Brilliant plan."

"Wait!" Meg protests. "Don't you even want to go inside?"

"I've already been," Geoffrey reminds her.

He was with her when they did the walk-through prior to closing on Friday morning. So was Cosette.

Neither was the least bit charmed by the cherry woodwork—painted over in shades of turquoise and pink; the vintage wallpaper—peeling; or even the oversized rooms—pronounced dark and drafty by Geoffrey.

"Drafty?" Meg echoed incredulously. "It's ninety degrees out."

"Wait until winter. Do you know how much it's going to cost to heat this barn?"

"You just don't want me to move," she accused.

"You're right, I don't. What am I going to do without you and Cosette?"

"We'll be an hour train ride away."

"It won't be the same."

He's right. It won't.

But Meg didn't want to dwell on that then, and she certainly doesn't now. Especially in front of Cosette.

She hasn't let her daughter witness a moment's doubt on her part—and there have been plenty of those since she made the offer on the house back in June, the very day she first saw it with Kris.

She's doing the right thing. She knows it in her heart. The right thing for herself, and definitely the right thing for Cosette.

It's just not easy to pull up your roots and leave behind the only home you've known for almost two decades.

Oh, really? You did exactly that, once before, without the slightest qualm. When you left Glenhaven Park.

But back then, she had only herself to worry about.

Now, there's a fifteen-year-old daughter who dramatically claimed she'd rather throw herself off the subway platform in front of an oncoming uptown express than move to "the middle of nowhere."

Meg didn't dispute that; Glenhaven Park *is* the middle of nowhere, relatively speaking.

That's the beauty of it.

Just beyond the town's perimeter are acres of nature preserve, unpaved roads, bridle paths that meander past ancient stone walls in the woods. These days, they also meander past massive estates occupied by bona fide blue bloods, Grammy-winning rappers, Wall Street superstars, and yes, the occasional ankle-bracelet-wearing white-collar criminal.

But there's still plenty of old-fashioned charm here in the hinterlands.

It's just too soon to make that point to a kid who is still lamenting the loss of her boyfriend—older man Jon broke up with her before the Fourth of July—not to mention the loss of her favorite hairstylist; and falafel readily available at all hours from a cart on the corner.

Meg pointed out, "You hate falafel."

"Not lately," Cosette shot back. "Lately, I love falafel."

Yes, she probably decided to love falafel right around the time she decided to hate Glenhaven Park.

And soccer.

Meg has already signed her up for a fall league, though, via the mail, thanks to a Glenhaven Park Recreation Commission booklet Kris sent her. It's time Cosette got some fresh air, physical activity, and wholesome new friends.

As for Meg . . .

Well, she'll settle in and eventually make friends here, too.

It just might be a little lonely at first—especially with Krissy on an Alaskan cruise until after Labor Day. Not that she and Krissy have much in common these days. The unconventional girl who planned to move to a commune out west now makes a living selling million-dollar showplaces and lives in one herself. There are occasional glimmers of the old Krissy, but she's no longer a kindred spirit.

Finding even one kindred spirit may not be as easy for Meg as it was in the city. Here, she'll be isolated, teaching voice right here at home.

Brad Flickinger's wife Olympia has already set up a meeting this coming week with the musically gifted Sophie, who has her heart set on a lead in the high school musical when school starts again. Meg called the Flickingers the moment she knew she was moving back to town.

A couple of Meg's Broadway contacts who happen to live in Westchester have also inquired about private lessons for their kids. They said she won't have a problem finding willing students.

She can't entirely support herself and Cosette, but it will be a good start, and she has Calvin's alimony and child support checks to fall back on.

Hopefully, her piano will be delivered on schedule as promised, in time for the Flickingers' appointment.

"Aren't you coming?" Geoffrey asks, turning back to Meg when he and Cosette are halfway to his car.

"Geoffrey! Do you know how long it's going to take to unpack this van?" She shakes her head in exhausted dismay. "I've got to have it back in White Plains before midnight, and I can barely remember how to get back to the rental place."

"Which is why you should have just rented it in the city, like I told you."

"That was too expensive, like *I* told *you*."

"I offered to spring for it. You wouldn't let me."

"That was very nice of you, and no, I wouldn't let you. I've got to do this myself."

Geoffrey sighs. "You've always done *everything* for yourself."

"Exactly."

"Come on, Astor. If you won't take cash, at least let me treat you to dinner. We'll all feel more like unloading the van once we've got some food in our stomachs."

"It's not Astor anymore, remember?"

"Oops! Sorry . . . I mean *Meg*. I don't know if I'll ever get used to that. But you know, the funny thing is, you're already starting to *look* like a Meg."

Holding the squirming cat with one hand, wiping another sweaty clump of hair from her face with the other, and glancing down at her grimy, mismatched clothing, Meg concludes he doesn't mean that as a compliment.

She thanks him anyway and tells him to go ahead to get something to eat and take Cosette with him.

Geoffrey has always been—if not a father figure for Cosette, then at least a big brother figure. He's certainly old enough to be her dad, but his relationship with Meg's daughter has always been more fun and conspiratorial than paternal. Hopefully, that will continue even now that they're moving.

"Oh," she calls after them, "I just remembered that there's a great burger place four blocks from here, across from the train station. They have the best battered french fries!"

"Sounds good, in a revolting way. Are you sure this place is still there?" Geoffrey asks.

"I saw it the other day from a distance . . ."

Then again, it might have turned into another yoga studio or something.

She still hasn't had much of a chance to explore her former—and future—hometown again since that first day.

The next time she came up a week later, it was to look at the house on Boxwood with Kris. The time after that—for Friday's closing—Geoffrey drove her straight to the house for the walk-through, then to the lawyer's office.

She's still itching to stroll down Main Street again—and she'll have plenty of time for that now. Home, sweet home.

"Do you want us to bring anything back for you?" Geoffrey offers, hand on the car door handle.

"Furniture would be good." She brought only the essentials up from the city, telling herself—and Cosette—that the style is too modern for the new place.

To which Cosette replied sarcastically, "Oh, right, we need a lot of dark, heavy stuff with velvet and mohair upholstery, fringe, tassels . . . Maybe somebody's great-great-aunt will be having a garage sale when we get there, and we can load up."

Actually, given the sorry state of Meg's household budget, visiting garage sales wouldn't be a bad idea.

"I'll help you decorate, but not today," Geoffrey informs her. "So no furniture. What else do you need? You know how I love to shop. Give me a list."

"You're going to be sorry you asked. I need a box cutter, toilet paper, toothbrushes and toothpaste because I didn't remember packing them, a case of bottled water, paper towels and cleaning stuff, a bucket, a cheeseburger, medium rare, and battered french fries," she rattles off. "Oh, and a side order of onion rings. With mustard."

"Gotta love a woman who eats like a trucker even in this heat. Where am I supposed to get the nonfood items?"

"Your guess is as good as mine. You're the shopaholic. Find one of those big suburban sprawl superstores people are always complaining about up here."

"Will do," Geoffrey calls with a cheerful wave, and they're off.

"Come on, Chita Rivera, before you pee all over me— or worse." Leaving the van at the curb, Meg carries the cat to the black iron gate.

On the other side, in the weed-choked yard, she can see fat bumblebees lazing among the dandelions. It's August. Bees are always plentiful at this time of year. And pesky, she remembers from her suburban barbecue days, when she was prone to shrieking into the house in terror as they dive-bombed her plate.

She takes a deep breath, trying to work up the nerve to step into the yard.

She isn't barefoot, and she isn't carrying a plate of chicken.

Come on, you know they won't bother you if you don't bother them, she reminds herself. *It's about time you conquered this irrational fear.*

The gate creaks loudly when she opens it.

Nothing a little WD-40 can't handle, she tells herself. The building super uses the stuff all the time back home.

Wait . . .

Make that *back in New York.*

This is home now.

She steps through the gate and it closes behind her with another protesting creak. Keeping a wary eye on the bees, who ignore her, she sets the cat on the cracked slab of grass-choked slate walkway.

"There. Now you can't run away."

The cat mews in protest, as though she had every intention of doing just that.

"Go ahead, find a nice spot to do your business."

Chita Rivera, who never in her life set paw outside before today, doesn't budge.

"Look, I know you're a house cat through and through, very dainty and ladylike and all that good stuff, but I have no clue where your litter box is," Meg informs her. "So get moving and do your thing so I can stick you in the house and get on with the unpacking. Just stay away from those evil-looking buzzing things over there, okay? They're the enemy."

Chita Rivera blinks.

"Go on. I didn't mean to scare you."

No response.

"Oh . . . do you want me to turn my back? You're modest? Is that it?" She folds her arms and turns away, coming face-to-face with her new home.

I can't believe this is mine, she thinks . . . and not in a pleased way.

No, more in a *what-the-heck-was-I-thinking?* way.

Porch half-hidden behind a broken-down trellis densely twined with overgrown wisteria. Sagging steps. Missing spindles. Dangling shutters. Peeling paint.

Yes, the place has oodles of potential, as Kris pointed out.

Though she didn't say *oodles.*

That's Meg's word, one she unfortunately used in a conversation in the company of the already-glowering Cosette. She immediately learned that cutesy words like *oodles* make glowering teenagers glower more fiercely.

Of course, it's a word she's actually never before uttered in her life. Along with several others freshly added to her vocabulary. Like *sapstain, radon,* and *sump.*

There were others, too, which she hasn't had occasion to use in quite some time: *deterioration, fungi,* and *architectural aberration* come most immediately to mind.

So the house has some problems. All houses do.

But it also has oodles of potential.

Far more potential than the cookie-cutter ranches in her price range fifteen miles up the commuter line. A house like this has character, and history, and . . .

And, well, just . . . lots of . . . er, potential.

For some reason, Meg is seriously determined to be optimistic about this gloomy old house.

"Gloomy?" That's not exactly optimistic.

No, but it's accurate. *Look* at it.

The place looks even more forbidding now than it did when she was a kid. It's even got that classic haunted house silhouette, thanks to the tall, mansard roof.

But it isn't *really* haunted . . . is it?

Gazing upward, she can swear she sees a sudden flicker of light in the attic window.

Which, of course, is impossible, because the house has been vacant for months. The new family never even took possession.

And why not?

Because they thought it was haunted.

She and Kris sure did have a good laugh over that.

Only . . .

Somehow, it's not quite as funny now.

"Let's go, Chita Rivera," she urges impatiently, turning on her heel.

Her command is dramatically punctuated by a loud rumble.

Meg gasps . . .

Then realizes that it's just thunder.

Which at this point is actually even worse than . . .

Well, other things that can make you gasp when you're hanging around a haunted house.

Meg looks up at the sky, hanging low and ominously gray above the distant hills that surround the town.

"Think it's going to rain?" she asks Chita Rivera, who merely looks royally peeved. "Yeah, so do I. Let's get moving."

*   *   *

"Right. That's one large pie, sausage and pepperoni, to 31 Boxwood. About how long?" Sam asks the pizza delivery guy, wondering why he's bothering. They always say the same thing.

"Half hour."

Yup, they say that whether it's going to be fifteen minutes or seventy-five minutes. Oh, well. Whatever. He's on his own for dinner tonight, so what does it matter when it gets here?

Hanging up the phone, Sam goes back to the book he was reading. A few paragraphs in, he hears a distant rumble of thunder and wonders whether it's supposed to rain— he didn't think so.

Then he wonders whether he remembered to close the windows on his Trailblazer when he got home a little while ago. The air-conditioning is on the fritz—in the midst of the dog days of August, of all times—and he's been driving with them down and the moon roof open.

"What do you think, Rover?" he asks the shaggy beige mutt lying on the rug beneath the raised footrest of his leather easy chair. "Did I close them, or not?"

Rover snores peacefully, as unfazed by questions as he is by thunder.

I probably didn't bother to roll them up, Sam decides, his open book poised in his hand.

Right, he was most likely thinking he'd just have to go out again later to pick up Katie. She's swimming in her friend Kelsey's pool over in Glenhaven Chase, the new development across town, and was supposed to just stay for dinner. But she called a little while ago and asked if she can sleep over. "It's so hot, and we're going to go swimming again before bed to cool off."

He reluctantly said yes, hating that he did it, in part, because he has an early soccer practice in the morning, and it's impossible to get Katie moving at that hour. Plus, she'll grumble the whole time about being bored and having to sit on the sidelines while Sam coaches and Ben plays.

Yes, he thinks somewhat guiltily, life will be simpler if Katie spends the night at her friend's.

But will Kelsey's mom know enough to get the girls out of the water at the slightest sign of a thunderstorm? Even if it doesn't actually rain, lightning could still—

Okay, stop it, Sam warns himself. *Just stop.*

He can't spend the rest of his life worrying that something horrific is going to happen to Katie, who, with her stick-straight brown hair and hazel eyes and boyish build, is the spitting image of Sheryl.

Or to Ben, who is at the moment down at Chelsea Piers hitting golf balls with his uncle Jack, Sam's younger brother.

Sam gave Ben so many preemptive cautions on his way out the door earlier that Jack finally intervened.

"Stop acting like a mother hen, Sam. He's fifteen."

That's pretty much what Jack said when he convinced Sam that it would be a good idea to put a box of condoms in the bathroom cabinet and let Ben know they were there . . . just in case.

"He doesn't have a girlfriend, and he's way too young for just in case," Sam protested.

"Really? How old were you when you lost your virginity? And did you tell Mom and Dad about it?" asked Jack, who was well aware of the answer.

Sam was sixteen that summer, and madly in love with older woman Molly Harper. At seventeen, she was a life-guard—tawny and toned—and on the rebound from her college-bound boyfriend.

Sam and Molly lasted all of one weekend. But what a glorious weekend it was. And no, his parents never knew a thing about it.

"I wasn't fifteen, Jack," he pointed out to his brother.

"Yeah, but this is over two decades later. Prices have to be adjusted to account for inflation. So do ages."

"For *inflation*?" He quirked a dubious brow at his brother.

"You know what I mean," said Jack.

"Well, Ben doesn't even have a girlfriend, so . . ."

"Sam, come on. Molly wasn't your girlfriend."

True, that.

"I don't want to condone my son having sex at this age."

"You're not condoning it. You're just being realistic. I bet you don't want to rock a grandchild this time next year, either."

Jack had a point there, too. As a high school teacher, Sam has seen more than his share of unplanned teenaged pregnancies. They usually happen to the nice, naive kids. The ones whose parents are in denial.

"Look," Jack persisted, "just get the condoms, stick them in the cabinet, mention it to Ben, then leave it alone."

That wasn't nearly as easy for Sam to do as it was for Jack to say.

It was also easy for Jack to say, amid Sam's many pre-cautions as he was headed to the city with Ben today, "Do you really think I'm going to lose him somewhere? And that even if I did, he wouldn't find his way back home again?"

Sam just shook his head.

Bad things happen in this world.

Children are kidnaped. Struck by lightning.

Their mothers walk out the door to go grocery shopping and never come back.

Sam squeezes his eyes closed in an effort to stave off the vivid memory of the crushed blue station wagon at the intersection. But he can't shut it out, nor a haunting echo of the wailing sirens that sounded less than five minutes after Sheryl left home that day. When he heard them, he somehow *knew.*

He just knew.

And he was right.

The nightmare had begun.

Widowed, devastated, he moved back into this house with his children—and dog—in tow. His mother had offered to move in with him instead, but he couldn't stand the thought of staying on in that house they rented in Pelham without Sheryl. Everywhere he looked, there were memories.

Here, at least, he stood a chance of eventually moving on.

So he came home to Glenhaven Park.

He commuted to his old teaching job in lower Westchester until, miraculously, a position opened up right here at his old school. Things had fallen into place within a year of Sheryl's death—he and the kids were settled in here with his mother, surviving.

Yes, there are memories in this house, too. Plenty of them. He grew up here, raised with his brother Jack under this very roof. Ben has his boyhood room now, and Katie has Jack's. Sam has his parents'.

Mom passed away two years ago. It was unexpected, though not the tragedy losing Sheryl had been.

In fact, at first, Sam reacted so numbly to the loss of his mother that Jack was worried about him. Gradually, the pain seeped in. But with it came an odd sense of peace. He bought out Jack's half of their inherited property, and this felt like home once again, in a way it didn't while he was living here with his mother.

Hearing another roll of thunder, Sam rises abruptly from his chair.

There goes the ball game, he thinks. The Yankees should be throwing out the starting pitch right around the time the pizza arrives. He was planning to watch the game, but the cable frequently goes out in thunderstorms. Plus, the Yanks are playing at home in the Bronx only thirty-some miles south of here—the game will be affected by the rain anyway.

It's going to be a long, dull, lonely night.

So what else is new?

Sam steps over Rover, plunks his open novel facedown on the coffee table, and bends over the back of the couch to peek out the front picture window.

The first thing he sees is the Trailblazer, parked on the driveway.

Yup, windows down.

And . . .

Huh. There's a big U-Haul truck parked at the curb in front of the Duckworth house next door.

Here we go again.

This time, the house wasn't even on the market all that

long. A FOR SALE sign hadn't yet been planted in the lawn before he heard the place had been sold again.

He has no idea who bought it this time, nor does he care. Why should he?

It won't be long before his new neighbors get wind of the rumors, fall victim to their imaginations, and go the way of the Delgados, and the Sterns before them, and the Blumbergs before them.

Seeing movement behind the truck, he spots a petite figure staggering backward, only half-visible beneath a towering cardboard box.

So the new people have children—and they've put them to work.

Well, that's good. Most of the kids around Glenhaven Park these days are the spoiled offspring of privileged parents.

Sam is thinking that it will be nice for Katie and Ben to have kids next door after all . . . until it occurs to him that it won't be nice at all when they move.

Maybe I won't even tell the kids about the new neighbors, he decides, wondering how long it will take before the resident ghost puts in its first appearance. For all he knows, these people will be gone before dawn.

At the window before him, the lace curtain stirs in a sudden gust through the open screen.

Then the still air is shattered by another reverberation of thunder. This time it's closer.

Yup, a storm is closing in.

Sam grabs his keys and heads for the door just in time to hear another loud crash.

Only this time, it isn't courtesy of Mother Nature—and this time, it's followed by a very human curse word.

He looks to the source and sees the newcomer just inside her black wrought-iron gate. She dropped the box she was carrying.

Uh-oh. Her mom isn't going to be very pleased about this. She's surrounded by shards of broken pottery, which she kicks angrily, with another curse—pretty salty language for a little girl, there.

"Need help, sweetheart?" Sam calls, stepping out onto his porch.

She looks up, startled.

Then she grins, and calls back, "That would be terrific, Honeybunch."

That's when he realizes that she isn't a little girl at all.

She's a woman.

A petite, curvy, beautiful woman.

A petite, curvy, beautiful woman whose eyes have just gone from mocking his mistake—he just affectionately called a strange *woman* "sweetheart"!—to wide with sudden recognition.

"Sam Rooney?"

He frowns.

"Sam? Is that you?"

He nods vigorously. Yup. He's positive he's Sam . . . and he's also pretty sure he's never seen this woman before in his life.

Though she certainly seems to know him.

Brushing off her red shorts and pulling down the hem of her orange T-shirt, she takes a few steps closer, toward the line of shrubs dividing their property.

"I don't believe it . . . it really *is* you. Hi!"

"Hello." His tone is meant to be friendly, but even he

can hear that it's unnaturally formal and fraught with uncertainty. "Uh, how are you?"

"Not great at the moment . . ." She laughs, indicating the broken pottery. "But generally speaking, I've been okay. How about you? Are you visiting your parents?"

"My parents?" he echoes, then shakes his head. "No, they, ah, passed away."

"Oh, no. I'm so sorry." She does seem to be genuinely sympathetic. But why? "When did it happen?"

"Dad died back when I was still in college. Mom died almost two years ago."

"I'm so sorry," she says again. "So then the house . . ."

"I live here now."

"Really?" She comes closer still.

Close enough for him to clearly see her features: big green eyes, pert nose, wide—like Julia Roberts's—mouth, straight white teeth.

All right, he has no idea who the heck she is, even now.

So maybe she's mistaken him for somebody else.

Then again, she does know that his parents used to live here, so . . .

"Are you . . . ah . . ."

"Meg," she supplies, thinking he's fishing for her name when what he was going to ask was *Are you sure we've met?*

"Meg," he echoes, nodding. "Right! Meg."

Still no clue.

Meg who?

"Meg . . ." He snaps his fingers a few times, as if it's on the tip of his tongue.

"Jones," she says, as thunder claps in the not-so-distant distance.

"Oh! That's it. Meg Jones. Now I remember."

"Really?" She takes a few steps closer, wearing a strange smile, her hands on her hips. "That's funny. Because it's actually not Jones."

"It isn't?"

She laughs . . . but frankly, she doesn't seem all that amused. "I was testing you. You have no idea who I am, do you?"

Uh-oh.

"No," he confesses. "I don't."

"We went to high school together."

"*Really?*"

He wonders why he never dated her. She's beautiful. Quick-witted. Spirited.

Definitely his type.

Or maybe—

Nah. He definitely *didn't* date her. He'd remember that.

"I graduated a year behind you. I'm Meg Addams."

"Really?"

"Really. Ring a bell?"

"No . . . but I have a lousy memory."

Total lie. He has a great memory.

That's why it's so shocking that he doesn't remember her.

Another clap of thunder, startlingly close, then fat raindrops begin splatting abruptly all around them.

"No!" Meg turns and hurries back toward the sidewalk.

"Isn't everything broken?" he calls, watching her scramble to pick it up.

"Not all of it. I'm going to save what I can. My daughter made most of it when she was little."

Daughter. Oh.

Well, maybe she doesn't have a husband.

His next thought: *Why do I care?*

The one after that: *How can I find out?*

"You have a daughter? Where is she? What about your husband? Did you hire movers? You aren't trying to do this entire move on your own, are you?"

Too many questions.

But he was trying to make the one about the husband a little less obvious.

And you did it so well it just got buried.

Meg looks up, apparently not sure what to answer first. "I, uh, no, they'll be back in a while, but I've got to—"

Lightning flashes. She jumps a little.

"Wait, I'm coming to help you," Sam calls, and stops at his Trailblazer first, mulling over her reply as he hurriedly rolls up the windows.

They'll be back in a while.

So she is married, with at least one kid.

Oh, well, Sam thinks, crossing to the gate to help her. It's not as though he's interested in dating her . . . or anyone.

Just . . .

For a moment there . . .

Well, he could have sworn when he looked at her that something stirred to life in a long-neglected, shadowy place deep inside him.

Chapter
4

He doesn't even remember me.

Wow.

But at least they had a real conversation.

All those years ago, when Meg was obsessing about Sam Rooney, it never occurred to her that it would take twenty years before she managed to connect with him.

Connect, as in, *talk to.*

Not connect as in . . .

Well, in the way a dreamy, infatuated young girl yearns to connect with the good-looking, athletic, charismatic student council president.

Sam Rooney.

He looks exactly the same.

Well, in a more manly way. He's still tall . . .

Of course he's still tall. Did you expect him to shrink?

Meg is utterly irritated with herself for even noticing his looks.

After all, he's a dad now. He must be, because when she and Geoffrey arrived for the walk-through on Friday morning, she saw a young girl riding aimlessly up and down the adjacent driveway on her bike, and several teenaged boys shooting hoops beneath the net on the detached garage.

Geoffrey, of course, had to comment on the scene. "Oh, happy joy, it's Kinder Kamp right in your own backyard."

"That's not *my* backyard."

"It might as well be." He looked around distastefully, hands tucked into the pockets of his black Armani silk slacks as though afraid he might contaminate them otherwise. "This is all very . . ."

"Suburban?" she supplied, when he couldn't seem to find the right word.

"I was going to say frightening."

Now, surreptitiously watching Sam Rooney stride toward the U-Haul, where she's pretending to survey the towers of boxes, she *is* a little frightened.

Of herself.

Of the strange, fluttery eruption in her stomach.

He looks the same as he did back in high school—tall, yes, and also lean and muscular. He's wearing his wavy brown hair a little longer and shaggier than he did back then.

And those killer blue eyes are just as piercing.

Looking at him, Meg is fifteen all over again.

Terrific. Is she doomed to go around with perpetual butterflies in her stomach whenever she sees the Dad Next Door?

Watching him approach, she wonders what his wife is like and is sure that *she* would never go around in ancient red shorts and an orange T-shirt. No, *she* probably looks as though she stepped out of a J. Crew catalogue.

Then again . . . Sam doesn't.

His no-frills wardrobe has seen better days: a plain old athletic-looking gray T-shirt (which reveals impressive biceps), blue running shorts (which reveal tanned, muscular, masculine-hairy legs) and white Nikes without socks (which reveal that he's been painting something in a reddish maroon color).

He looks like . . . a guy. That's the beauty of it. He's just a regular Joe, handsome through no conscious effort of his own.

In Meg's world—or rather, in Astor Hudson's world—guys like him simply don't exist.

The life she's about to leave behind is populated by beautiful men, yes. Some are gay, some are married. Most of the ones who aren't, she's fallen for—and been dumped by. Some are in show business and some aren't. What they all have in common is a highly motivated physical appearance.

They've got hundred-dollar haircuts; they've been waxed, massaged, manicured. They use *product* as opposed to plain old soap and shampoo to maintain their hair and skin. They knock around in designer clothes and wear custom-made shirts, and when they go without socks, their bare, pedicured feet are clad in Italian leather loafers. Their muscles are buff, strictly courtesy of the gym.

Somehow, Meg knows that Sam's aren't. No, he got them the old-fashioned way. Which is . . .

Well, how *do* regular guys get muscles?

She has no idea, but she really should stop looking at them.

Sam's muscles.

Stop.

She really should stop looking at *him.*

Even though *he's* looking at *her.*

Looking at her as though . . .

Well, as though he's interested.

At last.

Oh, sure.

Now that he's a married dad, he's finally, *finally* noticed her?

Unless . . .

Meg sneaks a peek at his left hand.

Bare ring finger!

Red alert: bare ring finger!

Wait a minute.

Is he just one of those guys who eschews jewelry of any kind?

Or can he possibly be . . .

Single?

A single dad?

Earth to Meg . . . come in, Meg. Did you forget that you've sworn off men?

"So . . . we'd better get busy," he says, reaching her side.

Busy.

Yes . . .

Oh. The boxes. He's talking about the boxes.

Right.

"Are you sure you don't mind helping me?" Amazing how laid-back she's managing to sound. "I wouldn't even accept the offer if I didn't have to get the truck back . . ."

"I don't mind at all. I'll carry the big stuff; you just direct me where you want it to go when we get it inside."

He doesn't even flinch as he reaches into the truck and lifts out a large, book-filled box that took all three of them—Geoffrey, Meg, and Cosette—to hoist into the truck.

Meg grabs a smaller carton and leads the way through the gate, which she has already propped open with a big rock. Plenty of those lying around the disastrous yard.

"Wow. I still can't believe it," she says mostly to herself, shaking her head at the looming monstrosity before them.

"Believe what?"

"That I just bought the old Duckworth place."

"So you remember it? Don't tell me—you didn't *live* in this neighborhood, did you?"

"No, but . . ."

But I spent a lot of time here. A few years, pedaling and strolling up and down this very street, hoping for a glimpse of you.

"Every kid in town knew about the haunted house," she says instead.

Following her up the walk, he asks, "Did you really believe it was haunted?"

Something in his overly casual tone makes her turn to look at him.

God, he's handsome.

He also seems to be holding his breath for her reply to his inane question.

"Did *you* think it was haunted?" she returns, unsettled by the memory of that glint she saw—or thought she saw—in the attic window a few minutes ago.

He grins at her across the boxes in their arms. "I asked you first."

"I sure did," she admits. "Whenever I went past it I used to—"

She breaks off. Oops.

"You used to what?" he asks, and starts up the uneven steps, eyes cast downward to avoid tripping.

Good. Then he can't see how red her face must be.

And he doesn't seem to realize that she had no legitimate reason to pass the Duckworth house, *ever.*

"I used to just rush by it and get away from it as fast as I could," she says briefly, and reaches for the doorknob. "Oh, careful when we go in . . . I don't want my cat to escape."

"Cat?" He doesn't exactly make a face, but . . .

"You don't like cats?"

Sam shakes his head with an unapologetic, "Nope."

A-ha! Definite deal breaker.

Even if Sam Rooney *did* turn out to be single and available—which he probably isn't—she could never fall in love with a man who doesn't like cats.

Fall in love?

Who said anything about love?

You're not allowed to fall in love.

Or even think about falling in love. Remember?

Yeah, well, anyway . . .

He's probably married. *Is* he married?

"Do you want to let your wife know where you are, or anything?" she offers lamely.

A strange look comes across his face. It takes him a moment to say, "My wife is . . . I'm not married."

He's not married.

But he hates cats.

But he's not married.

But she's sworn off men like him. Charming, gorgeous

men who can cause her to lose her head and her heart—and, ultimately, her mind.

She can't risk investing her emotions in another dead-end relationship. She's gone more than six months without falling in love, and six months without anyone breaking her heart.

It feels good. It feels healthy. She feels strong and independent at last.

So she's going to stick to her resolution.

Balancing her box on her raised knee propped against the jamb, Meg opens the door wide.

No sign of Chita Rivera.

She looks at Sam. "Come on in."

"Ladies first."

She shakes her head and smiles slightly. "Men bearing enormously heavy boxes first."

Watching Sam Rooney cross the threshold into her new home, Meg can't help but wonder just what she's gotten herself into.

Sam is about to unload the last box from the van in the pouring rain when he hears tires splashing down the street behind him.

Turning around, he sees the familiar domed Park Pizza roof sign on the car pulling toward the curb in front of his house.

That's right—he forgot all about the pizza he ordered for his solitary dinner.

He strides over and recognizes the kid behind the wheel as he opens the car door.

"Hey, Mr. Rooney, how's it going?" Jason Capellini is

a former student of Sam's, now working his way through community college.

"It's going just fine. How about you? Still in school?"

"Yeah, but after this semester I'm thinking of enlisting. My mother's freaking out."

"Mothers do that."

"Yeah, I know how it is."

With a pang for Ben and Katie, who will never know how it is, Sam fishes a twenty and a couple of ones out of his damp pocket and exchanges them for the pizza box.

"Did somebody move in there again?" Jason eyes the Duckworth place. "That'll last, what? A few weeks at the most?"

"Give or take." But Sam can't help wishing things could be different this time.

Why? Because you're attracted to the latest desperate housewife next door?

Jason drives away, and fat raindrops are falling on the red-and-white pizza box. Sam is about to carry it into his house before he moves that last carton for Meg, when he suddenly thinks better of it.

Wouldn't it be neighborly of him to bring it over there, instead? She's probably hungry, and her husband and kids might be, too.

He balances the pizza on top of the moving box and carries them both up onto the porch, noticing that dusk is falling.

He can see Meg through the screen door in the shadowy front hall, grouping the boxes. He admires the curve of her bare legs as she bends, back to him, and picks up her cat. Then she opens the door for him.

"I don't remember packing that." Her tone is the driest thing in the room as she eyes the soggy pizza box.

"Well, I'm glad you did. It even has sausage and pepperoni, my favorite. You guys aren't vegetarians, are you?"

She looks down at the cat in her arms. "Me and Chita Rivera? She prefers seafood, but I'm a carnivore."

He grins. She's sharp-witted. He likes that in a . . .

Married woman?

Only one way to find out for sure.

"When I said you guys," he clarifies, "I actually meant you and your kids and your husband. Nothing against your cat."

"Other than that you don't like her."

"Not just her."

"So you just hate all cats in general." She sets Chita Rivera on her feet and watches her trot away.

He opens his mouth—either to make a feeble protest about his newly acquired cat-hater reputation or to rephrase his inquiry about her family, he isn't sure which.

It doesn't matter; she speaks first, looking down at the tall carton she's sliding toward a pile by the stairs. "I guess it's just me. For pizza, I mean."

"What about the rest of your family?"

"My daughter went out to eat with my friend. He's supposedly bringing me back a burger. But God knows when that will be, so I won't wait for it."

So she didn't mention a husband, but her friend is a he. What does that mean?

Sick of dancing around the issue, Sam decides to come right out and ask. "Is your friend—you know . . ."

Even in the rapidly dimming light, he can see her eyes

flash indignantly as she looks up at him. "Yes, he is. Why? Is that a problem?"

"That you have a boyfriend? No, not at all. I just wondered what you meant by *friend*."

"Oh!" She laughs. "I thought you were talking about something else. You know, that you might have been asking me whether he's gay."

"No, why would I do that?"

"I don't know . . . Geoffrey's convinced the suburbs are full of homophobes, so I guess he's rubbing off on me."

"I'm not homophobic . . . and he's not your boyfriend, then?"

"No, he *wants* a boyfriend."

"Gotcha. So he's—"

"Right. How about you? You're not . . . ?"

"*Me?* No!"

"You look horrified. I thought you said you weren't homophobic."

"I'm not. I'm just . . . not . . ."

"Gay? No? That's funny, I really thought I remembered that you were, back in high school."

"*Really?*"

"Nope." She laughs, watching his face. "Kidding again."

He breaks into a grin and hears himself say, "So . . . no boyfriend. No husband, either?"

"Uh-uh."

"So do you want to . . ."

What are you doing, Sam?

". . . eat some pizza?" he concludes the question abruptly.

He could swear she looks a little disappointed. Almost

as if she were hoping he was about to ask her something else entirely.

I think I was.

Maybe I should, before it's—

"Sure," she says, "pizza would be good."

—too late.

In the fading daylight with rain pinging against the porch gutter just beyond the screen door, Meg's new foyer has taken on a cozy, old-fashioned charm. You can't make out that the antique gold wallpaper is torn away in spots, or that the baseboards have been painted many times over, most recently in a brassy coral color more suited to a tropical beach house.

The only place to sit, other than on the floor or wet cardboard boxes, is the stairway. It's wide—but not wide enough for both Meg and Sam to share a step with each other and the pizza box.

She sits near the banister on the third step up. He sits near the wall on the second step up. They balance the box between them, the cover folded back and propped below to almost make a little table.

Sitting here, eating pizza with Sam Rooney in the old-fashioned room with rain falling outside . . .

This would have been a dream date for Meg, a good twenty years ago. Now it's just . . .

Well, it could actually still be pretty dreamy if she were in that infatuated frame of mind, and if she were allowed to be infatuated.

Yes, if she didn't have this tremendous life-changing move to accomplish, and a daughter to worry about in the process, and a New Year's resolution to keep.

Things are complicated enough in her life without reigniting a long-extinguished flame. Speaking of which . . .

"I might need to borrow some matches from you," she tells Sam. "I'm pretty sure I know which box the candles are in, but I have no idea where the flashlight is. And I know I don't have lightbulbs." She gestures helplessly at the useless antique fixture high overhead, with its three empty sockets.

"So you don't have light in any rooms? Or just this one?"

"There's a ceiling bulb in the bathroom upstairs that works, and there's one in the front bedroom, too. Cosette and I will camp out in there tonight." She delicately nibbles the crust end of her second slice to make it last, wondering if it would be piggish to go for a third.

"What about your friend? Is he staying, too?"

"Geoffrey? He doesn't camp out—even indoors. He's headed back to the city."

"Do you have bedding handy?"

"Handy?" She eyes the towering stacks of brown cartons. "There are pillows and blankets in there somewhere, I think. I hope."

"You can—" Sam breaks off, hesitates. "You can spend the night on the pullout couch in our den, if you want to. Or—more privacy—I just remembered Katie's at a sleepover. You can have the bunks in her room."

"Oh, that's okay," she protests, surprised by the cordial offer. "I wasn't trying to get you to—"

"No, I know, but we've got plenty of room."

"How old are your kids?"

"Katie is twelve, Ben is fifteen."

"My daughter's fifteen, too."

"Really? That's a coincidence. What is she into?"

"Into?"

"Hobbies, interests . . ."

Hobbies. Hah. Meg tries to picture Cosette at a kiln, or learning to skate, or doing needlepoint . . .

No go.

"She hasn't really had time for hobbies. Her school is very challenging."

And they don't allow students to carry firearms; major bummer.

"What about boys?" Sam asks good-naturedly, reaching for another slice. "That's the usual hobby for girls her age, as far as I can tell."

"Oh, she likes boys." *And men.*

"Does she date yet?"

"She did, in the city. How about your son?"

"He's newly interested in the opposite sex, I think, but as far as I can tell, he hasn't done anything about it yet. Want more pizza?"

"Oh, no, thanks. I'm stuffed."

No you aren't. Why did you say that?

She still has a ravenous appetite.

For pizza, she thinks, watching him tilt his head back, holding his slice over his open mouth, nibbling a gooey string of cheese.

More pizza isn't all she's craving, though.

She watches Sam swipe a napkin across his luscious mouth.

Then he comments, "So I guess Ben is literally about to meet the girl next door, then."

Realizing he's probably picturing an America's sweetheart

type, as opposed to jaded Cosette, queen of the Goths, Meg hastily says, "Well, I don't know if I'd put it that way, exactly. Cosette is a little . . ."

Sam takes another bite of pizza and waits for her to go on.

Meg shifts her gaze away from him and ponders her vocabulary for the right word to describe her daughter.

Dark?

Edgy?

Moody?

Sullen?

All are accurate, but she isn't eager to undercut Cosette's reputation in the first hours of her new life. Anyway, things are going to be different here. More wholesome and down-to-earth.

Cosette might very well transform herself into a bona fide Girl Next Door.

Right, and Sam Rooney might tell me that he was lying earlier when he said he didn't remember me; that he's actually been pining away for me all these years, waiting for me to come back to him.

Uh-huh. Sure.

Meg watches Sam wipe his mouth again in that adorable way.

Adorable, Meg?

Yes, adorable, Meg.

And familiar.

It's all coming back to her now. She used to watch him in the cafeteria . . .

Among other places.

And she can't help but notice that Sam the Man shares certain qualities with Sam the Boy. He's still got the easy grin, the laid-back demeanor, the casual way of sitting with his legs straight out in front of him, heels against the floor at the foot of the staircase.

He used to sprawl like this back in their school days, she remembers: arms draped over the seat back, long legs stretched before him, a potential obstacle for anyone who happened to pass by him.

Meg did, often. And she was always careful not to trip . . . although sometimes she fantasized about tripping gracefully, if there is such a thing, and landing in Sam's arms.

And then, or so her fantasy went, he would hold her close and whisper something charming and romantic.

Something, she realizes in retrospect, no teenaged boy would ever utter.

No grown man, either, for that matter.

Something like, *"I've been crazy about you from the moment I first saw you."*

Or, *"If you don't let me kiss you right now, I'll die."*

And then he would—

"Meg?"

She blinks. "Yes?"

"You were saying . . . ?"

She was saying? What was she saying?

She has no recollection.

But she knows what she was thinking: that kissing him would be incredible.

Forbidden, yes.

Also incredible.

Hoping he can't read her mind, she changes the subject altogether, to something much safer.

"So, Sam . . . what do you do? I mean, for a living?"

"I teach physics at GPHS."

He teaches physics at GPHS.

Focus. Absorb.

Darn it, she can't seem to rid herself of the image of being in Sam's arms. All she can muster in response to his statement is, "You do?"

"I do."

"That's great."

What did he say he does, again?

Oh! He teaches physics at GPHS.

Think about that.

Think about anything other than kissing him.

He teaches physics at GPHS. Meg forces herself to picture him back at Glenhaven Park High, boyishly sprawled at the teacher's desk instead of behind a student one.

I bet all the girls in his classes have a crush on him, she decides.

"What about you?" he asks. "What do you do?"

What *does* she do?

Nothing at the moment, but . . .

Oh. That's right.

"I'm about to start teaching voice."

"Voice? So you're a singer?"

She nods.

"What do you sing?"

Assuming he's not looking for a rundown of her musical credits, she shrugs, and says, "Show tunes, mostly."

"I don't know many of those. Any, really." He sounds apologetic.

"Well, I don't know much about Newton's theory of relativity, so I guess we're even."

He gives her a blank look.

"You know . . . physics." He did say he teaches physics at GPHS . . . didn't he?

"I know," he tells her. "It's just that, uh, relativity wasn't Newton's theory. It was Einstein's."

"Oops. Well, I told you I didn't know much about it."

He laughs. So does she. Then they fall into an awkward silence.

He toys with his pizza. She nibbles her crust.

This is not going well.

Meg feels like she's in high school again, trying to think of clever things to say to Sam Rooney. Only back then, she never got the chance.

Now, he's a captive audience.

And all she can think of to say is . . .

"Wow, it's humid, isn't it?"

Sheer brilliance. When in doubt, resort to the weather.

"I'm used to air-conditioning," she continues. "You know . . . in the city."

"You should get a couple of window units," Sam replies. "I have them for my kids' rooms."

"Not for yours?" She tries not to picture him in bed.

"No. I like the heat."

Heat. Sam. Bed.

Stop.

"I hope the rain cools things down," she says, oh-so-astutely.

"It should."

"It's supposed to rain tomorrow, too."

"I hope not."

"So do I."

Ho-hum.

"I've got my first soccer practice in the morning," he says then, and she perks up at that.

"You play soccer?"

"No, I coach it. For the town rec board."

"Really? My daughter is playing."

"She's probably on my team, then. I've got the fourteen- and fifteen-year-olds who live in zone one."

"Zone one?"

"The town is divided into zones . . . from here to the Main Street green is one, from the green up to the Stonegate Condos is zone two, and from the train tracks over to Glenhaven Chase is zone three."

Stonegate Condos?

Glenhaven Chase?

She's never heard of either of those.

But on to more important details:

"So you'll be Cosette's soccer coach, then?"

He nods. "I guess. Ben's on the team, too. Did your daughter play soccer where you used to live?"

"Not for a few years, but she used to be pretty good. I'm sure she'll pick it up again easily."

As if he senses that she's trying to sound more opti- mistic than she actually feels, Sam offers, "Maybe she can kick the ball around the yard with Ben to get back into the swing of things."

"That would be good."

Meg has a pleasant flash of her daughter and Sam's son, kicking a soccer ball around in the autumn sunshine, laughing together.

Together.

What if . . . ?

Nah. If Ben's son is anything like he was—popular, athletic, wholesome—Cosette will eat him alive.

Too bad. It would have been great if she found a nice boy her own age to hang out with here, or even date.

Something bangs loudly somewhere on the second floor.

Meg jumps. "What was that?"

"I have no idea."

Chapter
5

As she and Sam gaze up the shadowy staircase, Meg's heart is pounding.

Oh, hell. This isn't just about strange sounds in a strange house. It's been pounding since she first laid eyes on Sam Rooney again.

"It must have been the wind blowing a door closed," Sam decides.

"No, all the windows up there are closed."

"Are you sure?"

"Positive. I tried to open a few when I went up, but I think they're painted shut, so I was going to wait for Geoffrey to give it a shot."

"I'll check it out." Sam brushes crumbs off his legs and moves the pizza box from the step.

"I'll come with you," Meg says hastily, not wanting to be left alone down here in the almost dark.

And, admit it, not wanting to be away from Sam.

Together, they make their way up the creaking staircase.

A few steps behind him, Meg can't help but notice that Sam seems a little hesitant as they get closer to the hot, stuffy second floor. The rain has stopped; now there is only a steady dripping sound coming from somewhere under the eaves.

"You don't really think this house is haunted, do you?" she asks, and wonders why she's whispering. But the circumstances seem to warrant it; she can't help but feel as though they might not be alone here.

"Haunted?" he echoes—also in a whisper, she notes. But he shakes his head adamantly. "No way."

Then why are they practically tiptoeing as they make their way down the almost eerily still upstairs hall?

They step into the first bedroom, the one Meg thought would be perfect for Cosette. She was charmed by the pair of dormered windows and the cozy alcove on one end where she plans to put a desk and overhead bookshelves.

Now, however, there's nothing the least bit charming about the room, even after she flips on the overhead light. The bulb must be low-wattage; its glow is far from cheery.

"So you tried this window?" Sam crosses to the one nearest the door.

"Yes, but it wouldn't—"

She breaks off, startled, as he effortlessly raises the sash. A cooling breeze instantly fills the room.

Meg gapes. "How did you do that?"

"Magic fingers." He grins and wiggles them at her.

"But I . . ."

"You probably loosened it for me. Or maybe it's less humid now. Let me try this one . . ." With a slight pull, he opens the other window.

She follows him from room to room, watching in disbelief as he opens one window after another with a mere tug.

Finally, in the back bedroom that's destined to become

her future study, he brushes his palms against each other, turns to her, and announces, "All done."

"I swear I didn't make it up," she says, baffled.

"You mean about the windows being stuck?"

She nods. "I really didn't."

"Why would you make it up?"

"I don't know . . ."

To play the helpless female role to your big strong man role?

If only he knew her well enough to realize that isn't her style. To realize that she's stronger and more independent than ever before.

But he doesn't know you at all, she reminds herself. *And you only think you know him. That was so long ago, and all you ever really knew was his image.*

Still, she has to admit, the nice guy image is pretty close to the real thing. At least, close to the man Sam Rooney grew up to become.

Hearing footsteps at the foot of the stairs, she realizes with a disappointed pang that Cosette and Geoffrey are back, and her time alone with Sam has come to an end.

"I'm up here, guys," she calls loudly.

To Sam, she says, "Thanks so much for helping me out. Now that they're back, I can release you from manual labor duty."

"Oh, it was no problem." He shrugs. "I've got nothing to rush home to."

Something in his tone makes her wish she could see his face more clearly, but there isn't enough light spilling in from the room down the hall.

She wonders why his marriage ended, and where his kids are. They must live with his ex-wife. But she must be here in town or at least nearby, if his son plays on his soccer team.

"I guess they're not coming up," Sam says after a moment, and she realizes Cosette and Geoffrey have yet to materialize—or speak.

All is silent below now; she can't hear them uttering a peep of complaint about the errands, or the rain, or the heat—which is unlike either of them.

"Guys! We're up here," she calls, stepping into the hall, then poising to listen.

Not a sound from below.

Frowning, Meg walks into the front bedroom and peers down at the street. Geoffrey's Prius is nowhere to be seen.

Goose bumps raise the hair on her arms. If Geoffrey and Cosette weren't downstairs . . . who was? She didn't imagine the footsteps.

Did she?

Sam seemed to have heard them, too.

And what about that slamming sound that drew them up here in the first place? What caused—

Hearing a floorboard creak behind her, she cries out and whirls around.

"Shh, it's only me!" Sam grabs her arms. "I'm sorry, I didn't mean to sneak up on you."

"It's okay," she murmurs.

Her heart is racing wildly.

Because he startled her?

Or because he's practically hugging her?

His big, reassuring hands are warm, firm on her shoulders. His handsome face—with that tantalizing mouth—is mere inches from her own.

She hasn't been this close to any man in ages. Over six months.

That's why her body is reacting to him this way: rippling with need.

Or is it simply because she's never been this close to Sam Rooney? Well, she sure has imagined it. All that buildup coming to unexpected fruition now, on the heels of fear-spiked adrenaline . . .

Is it any wonder she's aching for him to pull her closer, heedless of her resolve to stay away from men like him?

"Old houses make noises, Meg," he's saying, "you know? You just have to get used to them."

She nods, vaguely wondering if he's trying to convince her, or himself.

Wondering whether he's going to keep holding her, or let go.

Don't let go, Sam. Not yet.

"You can't let this scare you away."

She nods.

You're not scaring me, Sam. I've been waiting for this for longer than you can imagine.

"The power of suggestion can do strange things to a person, you know?" Sam tells Meg, who is looking up at him with those big eyes of hers: eyes that are the same translucent green of sunlit seawater on a warm afternoon.

"Mmm-hmm."

He should let go of her. He is well aware of that fact.

But there seems to be a vast chasm between knowing it and doing it.

How long has it been since he's been this close to a woman?

You know damn well how long.

Sheryl . . .

He waits to experience some sense of disloyalty to his late wife; oddly, there is none.

Still . . . he shouldn't be doing this. Shouldn't be holding her. Because if he doesn't stop, he's going to do something they'll both regret.

Okay, maybe *regret* is the wrong word—because he can't imagine regretting kissing a desirable woman.

But that would establish a romantic relationship between them right off the bat, and they're going to have to live next door to each other for years to come . . .

Unless, of course, she hightails it out of here just as all the previous occupants have.

Which, Sam assures himself despite a pang, would be fine with him. Because he definitely isn't interested in a relationship. He's learned his lesson the hardest way possible: when you love, you lose. When you lose . . .

You're shattered.

Pulling himself together emotionally—though still mysteriously unable to release his physical hold on her—he picks up his conversational thread. "So you do understand that your mind can play tricks on you, especially in an old house, in the dark?"

She says nothing, just looks up at him. In the yellow glow from the dismal bulb overhead, he can see that she's wearing a faraway expression that seems somehow to encompass him.

"Meg?"

"Hmm?"

"Are you . . . uh, *hearing* me?"

"What? Yes!"

"You just seem like you're a million miles away . . ."
And taking me there along with you.

She shakes her head a little. "I'm sorry. It's just a little overwhelming, being back here with you."

"*Me?*"

"What?"

"Did you say back here with me?"

"Oh. I didn't mean . . ." She looks momentarily flustered. "I don't know what I meant. Forget it."

He tries. But something shifts, then settles, inside him.

So she's feeling it, too. Whatever it is that he's experiencing, being so close to her—it's not one-sided. He's certain of that.

It isn't so much what she said, because she didn't really *say* anything other than to add that seemingly innocuous "with you."

But the emphasis on the "you" strangely seems to hint that there might have been something between them in the past.

And there definitely wasn't. He'd remember that.

"You must think I'm crazy."

"Crazy?" He looks at her. "Why would I think that?"

"A single mom with no real income, leaving behind a whole life and buying a rundown old house in my hometown, trying to duplicate this ideal childhood for my daughter . . . hell, *I* think I'm crazy. I've never even owned a car in my life until last week. How did I get myself into this?"

"You'll be fine. You'll see."

"You really think so?"

No. I think you'll get carried away thinking this place

really is haunted. Especially since you grew up here and knew all the rumors before you ever moved in.

So you'll get spooked, and you'll take off. Maybe tomorrow, maybe next week. You'll take your daughter and go back to the city where it's safe.

And when that happens, I'll miss you.

Huh?

Where did *that* come from?

How can you miss someone you don't even know?

"Listen to me," she says with a taut laugh. "Have you ever met a bigger wimp in your life? One day into my famous fresh start, and I'm already questioning everything about it."

"I don't think you're a wimp. I think the opposite about you. Most people don't have the guts to pick up and make huge changes when they aren't satisfied with their lives."

He realizes that her head is bent, and she's no longer looking at him . . .

Then he realizes why.

It's because he's . . .

He's . . .

He's half-stroking, half-massaging, her bare arms!

Mindlessly. Instinctively.

The way a man would touch a woman with whom he was physically involved.

"Sorry." Mortified, he releases his grip abruptly. "I don't know why I—"

"No!"

He looks at her in surprise. "No?"

It's Meg's turn to look embarrassed. "I mean, you don't have to . . ."

She looks flushed.

Hmm.

Is it the heat and humidity, or something else?

He doesn't have to . . . what?

Is she trying to say that he doesn't have to move his hands; that she wants him to go on touching her that way?

Maybe. He can't figure out how to get her to say it, though, now that she's stopped talking and started fidgeting uncomfortably, glancing everywhere but at him.

There's not much else to look at in this empty room, and it doesn't take long for her to reluctantly meet his gaze again.

"Are you okay?" he asks tentatively.

"Not really. I mean, in general, I am, but right this minute? I'm kind of . . . mortified."

"That's a coincidence," he says, "because so am I."

She laughs.

He relaxes a little. "I don't usually go around grabbing strange women and rubbing their arms. Just so you know."

"There's another coincidence," she returns easily, "because I don't usually go around letting strange men grab me and rub my arms. Just so *you* know."

He nods. "Glad to hear it."

"Then again . . ."

"Yes?"

"Technically, we're not strangers. At least, you aren't to me."

"So you've said. But I can't believe I never noticed you back in high school."

"I can't either. You must have been blind."

He's startled; superciliousness seems out of character for her. Then he sees that she didn't mean it that way—she's grinning.

"Not because I was drop-dead gorgeous," she clarifies, "because I *so* wasn't . . ."

He finds that hard to believe.

"What I mean is, you must have been blind not to notice me because I constantly detoured past your locker, rode my bike past your house, found reasons to be wherever you were. I threw myself into your path every chance I got, hoping you'd fall madly in love with me."

His jaw drops.

"I can't believe I just admitted that," Meg says, "but what the hell? It was so long ago, and it's really kind of funny. In a humiliating way. Basically, you had your very own personal stalker, and you were oblivious."

"So you . . . ?" He shakes his head.

"Yup. I used to have a crush on you, back in school. And just now, when you were . . . you know . . . touching me . . . I mean, for a second there, I felt like I was back there again. A kid with a crush." She laughs awkwardly. "Isn't that ridiculous?"

Ridiculous? Is it?

No.

It's charming, and flattering, and intriguing. That's what it is.

But not ridiculous.

And, touching her, he felt like anything but an insecure kid. He felt like a man who hasn't been with a woman in much too long.

"So now," Meg says in a brisk, case-closed tone, "you know my secret."

"Right. I just don't get why you didn't ever just come up to me and talk to me?"

She looks at him as though he's just asked her why she

never marched naked onto the football field with the band at halftime, carrying an I LOVE SAM ROONEY banner.

"I was shy," she says with a shrug.

He tilts his head, intrigued. "I thought you were a performer."

"That's different." She tilts her head in the opposite direction. Flirting.

"So you're saying you can sing onstage in front of thousands of people, but you can't make the first move with a guy you like?"

"Oh, I can now," she clarifies. "I just couldn't back then."

"Really." He finds himself folding his arms across his chest.

"Really." She mimics the posture.

"So these days, you don't ride your bike around lower Manhattan, hoping to catch a glimpse of your latest Wall Street crush? You actually make a move on him?"

"If I *had* a Wall Street crush, which I wouldn't—"

"Because?"

"Not my type."

He wonders if high school physics teachers could possibly be her type.

"And anyway," she goes on, "I'm on a permanent hiatus from stuff like that."

"Stuff like . . . flirting? Dating?"

"Right. All of it," she says firmly.

He can't help but wonder what happened to make her say that.

"But if you weren't on . . . hiatus . . . you'd just go right up to someone and let him know you were into him?"

"Yup."

"What would you say?"

"It's not what I would say. It's how I would act. Body language."

Whoa, it's getting steamy in here.

He should go.

No, he should stay.

He should definitely stay.

"Okay, then let's see," he challenges her.

"See what?"

"What you would do now, if you were into someone, and I was the person you were into."

"What?"

"You know what I mean. Go for it."

Okay, what the hell are you doing, here?

I'm flirting. And frankly, I'm surprised I remember how.

Well, now that you've refreshed your memory, you need to stop.

And go.

And I will. Just as soon as she makes her fake move on me.

"Go for it?" Meg echoes, and bites the edge of her lower lip, looking up at him alluringly.

Or maybe she doesn't mean to be alluring.

She just is.

"Right," he tells her, "just do whatever you would do if you were interested in someone."

"And you're the someone, right?" She takes a provocative step closer.

"Right. I'm the someone," he informs her in a voice

that suddenly resembles his own, a good twenty-odd years ago. When it was changing.

He clears his throat.

Which, as it turns out, doesn't matter, because he isn't going to be speaking again for a bit.

He won't be speaking because his mouth will be otherwise engaged.

Kissing Meg.

Or rather, letting Meg kiss *him*.

That's how it starts, anyway.

She rests her hands on his shoulders, stands on her tiptoes, and plants a kiss that is both bold and gentle on his lips.

"There," she says softly. "That's what I'd do."

That's it.

There.

No preamble, no pretenses.

Sam pulls her closer; they kiss again.

His mouth comes alive at the slightest brush against her lips. He closes his eyes and allows himself the pleasure, however fleeting, of kissing a desirable woman, after all these years, after all he's been through.

He might have forgotten what that's like, but he gets the hang of it fairly quickly. His body responds of its own accord; he pulls her closer, holds her against him; at once thrilled and dismayed by his own rigid need.

This is as far as it can go. Kissing. Tonight.

This is all he'll allow himself.

Tomorrow, they'll be nothing more than next-door neighbors again, and she can go back to her hiatus, but tonight—

Meg breaks the kiss and stiffens abruptly in Sam's arms

as downstairs, a door slams and footsteps tap across the hardwood floor.

Now my imagination is getting into the act, he realizes, still a little unnerved by the inexplicable slam they heard earlier.

Then a voice calls, "Mom?"

Heart still pounding from the unexpected kiss and what she thought was another haunting, Meg hurries to the top of the stairs with Sam on her heels.

She peers over the banister to see Cosette and Geoffrey, bags in their hands, looking up at her.

"Do you know how hard it is to find an onion ring in this burg?" Geoffrey demands. "Enough hummus, organic produce, sushi, pinot grigio, and espresso to supply a nation of soccer moms for a hundred years, but if you want—"

He breaks off, looking over Meg's shoulder, where Sam has presumably become visible.

"Hello," Geoffrey tells him politely, and casts a bit of a smug grin at Meg. She knows he's thinking about her New Year's resolution—and that he suspects she just violated it.

To Sam, Geoffrey says, "And you must be . . . ?" with obvious irony, as Geoffrey has no way of knowing who Sam must be.

Meg dares to dart a glance at Cosette and is surprised to see that she looks merely intrigued. And . . . impressed?

Looking over her shoulder, Meg can see why. Sam, with his shaggy hair and ruggedly handsome face, is . . .

Well, pretty much a total hottie, to borrow a favorite phrase of Cosette's. Or is it Geoffrey's?

No matter. It's been a while since Meg has personally

encountered a total hottie, but Sam Rooney definitely fits the bill.

Which is exactly why she should have run in the opposite direction.

Instead, you just kissed the living daylights out of him, she reminds herself, trying to fend off the sensation that what just happened between them was a dream sequence in some bizarre production.

"I'm Sam Rooney, an old friend of Meg's."

Startled back to reality by that unexpected—and basically untrue—introduction, she nods in vigorous agreement. "Sam was helping me move stuff."

"Really," Geoffrey says dubiously.

"Yes. All those boxes are so heavy that I couldn't get them up the stairs, so Sam . . . helped."

Never mind that there are no actual boxes on the second floor yet, which might lead Cosette and Geoffrey to wonder exactly what Meg and her hot old friend were doing in the bedroom.

"Sam," Meg says, heading down the steps with him right behind her, lest the newcomers venture up, "this is my daughter Geoffrey and my friend Cosette."

"Um, Mom? Hello?" Cosette waves a hand in her face as she arrives at the foot of the staircase, "*I'm* your daughter; *he's* your friend."

"Oh, right, whatever." Meg is becoming more discombobulated by the second—much, she sees, to Geoffrey's silent amusement. She prattles on, "Sam has a son your age, and he's going to play soccer with you."

"That's funny, I thought *Sam* was about my age," Geoffrey cracks.

"I was talking to Cosette."

"That's even funnier, because I told you I'm not playing soccer," Cosette retorts.

"Yes, you are. She is," Meg assures Sam, without looking at him.

She isn't particularly anxious to gauge his reaction to her daughter, who more closely resembles Edward Scissorhands than the mythical all-American girl next door.

"It's great to meet you, Cosette," Sam says so easily, she's relieved. "I think I'll be your soccer coach."

"That's nice, but I'm not actually playing. My mother is deluded."

"Cosette!"

"Mom!"

Fuming, Meg glares at her daughter. "You're not allowed to speak to me that way, and you're about to lose a privilege."

"Too late. I've already lost them all, now that we live here. Guess you'll have to figure out another punishment."

"Believe me, I will," Meg mutters.

"On that note," Geoffrey says after an uncomfortable pause, "I think I'll toddle back to civilization."

"And I've got to get home," Sam pipes up, following Geoffrey toward the door.

There, he pauses to ask, "Meg, do you want to spend the night? You and Cosette," he adds hastily, and tacks on a gratuitous, "because you don't have anyplace to sleep here."

"No, we'll be fine," she says reluctantly.

His offer is tempting for reasons other than the lack of sleeping accommodations here, but she isn't particularly anxious to further expose him to her sulky fifteen-year-old at this point.

He'll get to know Cosette soon enough. Unfortunately.

"Well, holler if you need anything. See you at soccer," he calls over his shoulder as he makes his exit.

"Definitely," Meg shoots a daggered look at her daughter as she returns with false cheer, "See you at soccer."

Chapter
6

Standing in the sunlit kitchen listening to morning birds chirping outside the screen and waiting for the coffee to finish brewing, Sam does his best to think of a good reason to go into the den.

Does he want to reread one of the dog-eared novels that line the built-in shelves?

Not particularly.

Does he need to pay a few of the bills stacking up in the basket on his desk?

Yes, but he can't. Not until after school starts next week and he resumes getting regular paychecks.

You could . . . um . . . dust! he tells himself triumphantly.

Yes, every room in the house can use a thorough dusting; he can't afford the Molly Maids service during the summer months. While he's fairly good about staying on top of the laundry, dishes, and vacuuming—a daily must with Rover shedding all over the place—he never pays much attention to the furniture.

Sheryl was always big on that. She'd bustle from room

to room with a wad of dust rags and a can of lemon-scented polish, spraying and swiping, making everything gleam and smell great.

Sheryl would want you to dust the den, he assures himself.

Yes, but not for the reason he's so eager to dust the den on this particular morning.

It happens to be the only room in the house—aside from Ben's room upstairs, where Ben just retreated after returning from his morning run—with windows that look directly over the old Duckworth place.

Rather, the new Addams place.

Yes, Sam is hoping to catch a glimpse of Meg again, somewhere other than in his own head. Last night was a restless one, and not just because he never sleeps well when one of the kids isn't tucked safely under his roof.

But when he finally did doze off, he dreamed of Meg.

Of kissing her, and . . .

More.

He woke up predawn feeling like a teenaged boy again: incredibly turned on by an erotic dream and frustrated as hell to realize that it wasn't real.

With a jingling of dog tags and toenails tapping on the hardwoods, Rover materializes in the kitchen.

"Good morning, boy." Sam reaches over to pet his head. "Hungry?"

Rover nods.

Well, not really. But master and mutt have been a team long enough for Sam easily to interpret the dog's needs.

He opens a can of Alpo, fills Rover's bowl, and sets it on the floor. "There you go, pal. Knock yourself out."

The dog fed, he remembers to turn his attention to filling a plastic cup to water the potted geranium on the windowsill. He bought the plant at the nursery on Mother's Day, when he took the kids to buy flowers for the cemetery.

When Sheryl was alive, they did that at his mother-in-law's grave every Mother's Day. Devoted daughter, devoted gardener, Sheryl would kneel in the dirt beside the granite headstone, crying and digging with her trowel as Sam and the kids and her father stood by helplessly. When she was finished, the bare earth was transformed into a blooming landscape; purged of her grief, Sheryl would brush herself off and move on.

Sam knew he had to take over the yearly ritual on her behalf, and he does. On the second weekend of May every year, he and the kids and his father-in-law cry and dig and plant. It's cathartic.

And every year, Sam buys an extra large geranium to brighten the kitchen window, the way Sheryl always did.

He's no gardener, but he's learning. He had to.

He still remembers the day they were packing to move here and Katie, sobbing hysterically, came to him carrying a clay pot filled with dusty clumps of dirt and a withered brown stalk.

It was the miniature rose she had proudly given to Sheryl for her birthday the month before she died. Then, it was covered in shiny foliage and delicate pink blooms. Sheryl tended to it daily.

Sam never even thought to water it after she died. It was all he could do to keep getting up in the morning with the kids, keep them fed and clothed, keep helping them with their homework and filling out the endless backpack paperwork, keep putting one foot in front of the other.

That was then.

These days, he has all that other stuff down pat. And he remembers to water the geranium on the windowsill a couple of times a week. No more, no less.

Ironically, the first year, he watered the geranium every day and watched the velvety leaves turn yellow, curl, and drop. Concerned, he watered it twice a day. It died anyway.

It turned out he had drowned them; the nice lady at the nursery—who fondly remembered Sheryl and always smiled sadly at the kids—told him geraniums don't like to be soaked.

"Why don't you try a different kind of plant for your windowsill?" she suggested. "We have some nice low-maintenance Melampodium over here . . ."

Low-maintenance.

She didn't think he could do it.

He was determined to prove her—to prove everyone—wrong.

It had to be geraniums.

It hasn't been easy to get it right: to water them just enough without flooding or forgetting.

This year, though, the big plant in the clay pot on the sill has made it through the summer with plenty of red blooms and curly deep green foliage.

He might just have the hang of it now. Sheryl would be pleased with the blooms in the kitchen and the garden on her grave.

Tossing the plastic cup into the sink, Sam yawns and checks the glass coffee carafe again: a mere two inches of fragrant brew in the bottom and a good couple of minutes before it'll be full.

It only takes a couple of minutes to dust a small room. Sheryl used to say that, back when she was irritated with his ability to overlook layers of dust along with other household blights.

How many times did he wonder, in the wake of losing her, why they had wasted all that time bickering about unimportant issues?

Yes, all married couples do it.

All husbands take their wives for granted at some point or another; it's human nature.

But now, knowing what he knows, Sam will never take anything for granted again.

There's guilt, too.

Guilt because their marriage, as good as it was, didn't entirely live up to his expectations.

He loved Sheryl. But in the year or two leading up to her death, he had begun to wonder if he was really in love with her.

They were best friends back in college; a friendship based on a number of elements. They were both secondary education majors; they lived in the same dorm; they were both athletic and had mutual friends, similar tastes in music, movies, books, sports.

Friendship eventually led to fooling around. That happened back in college. You had a few beers, you wound up kissing girls who were your friends and lived under your roof. Fooling around led to coupledom. That happened, too. It was convenient to have a girlfriend who was part of your group of friends, as opposed to some of his buddies, who were trying to maintain doomed long-distance relationships.

Coupledom eventually led, after graduation, to living together, to engagement, then marriage. That was the rhythm of life; it all made sense.

Sam did balk at getting engaged, when the time came to sink or swim.

But she gave him an ultimatum. She wanted to move on with their lives, or with her own.

It was either marry Sheryl or let her go.

Sam wasn't willing to let her go. They were too close, too entrenched in each other's lives. Everyone around them wanted—no, expected—them to get married. Their friends, their families, kept pointing out that there were so many reasons to stay together.

Meanwhile, Sam couldn't think of a compelling reason to break up.

Other than the nagging feeling he had that it was all too pat.

That there was supposed to be more to relationships than falling together like neatly interlocking puzzle pieces.

More . . . passion. Not just physical passion—though for Sam, married intimacy had faded into a comfortable, if lackluster and predictable rhythm by the time Katie came along. No, Sam also wondered if there wasn't supposed to be, between husband and wife, more of an emotionally charged connection fueled by fervent feelings.

But their marriage did work. Especially because the children were one more thing—the most important thing— they had in common. He and Sheryl were fiercely devoted parents, with Ben and Katie, they were a wholeheartedly cohesive family unit.

He just wonders what would have happened, had Sheryl lived, when Ben and Katie left the nest.

Would the vaguely restless, unsatisfied feeling have persisted, grown stronger?

Would he have forever wondered whether there was supposed to be . . . more?

Would he or Sheryl have had a midlife crisis at some point, and left the marriage to find out if there was more?

That would have been horrible: divorce. Not as horrible as widowhood, because at least his kids wouldn't be motherless. But horrible nonetheless.

And why am I thinking this way this morning?

I need some kind of distraction to break this mood.

Sam's gaze automatically goes to the digital clock on the microwave—8:06. Too early for Katie to be calling, ready to come home.

Sam's brother Jack showed up with Ben just after he'd left Meg's.

They were chatty about their golf outing at Chelsea Piers and dinner afterward at the famous Ben Benson's Steakhouse—"Where else would I take a kid named Ben?" Jack asked jovially.

Sam did his best to carry on a reciprocal conversation, but he was still trying to absorb what happened between him and Meg in that upstairs bedroom—and everything else about the evening.

He still can't figure out what caused the slamming sound he and Meg heard when they were on the stairs. And he has to admit, he did think he heard someone down in the hall the first time, just as Meg did—when there was nobody there. He still doesn't believe in ghosts. But realizing that he, too, is susceptible to the myth really threw him for a loop.

So, for that matter, did kissing Meg.

As did meeting Meg's daughter, who wasn't at all what he expected.

All right, he admittedly didn't give that much consideration before he encountered Cosette. But as a teacher and a parent, he knows enough girls her age to have a perpetual stereotype in mind.

Meg's daughter shattered it.

Teenaged girls her age—most girls Sam knows, anyway—are insecure and spend a lot of time acting like they aren't. They're wrapped up in how they look and do their best to make the most of their God-given physical attributes. Their conversations are liberally sprinkled with *like* and their remarks frequently sound like they're ending in a question even when they're not asking one.

Cosette, however, exuded a centered confidence and articulation. And although anyone can see that there's a pretty girl lurking somewhere beneath the unnatural hair and makeup and baggy black wardrobe, she is obviously bent on keeping it well concealed.

As far as Sam can tell, the only cliché Meg's daughter personifies at this point is her antagonistic attitude toward her mother.

Unfortunately, the moment he laid eyes on her, he knew Ben—whose budding interest in girls is apparently limited to surface appearance at this point—would probably want nothing to do with her. The girls Sam has caught his son checking out are your garden-variety high school cheerleader/prom queen types.

The same kinds of girls Sam used to date.

He wishes he could retract his offer to have his son kick a soccer ball around with Meg's daughter.

Not that Cosette is likely to have any interest in that, anyway.

But her mother seems hell-bent on having her play on the team.

And, lucky me, I get to be her coach.

Naturally, Sam checked his list of players first chance he got last night. At first he thought she wasn't on it.

The list goes alphabetically by last name, and there is no *Addams, Cosette* at the top.

There is, however, a *Hudson, Cosette* a third of the way down, and the address is 33 Boxwood Lane.

That's her.

Sam also, embarrassingly, got online as soon as Ben went to bed, and Googled Meg Addams. He figured that if she'd been on Broadway, there would be a wealth of information about her.

There was nothing.

Remembering the soccer team list, he then checked Meg Hudson, figuring she might have used her ex-husband's name on stage.

Still nothing.

Which *means* nothing, really . . .

Other than that Sam is feeling more and more like an infatuated teenaged boy.

Now, reaching into the cupboard below the sink to find a can of Pledge and a dust rag, he abruptly stops himself.

What are you doing?

Act your age.

You're a grown man.

And you absolutely cannot let things go any further with Meg than they did last night.

If only he could remember, in the bright, promising light of day, exactly *why* that can't happen.

*   *   *

Driving—as opposed to, say, kissing—doesn't come right back to you when you haven't done it in a while.

Late last night, Meg was nervous behind the wheel of her new used Hyundai on rain-slicked roads after leaving the truck rental place in White Plains. Cosette glowering in the front seat didn't help matters much.

Now, as she steers the car through the streets of her old hometown, the sun is shining, and the roads are dry, but Cosette is still glowering in the front seat with her, and Meg's driving skills are still rusty.

Not only that, but things around here are unnervingly unfamiliar.

There's a whole strip of chain stores on what was once a sleepy stretch of tree-lined highway. There are lights at intersections where there used to be four-way stops, and it's much harder to make left turns than she remembers— not because of her driving skills but because of all the traffic. Chestnut Street is now one-way—which she discovered after a near-head-on collision that would have been her own fault.

Even worse, nobody seems to obey the right-of-way or speed limit laws.

Were people always this impatient? Meg wonders, as yet another supersized SUV tailgates her for a couple of blocks before swerving around her at the first opportunity.

By the time they've reached Glenhaven Memorial Park, a wooded thirty-acre plot on the edge of town, Meg feels as though she's driven a couple of legs of a road race—and lost.

Oh, well. Time to stop worrying about her driving skills and turn her attention to her parenting skills . . . or lack thereof.

"I swear, Cosette, if you embarrass me in any way, shape, or form, you're going to regret it," she informs her daughter as she pulls into a space in the crowded lot adjacent to the athletic fields.

Slumped in the passenger's seat in her usual position— spine resting against the seat bottom, knees propped against the dash, arms folded stubbornly—Cosette retorts, "That seems really unfair, considering that everything about this embarrasses me in every way, shape, and form, and you don't seem to regret that."

Meg ignores that.

She also ignores Cosette's heavy sigh as she turns off the engine and pulls the key from the ignition. "Let's go."

"I can't believe you're making me do this."

I can't, either. But . . .

"It's for your own good."

And I can't believe I just said that.

That was Meg's parents' favorite phrase when she was growing up—and one of the many she swore she would never, ever, *ever* use on her own children.

It's for your own good.

Mom and Dad said that whenever they made Meg do something she didn't want to do, like eat beets or get a shot or take swimming lessons.

They also said it whenever they wouldn't let her do something she was longing to do, like trade Glenhaven Park High for a private school specializing in the performing arts. Or audition for a European tour of *Annie*. Or even study voice in Manhattan.

Her parents weren't trying to smother her creativity, though—as she accused them of doing on more than one occasion. They just wanted to protect her, to keep her healthy and happy and close to home—and them—for as long as they could.

Which is exactly what I want for Cosette.

She climbs out of the car, starts across the gravel past the row of shiny parked vehicles, and promptly notices that hers seems to be the only Hyundai in the lot. The others all seem to be either massive sport utility vehicles—including Hummers—plus Volvo station wagons, expensive sports cars, and glossy sedans.

She watches a pair of fashionably dressed, impeccably groomed Fancy Moms emerge with Starbucks cups from an SUV big enough to transport the entire cast of *A Chorus Line*. Meg momentarily wonders if she knows either of them, then dismisses the thought.

Probably not.

Krissy said there aren't many locals left in town. After running into her, then Sam, Meg figures her resident acquaintances are most likely tapped out.

Sam.

She's about to see him again.

Her hand immediately goes to her hair. If only she'd had time this morning to fix herself up a little.

Not that she's trying to be seductive.

What happened between her and Sam last night won't be happening again.

At least in the city, after a bitter breakup, she didn't have to cross paths regularly with her ex-boyfriends.

But if she allows Sam into her life, only to have him turn it upside down and walk away, he can't walk far.

It was hard enough nursing one-sided feelings for him back in high school, when he didn't know she was alive. It would be torture to let this flirtation go any further now, then be forced to spend wistful years watching him live his life right under her nose.

Then again. . . .

Maybe that wouldn't have to happen.

Maybe for once . . .

Suddenly, Meg realizes Cosette isn't walking with her. She turns and sees that her daughter is still sitting there in the Hyundai with the door closed, sulking.

With a weary sigh, Meg marches back over to the passenger side, jerks open the door, and orders, "Get out."

She's prepared for a battle, but Cosette scowls and gets out.

That's probably because she's overcome by the heat in the car with the windows rolled up—especially when she's wearing all that black: long spandex shorts, a sleeveless T-shirt, socks, and high-tops.

Having learned to choose her battles, Meg didn't bother to criticize her daughter's unorthodox practice gear this morning. She'll leave that up to the coach.

Sam.

Sam Rooney.

So you're back to this, are you, after all these years? Back to palpitations and a butterfly-filled gut every time you so much as think about him?

How ironic. She came to Glenhaven Park for a fresh start, but here she is, feeling as though she's picked up her old life where she left off years ago.

Still infatuated with Sam Rooney . . .

And still feeling as though she doesn't fit in.

She watches another pair of Fancy Moms disappear around a clump of trees and knows there are probably more where they came from. Even here, it's going to be just like it was in the city, with Meg and Cosette on the out-skirts of the socially "in" crowd.

So what?

Why do you care? This isn't high school . . .

Well, it is for Cosette.

Remembering the painful bullying experience they left behind, Meg wonders if she's made a big mistake. Is it going to be even worse here in the suburbs?

This was supposed to be her small-town safe zone, a place where all the bad stuff can fade away.

She glances at her daughter, whose face is clearly visible, for a change, because she's got her black hair pulled back in an elastic. Her jaw is tense, and she's looking straight ahead toward the crowd at the edge of the soccer field, wearing a grim expression.

"Are you okay, Cosette?"

"No. I hate this."

For a second there, Meg was certain she was going to say *you* instead of *this*.

That she didn't gives her a flash of maternal hope.

"I know you hate it," she says, and reaches out to touch her daughter's arm.

Cosette flinches.

Meg releases her. "Listen, it's going to be hard, but in the end, everything will be okay. I promise."

"You can't promise. You don't know."

There was a time when Meg would have contradicted that statement. Like when Cosette turned to her for reassur-ance after the 9/11 attacks. They had a similar conversation then, tightly holding hands, standing on their building's rooftop, watching the black smoke from the ravaged twin towers curl into the clear blue September sky.

Cosette was frightened. Crying.

So was Meg.

But she said, *I promise you, sweetheart, that everything is going to be okay.*

You can't promise, Cosette protested. *You don't know.*

Yes, I do, Meg said firmly, and her daughter was young, and idealistic, and naive enough to believe the lie.

Not anymore.

Now, Meg merely admits, "You're right. I don't know. I just hope."

"Hope is stupid."

Meg bristles at that.

Sometimes, hope is all you have.

That's what she wants to say, but she keeps it to herself. Under the stressful circumstances, she'll cut Cosette a bit of slack.

As they walk toward the athletic fields, she notes that some things around here, at least, have remained the same. The park itself is virtually unchanged, right down to the familiar gravel pathways, deer netting around some of the newer shrubs, and a cluster of stone and timber picnic shelters.

Meg makes sure to give a wide berth to the trash cans around the shelters. She can see bees and wasps buzzing around them even from here.

"Careful," she cautions Cosette, who refuses to walk at her side and passes close to the cans. "You'll get stung."

"No, I won't. Bees don't bother you if you don't bother them."

"Sometimes you bother them without meaning to." Meg shudders, remembering the hive incident from her childhood.

She's told Cosette that story enough times, though, that her daughter rolls her eyes whenever she brings it up.

"Get a grip, Mom," Cosette tells her now, and marches defiantly closer to the trash barrels and the bees . . . without incident.

So far, so good, Meg thinks, trying to relax.

They emerge from the wooded pavilion area into a wide, sunny meadow bordering the soccer field.

She looks around for Sam and spots him almost immediately.

There he is, kicking a ball around with a couple of other boys . . .

Wait a minute! That's not Sam.

But it could have been, if this were twenty years ago.

The boy on the field looks exactly like the Sam Rooney Meg once adored from afar. So much so that she's positive he must be Sam's son. She watches him for a minute, smiling. Even from this distance, she can see that he has not just his father's looks, but his easygoing, good-natured disposition.

As for the real, grown-up Sam . . .

She takes another quick look around and spies him standing near the bleachers. He's holding a clipboard and wearing athletic shorts, a white T-shirt, sneakers. He's tanned and muscular and his wavy-could-stand-to-be-cut hair pokes from beneath a baseball cap that shades his good-looking features.

Whoa.

Palpitations. Butterflies.

I actually kissed him, she thinks incredulously—for the hundredth time since she woke up this morning. *And he actually kissed me back.*

That the kiss was just as good as she always imagined it would be probably isn't a great thing.

If kissing Sam Rooney hadn't lived up to her expectations, she'd have gotten him out of her system once and for all.

But it did live up to them . . . and then some.

As a result, he seems to be even more firmly entrenched in Meg's . . . uh, *system* . . . than he was back in high school, when she was in full-blown obsession mode.

She sees him glance around, almost as though he's looking for someone.

Then he shades his eyes in her direction, and waves.

He sees me, she realizes, quickening her pace. *But he wasn't looking for me.*

At least, that's what she needs to remind herself, trying to keep a silly grin off her face as she waves back at him.

"Mom, jeez, will you stop?"

"Stop what?" She looks at Cosette and finds her glaring.

"Stop flailing your arms all over the place like that. Everyone is staring at us now."

Meg automatically says, "No, they aren't."

But, oh yes they are.

She lowers her arm slowly, acutely aware that clusters of Fancy Moms and a couple of dads are watching her and Cosette approach.

Even the kids turn their heads, although after shooting curious glances at the newcomers, they quickly go back to whatever it was that they were doing. For the girls, that's gossiping with their friends and hoping the boys will notice them; for the boys, it's anxiously shuffling their feet and stealing glances at the girls.

It's as difficult to picture Cosette slipping seamlessly

into this bunch as it is for Meg to imagine herself sitting in the bleachers with a tasteful blond pageboy, a manicure, and a grande nonfat iced caramel espresso.

Not that she doesn't enjoy the occasional upscale coffee drink. But for the time being, her budget won't allow for anything more than Maxwell House, brewed at home.

Which reminds her, she has yet to find the box that holds the kitchen appliances. What she wouldn't have given for a cup of coffee this morning.

Luckily, though, she found the bedding last night. And some of her clothes—although she can already see that her cutoffs, drugstore flip-flops, and Old Navy T-shirt leave something to be desired in this crowd.

Too many of the other moms are showing off their summer tans in cute resort wear.

Well, at least I have fresh breath, Meg thinks, grateful that she also located the box that held the toothbrushes and Listerine.

Just in case Sam feels the urge to kiss me again.

Ha.

She covers the last couple of yards between them, widely sidestepping a couple of fat, lazy bumblebees among the dandelions, and a toddler plugged into an iPod.

She does a double take at that, and realizes the little girl is also wearing a Lilly Pulitzer sundress.

Perfect for Palm Beach.

But a suburban soccer field?

She recognizes a tiny blond woman clad in pink silk who's on the sidelines with a tinier blond version of herself. It's the Hummer-driving, yoga-doing, diamond-flashing, supposedly Sharing and Caring Laurelle again, and obviously, she's with her daughter. The two of them definitely aren't having a warm, fuzzy moment over there. The girl looks sullen, the mom pissed off.

So we do have something in common after all, Meg thinks, as blondie throws her hands up in exasperation and stalks away, toward the bleachers.

"Hey."

Recognizing Sam's voice, Meg turns to see him smiling at her.

"Hey," she returns, glad her eyes are concealed behind her sunglasses—Duane Reade, $12.99.

Cosette, of course, is lagging several steps behind Meg, head down, undoubtedly furious.

"I'm glad you made it. We were just about to start the drills. How did you sleep last night?"

"Oh, we were fine," Meg replies, conscious that everyone in the vicinity is eavesdropping on their nonconversation. "I slept like a rock."

She did, surprisingly—even though it felt as though she were sleeping *on* a rock.

By the time she and Cosette had returned the truck, driven home in their car, located the bedding, pajamas, and toiletries, she was utterly exhausted. Too exhausted to worry about much of anything, including ghosts. Even kissing Sam didn't deter her efforts to drift off, and she slept soundly, straight through, until about forty-five minutes ago.

"Cosette, we'll do introductions on the field in a bit," Sam says. "For now, just let me introduce you to my son . . . Ben! Come here!"

Sure enough, he's waving at the Sam clone Meg mistook for her old crush during her mini time warp episode.

The boy picks up the ball, tucks it under his arm, and obediently trots toward his father.

Impressed, Meg realizes her daughter hasn't promptly responded to her own requests since she was . . .

Well, has she ever?

Not really. Even as a toddler, Cosette was a willful free spirit, resenting interruptions and resisting commands.

Meg is afraid to glance at her now, certain she's still glowering, or is applying black lipstick and more eyeliner, or has disappeared altogether.

"Ben, this is Cosette—she just moved in next door to us— and this is her mom, Mrs. . . . . " Sam trails off questioningly.

"You can just call me Meg."

"Nice to meet you." The boy has his father's easy grin and laid-back demeanor—even when he glances at Cosette.

Thank God he isn't staring at her in disdain.

Making sure Cosette isn't staring at Ben in disdain, Meg turns her head and sees that her daughter has momentarily lost the glower as she mumbles a suitable greeting.

Not that she's congenial as a Georgia beauty queen, but at least she isn't treating Ben and his father with open hostility.

No, that's just reserved for me.

"Okay, guys, let's go," Sam calls. He blows the whistle hanging around his neck and begins herding the kids out onto the field.

You're on your own, Meg thinks, watching her daughter fall in with the crowd.

Turning back toward the bleachers, filling with Fancy Moms, she thinks, *And so am I.*

Chapter
7

Laurelle! Hi!"

Seeing the blank expression on the other woman's face, Meg wishes she hadn't spoken up as she approached the bleachers, where Laurelle is seated on the bottom row.

"I'm Meg . . . Remember, Krissy introduced us a while back . . ."

Still blank.

"Krissy Rosenkr—I mean, Kris Holmes."

The light dawns, but just barely. "The Realtor?"

Meg nods.

"Oh! You're the woman who came to clean that time. Thanks, but I'm afraid we've gone in another direction."

"Excuse me?"

"You know, I should probably just come right out and say it. I'd be doing you a disservice if I didn't." Laurelle sighs and shakes her head. "I don't consider myself all that fussy, but when I come home to a supposedly clean house and find a hair—that isn't mine—on the white tile floor, I don't give second chances. And anyway, I prefer a live-in."

Okay, this is potentially embarrassing all around.

Meg tries to think of the best way to let Laurelle off the hook. "Actually, I'm not Kris's maid," she says, almost apologetically.

"You're not?" Laurelle asks—thinking she must be mistaken about her identity, judging by the look on her face.

"I'm not," Meg says firmly. "I'm Kris's friend."

"Her friend?"

"We met that day when you were on your way to yoga . . ." She prompts.

"I take yoga every day, so . . ."

"We were parked on Boxwood," Meg adds helpfully, wondering why she's bothering.

"Oh. I remember!"

No, you don't, Meg tells her silently, seeing the still-blank look in her brown eyes. *You just want me to shut up and leave you alone.*

"Well . . . it was nice seeing you again!" Laurelle says in that fake-bright tone people use with annoying children who keep asking questions.

"Nice seeing you, too."

"Have fun watching the practice," Laurelle adds, without bothering to ask why she's here, or whether she has a child on the team, much less making room on the bench beside her.

"You have fun watching the practice, too." Meg wishes she could flee, but her path is temporarily blocked by a pair of women in designer sunglasses and heels trying to strategize where they're going to sit. It seems that between the two of them, they're holding grudges against half the female population in the bleachers.

There's nothing for Meg to do but linger. She says to

Laurelle, because it's less awkward than saying nothing, "Have a nice day."

Maybe it isn't better than saying nothing.

"Oh, I will. And I'm sure I'll see you . . . around. So . . ."

For the love of God, stop! Meg wants to shout. *I'm going, I'm going.*

The two women blocking her path seem to have finally picked a destination, freeing Meg to move past Laurelle at last.

I should have brought something to read or do, she thinks, watching the horde of other women—most of them Fancy Moms—settle into chatty rows on the tiered wooden benches like pigeons on a telephone line.

No, not pigeons. They're much too bourgeois.

More like peacocks, or something equally beautiful and exotic.

And mean.

Wait, are peacocks supposed to be mean? Or is that blue jays?

Anyway, you don't know that these women are mean. You're just imagining that they are because of your own insecurity. For all you know, they're going to take you under their wings—as it were—and become your new best friends.

"Hi, Meg."

It takes her a moment to realize someone is calling to her—in part, because she's accustomed to answering to Astor.

Even when she recognizes her new—old—name, she doubts the male voice is addressing her, because she doesn't know anyone here, other than Sam.

"Meg?"

Oh, yes you do.

Turning, she recognizes Brad Flickinger, wearing a linen shirt and madras shorts, holding a camera bag in one hand and a cell phone in the other. With him is a woman— an obvious Fancy Mom—clad in an effortlessly chic Caribbean aqua silk sleeveless shift and matching sandals. She can only be his wife Olympia.

Sure enough, Brad says, "Olympia, this is Meg, Sophie's new voice teacher."

"Voice *coach*," amends Olympia, a slender brunette with classic, elegant Grecian features. "And remember, we're actually still in the interview stage, Brad. We need to find the best coach to help Sophie land the lead in the all-school musical."

Meg is well aware that the Flickingers and Sophie have placed themselves in the interviewer role, rather than inter-viewees. Their attitude is that anyone would be fortunate to have a fledgling star in her tutelage.

"It's very nice to meet you," Olympia says belatedly, stretching out a bare, tanned, toned arm with a dazzling tennis bracelet at the wrist and an even more dazzling array of diamonds on the ring finger. "Is your daughter playing soccer?"

"Yes, she is." Meg resists pointing out Cosette on the field—not that Olympia has asked which one she is, or so much as glanced in that direction.

"That's nice."

"Is your daughter . . . oh, wait. She's only thirteen, right?" Meg remembers that Sam said this was the fourteen- and fifteen-year-old league, and wonders what the Flickingers are doing here.

"Yes, she's thirteen, but she's on the team," Brad says, keeping one eye trained on the players.

His wife comments, keeping one eye trained on the social activity in the bleachers, "Sophie has been playing soccer for years, and she's beyond the twelve- and thirteen-year-old team. We wanted her to be challenged, so we had her moved up to the next level."

"It's nice that they're willing to do that," Meg murmurs.

"I wouldn't say *willing*," Olympia amends, and her pink-frost-glossed lips curve into a smile.

"When my wife wants something accomplished, no matter how unrealistic it might be, she keeps at it until even her adversaries become accomplices in the end."

Meg notes that Brad says it proudly, as though getting others to bend to your unreasonable demands is the utmost quality in human character.

She's beginning to think she doesn't particularly like the Flickingers. Maybe she shouldn't consider teaching their daughter. All she needs is for Olympia to decide that Sophie should be in an accelerated voice program of some sort . . . or, God forbid, onstage in the next Andrew Lloyd Webber musical to hit Broadway.

Convinced she's dealing with a potential Stage Mother from Hell, Meg says, "Well, it was very nice seeing you"—to Brad—"and meeting you"—to Olympia. "Let me know if your interviews with other instructors don't work out, but I'm sure that you'll find—"

"Oh, we're still planning on keeping our appointment this week," Olympia cuts in. "We'll make our final decision after we've met all the candidates."

"That's great." Meg smiles brightly and tells herself she has no choice . . . she needs the money.

And the Flickingers certainly have it.

If they hire her to teach their daughter, she'll at least have a slight income coming in fairly soon.

"I'm going to have to shift a few things around in the schedule to make this work," Olympia says, "because we've got so much going on, and it's getting more and more impossible to squeeze everything in."

"Do you work, then?"

"Me?" Olympia looks at her as though Meg just asked if she has her period. "Oh, not anymore. I haven't worked since Sophie came along."

"What did you do?"

"I was a senior vice president at IBM."

"Oh. That's . . . great."

That's great? Is that the best Meg can do?

"All those executive skills come in handy even when you're out of the workforce," Brad puts in. "My wife manages our household the same way she managed her job."

Meg opens her mouth but can't come up with anything more original to say in response than, "That's great." Again.

"Listen, why don't you come sit with us in the bleachers?" Brad offers. "Olympia can introduce you around to everyone."

Everyone consists of the very women Meg was just watching . . . the beautiful, exotic, mean peacocks on the bench.

She can hardly say no.

Nor can Olympia, though she looks as though she'd like to. But she graciously pipes up, as though it were her own idea and not her husband's, "Yes, come sit with us. You can meet the other moms."

"And dads," Brad points out.

Meg looks over at the scattering of men and wonders why they aren't working on this nonholiday Monday morning.

Maybe they're teachers, like Sam.

Nah. They don't look like teachers. They all have that businessman air, like Brad does. Olympia too, for that matter, now that Meg knows about her corporate background.

These people obviously have the luxury of taking time off for things like soccer practice. How different it is from the old days, when Meg was growing up. The men worked, and some of the women did, too, and you would never find parents at midday soccer practice together—with cameras, no less.

So this is a good thing, Meg tells herself. *Parents who have enough money and time to indulge their interest in their children. Definitely a good thing.*

Isn't it?

"*You* can introduce Meg to the dads," Olympia tells her husband. "Or maybe you shouldn't." She turns to Meg. "You're single, right?"

"Right." *And not ashamed of it. Really.*

"You don't want to meet these men, then. They're all married with children. In fact, there aren't very many single men in town, so you might be disappointed here."

"Oh, I'm not here to meet men." Meg glances up at the contingent of Fancy Moms again and wonders why she's feeling as though she's about to confront the Harper Valley PTA.

"Are you involved with someone, then?"

"No!" She's careful not to turn her head toward the soccer field . . . and Sam.

Anyway, she isn't involved with him.

She kissed him, yes.

You even made the first move, she reminds herself, glad Olympia Flickinger can't possibly read her mind.

She kissed Sam, but they aren't involved.

For her, that was just . . . closure.

Even though it felt like the opposite.

"I'm sorry, I didn't mean to be so insensitive," Olympia is saying apologetically. "I completely forgot."

"Forgot what?" she asks, as Brad takes out a camera with a paparazzi-worthy telephoto lens and aims it at the field.

"Of course you aren't involved with anyone, or interested in dating. You're in the middle of a divorce."

"I am?" Meg shakes her head. "I mean, no, I'm not."

"Oh! I assumed that might be why you were moving here. You know . . . to put some distance between you and your ex. People do that."

Meg would love to tell her that there's more than enough distance between herself and Calvin. Not just an entire continent, but also a jet-setting lifestyle, a vast personal fortune, and an ego the size of the famed Hollywood sign.

But she's already made up her mind not to let anyone in her new life know that Cosette's father is a movie star.

Not, however, because she doesn't want to brag.

More like, because she can already sense that it would be some kind of social stigma here in the new Glenhaven Park.

Meg is fairly certain that people of the Flickingers' ilk won't be impressed by celebrity. They're impressed by wealth, she suspects, and only when it's earned the old-fashioned way: through inheritance or savvy investment.

Not that Meg wants to impress them. And she doesn't really care whether she fits in here or not.

But she's got to try, for Cosette's sake. She can't bear the thought of her daughter being ostracized here the way she was in the city.

"Actually, my divorce is ancient history," she informs Olympia, wishing she could exit this conversation already. "I moved here because it's my hometown."

"Oh, that's right. Brad mentioned that you lived in our house." She shakes her head. "Can you believe what the last owners did to it? When I saw that tacky ceramic tile back splash in the kitchen, and that overgrown wildflower garden by the back door, without any kind of plan, just all kinds of flowers thrown in wherever—well, I nearly lost it. What were they thinking?"

They were thinking that wildflowers are beautiful. That they shouldn't be in ordinary rows; rather, a riot of glorious, meandering color.

They were thinking that ceramic tile is cheaper than marble, making more room in the family budget for a little girl's sequined ballet costumes and toe shoes.

Meg knows, because she shopped with her father for that tile, and she planted that cottage garden with her mother.

She has the same sick feeling that she did back in fourth grade, when Bobby Baxter asked her why her mother's hair was gray.

"She looks more like a grandma," he declared.

Meg, who was already painfully aware that her mother was about fifteen years older than her friends' mothers, tripped him the next time she saw him coming down the hall. That helped a little.

"Get closer," Olympia says abruptly to Brad, who, with his camera focused on the field, is clicking away like a fashion photographer.

"I'm using the telephoto."

"Well, make sure you do some digital ones, too, so I can e-mail them to everyone later. You did bring the digital cameras, didn't you?"

He nods.

"Get some video, too."

He nods again.

Meg is bemused. *Make sure you do some digital ones, too, so I can e-mail them to everyone?*

Who are these unfortunates, and why in the world would they want to see pictures of somebody's suburban soccer practice?

Well, maybe the Flickingers are documentary filmmakers, Meg decides.

Either that, or just insufferable.

"He sure is taking a lot of pictures," Meg comments. "It's nice that he can be here."

"Brad doesn't miss a practice or a game. Or anything else Sophie is involved in, for that matter."

"Does he work from home, then?"

"No, he commutes to the city."

"He's off today?"

"He took a personal day."

For soccer practice?

Apparently so, because there is no elaboration.

Meg watches Olympia watch her husband, the intrepid photographer, for another couple of seconds.

Then, with an air of *my work here is done,* she turns to Meg, and announces, "I'm going to go sit down. My feet are killing me."

Of course they are, in those strappy sandals with heels.

"How about you?" she tacks on.

"My feet are fine."

Olympia looks down at Meg's feet.

Meg hopes her toes aren't dirty.

When Olympia looks up at her again, she's wearing an expression that hints that they might be. "I meant, do you want to come sit with me?"

Unable to think of a plausible excuse, Meg follows her to the bleachers.

As they walk, though, she fights the urge to stick an unpedicured and possibly soiled foot, in a drugstore flip-flop, in front of Olympia's polished toes in their designer sandals, and send her sprawling like Bobby Baxter.

"Oh, and you can all pick up your uniforms at Crawswell's Sporting Goods on Main Street starting tomorrow morning," Sam remembers to add before dismissing the players from practice. "I want everyone in uniform for Saturday's practice. Got it?"

Everyone nods.

Rather, the kids nod.

Their parents are busy chatting to each other or on their cell phones. Loudly.

All except Meg.

She stands a little apart from the others, looking wholesome by contrast in her simple clothing, her glorious mane gleaming in the late-summer sun, unfettered by spray or pins.

She doesn't belong in this self-absorbed crowd any more than I do, Sam finds himself thinking.

But, he reminds himself sternly, *she doesn't belong with you, either.*

That reprimand is necessary because he's spent the last hour and a half trying to keep his focus on the field and not the bleachers, where Meg was sitting with Olympia Flickinger and her cronies.

That surprised him.

Especially since Meg seems down to earth, while Olympia is a tremendous pain in the—

"Excuse me, Sam?"

Speak of the devil.

Rather, the devil's spawn.

Sophie Flickinger, a perfect clone of her mother—not just physically—briskly informs him, "I'm going to come to the next practice a half hour early."

He nods, and transmits that to the other kids, whose collective attention is beginning to dissolve at this point. "It's good to be early . . . a half hour isn't necessary, but—"

"No," Sophie interrupts, "I want to be early so that we can go through some drills together."

"That's what the practice is about, Sophie. I don't think we can ask the entire team to come early so—"

"No, not the entire team. Just me."

"Just you?" Good Lord. It's day one of the season, and it's starting already. He's been down this road before, as a soccer coach and as a teacher.

"Why do you want to come early, Sophie?"

"I need some one-on-one coaching."

"Actually, you're doing just fine."

"Just fine?" Brad Flickinger has materialized at his

daughter's side. "Don't you want to encourage the kids not to settle for status quo, Sam?"

"Of course I do, but we've only had one practice, and—"

"Olympia and I want to get her here early Saturday so that you can spend some time going over the drills with her, if she feels she needs it," Brad informs him.

"Fine," Sam says helplessly, because how can he argue with a child's incentive? It's better than apathy, isn't it?

He glances at Cosette Hudson, standing a few feet apart from the other kids, just as her mother is from the other moms. Cosette's head is bowed, and she's kicking the grass with a black sneaker.

The moment she showed up, pale-skinned, clad in that funereal gear, Sam found himself thinking that she'll look as at home in a soccer uniform as Ben would in a dress.

He tried to give her the benefit of the doubt, for her sake—and for Meg's.

But his hopes sank as she merely went through the motions on the field.

Finally, though, when the ball unexpectedly came her way, she impulsively leapt toward it with a mighty kick and sent it sailing toward the goal.

Sam could distinctly hear Meg's thrilled screams from the sidelines, and smiled. As a fellow parent, he knows that witnessing a child's triumph is far more exhilarating than achieving your own. He and a few of the other kids, including Ben, cheered wildly, too. Cosette looked momentarily pleased . . .

Then reverted right back to indifference.

But that glimmer of athletic brilliance was enough to give Sam confidence that Meg's daughter might actually have what it takes to play on the team—and win over the other kids' respect, if not their friendship.

Now, as the players and their parents disperse at last— including the dauntless Flickinger clan and their heap of photographic gear—Sam watches Meg drape an arm around her daughter's shoulders.

Cosette immediately shakes it off.

Not surprising.

No kid wants a parent touching her affectionately in front of other kids, in public.

But, catching a glimpse of Meg's troubled expression, he senses there might be something more going on in their mother-daughter relationship.

And whatever it is, it's none of your business, he tells himself firmly.

Still, as he gathers the equipment from the field with Ben's help, he can't help but keep one eye on Meg and Cosette as they walk away, toward the parking lot. Cosette is several feet in front of her mother.

To his surprise, he catches Meg shooting a backward glance over her shoulder.

At him.

Or maybe just at the field, to see if . . .

What?

Come on, you've been around long enough to know she wasn't looking at the field.

She was looking at you.

And you were looking at her.

So what are you going to do about it?

Ignore it, he decides, turning away and reaching for a mesh bag filled with soccer balls.

Because if he doesn't ignore it, he'll have to do something about it. Which is out of the question for more reasons than he can count.

"Come on, Ben," he says, slinging the bag over his shoulder. "Let's go pick up Katie."

As they walk off the field, he can't help but ask his son, "What did you think of the new girl?"

"Collette?"

"Cosette."

"Oh. Right. She was okay."

"Yeah?"

"I guess."

"She doesn't know anyone. I was thinking maybe you can—"

"I don't think so, Dad."

"You don't even know what I was going to say."

"I bet I do. You want me to introduce her around."

"Right. Why don't you want to do it?"

Ben shrugs uncomfortably. "She's just different."

Ah. *Different.* The ultimate adolescent curse.

"Different is good, Ben," Sam points out, adapting his bordering-on-reproachful schoolteacher tone. "You need to respect people's differences."

"I know. I do."

"Cookie cutters are boring," Sam persists. "Some of my best students are the ones who refuse to conform."

"Yeah, but are they happy? Do they have a lot of friends?"

Sam opens his mouth to answer—how, he has no idea. Ben does it for him. "Trust me. They're miserable."

"I don't know about that."

"I do."

Sam shrugs and shakes his head.

"Come on, Dad . . . you're saying that if you were me, you'd take that girl under your wing and try to make her a part of things?"

"Yes, I absolutely would." Sam ignores a pinprick of conscience. "And I'd hope you'd have the character to do it, too. Otherwise, you might miss out on getting to know a terrific person."

There's a long pause.

Then Ben asks, "Can we talk about something else?"

"Sure."

Sam pushes the unsettling thoughts of "different" Cosette and her "different" mother—whom he failed to notice in high school, despite her reportedly throwing herself into his path—out of his head.

For now, anyway.

At dusk, Meg carries yet another full garbage bag out the back door, careful not to trip on the uneven tread as she walks down the steps.

There's yet another thing that needs to be fixed around here, before somebody gets hurt. It seems that every time she makes a move, she stumbles across yet another hazard or eyesore that requires attention.

She'll have to find room in her household budget to hire someone to start making repairs around here right away, before the whole place falls down around her.

Okay, it's not that bad, she tells herself, realizing she's just on the verge of exhaustion. Things will look much brighter in the morning.

At least, that's what she just promised Cosette before she left her upstairs grumbling that there aren't enough outlets in her room to plug in any of her stuff.

Outside, Meg instantly feels lulled by the silver-black sky, chirping crickets, and sweet green aroma of freshly mown grass.

It's going to be fine, she reminds herself as she lugs her heavy black plastic bag to the lattice-bordered nook beside the angled horizontal doors perpendicular to the foundation. They lead to the basement, which she hasn't even begun to tackle yet. She poked her head down there this morning, saw the cobwebs and smelled the earthy, musty scent of forgotten junk, and closed the doors.

There's just way too much to worry about in the house.

And outside the house: Both trash cans there are well beyond full, with the overflow bags leaning against the house.

One of these next few days, she'll have to lug it all out to the curb . . . but which day? She should have thought to ask Sam when garbage pickup is.

You can always call him, she tells herself, glancing toward his house beyond the border of shrubs and trees. It looks like he might be at home; lamplight spills from several windows on the first and second floor.

But she didn't get his phone number—and he probably isn't listed. High school teachers rarely are. Too many prank phone calls.

Okay, then you can knock on his door and ask him.

After all, it's a legitimate reason to go over there.

Right. And you've just spent the entire day trying to come up with one.

Which is precisely why she has to stay away from Sam.

She's in danger of becoming obsessed with him all over again. And that's even riskier for a single mom with a lot to lose—including a fragile heart—than it is for a quirky, insecure high school girl. Heartbreak is pretty much guaranteed.

You don't know that for sure, she reminds herself.

Oh, come on. Yes, you do. Because you sure as heck aren't going to marry Sam Rooney and live happily ever after here in Glenhaven Park.

This is her life, not a movie. Romantic happy endings like that don't happen in the real world.

Maybe that's why she tried to escape the real world . . . as if her hometown weren't a part of it.

But it is.

Slowly, she's realizing that in some ways—too many ways—things are no different here than they are in the city, or anywhere else.

There are still complications and snobs. She still doesn't have enough money or time; there's still more than enough traffic and pressure.

Well, what did you expect to find here?

Meg stares absently into the shadowy thicket between her yard and Sam's, shaking her head at her folly.

She expected to relive her childhood—or at least, to duplicate it for Cosette.

How could she not have fathomed that it's impossible?

She's not a fiftysomething housewife who's a wiz in the kitchen and the garden, and she's not married to the man who fathered her child and keeps a roof over their heads, food on the table, and a smile on his face no matter how hard his day was.

I was so lucky to grow up the way I did. And I never even realized it.

On the heels of that thought automatically comes another, more familiar one: *Poor Cosette . . . She gets to grow up without a father in her life, and with a crazy mother who makes impulsive decisions.*

Like giving up a career, an apartment, a life, and moving to a haunted—

Meg goes utterly still as she spots something moving stealthily in the shrub border.

Can the yard be as haunted as the house is? she wonders, just before a young girl steps out onto her lawn.

She certainly looks very much alive . . . and sheepishly guilty.

"Hi," she calls, waving.

"Hi." Meg wonders if she can possibly be Sam's daughter.

"I'm really sorry I'm in your yard." The girl comes a little closer, bending her head and rapidly brushing at her hair as if she's afraid something might be crawling in it.

"That's okay. Are you . . . okay?"

"I'm fine. I was just over there"—she motions at Sam's yard—"throwing a Frisbee for my dog to catch and it landed in here somewhere. Now I can't find it and my brother's going to kill me because it's his and he told me not to touch it."

"Uh-oh. That's not good. I'll help you look." Meg smiles and walks toward her, heedless of her bare feet. The grass is damp, but it's too late in the day to worry about stepping on bees.

She pushes aside a couple of leafy branches to peer into the dark thatch of pachysandra, saying conversationally, "My name's Meg."

"I'm Katie."

"Is Sam your father?"

"Yup. You met my dad?" She sounds surprised.

"He's coaching my daughter's soccer team." Meg decides not to mention she also knows Sam because she grew up nursing a ferocious crush on him and, oh yeah, kissed him last night.

"You have a daughter? My dad didn't tell me that."

"What did he tell you?" She's afraid to ask.

"Just that the new people are here and that you probably won't stick around."

Meg's heart sinks. "Really."

"Yeah, 'cause new people never do." Katie stoops to poke into a clump of weeds. "They always start seeing things and hearing things and get scared and run away. My dad says they're all crazy."

"The people who leave? Why is that?"

"Because he said there's no such thing as ghosts." She pauses, not lifting her head when she adds decidedly, "But there is."

"You've seen ghosts?"

"Just one." Looking up at last, Katie's face is illuminated in the light of the rising moon.

She's wearing a strangely solemn, cryptic expression.

"Was it here?" Meg indicates her new house.

"No. It was there." Katie gestures at her own house. "But please don't say anything to my dad about it, because he'll get all upset."

"Because you believe in ghosts and he doesn't?"

"Yes."

But her tone is cagey.

It's more than that, Meg realizes. Yet she senses that the subject is best dropped.

They poke around for a few more minutes, chatting and looking for the Frisbee.

"How old is your daughter? Fifteen?"

"How'd you know?"

"I figured it was either that or fourteen if my dad's coaching her. Did Ben meet her?"

"Ben is your brother?"

"Yeah. He's really mean."

Meg hides a smile. "He did meet Cosette today, yes."

"I bet he was nice to her. Ben likes girls, except for me."

"That's how brothers are."

"You have a brother?"

"No. But that's what people say."

"Do you have a sister?"

"Nope."

"How about a mom?"

"Yup—hey, look, I found it!" Meg interrupts herself triumphantly.

"Wow, great. Thank you." Katie accepts it, but she looks less enthusiastic than Meg expected.

"Well . . . you should probably go give that back to your brother," she suggests.

"Yeah, I should. Thanks for helping me look. You must be really busy getting your stuff moved in."

"It's been a little crazy," Meg admits.

"Do you want some help? I'm not really doing anything if you need me. I've been kind of bummed all night because my dad said I can't go with my friend and her family to stay overnight at this resort in the Catskills for two nights to celebrate the last week of summer."

"Why not?"

"My dad said it's not safe."

"Are you going to be *climbing* the mountains?"

"Huh?"

"Skydiving? Bungee jumping?"

Katie giggles. "Nope."

"Well, that's good." Meg grins. "But, listen, your dad loves you. He probably thinks that's too far away for you to go on your own."

"I wouldn't be on my own. I'd be with my friend Erin's mom and dad. They're really responsible. They eat healthy stuff and they go to church every single Sunday."

Clearly, this is an excerpt from a prerehearsed speech she gave to her dad earlier.

"They do sound responsible."

"Can you tell that to my dad? He and my brother are inside watching the Yankee game, and maybe if you told my dad that I should be allowed to go—"

"Sorry. Can't do that."

"I figured you wouldn't. But can I still come help you unpack if my dad says it's okay?"

Meg finds it all too easy to picture Sam lounging in front of the television, engrossed in a ball game. Maybe he's bare-chested . . .

She wonders how he'd react if she stuck her head in to ask if his daughter can come over for a little while. Katie's loneliness is palpable.

Then she remembers what Sam said about her moving in here. That she probably won't stick around.

Oh, yeah? Watch me.

Ghosts or no ghosts, she's going to see this through.

Yes, and she'll prove to herself that it wasn't a rash, impulsive decision to move here.

She'll also do her best to steer clear of temptation so she can't possibly make any decisions that *are* rash and impulsive—like kissing Sam again.

"You know what, Katie? It's late, and I'm finished with

the unpacking for tonight. But maybe you can help me another time," she adds, seeing the disappointed look on the girl's face.

"Okay. It was nice meeting you."

"You, too."

Meg watches her start back to her own yard.

Then she turns on her heel and marches back to her haunted handyman special.

Sam is reaching again into the bag of chips Ben holds out from his sprawled perch nearby when Katie bursts into the house with Rover.

"Dad?"

"In here."

She appears, all breathless and excited. She does this sometimes, being a dramatic adolescent girl. It doesn't take a lot to get her worked up.

Sam keeps his eyes on the game—three men on, two outs, bottom of the sixth—until he realizes that the source of Katie's bubbly enthusiasm is "the new mom next door."

Not "the new kid next door."

The *mom*.

"She was so nice to me," she chatters, helping herself to chips, loudly rattling the bag and crunching as she talks.

The batter swings and misses. Strike one.

Ben shushes his sister.

Naturally, that encourages her to press on defiantly. "She was really nice to me when she saw me, and she even helped me look for—"

She breaks off and shoots a guilty look at Ben, who's glued to the screen and doesn't notice.

Uh-oh.

The batter swings again. Strike two.

Rover trots into the room and settles in his usual spot on the rug.

"And she was so beautiful, with the most gorgeous long curly, wavy hair . . . I would kill to have hair like that."

"Your hair is beautiful," Sam says automatically.

Katie has Sheryl's hair, and Sheryl's eyes, and Sheryl's lanky build. But she doesn't have Sheryl's calm, quiet, reasonable disposition. She's far more fiery and passionate than either Sheryl, or Sam.

Meg is like that, too, though.

Huh?

Where did that thought come from? How the heck would he know that Meg is fiery and passionate?

He wouldn't.

In fact, he could have sworn that it wasn't his own mental voice that thought it.

He could swear that it was Sheryl's voice, talking to him in his head the way it sometimes does.

Yes, there are times when he can almost hear her saying things like, "Don't heat a Styrofoam coffee cup in the microwave," or "Don't forget to buy cupcakes for Katie's class on her birthday, and bring napkins."

Stuff like that.

"All right, come on," Ben mutters.

"And she said her daughter's on your soccer team so maybe I can come to the next practice, Dad, and meet her."

"Maybe."

Another pitch. Ball one.

"And she said I can go over there and help her unpack," Katie is saying. "But not tonight because it's late. And she said Ben met her daughter, too. What was she like?"

Ben shrugs, eyes on the batter.

The batter swings again. Strikes out.

Commercial.

"Jeez, do you ever shut up?" Ben asks his sister.

"Dad! Ben just told me to shut up."

"No, I didn't."

"Yes, you—"

"No, he didn't," Sam says wearily. "He said—"

"He said to shut up."

"I did not. I posed a rhetorical question about you and your big mouth."

"Ben." Sam gives him a warning look.

"You should tell him he can't watch the rest of the game for that, Dad."

"For what?" Ben demands.

"For being mean to me. You're always mean to me. That's what I told Meg. She said big brothers are like that."

Meg.

Again.

This isn't good for anyone.

Especially not for Katie.

"I don't want you over there, bugging . . . Meg." Sam is reluctant to even allow her name to settle on his tongue. "She's busy trying to get settled in. The last thing she needs is an extra kid underfoot."

"No, she said that I could come over and help her. She needs me."

No, Sam thinks sadly, *you need her.*

Pop psychology 101.

Desperate for a female role model, Katie has latched on to Meg.

That's happened before—but usually with other girls.

Never with an adult woman.

Why now?

Why Meg?

It can't be that she reminds Katie of Sheryl, because the two women couldn't be more opposite.

Sam can't imagine pragmatic, conservative Sheryl moving into a run-down old house, or wearing cutoffs, or talking too much when she got nervous, the way Meg did when she introduced Sam to her daughter and her friend.

No, Sheryl was always quieter. More serious. More centered.

That's what I need, Sam tells himself firmly.

And that's what Katie and Ben need.

If any of them get attached to the new neighbors in more than the most casual way, it can only lead to trouble.

It's one thing for Sam to take risks with his own emotional well-being.

It's quite another for him to allow the children to do that.

Yes, it would be irresponsible of Sam to allow Katie to spend any amount of time with Meg. She'll only get hurt.

We'll all steer clear, he concludes.

That's the only way to protect his kids from getting hurt.

"Hey, Katie," he says thoughtfully, "I've been reconsidering Erin's family's invitation to take you to the Catskills . . ."

"You have?" She sucks in a quick breath.

He nods. "Maybe I shouldn't have said no right away."

Katie squeals. "Daddy! Are you serious? I can go?"

He nods, trying to hide his reluctance.

"*OhmyGodohmyGodohmyGod!* I've got to go call Erin!" She bounds out of the room.

Crisis averted.

For now, he thinks grimly.

And on television, the batter for the opposing team leads off the inning with a home run.

In the upstairs bathroom, Meg turns on the faucet and waits for the water to heat up for her shower. That takes much longer in this old house, she's noticed, than it did back home in Manhattan.

Old pipes, probably, she thinks, picking at a rubbery thread of caulk that's come loose from the tiles alongside the tub.

This whole wall should probably be recaulked.

That, or retiled, she amends, noticing that a number of the tiles are cracked. Anyway, avocado green isn't exactly her favorite color scheme. It would be nice to go with something neutral, like white or even—

Frowning, Meg notices that the water running into the tub is already steaming hot.

That's strange.

Yesterday she had to run it for a full minute before it even got warm.

Then again . . .

The steam—which looks more like a mist, really—doesn't seem to be coming from the water streaming from the tap, exactly.

It's more like . . .

Hovering above the tub, and over a bit.

Meg reaches gingerly toward the water to test the temperature, poking one finger cautiously into the spray lest she get burned.

Burned?

It's still cold.

In fact, not only is the water cold, but the temperature in the room seems to have dropped a good ten or fifteen degrees in the last few seconds.

What the . . . ?

Heart pounding, Meg uneasily turns again to look at the steam. Which is more of a mist.

Which is slowly taking shape into an almost . . .

Human form.

"Oh my God," Meg whispers, throwing her hands over her eyes and pressing down, hard.

This isn't happening.

You are not seeing some kind of creepy . . . ectoplasm, or whatever it's called.

It's plain old steam. That's what it's called.

Right, steam. From water that's downright chilly.

That makes total sense.

Well, does a ghost make any sense, either?

Hell, no.

Hands still covering most of her face, she cautiously spreads her fingers a bit and opens her eyes to peer through the slits.

The mist—or steam—or ectoplasm, or whatever it was—is gone.

Of course it's gone.

Because it was never there.

Maybe she won't take a long, hot, soothing shower after all.

Maybe she'll jump right into bed and pull the covers over her head.

Come on, don't be such a baby, she tells herself. *You know it was just steam. See? It's everywhere now.*

That's true. The bathroom is filling with wisps of mist that hover above the running tap and disperse through the room, fogging over the mirror above the sink.

That's what happens when you run hot water in a small room with no fan ventilation.

She knows that. She's always known that.

Then why was there steam when the water was cold?

The air was cold, too.

Not anymore. Now it's warm and humid.

Maybe the chill was her imagination.

Maybe it wasn't, and the house is haunted.

What are you going to do about it if that's the case?

You can't move. You have nowhere to go.

Haunted or not, Meg reminds herself grimly as she strips off her clothes for her shower, *this place is home sweet home from here on in, so you'll just have to make the best of it.*

Chapter
8

Looking out the window, wiping a trickle of sweat from his brow, Sam decides he can put it off no longer.

He has to mow the grass.

His lawn is embarrassingly overgrown compared to the others on the street—well, with the drastic exception of the one next door.

Which, ironically, happens to be the very reason he hasn't mowed *his* lawn these last few days.

He doesn't want to run into Meg.

Nor does he want Katie to run into Meg.

Which can't happen in the immediate future, since she is safely in the Catskills with her friend Erin's family, and won't be back until tonight.

Safely in the Catskills?

Hah.

Sam hasn't stopped worrying about her since she left.

It didn't help matters that her parting words just before Erin's dad pulled into the driveway to pick her up yesterday morning were, "Don't worry, Dad. I'll be fine. I'm glad you let me go. And Meg didn't even have to help me convince you!"

"*Meg?*"

Katie nodded. "She said the Catskills are safe, unless you're climbing them, and since I'm not, she thought you should let me go."

"She did, did she?" Sam muttered.

"Well . . . more or less."

That conversation keeps ringing in his head.

Meg has no right to interfere in his relationship with his daughter, that's for damned sure.

Then again . . .

More or less.

Katie does have a tendency to overexaggerate things. For all he knows, she was complaining to Meg about his not giving her permission for the trip, and Meg said something vague like "Uh-huh," and Katie interpreted it as a preorder for a Team Katie T-shirt.

Whatever.

None of it changes the fact that the house next door is off-limits.

But you can't hide inside forever.

No, he really has to mow the lawn. Quickly. Before the midday heat can set in . . .

And before he runs into Meg and a different kind of heat can set in.

Anger, he reminds himself. *You're thinking about the heat of anger. Not the heat of . . .*

Passion.

*   *   *

Meg nearly jumps out of her skin at a loud sound before she realizes that this time, it's nothing remotely supernatural.

No, what she just heard was a pair of car doors slamming just beyond the screened windows of her new living room

That's a relief.

There have been more than a few unexplained creaks and slams these past few days, and it's left her more than a little jittery.

Setting down the box she was about to carry into the kitchen, she hurries over to look out, asking, "You don't think it's them already, do you, Chita Rivera?"

Chita Rivera, who is curled on the floor against one of the boxes, sends her a calm look that says she does indeed think it's them.

Sure enough, Olympia Flickinger and her daughter Sophie have just climbed out of a gleaming black Range Rover. Olympia is wearing a cream-colored sleeveless top and matching slacks that set off her golden skin. Sophie is in a sundress. Both have their hair in ponytails that look crisp and chic.

Meg's hand goes to her own ponytail, which is anything but. She pulled it back hastily with a rubber band first thing this morning because her hair was hot and sweaty against her neck. For all she knows, she has dust and cobwebs in it by now.

She looks at her watch . . . which she's wearing only because she already lost it once in the past few days. The house is still so upside down she doesn't have any place specific to leave it when she takes it off.

It's only eight-thirty-five. The Flickingers are twenty-five minutes early.

"It figures," she tells Chita Rivera, who wisely leaves the room as if she can't bear to witness what's going to happen next.

Meg was hoping to at least have cleared the living room of boxes. The piano arrived yesterday, but she was too busy out shopping for furniture to organize the room.

At least she managed to order couches, tables, chairs, bureaus, and beds . . . all of it purchased from the enormous Crate & Barrel store down at the mall. The good news is that it was all pretty affordable. The bad is that none of it will be delivered for at least a couple of weeks . . . longer for the upholstered stuff.

Thus, the only seats she can offer the Flickingers are the piano bench or a couple of cardboard cartons that have sufficed for Meg and Cosette so far.

As Olympia and Sophie descend through the gate, Meg stands on her tiptoes to see into the tremendous built-in mirror above the fireplace and immediately wishes she hadn't.

Her hair is unkempt, her face is flushed and shiny.

Is it any wonder she looks this bad? She's been trying to unpack and organize since she rolled out of bed—or rather, hoisted herself from the floor—a few hours ago.

It's got to be almost ninety-five degrees this overcast morning already: the kind of still, muggy late-summer heat that threatens to build, then erupt into thunderstorms as the day trudges on.

Meg hurriedly removes the rubber band from her hair, attempts to fluff the matted curls with her fingertips, and cleans the streak of dirt from her chin with the spit-dampened hem of her T-shirt.

There.

Yeah, right.

If it were anyone but the Flickingers, she wouldn't care about feeling quite so . . . grimy.

Well, the Flickingers, or Sam Rooney.

But she hasn't even caught a glimpse of him since soccer practice a few days ago, which is strange, considering that he lives right next door and his car has been in the driveway.

His son has been shooting hoops, and his daughter has been reading on the porch and riding her bike up and down the driveway, but no sign of Sam.

Not that she should be looking for him.

Well, old habits die hard.

The doorbell rings.

So much for being presentable.

Meg turns away from the mirror, kicks a couple of the lighter boxes into the corner, and starts for the door.

The bell rings again before she reaches it.

"Coming," she calls, trying to keep the irritation from her voice.

She opens the door and pastes a smile on her face. "Hi, Olympia. And you must be Sophie."

"It's nice to meet you," the girl says politely, reaching out to shake her hand.

"You, too." Meg is impressed with her manners and resists the urge to wipe off her own sweaty, dirty hand on her shorts before shaking Sophie's dry, clean one.

Sophie, however, does no such thing. The moment she releases Meg's grasp, she wrinkles her nose distastefully and runs her palm along the side of her dress.

"I'm sorry . . . I should have called to confirm the appointment," Olympia says. "You have so much going on with the move, it's completely understandable that you'd forget."

"Oh, I didn't forget. I'm just . . . running a little late."

No, you aren't. They're running almost a half hour early. Why are you letting them off the hook? Being that early is just as rude as being late.

"Do you want us to wait on the porch while you . . . get ready?" Olympia offers dubiously.

"No, that's okay. I'm ready. Come on in."

"Thank you." As the Flickingers primly cross the threshold, Meg hears a mower start up next door.

Glancing over at Sam's house beyond the hedge, she spots him in the yard, shirtless.

Whoa.

It's all she can do to pry her eyes from the sight of his glorious, sun-bronzed chest, muscular arms, and washboard abs just above the waist of his white cotton shorts.

That his honed physique is visible even from this vantage point is blatant testimony that the man is still in amazing physical condition, just as Meg suspected.

Suspected?

You dreamed it.

Last night, and the night before.

Yup, she's been dreaming vividly about Sam, shirtless, looking just like that. Only he was much closer, in her dreams. Closer, and he wasn't wearing the shorts. Or the sneakers. Or anything else.

Unfortunately for Meg, she's been so exhausted she's been sleeping more soundly than ever before in her life. Deep R.E.M. sleep, the kind that's most conducive to dreaming.

Which would be welcome under any other circumstances. But regularly seeing Sam in her comatose hours only fuels a perpetual longing to see him when she's wide-awake.

Not just *see* him . . .

Because she's not just seeing him in her dreams.

She's . . . well, actively engaged.

And it has to stop.

Simultaneously pushing Dream Sam from her thoughts and turning away from Real Live Sam, Meg closes the door.

With any luck, she'll have trouble sleeping tonight.

Sam has just settled onto his king-size mattress with the newest issue of *Sports Illustrated* and a rotating floor fan aimed at the bed, when somebody screams.

The sound is faint but shrill, coming not from under his own roof, thank God, but from somewhere outside.

He bolts toward the screened window across the room, the one that looks out over the street.

Nothing unusual there.

It's after midnight. Deserted.

He waits, poised, listening. All he can hear above the hum of the floor fan is the steady chirping of crickets and the distant rumble of a Metro-North train.

But he's pretty sure that scream wasn't his imagination.

So sure that, heart pounding, he hurriedly pulls a pair of jersey shorts over his boxers and hurries down the hall. Though he's confident the scream came from outside, he stops to open bedroom doors and look in on Ben and Katie.

They're both safely, soundly asleep in their beds. Of course; they wouldn't have heard a thing, thanks to their closed windows, where air-conditioning units hum loudly, obliterating night sounds.

He closes their doors, leaving them to slumber in pleasantly cool rooms.

Then he hurries downstairs, turning on lights as he goes, wondering if he should dial 911, wondering about Meg.

It's not as though she was far from his thoughts in the first place, when he heard the scream.

He's been thinking about her pretty much nonstop these last few days, in fact. It's as if the more he tells himself not to even acknowledge her presence next door, the more he dwells on the fact that she's there.

But he hasn't seen her.

Not unless you count the surreptitious glance he stole at her as she admitted the Flickingers to her house this morning.

That surprised him.

Not just that the regal Olympia Flickinger would befriend someone like Meg, who obviously doesn't conform to Glenhaven Park's nouveau social network . . .

But also because he wouldn't expect the seemingly down-to-earth Meg to befriend someone like Olympia Flickinger.

He can't help but feel vaguely disappointed about that—and annoyed that he allows it to bother him.

Who cares if Meg doesn't exhibit a more discriminating taste in her selection of new friends?

He has no business worrying about that.

He does, however, have business worrying that she might be screaming in the middle of the night. It sounded as though it came from the direction of the Duckworth place.

Which is why, rather than stopping to dial 911, Sam decides to head directly next door.

He can see that several lights are on upstairs, meaning somebody must be awake.

But what if the scream really didn't come from here?

Sam stops on the walk just inside the gate, unsure what to do.

Does he dare knock on someone's door in the middle of the night?

Does he dare not to?

He takes a couple more tentative steps through the inky shadows toward the house . . .

Then suddenly, finds that he's no longer in the dark.

A light has gone on inside the house, this time downstairs. Its glow spills through the windows, partially illuminating the walkway.

Inside, someone passes by the nearest window to Sam—Meg, he realizes.

There are no curtains or shades to obstruct his view; he can see her clearly. The first thing he notices is that she's wearing skimpy pink cotton pajamas: a top with spaghetti straps, and short shorts.

The next thing he notices is his body's predictable reaction to the sight of her in said skimpy pajamas.

He's so focused on trying to tame it that it takes him a moment to remember why he's here—and realize that Meg is obviously agitated.

She rakes a hand through her long hair and shakes her head.

"I know, but I'm sure you were just dreaming," Sam hears her say—apparently to Cosette, whom he can't see.

He can hear her, though. Loud and clear.

"I was not dreaming! You don't dream when you're wide-awake."

"Maybe you just thought you were awake. That happens." Meg's voice, fainter and more reasonable than her daughter's, floats to Sam through the screen.

"It does happen, but not when it's a hundred freaking degrees and as humid as a swamp. Who can sleep in this weather?"

"I can."

"Good for you. I can't. And I'm telling you, someone walked into the room and was standing over me, watching me."

Sam immediately comprehends the source of the scream—Cosette—and the reason behind it.

Apparently, she got wind of the haunted rumors and now she, too, is falling under the spell of suggestion.

"Think about it, Cosette—this is irrational," Meg says, obviously trying to sound reasonable.

But even from out here, Sam can hear the telltale waver in her voice.

"Irrational? Thanks a lot, Mom. Next time a harmless little yellow bumblebee scares you shitless, I'll remind you that you're irrational."

"Don't use that language."

"Irrational?"

Sam perceives parental exasperation taking over as Meg says, "I think we should just go back to bed and try to get some sleep. You have soccer practice tomorrow, and—"

"I'm not going back up there," Cosette interrupts—sounding almost tearful.

Maybe she is tearful, because Meg walks toward the

sound of her voice with outstretched arms, disappearing from Sam's view.

For a moment, there's silence. Mother is presumably comforting daughter.

She's got things under control here, Sam assures himself. *You should go home. They'll be fine.*

He turns toward home.

Then he hears another scream—this time, from Meg.

"What?" Cosette shouts. "What is it?"

"Nothing, I just thought I saw . . ."

Either Meg doesn't finish the sentence, or Sam can't hear her voice from wherever she is. No matter. The implications are clear.

Something has scared her.

How can Sam walk away?

He can't.

With a purposeful stride, he walks up the steps and rings the bell.

This time, both Meg and Cosette shriek.

"What was that?" Cosette asks, clinging to her mother as she hasn't since she was a young child in rough surf at the Jersey Shore.

"It was just the doorbell," Meg realizes.

Not that a ringing doorbell in the middle of the night should be reassuring in the least.

"Maybe the ghost did it."

"No, Cosette, there's no ghost."

"You know there is."

Cosette is right.

She *does* know there is. She saw it with her own eyes: a

glimpse of a shadowy figure watching them from the foot of the stairs just now.

It was little more than the outline of a human being, really—she couldn't make out its gender, much less its features.

And when she screamed, it vanished abruptly.

But it was definitely there.

And if she had any doubt that someone—something—was hovering over her daughter upstairs, she no longer does.

This place is haunted.

They've got to move.

"Meg?" a voice calls from the porch.

A human voice.

"Oh my God, it knows your name!" Cosette says in a high-pitched, terrified whisper, clutching her arm.

"That's not the ghost." Meg hurries toward the door, Cosette right with her. "It's Sam."

"*Who?*"

"Sam Rooney. From next door."

"What's *he* doing here?"

Meg has no idea, but when she opens the door, she realizes that she's never been so glad to see anyone in her life.

"I heard someone scream over here. Are you okay?"

She appreciatively takes in the sight of him, barefoot, bare-chested, wearing just a pair of shorts.

Amazing how, even in a moment of stark fright, one can still manage to shamelessly lust after someone.

"Are you okay?" Sam repeats, not meeting her eyes.

"I'm . . . not sure."

"*I'm* sure. We're not," Cosette puts in. "This place is haunted."

"Really." Sam's gaze flicks from her back to Meg.

Looking into his blue eyes, she silently asks him not to mention what happened here the other night.

The disembodied slamming, creaking, footsteps . . .

The kissing, either, for that matter.

Sam lifts his chin a fraction of an inch in a half nod that seems to promise that their secret is safe.

She gives him a return half nod of appreciation.

Then, remembering that she's scantily dressed in summer pajamas, she glances down, hoping that everything that should be covered is covered.

Yes, but barely.

She really should throw on something over this.

Unfortunately, there's no robe hanging conveniently on a hook beside the door. All she can possibly do in the moment is hope Sam's eyes don't wander below her neck.

So far, so good. In fact, despite his heroic presence here and the look that just passed between them, he seems almost . . . professionally disengaged.

"Well, if you two are okay, I'll go."

If he were wearing a hat, Meg thinks, he'd be tipping it politely right about now.

"We're fine. Thanks for checking in."

"You're welcome."

Wow. He couldn't seem more detached if he were a professional ghostbuster she'd summoned on a hotline.

"I'm not staying here." Cosette's voice quavers then, propelling Meg instantly back into maternal mode.

She turns to see that her daughter is shaking her head adamantly, eyes wide with fear. In her pastel summer pajamas, with her face scrubbed free of extreme makeup and her hair hanging loose around her face, she looks like a frightened little girl who needs a hug.

Meg gives her one.

And for once, her daughter lets her.

"Listen, Cosette," she says, "I know that you're scared, but we can't just pick up and leave in the middle of the—"

"Mom, you can stay if you want, but I'm leaving."

Meg purses her lips. "Where are you going?"

"Back home to the city."

Conscious of Sam's silent presence, taking it all in, she says, "Okay, you have to be reasonable here."

"I am being reasonable."

"You're *not*. For one thing, it's the middle of the night, and you don't drive."

"You do. And we have a car now."

"I'm not driving you to Manhattan."

"Then I'll take the train."

Ignoring that, Meg goes on, "For another thing, somebody else is living in our apartment now, remember?"

"Then I'll go to one of my friends' apartments. At least they'll have air-conditioning. And no ghosts."

Meg doesn't have the heart to remind Cosette that the few friends she retained after the school disaster have all but ignored her since they found out she was moving to the suburbs.

Why bring that up again? They've been through that repeatedly, anyway, with Cosette blaming Meg for ruining her life and making her an outcast.

Tension hangs more densely than humidity in the sultry night air.

Then Sam pipes up unexpectedly, "You guys can stay at my place, if you want."

Surprised, she looks at him.

Something flickers in his eyes; he seems ambivalent about having made the offer.

Yet he continues, almost as if he can't help being a nice guy, "We have air-conditioning—well, in a couple of rooms—and no ghosts."

Spend the night with Sam?

The tension thickens.

"Great," Cosette says, as though it's a done deal. "Thanks. Let's go."

"We can't do that," Meg protests. "There's no reason to do that."

"Fine, if you believe that, you can stay here, Mom, and get haunted all night. But I'm out of here."

Sam catches Meg's eye. "It's okay. Really. You guys can come over, and at least get a good night's sleep."

"But . . ." Meg fumbles for a plausible protest to an offer that's all too tempting. "We don't want to inconvenience you."

"It's no inconvenience. Really."

Meg wants more than anything to say yes. For selfish reasons that have nothing whatsoever to do with ghosts and everything to do with him.

Right.

Like *that's* going to happen—like she and Sam are going to have a romantic evening together at his place.

Knowing that with three kids underfoot it's guaranteed to be anything but, Meg shrugs and nods. "Okay. We'll come with you. Thanks, Sam."

What can possibly happen?

"No problem. Do you want to get your stuff?"

"I'm not going back upstairs," Cosette says firmly.

Meg sighs. "I'll get it."

She turns toward the staircase and remembers the reason they're leaving.

Terrific. Why did she volunteer to go back up there alone?

Heart pounding, conscious of Sam and Cosette watching her from behind, she gingerly climbs the steps. As soon as she's out of their view, she darts into the bathroom, grabs their toothbrushes, then snatches some clothes from the duffel bags on the floor in the side bedroom.

She looks for her robe, but of course she can't find one. It's probably still packed. It's been too hot all week to even miss it until now.

She'll have to find something else to—

"Mom? Are you okay?" Cosette calls anxiously from downstairs.

"I'm fine."

"Well, can you please hurry? I really want to get out of here."

"I'm trying, Cosette!"

Meg conducts another quick, fruitless search for even a sweatshirt to pull on. The best she can come up with is a wool cardigan, and there is no way in hell she's putting that on in this weather.

"Chita Rivera?" she calls as she hunts for something else to wear over her pajamas. "Where are you, kitty?"

No reply.

Chita Rivera likes to get her beauty sleep, but you can usually rouse her with a high-pitched "Here, kittykittykitty-kitty."

No sign of the cat.

That's unusual.

"Mom! Please!"

Oh, well. Shoving her feet into flip-flops and grabbing a pair for Cosette, Meg tells herself that she'd be wearing less clothing than this at the beach. So it's not as though she's indecent.

As for Chita Rivera, she couldn't have come to Sam's anyway. He hates cats.

It would just be nice if Meg knew where she was before she left the house.

She flips off all the lights and hurries back down the stairs, where she finds that Cosette is already out on the porch.

"I forgot pillows and blankets," Meg remembers belatedly.

"It's okay. I've got all that stuff. Come on." Sam holds the door open for her.

"What about Chita Rivera?" Cosette asks.

"I can't find her."

"Well, cats are afraid of ghosts," Cosette announces. "And she's been acting weird ever since we moved here. Jumping around, skittish, looking at nothing like she's seeing something . . ."

She has been doing that, Meg realizes as she grabs the key from the jagged nail beside the door. She's been using it as a hook but she really should pound it in so nobody gets caught on it.

She really should do a lot of things around here.

Handyman. I need a handyman.

But not tonight.

She flicks the last light switch, and they make their exit. As they walk away, down the path through the hot, muggy night toward the gate, she looks back over her shoulder at the house.

That's funny.

She could have sworn she turned off all the lights upstairs.

But there seems to be a faint glow coming from the front bedroom window, almost as though it's illuminated from a night-light.

Only . . . there is no night-light in the room.

Chapter 9

"Are you sure this is okay?" Meg whispers uncertainly to Sam.

"It's fine," he assures her in his regular voice as Cosette settles into the top bunk in his daughter's dim, air-conditioned room.

The only sign that anyone occupies the bottom bunk is an oblong lump huddled beneath the patchwork quilt. Katie didn't even stir when they slipped into the room just now.

"She sleeps through anything," he informs Meg. "And she'll be thrilled when she wakes up in the morning and finds out she has an overnight guest here."

"Even if it's a complete stranger?"

Sam wants to point out to Meg that it's a little late now to pluck Cosette from the bunk and go home.

Instead, he just says, "Katie has been wanting to meet her."

Which is semitrue.

She did say something about wanting to meet the new girl next door when she got home from her trip tonight.

Then she caught sight of Cosette in the yard at dusk, and her enthusiasm faded.

"I just saw the girl next door," Sam heard Katie telling Ben.

"You mean the ghoul next door."

"Yeah! Is she a witch or something?"

"Dunno," he replied helpfully. "Maybe."

"Well, she looks like one. She freaks me out."

Sam fought the urge to pop into the conversation and admonish his kids, knowing that wouldn't do much good.

Now, he can't help but worry about how Katie will react in the morning when she finds that the ghoul next door—rather the girl next door—is her roommate.

With any luck, she'll stagger out of bed without noticing. She's not exactly a morning person.

"Where are you sleeping?" Cosette asks her mother, peering over the rail.

Meg looks at Sam, who wants to say, *not with me*!

Just in case that's what her daughter was thinking.

Her daughter? Who are you kidding?

You're worried that that's what Meg's thinking.

No, that isn't it, either.

He's worried that Meg might somehow sense that it's what *he's* thinking.

Yes, that's it exactly. He does his best to rid his mind of salacious thoughts as he says, "Your mom will be down the hall in my room."

Cosette's jaw drops.

Realizing belatedly what he just implied, Sam stutters, "I, uh, I-I—no, not, you know, with me, I mean, I'll be downstairs on the pullout couch and, uh, your mother—"

"Right. Gotcha." Cosette all but winks. "G'night," she

adds, and rolls toward the wall in a clear signal that it's time for Meg and Sam to leave the room.

"G'night," they say in unison.

Sam leads the way out to the hall. A wall of heat greets them. The T-shirt he donned a few minutes ago seems to instantly stick to his skin.

"Whoa," Meg says as he shuts Katie's bedroom door. "I almost forgot for a minute that it was sweltering tonight. I wonder when this heat wave is supposed to break?"

"Saturday," Sam tells her. "We're supposed to get a lot of rain from a tropical storm and after that things are going to cool off."

"That's good."

"I wish my room were air-conditioned," he says. "Unfortunately, it's not. I usually don't mind it, but on a night like this . . ."

"It's okay," she says quickly. "Honestly, the heat doesn't bother me all that much. I was sound asleep before Cosette freaked out."

"Right . . . what do you think happened?"

"I think the house is haunted."

Her prompt, straightforward reply surprises him—but it shouldn't. After all, she's not the levelheaded, common-sense type.

What do you expect?

Trying not to sound as if he's scoffing, he asks, "Are you serious?"

He doesn't sound like he's scoffing. He sounds concerned.

More concerned than he should be about someone with whom he's trying to maintain a platonic distance.

She nods vehemently. "I saw it myself."

"A ghost?"

"Something. *Someone.*"

Sam shakes his head.

"You think I'm crazy?"

"I didn't say that."

"But you're thinking it."

"How do you know what I'm thinking?"

"I read minds," she says with a shrug and a glint of amusement in her eyes.

She's kidding, he assures himself, but a ripple of alarm shoots through him anyway.

"It's just that I don't believe in any of that stuff," he says, trying to keep his thoughts pure just in case she really can read them.

"Stuff like . . . ?"

"Spirits. Hauntings."

"Why not?"

Because if there were any way a person who died really could come back, Sheryl would have done it. She would have let me and the kids know she's all right, and she would have found a way to say good-bye.

But now isn't the time to bring up his late wife—or the tsunami of complex emotions that rise along with thoughts of her.

He answers Meg's question, "Because there's no evidence that ghosts exist."

"I just told you I saw one."

"Maybe if I saw it with my own eyes . . ."

"You don't believe me?"

"It's not that . . ."

"Either you think I'm lying, or you think I'm telling the truth."

"It's not that simple, Meg." The sound of her name on his lips gives him pause.

Meg.

It's run through his mind countless times since they met, and he even said it to Katie the other night . . . but has he ever said it to Meg?

Never.

Now he finds himself wanting to say it again.

He refrains.

"I think you believe you saw something. In a strange house, in the middle of the night, on the heels of your daughter's screaming about a ghost . . . well, it's not really surprising that you think you saw one."

"I don't think I saw one. I know I saw one," she persists stubbornly.

He shrugs.

Then he realizes they're just standing here in the hallway, talking, when he should be showing her where everything is.

Getting ready for bed.

Maybe he should take a cold shower first, before he hits the couch.

"*Anyway* . . . that's my room," he says, motioning at the door he left ajar down at the end of the hall. "You can—oh."

"What?"

"I should change the sheets. Sorry. Being a gracious host doesn't come naturally." He smiles.

She returns it. "That's okay."

"The only trouble is . . . the only other king-size sheets I have are flannel. And it's too hot for flannel, right?"

She politely avoids answering. He can't read minds, but

he'd bet his life she's thinking, *there's no way in hell I'm sleeping in flannel sheets tonight.*

"There was another set of king sheets, but I used them for a drop cloth last spring. They were so worn-out they had holes in them," he feels the inexplicable need to elaborate. "I guess I'm still not used to shopping for stuff like that. I don't do sheets, or towels, or place mats . . . I mean, I wash them, but I don't buy them. That was always my wife's—"

He breaks off, realizing he's gone and introduced the taboo subject.

"Your wife's department?" Meg asks helpfully, without missing a beat.

"Right."

"I know how that is. There are certain things that are a man's department, too."

"So you know what it's like, then. Trying to get used to doing things that your husband used to do."

"Not really. The only thing my husband used to do was plot his escape."

"What?"

"Never mind. He was a loser, that's all."

"How long ago did he . . . ?"

"Escape?" she supplies. "Before Cosette was even born."

"He never . . . ?"

"No. He never stuck around to see his own child into the world, which should give you some idea of his character."

Sam nods, feeling sorry for Meg even though there isn't the slightest indication that she feels sorry for herself.

"I'm guessing your wife stuck around for your kids' births," she says dryly, catching him off guard.

"Oh . . . right. She did." His attempt at a laugh is a pathetic staccato choke.

"I'm sorry. I shouldn't joke about your divorce, even though mine was long enough ago that it sometimes seems almost funny. In a humiliating kind of way."

"I understand. It's just . . . I'm not divorced."

Her eyebrows shoot up and she actually takes a slight step back from him.

"You're married?"

"No!"

"Then . . . ?"

Sam takes a deep breath. "My wife was killed in a car accident."

Meg's hands fly to her mouth as she gasps. "Oh, God. I'm so sorry, Sam. I just assumed . . . I mean . . . I'm an idiot. I had no idea."

"I know you didn't. How would you?"

She touches his arm, and he's startled to realize that he's trembling. It isn't so much from grief or emotion as it is from relief.

There.

He's said it, without breaking down.

My wife was killed in a car accident.

That's not something he voices very often anymore, now that he's been living around here for four years. But back in the beginning, when he and the kids had newly moved back in with his mother, he was forced to say it almost constantly.

He cried every time.

Not this time, though. This time, he feels as though he's just set down a box of bricks he's been lugging around.

"I wish I had known," Meg says softly. "About your wife."

Does she mean that she wishes she had known back when it happened—before he even knew her?

Or does she mean now, since they met a few days ago?

"Why?" He can't help being struck by the tide of genuine sympathy in her eyes. It washes away his misgivings about her, try as he might to cling to them.

"I don't know . . . I just wish I could have . . . done something. I know it sounds crazy, since you didn't even know me, but . . . well, I would have helped you, if I could."

It's a bizarre thing for her to say, really. They're strangers even now.

Yet somehow, Sam is tremendously comforted.

For a moment, they just look at each other.

Then, remembering that he's supposed to be helping her get settled, he clears his throat. "Do you, ah, want me to just put a clean blanket over the sheets that are already on the bed, or something?"

"What? Oh. No, I'll be fine."

He nods, finding an odd intimacy in the notion of her naked limbs settling into the tangle of sheets he just vacated.

"Where are you going to sleep?" she asks him.

"Downstairs, on the pullout couch." He pauses. "I'll let you get some sleep, then. You must be exhausted."

"Not really. Must be the adrenaline. I feel wide-awake."

"Me, too. Do you want . . ."

Watch it, Sam. What are you doing?

"Do you want to come down and watch TV with me?"

he offers, and wonders why he feels as though he's just made an indecent proposal.

It's TV.

Nothing more.

Really.

Oh, well. She'll undoubtedly say no. At this hour of the night, who wants to stay up?

Meg does, apparently, because she responds with an enthusiastic, "Sure."

You should have gone to bed, Meg scolds herself as she watches Sam take two beers from the fridge and open them.

But she wasn't the least bit tired.

Well then, I should have at least said no when he asked if I wanted something cold to drink. Or asked for ice water.

She distracts herself, looking around the kitchen. It's comfortably worn, the appliances dated and a harvest gold shade that hasn't been popular in a few decades. The fridge is covered with paper reminders and invitations held in place by colorful magnets. There's a stack of newspapers and mail on the laminate counter, alongside a couple of paintbrushes and a pair of sneakers.

This isn't a woman's kitchen, Meg thinks, smiling to herself.

Then she sees the lush, potted geranium blooming on the windowsill. It seems out of place here. Somebody's obviously tending to it, though. Sam? Or maybe . . .

It occurs to her suddenly that he might have a girlfriend.

Why wouldn't he? He always did.

He turns to her and holds out a beer.

"Thanks," she says, and finds herself gesturing at the plant. "That's beautiful. Who takes care of it?"

There's a note of sadness in his grin. "Who do you think?"

"You?"

"Yup."

That doesn't mean he doesn't have a girlfriend. And Meg shouldn't care if he does.

But she finds herself feeling pleased.

A finger of frosty air curls above the neck of the open green bottle in her hand.

"Cheers," Sam says, and clinks his own bottle lightly against it.

"Cheers." She tilts the bottle to her lips and sips.

The sip quickly turns to a swig.

There has never been anything as refreshing as this fizzy, ice-cold brew. She drains a third of the bottle before lowering it to find Sam grinning at her.

"What?"

"Nothing. I was just trying to picture most of the women I know drinking a beer from the bottle, and I couldn't."

"Then you're not hanging out with the right kind of women," she says lightly, trying not to imagine Sam hanging out with women. Any women. For any reason.

Jealous? asks an inner voice.

Absolutely.

Yes, old habits die hard. She vividly recalls the envy she used to feel whenever she spotted Sam leaning in his usual spot against the radiator in the science wing at school, his arm draped around some cheerleader's shoulders.

"Actually," Sam says, "my choice of women to hang out

with in this town is seriously limited to fancy wine drinkers."

"I like wine."

"Fancy wine?"

Meg shrugs. "Any wine. I'm not a Fancy Mom."

"A Fancy Mom. There are plenty of those around here."

"No kidding. The scariest one of all was at my house today."

"Olympia Flickinger?"

"How'd you know?"

"I saw her car," he admits, looking embarrassed, as if she just caught him spying on her.

Maybe she did.

She sips her beer, trying to figure out what, if anything, that might mean.

"Why was she there?" Sam asks.

"Long story short, I'm going to be teaching her daughter to sing, if she'll have me."

"Poor you."

"No kidding."

There's a pause.

Not an awkward one, though. Just a pause.

"Want to go watch Conan or something?" Sam asks.

"Sure."

She follows him back to the front of the house, taking in every detail as they go. She can't help it, she's been fueled by curiosity about his private life ever since she walked through the front door she stared at longingly and surreptitiously so many times in the past.

The place has a comfortable, lived-in aura. Not a showplace, not a bachelor pad. Something pleasantly in between.

There are old family photos on tables and walls, probably left over from Sam's parents' occupancy of the house. Meg wants to look more closely at them, but she can't do it in passing, and she doesn't want to seem nosy.

The furniture is comfortable oak that looks more country than Victorian, which contrasts with the window treatments. Those, Meg suspects, are probably courtesy of his mother's reign here as well.

If Sam doesn't "do" sheets, he probably doesn't do curtains, either.

The French door to the living room, covered in an opaque lace panel, is closed.

"If I don't shut it when I go upstairs at night, the dog wants to sleep on my bed," Sam explains, opening it.

He flips on a light, and they cross the threshold. Meg hears a jingling sound.

"That's Rover," Sam says unnecessarily, closing the door behind them.

Meg spots a sleepy dog looking up from his spot on the rug.

"Hi, Rover," she says cautiously.

Rover responds with a halfhearted wag of his tail, then closes his eyes again.

She tries to think of something positive to say to Sam. "Friendly dog."

"Rover is a sweetheart."

Not much of a watchdog, though, is he? Meg wants to point out. The dog didn't so much as bark when Sam came traipsing into the house with her and Cosette.

She thought dogs were supposed to come yapping around whenever strangers are afoot.

Oh, well. She'll take a laid-back, indifferent mutt over a growling, barking watchdog any day.

Meanwhile, as Cosette pointed out, their own cat has been practically bouncing off the walls next door. Maybe she should spend a little time with Rover and take a refresher course in how to chill.

Either that, or maybe we should take a cue from Chita Rivera and get the heck out of that haunted house.

"Have a seat," Sam offers, apparently looking around for the remote.

After brief consideration of her choices, Meg settles on the couch.

That way, she's farthest from the dog.

Yes, and that way, Sam can sit next to you.

That isn't why, she argues with herself, and takes another gulp of her beer.

But she isn't disappointed when he locates the remote and sinks onto the couch beside her. Not thigh-to-thigh beside her, but close enough.

Close enough? He's too close.

You should get up and move, before it's too late, Meg cautions herself.

But her body doesn't budge.

Get up and move, she commands, but she might as well be a helpless puppeteer whose marionette's strings have been slashed.

Now what?

Chapter
10

Powerlessly mired inches from Sam on the couch, Meg watches him aim the remote at the television and press a button.

Nothing happens.

"What's up with that?" Sam mutters, and presses it again.

This time, the television flicks on, but the screen is filled with snowy static.

Sam curses.

"What's wrong with it?" Meg asks.

"The cable must be out again. It happens. Usually only when there's a storm, though."

They both look toward the window.

Beyond the screen, everything is still. Not even a gust to stir the curtains.

Sam clicks off the television again. "We'll try it again in a few seconds."

"No big deal. I don't watch much television anyway. In fact, I haven't even hooked up our cable service yet."

"And your daughter isn't freaking out?"

Meg shakes her head and sips her beer.

"That would drive my kids crazy. They both watch too much television—I probably do, too."

"Cosette reads a lot. What do you watch?"

"Baseball games, sitcoms, a couple of reality shows, some HBO series, movies . . ."

"Which movies?" asks Meg, hoping to find some common ground. On the rare occasions that she does watch television, she watches movies.

"You know . . . whatever's on. New ones, old ones."

"Old ones? I like old movies. What are some of your favorites?"

"*Meatballs* is good," he says promptly. "And I like *Top Gun*."

So much for common ground.

"What about you?"

"*Philadelphia Story, Citizen Kane, It Happened One Night,* anything with Joan Crawford, or Henry Fonda . . . And I love old musicals."

"Like *Grease*? Have you ever seen it?"

Seen it? She debates whether to tell him that she played Sandy for over a year in a revival. Nah.

"I meant more like the old musicals from the thirties and forties."

"Oh. I don't think I've ever seen one of those."

Meg has seen them all. In fact, she and Geoffrey had a Judy Garland movie marathon just last week, before she moved. They kicked it off with popcorn and *The Wizard of Oz,* wound it down with a nightcap and *Meet Me in Saint Louis.* A perfect evening, in Meg's opinion.

Something tells her Sam might not agree.

I miss Geoffrey, Meg realizes suddenly, overcome by a wave of nostalgia for her old life.

She drains what's left of her beer and sets the bottle on the coffee table.

She misses Geoffrey, and her apartment, and gossip about people who populated the world she left behind, and the city itself, and yes, her work.

Certain elements of it, anyway. She doesn't miss auditioning, or cutthroat competition, or the rigors of keeping her voice and body in peak performance condition. But she does miss being immersed in musical theater, and singing, not to mention the regular paychecks.

Basically, she's homesick.

And it hasn't even been a week.

"What are you thinking?"

She looks up, startled by Sam's question. She had momentarily forgotten where she was.

"Why?" she asks, instantly aware again of his presence.

In the soft amber lamplight, with his summer tan and slightly flushed, damp skin, he seems to glow. And he's close enough for her to smell him: a heady scent of the clean fabric softener emanating from his cotton T-shirt, and the earthy heat coming off him. Not perspiration, just the appealing cologne of masculine warmth.

"I asked because you look distracted," he tells her. "And sad."

"Oh . . . don't mind me. I was wondering if I just made a really bad move."

"You mean not using a coaster?"

Baffled, she looks at him.

His mouth quirks into a half smile. "It was a joke. I meant setting the beer bottle down, no coaster, bad move . . . Forget it. Stupid joke. You meant bad move, as in leaving the city and moving up here?"

"Right. What do you think about it?"

"I don't know you well enough to have an opinion."

No, he doesn't. She keeps forgetting. Not only does he feel like an old friend, but he suddenly feels like her only friend.

"It's just that I don't know what to expect from here on in," she confides. She's not sure why. She just needs someone to talk to. Someone who isn't hostile and hormonal and fifteen.

Anyone would fit the bill, really, she insists to herself. It doesn't have to be Sam. He just happens to be here.

So you're not going to make him your new confidant, or anything more.

No.

But tonight, he's all you've got.

Yes.

And you might as well talk to him, because you can't do anything else with him, lest you forget.

She didn't. Not even for a second.

"You should have some idea of what this is going to be like, though," Sam is telling her. "It's not like you're a stranger in a strange land. You grew up here."

"I know, but it feels like a strange land," she says, thinking of the Flickingers and their wardrobes and cameras occupying her childhood home. And of the Fancy Moms, and the trendy new businesses that have pushed out the old ones on Main Street. And of the haunted house next door where her belongings are currently parked.

"I know what you mean. When I moved back here again, it did take some getting used to."

"Moved back? You mean you left?"

He nods. "After college—I went to a SUNY school upstate . . ."

She nods. She knows. The State University of New York at Fredonia, where he majored in education. She kept track of him after he left Glenhaven Park High—until she left town herself.

"I went to grad school in Manhattan," he continues. "We lived there for a few years and I taught in the Bronx until Ben was born. Then we moved to Pelham."

Meg tries to absorb this mini–biographical sketch. Tries to absorb the *we*.

And . . .

Manhattan? So he was right under her nose for years, living in the same city, and she never even knew it.

Yes, with his wife and child, she reminds herself. *They're the "we."*

"Did you meet your wife in college?" she asks, and he nods.

"She was a teacher, too. But mostly, she wanted to be a mom."

Meg smiles faintly.

So does Sam, but his is ominously shadowed. Her heart goes out to him.

"So you moved back here a few years ago?" she asks, to keep him talking.

"Yes, the kids and I moved in here with my mother after Sheryl . . . passed away."

Don't go to that dark place, Sam.

"That must have been a difficult adjustment," Meg says, trying to think of a way to steer the conversation back to a less painful topic for him.

"It was. But I honestly don't remember much of it. I just knew things had changed around here, but it didn't matter much to me."

"That's understandable."

He falls silent, lost in thought.

Come back, Sam.

"For me," she says, "I'm starting to think it might have been almost easier if I had moved someplace where I had never lived before."

Except that Sam wouldn't be there.

That would be a good thing, because she can't fall for him, and she feels as though she could. If she let herself. Which she won't.

But still . . .

"Why do you think it would be easier someplace new?" Sam asks, rolling his empty beer bottle back and forth between his palms.

"Because I wouldn't have had all these expectations about what it was going to be like. I guess I was trying to, you know . . ."

"Go home again."

"Yes."

"And you just found out that you can't."

"Right. You can't go home again."

"Hey, great saying . . . you should put it on a T-shirt," he says with a smile, and stretches. "Want another beer?"

Yes, she does.

But she'd better not. She never had a chance to eat dinner tonight, and the one she just drank went down much too easily. One more, and she might drop her guard.

Yes, the next thing she knows she'll find herself crying

on Sam's sturdy shoulder, or encouraging him to cry on hers.

Or something worse.

Worse?

All right, better. Infinitely better.

She isn't exactly repelled by the image of herself in Sam's arms.

"Meg . . . ?" he asks tentatively.

Her breath catches in her throat. "Yes . . . ?" she asks, just as tentatively, wondering if he's going to ask if he can kiss her.

"The beer?"

"Oh! Beer! No!"

He looks taken aback by her vehement response. "Wow. You really don't want one, do you."

She laughs nervously and lifts her hand to shove her hair from her face. "No, I just . . . I'm good. Thanks."

"Are you sure?"

She catches him watching her move her arm and remembers that she's barely dressed. He seems to have noticed that, too.

"I'm positive. I'd better not drink anymore," she says hastily.

"Why not?" He looks pointedly at her and slides an inch closer on the couch. "Afraid you might do something reckless?"

Startled by his provocative question, she realizes that he might be startled as well.

He follows it up with a slightly nervous-sounding, "I don't know why I said that."

"It's okay. You were right."

Now it's her turn to feel as though someone is putting a barrage of dauntless words into her mouth.

"I could definitely swerve into reckless territory tonight if I'm not careful. It's been a stressful week . . ."

"And . . . ?" It sounds as though he's holding his breath.

"And I just . . ."

"What?"

"Don't trust myself."

"Then I shouldn't trust you either."

She smiles. "Probably not."

"So you're going to hurl yourself at me and beg me to let you have your way with me?"

"Probably not," she repeats lightly, and he feigns a little-boy pout.

"Then again," she adds, tossing him a coquettish up-and-down glance, "you never know."

"Really?" He sounds . . . hopeful. Intrigued.

Yet she senses the wariness in him that she feels herself.

He's afraid too. And her own reservations are lost in a flood of captivated concern for his emotional well-being.

"So hurling and begging might occur?" He says it teasingly, but they're both aware that they're venturing into uncharted territory.

For a moment, they just stare at each other.

Then, all at once, Sam leans in and captures her mouth, swiftly, sweetly, with his own.

When he pulls back, she sighs. "Now I'm not sure of anything at all."

"You're not the only one."

"I swore we wouldn't do this tonight, Sam. Or ever again."

"So did I."

She wants to ask why.

But before she can, he reaches out and runs his hand down her bare upper arm. She gasps as a shock sends a current surging through her bloodstream . . .

But that's impossible, she reminds herself. Static electricity doesn't occur when you touch someone on a humid summer night.

Yet that's exactly what it felt like when his fingertips made contact with her skin.

Rather than removing his grasp, Sam tightens it. Then, with his other hand, he brushes a curtain of hair gently away from her face.

"There. Now I can see you," he murmurs, his eyes fastened on hers.

She knows somehow that she couldn't break the connection if she tried. Not that she's going to.

Magnetic force, electrical force . . .

An incredible stream of energy seems to be sizzling between them.

Sam leans closer, and she closes her eyes, waiting for his kiss.

All coherent thought flies from her head as his lips make contact again.

More magnetic, electrical energy.

She leans back against the couch cushions, taking him with her. He's cupping her face in his hands, holding her fast, kissing her more deeply when she opens her mouth willingly.

He groans deep in his throat, and the sound sends a hot surge of need to ooze and pool within her.

This is really happening.

It isn't some adolescent fantasy fueled by an unrequited crush.

This is real.

And we should stop.

There are so many reasons not to do this . . .

But right now, she can't remember any of them. She doesn't want to.

So don't think.

Just feel.

You can think all you want, later.

But you might never get to feel this way again.

Sam's face is against her neck as he nuzzles a moist, molten trail past her collarbone. She can feel the rough texture of his stubble and the silken stroke of his lips. Then he shifts his weight, and she can feel much more than that.

She can feel it lower, below her neck . . . below her waist.

Rigid angles meet pliant curves, and she hears his sharp intake of breath as she settles herself against him.

"Do you know what you're doing to me?"

"Yes," she says simply, and her fingertips wander beneath his T-shirt, where at last she is able to touch him the way she used to dream about.

Running her fingertips over impressive planes of warm, hard muscle, she feels his lips resume their heated journey, dipping into the hollow beneath her shoulder blade.

He lingers there, but not for long, lifting his head briefly as he pushes aside the thin strap of her top, slipping it down over her shoulder.

Meg shudders when she feels his wet mouth on her bare breast, and again when his tongue teases its taut, puckering peak.

She wriggles against him, aching to be closer. He groans at the intimate contact, lifts his head, kisses her again, long and hard.

Dragging his mouth from hers, he asks raggedly, "Do we need to stop? Because if we do, we should . . . now."

Yes, she comprehends as the fog of passion lifts slightly. This is the point of no return.

Do we need to stop?

Her head is swimming. She can barely remember her name.

Astor Hudson? Meg Addams?

Who am I?

What do I want?

Do we need to stop?

Too many questions.

Sam's blue eyes are probing hers for an answer to just one.

"No," she says, "we don't need to stop. Unless . . ."

"What?" He's gone from visibly elated to deflated in the space of the split second it took her to utter that word.

"Unless . . . ?" She gestures helplessly overhead.

"Unless . . . the ceiling caves in on us?"

Still panting from the exertion, a laugh—more of a giggle, really—escapes her as she shakes her head. "No, I meant, what if one of them comes downstairs?"

"Oh. The kids. Wait here, I'll be right back."

"I'll be here."

She watches him leave the room, scarcely able to believe where she is and what she's doing.

Rather, about to do.

Should I?

She knows the answer to that.

Then why is she ignoring it? Why has she allowed herself to cast aside everything—her resolution, her better judgment, her decorum, just so—

She hears a jingle and catches Rover lifting his head to glance over at her from his spot on the rug.

Is it her imagination, or does he seem to disapprove?

Who cares what the dog thinks? She turns away from Rover's reproachful gaze.

Who cares what anyone thinks?

Who cares about *shoulds*?

Meg's life since motherhood has been riddled with them; it's time to let go of all that for once.

For once? Until her big New Year's epiphany, she was heedless of shoulds when it came to men.

Well, everyone's allowed to lapse from time to time. So she's going to put it all aside.

Just for tonight. Just for a little while, even.

What's wrong with indulging in a wanton romp she's anticipated her whole life? Especially if she allows no expectations about what will come of it.

Nothing will come of it, she reminds herself, even as a pang of misgiving slips in.

Why can't anything come of it?

Why can't she allow herself to imagine that she and Sam are somehow meant to be? That after all these years, they might fall in—

No! Don't even think that word!

She hears footsteps creaking overhead; Sam is coming back down the stairs. Quickly. *He's almost running,* she notes, and her body feels charged again; tingling with anticipation.

He reappears in the doorway, pauses, and snaps his fingers. "Rover. Come here."

The dog gets to his feet obediently and trots over without casting a backward glance at Meg. Still, she senses smugness, almost as though he's silently telling her, *See? He's calling me, not you.*

Yes, I do see that.

Has Sam changed his mind?

Is he taking Rover out or something? Is dog walking the Sam Rooney equivalent of a cold shower?

Rover crosses the threshold into the hall.

Sam disappears with him.

Meg is riddled with doubt.

She should probably just go home.

No shoulds, remember?

Anyway, there are ghosts over there. She doesn't want to venture back alone in the middle of the night.

You'll have to go sooner or later, though. That, or sell the place and move.

But where would she go?

And how could she leave Sam?

Huh? Leave Sam?

Sam should have nothing to do with whatever she decides is best for herself and for Cosette. Nothing whatsoever.

She hears footsteps and he's back. There he is, a grown man, exuding teenaged-boy anticipation and vulnerability when he looks at her.

Meg's misgivings evaporate like the figure she spotted at the foot of the stairway next door.

"Where's Rover?" she asks him.

"Having a snack in the kitchen."

"He was hungry?"

"He's always hungry. That comes in handy whenever I need him to be somewhere other than where I am."

"Oh." She smiles, relieved.

Standing on his tiptoes, Sam runs his fingers along the top of the molding above the French door.

"Where . . . ? There. Got it."

Meg sees that he's holding a key.

He swiftly locks the door and turns to her wearing a smug grin. "Where were we?"

"You were right here." She can't help smiling, either, as she pats the couch beside her. "Did you check . . . ?"

"Upstairs? Not a creature is stirring, not even a mouse. And believe me, we do have them."

She shrugs. "Most old houses do."

"You're one of those hearty beer-drinking girls who's not afraid of mice, then?"

"Not of mice. Just bees," she admits, as he settles beside her again.

"And ghosts."

"I thought you said there was no such thing."

"What I say doesn't matter. If you think they exist, then they do for you. And you're allowed to be afraid of them."

"Gee, thanks." She snuggles a little closer as he settles his arm around her and pulls her closer. "So . . . what are *you* afraid of?"

"Me? Nothing."

"I don't believe you." She strokes his cheek, giddy that she can actually do that, after all these years.

That, and more.

"Okay," he admits, "I am afraid of two things."

"What are they?"

"Something happening to one of my kids."

"That's universal. Isn't everyone?"

"Probably."

But not like I am.

That blatant message is clear to read in his eyes.

His wife was killed. No wonder he worries about losing his children.

Oh, Sam.

She encircles his neck with her arms, wishing she could take the pain away.

"What else?" she asks gently.

"What else, what?"

"What's the other thing you're afraid of?"

His voice is hushed as he says, "This."

He grazes his lips against her lips, her throat, her shoulder, whisper-soft.

"Then . . . do you not want to?"

"No. I *do* want to." He shifts her in his arms so that she's lying down, and he's stretched out alongside her, the length of his body pressing the length of hers. "I want to so much that it scares me."

"For what it's worth, I'm scared, too."

"So that's three things, total?" he asks, chuckling quietly, tracing her cheek with his fingertip.

"Hmm?" She lets her own hands wander beneath his shirt again, back to warm skin and muscles.

"Bees, ghosts, and making love?"

"Not in general," she amends, trying to maintain the playful tone as her heart skips and starts at the mere phrase *making love*. "Just with you. With you, I'm terrified."

"Should I be honored, or offended?"

"Honored. Definitely."

"Well, you know what they say, don't you?"

"What do they say?"

"That the only way to conquer your fear is to face it head-on."

With that, he kisses her deeply. A fierce longing soars within her, and she presses herself urgently into his embrace.

The pace quickens, an unmistakable prelude to love-making.

Tongues duet in an age-old dance; hands roam; limbs intertwine.

Clothing is cast away; with it go lingering reservations and shoulds and fears and logic.

Now there is nothing but moist, heated kisses and warm, slippery skin and ripples of pleasure.

At last, Sam, breathing hard, gasps, "Wait a second." He leans over to fumble around for his discarded shorts.

Panting, rubbing her sweat-dampened hair back from her forehead, she watches him retrieve the square foil packet he got when he went upstairs. The sight of it fills her with capricious expectation.

Sam sees her watching and glances a question at her. She nods the answer, too overcome to speak. She feels as if she dipped a toe into a refreshing stream and was suddenly caught up in a raging current, swept toward the brink of a waterfall, with no going back even if she wanted to . . .

And I don't want to.

Within moments, he's sheathed and poised above her, looking into her eyes again.

"Okay?" he asks in a hoarse whisper.

She nods, unable to speak.

Their eyes lock as he grazes the aching core of her that yearns for fulfillment. She reacts as if maddeningly tickled by a feather. Her hips lift, seeking him, and with a groan, he enters her at last.

Never before has it been like this for her. Never before has it felt this right.

She whispers his name in wonder, scarcely able to grasp that this is really happening, that she's here, now, with him.

She's a delicate instrument coaxed to a new range by a masterful musician, and nothing could ever be better than this. Sam plays her with notes sweet and tender, then bold and deep, ultimately crescendoing to an exquisite and pure climax. Every nerve ending in her body seems to erupt in dazzling sensation.

Lying against the cushions, Sam's head cradled against her breast, his fingertips playing lightly up and down her hip, Meg realizes that *this* is as good as it gets.

"Still afraid?" he asks, lifting his head and flashing her a lazy Sam smile.

"No."

But that's a lie.

Somewhere in the back of her mind, she's more terrified than ever. But coherent thought is held at bay by shimmery ripples of afterglow.

"We should sleep," she tells him drowsily after a while.

He responds with a deep yawn and snuggles her against his chest. "I know."

"But not here . . . not together."

"No. I know. You have to go upstairs."

"I will." She begins to disentangle herself from him.

"Wait." He pulls her back and kisses her deeply.

A new ache promptly makes itself known.

"I have to go," she protests, laughing a little.

"I know. And you can. Just . . . not yet."

*　*　*

The first light of dawn is creeping into the house by the time Meg climbs into Sam's bed upstairs . . . alone.

Yet as she sinks her head into the pillow and pulls the sheet around her shoulders, his scent billows up to envelop her like a hug.

Her final thought before she goes to sleep is that for the first time since she moved back here, she really does, at last, feel like she's come home.

Chapter
11

Jauntily whistling an old Van Morrison song, Sam slips a spatula beneath the edge of an oversized chocolate chip pancake on the griddle. He flips the raw, holey side face-down into sizzling butter beside the other three he's just turned.

Then, hearing footsteps creaking on the stairs, he drops the spatula, turns down the flame, and sticks his head out into the hallway.

"Hi, Daddy," Katie says cheerfully, appearing in her usual summer morning getup of shorts, a tank top, and flip-flops.

"Hi, sweetie."

He kisses her on the head, hoping he didn't sound disappointed when he realized that it was only her.

He probably shouldn't have been expecting Meg; she went upstairs pretty late. She'll probably sleep for a while longer.

Even Ben seems to have slept in today. He's usually up bright and early most mornings to go for a run. Sam often finds him in the living room catching up on last night's scores on ESPN.

Not today. No sign of Ben up and about. And Sam just got up himself about fifteen minutes ago. He grabbed a quick shower, then decided to make a decent breakfast for a change. Cold cereal is the norm in the Rooney household.

"Pancakes?" Katie grins. "Yay! Why are you making them? Is it somebody's birthday?"

"No. We have company."

"Where?" She looks around as though expecting to see that someone has slipped in and pulled up a chair at the table.

So she didn't notice that somebody was sleeping in the bed above her.

"They're upstairs. Cosette and her mother, from next door."

"Meg is here?"

He nods reluctantly, remembering all the reasons he wasn't supposed to do what he did last night.

Ah, the cold cruel light of day.

"Where *upstairs*?" Katie asks excitedly. "And why are they here?"

He chooses to ignore the why. "Meg slept in my room—I slept on the couch," he is compelled to add hastily, "and Cosette actually slept in the extra bed in your room."

"No, she didn't."

"Yes, she did. You were sound asleep, so—"

"There's nobody in the bed above mine."

"How do you know?"

"Because I was just crawling around up there, looking for my brush."

"Why would it be on the top bunk?"

"Because I looked everywhere else," says Katie, whose cluttery habits, even as an eight-year-old, used to drive neatnik Sheryl crazy.

Sheryl.

Sam hasn't allowed himself to think of her all morning. Nor did he think of her last night, when he was with Meg.

He waits to be seized by guilt, but it doesn't happen.

"Dad?"

"Hmm?"

"Are you okay?"

He looks up at Katie. "I'm fine. I'm just wondering where Cosette went if she didn't spend the night in your bunk."

"Maybe she spent the night, but she already got up."

"Maybe. But where would she have gone?"

"Home?"

"I doubt that," he mutters, remembering the so-called haunting.

But where else could Cosette be?

Maybe she crawled into his bed with her mother.

He doesn't feel comfortable knocking on the door to check.

Instead he strides toward the den, to look out the window and see if he can spot any sign of activity next door.

Hmm. The door to the den is closed, which is unusual.

Sam opens it to peek in . . . and is greeted by the last thing he ever expected to find.

*   *   *

"They were *what*?" Meg sits up groggily in Sam's bed, rubbing her eyes in the bright morning sunlight.

"Kissing."

"Wait . . . *who* was kissing?" she asks, just to be sure she heard right.

"Ben and Cosette. In the den. On the couch." Sam sits gingerly at the foot of the bed.

He's clean-shaven, his wavy hair slightly damp, and he's wearing gray jersey shorts and a navy T-shirt with faded white lettering that reads GLENHAVEN PARK BULLDOGS.

"I opened the door," he tells Meg, "and there they were."

"What did you do when you saw them?"

"Nothing. I closed the door and left. They didn't even know I was there."

Meg tries to digest what he's telling her, but she's as caught off guard by his appearance in her bedroom—no, *his* bedroom—and by the recollection of just what happened between them last night—as she is by the news about her daughter and his son.

"I mean, it's not that big a deal," Sam says, getting up and pacing across the bedroom as though it is, *indeed,* a very big deal. "At least it was broad daylight, and they weren't doing anything else."

Unlike their parents.

Pushing that disruptive thought from her head, Meg asks, "Are you positive they were really kissing?"

"Unless one of them almost drowned and the other was giving mouth-to-mouth—but only after changing them both into dry clothes—yes," he says dryly, "they were kissing."

She shakes her head. "That's so . . . bizarre."

"Yeah."

For a moment, they're both silent, digesting the facts.

"I mean . . . they just don't seem to have much in common." Meg sits up straighter, pulling the sheet with her to cover herself in her strappy pajama top, which she realizes is almost laughable, considering he saw much more than her shoulders and a hint of cleavage a few hours ago.

"Yeah, well, they're both fifteen, attractive, and hormonally charged. I'd say that's something."

She smiles. "Thank you for saying that."

"For saying what?"

"*Attractive.* Underneath all that black, Cosette really is a pretty girl. Most people don't see that, though. Not that she cares what anyone thinks of her. For over a year now, she seems to be doing her best to make sure that she looks as hideous as possible."

"Why is that?"

"I have no idea. I gave up on trying to figure her out. I decided I should be glad she's a nonconformist."

"You should be."

"I would be if it didn't seem to make things even more painful for her." She briefly describes the bullying incident, all the while acutely aware of what happened between her and Sam last night.

How is it that she can possibly be sitting here carrying on a coherent conversation while a series of steamy fantasy images parade through her head?

"We take stuff like that really seriously at school," Sam tells her. "If Cosette has any problem at Glenhaven Park when she starts, we'll be on it right away."

"That's good to know. Hopefully that won't happen again."

"I hope not. And at least I'll be around to keep an eye on things for you."

Those words—*I'll be around*—send a shiver of contentment through her in one moment, and dismay in the next.

He'll be around . . .

But he doesn't mean it the way you wish.

Wish? Does she actually wish Sam were talking about a long-term relationship?

Well, maybe.

But he isn't. He means he'll be around for Cosette, as a faculty member at school.

That should be reassuring. It should be enough to make her feel a little more at ease about staying here in Glenhaven Park.

Before last night, she was filled with doubt about it.

She's just so stressed by all that needs to be done with the house . . .

But you did order furniture and unpack a few more boxes, she reminds herself. *And you should ask Sam for the name of a good handyman.*

Well, it isn't just about the house. It's about the latest visit from the resident ghost . . .

Although Sam seems convinced that was her imagination, and in the bright light of day, she can almost convince herself it might have been.

Well, regardless of any of that, Cosette is miserable here . . .

Yes, but now that she's kissing the boy next door, she might perk up considerably.

Generally, though, the fresh start isn't what Meg hoped it would be. She's lonely, and overwhelmed, and rapidly going broke.

And yesterday's meeting with the insufferable Flickingers didn't help matters.

Sophie isn't tone-deaf, exactly . . . but she's hardly the next Maria Callas. Then again, both she and her mother have the prima donna persona down pat. By the time they left, Meg was thinking that she'd rather wait tables for a living than give voice lessons to the likes of Olympia's daughter.

But not all her prospective students are going to be like that . . . are they?

Thinking of the Fancy Moms she met on the bleachers at soccer practice the other day, she doesn't feel particularly optimistic.

"What do you want to do about this?" Sam is asking.

"I have no idea," she replies, and she isn't just talking about the apparent fledgling romance between their kids.

"Well, I don't think we should acknowledge that we know what's going on."

"Right." Looking at him, she's back to remembering last night . . . and wishing it could happen again. Right now.

"We should probably just . . . keep an eye on them."

"Right."

"It'll probably fizzle right out anyway," Sam goes on, and her heart sinks fleetingly before she realizes that he's talking about what's going on between the kids.

Oh . . . good.

Then again . . . he might as well be talking about the two of them, as well.

Because this can't go any further. And she doesn't expect it to.

Just for tonight—that's what she told herself it would be.

And now, the night is over.

She had her glorious encounter with Sam.

There won't be another one, because that would lead to her wanting more, and more . . . and ultimately, getting hurt.

She saw the pain in Sam's eyes, heard it in his voice. He came right out and told her he was terrified.

No, he's not any more willing to invest in a relationship than she is.

When Sam returns to the kitchen, Ben is pouring two glasses of orange juice. Cosette is nowhere in sight, but music is coming from the den. One of Sam's CDs.

Sam asks, in a low voice, "What are you doing?"

"Pouring juice."

"Two glasses?"

"One's for Cosette."

"Oh."

Ben refuses to look him in the eye, but Sam sees his hand shaking a little as he returns the Tropicana carton to the fridge.

Poor kid. He's trying to be cool about whatever it is that just happened. He doesn't need his old man giving him a hard time.

"Hey." Sam lays a hand on his son's shoulder. "Where is she?"

Ben tilts his head toward the den. "We were just . . . listening to music."

"Yeah? That's good. You like the same kind of music?"

"Yeah. Why? Does that surprise you?"

Sam shrugs. He tries to think of something else to say, but can't.

You're the one who told him to give her a chance, he reminds himself, watching his son return to the den and close the door.

And, hey, aren't you also the one who was supposed to keep Meg away from Katie?

He just passed his daughter on the stairs. She said she was going to go change her clothes before breakfast, but he has a pretty good idea that she's hoping to run into "the Mom next door."

Meg's in the shower now; he can hear the water groaning in the pipes overhead.

Sam's body reacts promptly at the thought of her, naked, lathering herself under a stream of spray.

Before he left the bedroom upstairs, she said she's going home after breakfast.

He was disappointed when she told him that, but now he thinks, *the sooner, the better.*

He offered to go back over with her, just to make sure everything is okay.

She turned him down.

"I'm sure everything is fine," she said, and added wryly, "But don't worry, if I see any ghosts, I'll holler."

"Make sure you do."

He hopes that she doesn't, though.

Not just because he wants to spare her further trauma, but because he wants to spare himself further temptation.

Pancakes at the round table in Sam's sunny kitchen.

Meg can't help but notice that Cosette seems to have undergone a vast transformation since last night.

Of course she still isn't wearing makeup, and her dark hair falls becomingly in loose waves around her face. The jet-black color seems less intense without the thick jet-black eyeliner to enhance the dramatic effect, and her skin seems more porcelain than pallid. She's still wearing her summer pajamas, which consist of a pale lavender sleeveless cotton top and boxer-style shorts in a lavender print. Ordinarily, she wouldn't be caught in pastels outside the house, but she seems to have forgotten what she has on.

For that matter, she seems to have forgotten anyone exists in the room other than Sam's son Ben, and vice versa.

He's looking at Meg's daughter the way his father looked at Meg just hours ago.

As for Sam, he's made a conscious effort to avoid eye contact altogether this morning. A wall seems to have gone up between them again, more impenetrable than the overgrown hedge border on the property line.

Katie, however, seems to have taken a giant leap and landed cleanly on Meg's side of the hedge. She chatters nonstop as they eat their pancakes, telling Meg all about her trip to the Catskills, and her friends and her hobbies, and the new clothes she wants to buy for school's start next week.

"My dad said he'll take me to get some new outfits, but he still hasn't. He hates to shop," Katie says, flashing an accusing look at Sam, who shrugs.

"What can I say? I'm a guy. Assembling new outfits isn't my all-time favorite pastime, but I promise I'll take you this weekend, okay?" Sam sips his coffee moodily.

"Yeah, but Ben will have to come and you'll both be bored and I'll have to rush and nobody will be able to come into the dressing room to tell me what looks good on me and what doesn't."

That does it.

Meg takes the bait. She can't help it. She feels sorry for Sam's motherless daughter.

"Katie, why don't you come shopping Saturday with me and Cosette?"

Instant delight. "Can I really?"

"Sure. I'd be happy to help you pick out some clothes."

"That's not necessary," Sam says stiffly.

Startled, Meg looks at him and finds that he's shifted his gaze to her at last.

"I can take her shopping," he informs her.

"But you hate it, Dad."

"No, I don't."

Meg doesn't believe that any more than Katie does.

"Dad, come on," she protests, "who are you trying to kid? You hate shopping for clothes. You say it all the time. Meg loves it. Right, Meg?"

Torn, she says, "Well, I wouldn't say I *love* it, but . . ."

"You certainly don't have to take my daughter for her school clothes."

"I know, but I don't mind at all. I'm going anyway."

"See, Dad?"

Sam looks dubiously at Meg, who shrugs.

"I really was planning on taking Cosette shopping Saturday afternoon."

"We have soccer practice."

"I know, but it's supposed to rain." He's the one who told her that—a tropical storm blowing through to break the heat wave. "Do you have practice in the rain?"

"Not if it's torrential," Sam concedes.

"Well, if it's not, we'll still go shopping after practice. Cosette wore a uniform to her old school in the city, so she needs a new wardrobe for September."

She can't help but notice that her daughter doesn't even glance over at the mention of her name. Sitting there across the table, she and Ben are lost in each other's eyes.

Meg can't decide if their newfound romance is sickening or cute or alarming.

A bit of all three, really.

"Dad, you have to let me go shopping with Meg and Cosette. Please."

Meg turns back to see Katie fixing her father with an imploring gaze to match her tone.

This isn't just about shopping, though. There's something more going on here. She can see it in Katie's eyes, and in Sam's expression.

She wisely keeps her mouth shut, refusing to engage in the father-daughter power struggle, having endured her share of similar battles with Cosette.

"Dad, I never get to do girl things," Katie goes on. "All my friends have moms and sisters to shop with, and I don't have that."

The pain and vexation in Sam's eyes is blatant. "I can't give you a mom and a sister, Katie."

Katie is oblivious, turning the knife deeper. "I know you can't, but you can let me go with Meg and Cosette, and that will be the next best thing. Please, Dad? *Pleasepleaseplease?*"

"It really is okay, Sam," Meg says, and wishes that she hadn't.

He turns to her with thinly veiled animosity. "It really isn't okay, Meg."

"I'm sorry."

"I like to take her shopping for her school clothes."

She doesn't believe that for a second.

"I take her every year. I get her whatever she needs. And then I take her to eat at the Cheesecake Factory. Her and Ben. We do that every Labor Day weekend, the three of us. It's a family tradition."

"You never said that," Katie tells him, and has the grace to look slightly remorseful. "I didn't know it was a tradition."

"We do it every year. Of course it's a tradition."

"But you act like you hate it."

"Well, I don't."

But he does. Meg can tell. And she knows why.

It's because his wife isn't there to share it with them, the way she should be.

She knows, because there are certain rituals that make her acutely aware that Cosette should have a father. Soccer games on Saturdays in the city, when the other dads would cheer their daughters on. And Christmas morning, with toys that require a toolbox and infinite patience to put together. And the action and horror films Cosette loves to go see—unless, of course, her father is in them. Meg goes, but she prefers romantic comedies.

Meg does a lot of things she would relegate to a dad, if Cosette had a real one.

Just as it's obvious Sam does a lot of things that would have been Katie's mom's territory.

I can't step into that role, Meg tells herself. As simple as it would be in theory for her to take Katie along with her, it would be terribly complicated in other ways.

Yes, that would have huge implications on the dynamic between herself and Katie, between Katie and Sam, between Sam and herself.

Things are rapidly becoming complex enough, judging by the way Cosette and Ben are looking at each other.

"Please, Dad?" Katie persists. "Please let me go with Meg, just this once?"

"No," he says firmly.

"But—"

"Katie," Meg cuts in, and feels Sam's wary gaze immediately on her. "You need to listen to your dad. You don't want to break a family tradition, do you?"

"No," she says in a small, disappointed voice. "I guess I don't."

She halfheartedly cuts off a piece of pancake with the edge of her fork and thrusts it into her mouth, chewing glumly.

Meg sneaks a peek at Sam.

Their eyes crash into each other, and her heart skips a beat. There's a whole new layer now to what she was feeling for him before. The attraction isn't just physical anymore. It's emotional.

There was a time, not so long ago, when Meg would have found that to be reason enough to stay.

But not anymore.

Now, it's reason enough to walk away.

She pushes back her chair.

"Come on, Cosette," she says, and for the first time her daughter tears herself away from Ben's eyes, looking startled.

"What?"

"It's time to go home."

Cosette is about to protest, but seeing the look on her mother's face, she mercifully doesn't.

"Thank you for everything, Sam," Meg says, as they step out into the muggy August morning.

"You're welcome. Good luck."

It must be ninety degrees out, Meg notes, hearing him close his front door firmly as she and Cosette make their way toward home, but as far as she's concerned, the heat wave—hers and Sam's—has already broken.

Chapter

12

Meg wakes up Saturday morning to see rain pouring down the bedroom windowpane.

She climbs off the mattress that was delivered yesterday afternoon—still no bed frame, but this is luxury compared to the hard floor—and looks out. What a dismal day.

She reaches over to turn on a lamp to dispel the gloom, then waits for it to flicker out again. That happened a few times yesterday, in various rooms in the house.

Either the ghost has been up to new tricks, or there's a problem with the wiring.

Meg decided to go with the wiring.

This time, the light stays on. Good.

She's determined not to experience another haunting episode like the one that sent her straight into Sam Rooney's arms the other night.

To her relief, there have been no further incidents.

After what happened, she expected Cosette to put up a fuss about staying here, but she hasn't. In fact, she's been almost docile the last day or so. She was particularly happy to get her computer set up on a makeshift desk in her room, and has been spending her spare time in there, apparently surfing the Net and reading. She said she wants to get caught up on the summer book list she picked up from the library back in New York in June. She spent a lot of time there these last few months, with little else to do.

Meg was thinking she might be bored enough at this point that she won't complain about going to soccer practice today, but there's absolutely no way in hell that she's going to have it in this weather anyway.

She says as much—without the "in hell" part—when she pads barefoot into the kitchen to find her daughter standing by the counter wearing jeans and a T-shirt. The shirt is black, but the jeans are not. It's an old, faded pair Cosette hasn't worn in at least a year.

Meg bites back a comment about the attire, knowing better than to call attention to her daughter's welcome addition of color, even if it is just denim.

"Yeah, I already know, practice is canceled." Cosette peers into the toaster, waiting for it to pop.

"Officially?"

Cosette nods.

"How do you know that?"

"Sam told me."

Meg's heart skids into a brick wall at the mention of his name.

She's successfully avoided hearing and saying it, not to mention seeing him, since she left his house after the pancake breakfast.

"When did you see Sam?" she asks, trying to sound casual.

"He was up walking the dog when I went for a run with Ben this morning," Cosette says, just as casually.

Meg's jaw drops at this bombshell.

The "run" part is surprising enough. Cosette hasn't shown any interest in athletic pursuits in ages.

But . . . Ben?

That's the real shocker.

As far as she knew, Cosette hasn't had any more contact with Ben than she herself has with Sam. She half expected to see Cosette mooning around, looking for him. When it didn't happen, she chalked up both her daughter's romantic interlude and her own as getting caught up in the heat of the moment. When the moment was over, so was the heat—or so she believed.

So much for Meg's intuitive skills.

"I didn't know you went for a run with Ben," she says as the toast pops up.

"How would you?"

"I'd know if you told me. I guess you didn't want me to know."

"I guess I didn't. Ow!" Cosette burns her fingers. "Where are those wooden toaster tongs?"

"Wherever the alarm clock, the raincoats, and my Tony Award are."

"You mean still lost in some box somewhere?"

Meg nods. "And we're going to need that stuff."

"The Tony Award?"

"Especially that," she says ruefully.

Olympia and Sophie are coming here on Monday afternoon for Sophie's first voice lesson, and Meg really wants to have the Tony sitting out on the mantel when they get here.

Normally, she doesn't flaunt it, and she frowns upon her fellow award-winners who make a big deal out of it. She hates that she feels as though she has something to prove, but she does with Olympia Flickinger.

When the woman called yesterday to regally announce that she and Brad had agreed to allow Meg to give Sophie a trial lesson, Meg wanted to say, "Don't do me any favors."

She managed instead to say graciously, "I'm so glad. I'll look forward to working with her."

She desperately needs the money. The handyman she found in the PennySaver will be charging her a fortune, but at least he's available to come next weekend, which is late, but better than not at all. The first six handymen she called weren't free until mid-to-late September.

Apparently, the home improvement industry is thriving in northern Westchester County. Surprise, surprise.

Anyway, Meg figures it can't hurt to display her coveted Tony and show Olympia Flickinger that she's more than qualified to teach voice to a thirteen-year-old aspiring diva. Especially at the astronomical rate she's charging.

When Olympia—after proving herself to be the most high maintenance potential client imaginable—asked about Meg's hourly rate, she more than doubled the one the handyman had just quoted, hoping to scare her off.

Alas, Olympia didn't bat an eye, and even offered to pay for the first session in advance, to secure a spot. An hour after she left, two of her friends called to inquire about Meg taking on their children. So things are looking promising.

But if somehow the voice lessons don't bring in enough cash, I can always become a handyman, she decides. That, or learn a trade. Plumbers and electricians are also in high demand around here. She can't get anyone to come take a look at the leaky pipes or faulty electrical outlets until after the weekend.

"So should we go shopping today?" she asks Cosette.

"Definitely," is the swift reply, catching her off guard. "Let's go to the mall down in White Plains."

"Great." Meg smiles.

Just the two of them, mother and daughter, shopping for back-to-school clothes together.

That'll help take her mind off Sam.

"Yeah, that sounds good," Sam tells Ben across the breakfast table, thinking a trip to the mall will at least get him out of here and help to take his mind off Meg.

He can't help but think about her every time he sees her house. Or the couch where he made love to her. Or his bed, where she slept. Or a bottle of beer, or a remote control, or any number of ordinary household items that now remind him of her.

"And afterward, we'll go to Cheesecake Factory, right, Dad?" Katie pipes up around a mouthful of Cap'n Crunch.

"Of course. It's a tradition." He smiles weakly.

Maybe he shouldn't have made such a fuss about her going with Meg instead of him. He couldn't help but feel a little ridiculous about it afterward.

He's pretty sure nobody—least of all Meg—bought his story about enjoying those yearly back-to-school shopping trips with Katie.

The truth is, he dreads them.

Not just because it's no fun to sit, bored, in the department store man-chairs while his daughter spends hours in dressing rooms.

It isn't fun.

But shopping for clothes for their daughter without Sheryl is a torturous reminder of what Katie is missing. He has to watch other moms and daughters parade past in pairs and threesomes, sometimes laughing and chatting, sometimes arguing, but always together.

Katie is alone.

Not alone . . . she has you and Ben, he reminds himself.

But what do they know about dresses and shoes, proms and weddings? All those milestones in Katie's motherless future loom before Sam every time he sets foot in a mall with his daughter. Things other parents look forward to, he dreads.

It isn't fair.

But that's the way it is. He has to accept it.

And you have, he points out stoically. He rarely allows himself to wallow.

He won't today.

But enjoy it?

That's not going to happen.

Every man, woman, and child in suburban New York is at The Westchester on Saturday at high noon.

At least, that's what it feels like to Meg.

It's a rainy Labor Day weekend, so she should have realized that the upscale, elegant mall would be jammed with back-to-school shoppers. It wasn't this crowded when they were here the other day to order the furniture from Crate & Barrel.

"Let's just valet park," Cosette suggests on their third fruitless journey through the packed parking garage.

"Valet park?" Meg echoes incredulously, and her daughter points to an elegant Scarsdale-type matron emerging from her white Lexus sedan and handing over the keys to a uniformed attendant.

"I don't think so," Meg mutters, steering the Hyundai in the opposite direction. "This is crazy. Maybe we should just go home."

"No!" Cosette's tone is so forceful that Meg nearly hits the brakes.

"Since when are you so into shopping with me?" she asks.

"Since I don't have anyone else to shop with," is the prompt reply.

Oh.

"You'll make some friends as soon as school starts Wednesday," Meg assures her. She adds, fishing, "Anyway, you already know Ben."

"Yeah."

No new info gleaned from that comment.

But Cosette did admit to jogging with him, but insisted he was just a friend. She wasn't very convincing.

Meg has been wondering just what her daughter has been up to when she's behind the closed door of her bedroom. She has her cell phone, and she also has her computer, with dial-up Internet access, thanks to the phones being turned on. For all Meg knows at this point, Cosette has been in constant contact with Ben Rooney since she kissed him.

But if she has, she's not letting on. What can Meg do besides snoop? And snooping isn't her style.

"Mom! Hurry!" Seizing her arm, Cosette gestures at a Chevy Tahoe vacating a spot a few feet away.

Meg flips on her turn signal and prepares to pull in when it pulls out, but a Mercedes SUV appears out of nowhere and slips into it first.

"Hey!" Meg shouts out the window in frustration.

"Mom!"

"That person just stole my spot." Steaming, Meg watches a pair of Fancy Moms emerge from the Mercedes, clutching designer handbags and effortlessly unfolding designer strollers for their designer-dressed toddlers.

"We need to go," Meg decides abruptly. "Let's go down to the city and shop on West Broadway instead."

"No! Come on, Mom, you hate driving in traffic in the rain."

True.

But she also hates mingling with self-centered, arrogant women, and the mall promises to be filled with them today.

"Cosette, I don't see how we're going to shop here if we can't even find a parking—"

"There!" Cosette indicates a Volvo station wagon pulling out of a spot just yards from them. She reaches over and flicks on Meg's turn signal. "Get in there, Mom. Hurry."

Meg spots a shiny black sedan coming around the corner in the opposite direction. Seeing the Volvo pulling out, the driver brakes. Puts on her turn signal.

"She's going to steal your spot, Mom!"

"No, she isn't!" Meg guns the engine and screeches the car forward, just barely missing the exiting station wagon as she swerves in triumphantly.

Take that, you . . . you Fancy Mom, she wants to shake her fist and shout.

"Next time," Cosette says, as they head toward the elevator, "We'll valet park."

Over my dead body, Meg thinks.

There was no valet parking at malls when Meg was a kid. In fact, this particular mall wasn't even here when

Meg was a kid. Her parents took her to Caldor for her back-to-school wardrobe, where they could pick up school supplies and lunch box snacks as well, all under one roof.

Under the towering, skylighted ceiling at The Westchester are tony stores one finds on Fifth and Madison Avenues in Manhattan: Coach, Tiffany, Gucci . . . there's even an Elizabeth Arden spa. Elegant white pillars line the marble-floored and carpeted corridors, which are filled with natural light, unlike most malls. Sculptures, fountains, and lush greenery are tucked along with designer boutiques.

No lunch box snacks here, Meg thinks with regret as she and her daughter survey the directory on the main floor.

"Wow, Mom. *Ch-ching.*" That's Cosette's verbal shorthand for a whole lot of cash . . .

Which is what one definitely needs to shop here.

Which we don't have, Meg acknowledges.

"Let's go to the Gap," Cosette suggests, to her relief.

Okay, so far, so good. Maybe she'll want to buy some regular jeans—*blue* jeans—and T-shirts. T-shirts in white and blue and gray.

To Meg's surprise, Cosette does just that. She picks up some more black jeans and black T-shirts, too . . . but Meg is so pleased by the unexpected addition of color to her wardrobe that she doesn't protest.

She's also noticed that her daughter has gone a little lighter on the eye makeup today. It's still there, and still black, but not quite as startlingly. And she's tucked her long hair behind her ears for a change.

She doesn't look wholesome . . . not by a long shot.

But she doesn't look like Marilyn Manson, either.

"You should get some new jeans, too, Mom," Cosette

suggests, checking her watch as they make their way toward the register.

"I have plenty of pairs of jeans."

With a pointed downward glance, Cosette informs her, "Yours are cut wrong."

"What do you mean by that?"

"You know . . . they're not in style anymore."

"I just bought these last year."

"Exactly. Here, try these." Cosette expertly plucks a pair from the nearest stack and thrusts them at her.

"I thought we were ready to pay and get out of here."

"Yeah, but you should get some new jeans first." She sneaks another peek at her watch. "Go ahead, Mom. I don't mind waiting."

Meg glances dubiously at the jeans. "You didn't even check the—"

"Yes, I did. They're a six. Exactly your size. Go ahead, try them. And if they fit, buy them. And get some other stuff, too."

Meg wants to protest. They're shopping today to buy clothes for Cosette, not her.

Then her gaze falls on a nearby woman. She's fortyish, a married mom, with a pretty face and slender figure. But it's her style that makes her eye-catching. Her sleek, well-cut clothes aren't last *season's* fashion, let alone last year's.

I am feeling a little frumpy, Meg decides.

How ironic that in cosmopolitan New York City, she rarely felt that way. Mostly because she traveled in artistic circles there. You went to rehearsal in sweats, and so did everybody else. And nobody on the subway or in Hell's Kitchen or the East Village gave your wardrobe a second glance.

In Glenhaven Park, however, they do. Running to the A&P for milk and eggs and bread last night, Meg was very conscious of her no-frills shorts and tops and her no-makeup, no-manicure state . . . and so was everybody else in the store.

I need to step it up a little, Meg thinks.

Not, she adds defiantly, *because I want to become one of them.*

No, it's because she doesn't want to call negative attention to herself, for Cosette's sake and because you can't launch a successful career if your clients don't respect you. She wants to make a living teaching voice here in the suburbs—not just because she needs to supplement her alimony and child support checks, but because she could use the self-esteem boost after leaving behind her stage career.

All right, then. It can't hurt to try on the jeans.

Anyway, it's not as if this is Chanel. It's the Gap, for Pete's sake. She can buy something for herself here. It doesn't mean she's defected to Team Fancy Mom, at risk for becoming shallow and self-absorbed.

Not just self-absorbed, but child-absorbed, too. Women like Olympia Flickinger don't just dote, they obsess, micromanaging every detail of their children's lives.

I'll never be like that, Meg thinks, and for the first time, she doesn't lament Cosette's foray into gothdom. *At least I've given her the space to breathe, and experiment.*

She suspects that's more than Sophie Flickinger will ever have.

In the dressing room, she quickly sheds her old jeans and pulls on the new.

Surveying herself in the mirror, she's startled to find that she feels transformed. Not just outside—the jeans are lean and sexy—but inside as well.

When was the last time she bought something for herself?

I wish Sam could see me in these, she finds herself thinking as she turns and looks over her shoulder to survey her behind in the mirror.

What? Sam?

You're not allowed to think about Sam.

Remember?

"Let's see, Mom," Cosette calls from out in the store.

Meg ventures from the dressing room.

"Wow. You look great," Cosette says approvingly.

"You do look great," a male voice echoes.

Meg swivels her head to find Sam Rooney looking appreciatively at her from across a clothing rack, as though she'd made a wish and he just materialized in a puff of magical blue genie smoke.

"What are you doing here?" Meg asks Sam, wide-eyed, before he can inquire the same thing of her.

"Shopping," he says, and gestures with his head. "Ben and Katie are in here someplace. I was just going to find a chair and sit."

He sees Meg's daughter—who didn't look the least bit surprised when Sam turned up in the Gap just now—turn slightly to seek out Ben.

Spotting him, Cosette slips away in that direction, but only after sneaking a peek at herself in the nearby mirror and patting her hair into place.

He can't believe what he just said to her about looking great in those jeans. He saw her, and it just slipped out. But she really does look great in them. They're snug but not tight, gently hugging her curves in all the right places.

I wish I could do that.

For God's sake, get your mind off that. You're a grown man, not a teenaged boy.

On that note, he looks over to see his son ducking his head and pushing his hair back from his forehead the way Sam's noticed he does when he's trying to impress a girl.

And that girl is Cosette.

"I didn't know you were coming here today."

He turns his attention back to Meg, who looks vaguely embarrassed. Or is it defensive?

"I didn't know you were, either," he replies, and tries hard not to allow his eyes to slip down past her neck again.

"Well, I have a feeling somebody knew," Meg says, and he sees her gazing across the store at Ben and Cosette, who are chatting over a stack of sweaters.

"You think they orchestrated this accidental meeting?"

"I was already planning on going shopping somewhere today."

"So was I, and we always come to this mall," Ben tells Meg. "The Cheesecake Factory is near here. Remember I told you . . . ?"

"Right. Your family tradition. I remember."

"Why are you *here*?" Of all places. Why not some other mall? There are so many others in relatively the same distance of Glenhaven Park: Jefferson Valley, Danbury, Woodbury Common, Stamford, the White Plains Galleria . . .

Why here?

Why now?

"It was Cosette's idea to come to The Westchester," she

admits. "So you really think they planned on hooking up here?"

"I wouldn't be surprised. But Ben says they're just friends. Anyway, they were going out for a run together this morning when I came back from walking the dog."

"In the rain?"

He shrugs. "It wasn't raining that hard. And there are worse things they could have been doing. Running is healthy. Wholesome." He flashes her a grin and tries not to think unwholesome thoughts about what *he* could be doing with *her.*

"I know. Running is fine. But . . . well, have they done anything else? I mean, did they see each other last night, or yesterday?"

"Not that I know of. Not that I would know, though. Ben is alone in his room a lot, on the computer."

"So is Cosette."

"You know, things are different these days than they were when we were young. Kids carry on entire relationships over the Internet."

"That's what scares me," Meg says, shaking her head.

"Ben is a good kid," he assures her.

"So is Cosette. I guess I'm just surprised."

"He's not her type, right?"

"I don't know if she has a type. I don't even know if she *is* a type. Until the last day or two, I thought I had her pegged. Brooding rebel. But now all of a sudden—"

"Dad, there you are. I can't decide on these jackets, so can I get all—" Appearing around the rack, Katie stops short. "Meg! What are you doing here? Hey, great jeans!"

"Hi, Katie. Thanks."

"Are you getting them?"

"I don't know," she says, looking self-conscious.

"You definitely should."

Yes. You definitely should, Sam thinks, and reluctantly hauls his errant eyes up to Meg's face again.

"Meg, I need your help," Katie tells her. "I like all three of these jackets, but unless my dad says I can buy all of them . . ." Her gaze slips hopefully to Sam.

He shakes his head. "Nice try, but no."

"So I can only get two. But which two?"

"You can only get one," Sam amends.

"But Dad, I can't pick just one. Look, this one is waterproof, so it would be good if it rains, and this one has the zip-in lining for cold nights."

He shrugs. "They're both great. Just choose one."

"But which one?" Sam notices that Katie is asking Meg, not him.

"Get the waterproof one." Meg is as decisive as Sheryl would have been, he can't help but notice. Maybe it's a female thing, because she and his late wife don't seem to have much in common, otherwise.

"Are you sure?" Katie asks.

"I'm positive."

To Sam's surprise, he finds himself grateful, rather than resentful, about Meg's input.

"What about cold nights?"

"Dress in layers underneath."

"That's a *great* idea!" Katie sounds as though she's congratulating Marconi on inventing the wireless.

Warning bells are going off in Sam's brain as he sees his daughter's blatant admiration for Meg, but what is he supposed to do about it?

You have two options.

*You can grab Katie and drag her out of here and tell her
never to speak to Meg Addams again . . .*

*Or you can let her get attached to Meg the way she got
attached to the kids who have moved in next door in the
past—only worse this time, because Meg is a mother
figure—and then you can watch her heart get broken when
Meg leaves.*

The answer should probably be obvious. So why isn't it?

"Meg, can you come look at something back here with
me?" Katie asks. "I'm trying to decide about something
else."

Meg has the courtesy to hesitate and look to Sam for
guidance.

"I'll come look at it with you," he says firmly.

"No, I really want Meg."

"Katie, I'm your dad. Just let me see it."

"Dad—"

"Katie—"

"It's a bra, okay, Dad?" she says, looking mortified. "I
need help figuring out if I need to get one."

"Oh."

Boy, is my face red.

Sam doesn't dare look at Meg as he asks her, "Would
you mind . . . ?"

"Not at all. Let's go, Katie."

As they head to the Gap Body section, Sam sinks into
the man-chair.

Maybe the choice—about allowing his daughter to treat
Meg as a confidante—will be easier to make than he
thought.

There are certain things a girl needs to talk about with a

woman. Certain things that prove Sam is decidedly out of his element when it comes to raising a teenaged daughter.

Maybe having someone around close by—someone for Katie to turn to—will turn out to be a good thing.

As long as Meg doesn't move away, and Katie doesn't feel abandoned all over again . . .

And as long as Sam himself remains detached from Meg . . .

Well, this might not have to be disastrous.

It would be a different story if he and Meg were dating . . .

Which we aren't.

And we won't.

That would be disastrous, for sure. In Sam's world, after all, relationships either end in marriage or in breakups. There is no in-between.

And since he has no intention of getting married again, of tempting fate with stagnant restlessness again—it would have to be a breakup. A breakup that would ultimately hurt him, and could destroy vulnerable Katie. Especially if she were entertaining fantasies about having Meg as a step-mother.

So, no go as far as he and Meg are concerned.

But it's not as though she's beating down his door, try-ing to seduce him, either. If she were interested in pursuing something, he'd know it.

Maybe we can just be neighborly friends, he tells him-self, relieved to have drawn that obvious conclusion.

What happened the other night was an aberration.

It won't be happening again.

* * *

Feeling a little dazed by all that's transpired today, Meg settles into her seat in the Cheesecake Factory.

It's as jam-packed as the mall, of course. They had to wait over an hour for a table for five.

The five being Meg and Cosette, plus Sam and Ben and Katie.

The path that led from the mall to the restaurant is a muddy, twisted one.

They could have parted ways with the Rooneys right there in the Gap, if Sam hadn't said something about having to buy Ben some new sneakers. Katie immediately asked her father if she could branch off with Meg and Cosette. She said she still needed to buy a bra; they didn't have her size in the Gap. And she wanted to get some panty hose instead of the tights she always used to wear.

Meg expected Sam to turn down Katie's request.

To her surprise, he didn't.

"Would it be all right if you helped her get that stuff?" he asked, quite possibly a little chagrined by the phrases "bra" and "panty hose."

"I'd be happy to."

"Can I get some outfits, too, Dad?"

"I guess you might as well get everything you need." He handed Meg a wad of cash and warned Katie, "When that's gone, it's gone."

It was gone quickly in this mall, where Meg observed plenty of people dropping thousands of dollars in single purchases on most cash register lines while they waited.

She helped Katie learn how to look for sales, though, and with Cosette's help, talked her out of several purchases that would have been either too babyish or too mature for her.

Meanwhile, Katie talked Cosette into buying an aqua-colored sweater by casually holding it up, and saying, "This is Ben's favorite color. He says it reminds him of the Caribbean Sea. We went there once with my parents, before my mom got killed."

Meg's heart sank for Katie at those words, and again for Cosette when she bought the sweater.

Is she trying to conform to impress Ben?

Is that any more preferable to being a vehement non-conformist?

Between her daughter's newfound, obvious infatuation and Katie's constant questions and chatter, Meg's head was spinning by the time they met up with Sam and Ben.

Ben mentioned that he was starved, Cosette chimed in that she was, too, Katie suggested that they all go together to the Cheesecake Factory, and here they are in a booth, like one big happy nonfamily.

Katie wanted to sit by Meg, so she finds herself sandwiched between her and Cosette on one side. Ben positions himself directly across from Cosette. The two of them might as well be at another table for all their awareness of the others. They seem to be carrying on a private conversation without saying much of anything at all. At least, little that Meg can overhear, and what she does hear sounds fairly innocuous, about Sam's new sneakers, the food, and the menu choices.

As for Meg, she doesn't have to worry about making conversation with Sam. Katie talks enough for all five of them.

"What are you ordering, Meg? You should try the avo-cado egg rolls. They're so amazing. Do you want to share some with me? Dad and Ben hate them and there's such a big order . . ."

"Sure."

"Do you like pasta? Because the angel hair with shrimp is really good."

Before Meg can answer, Katie adds, "They have the best burgers, too, if you like burgers. My dad and Ben love burgers. Hey! Dad, we should have a cookout so you can make Meg one of your famous bacon double cheeseburgers. Let's do that tomorrow."

"We can't tomorrow. We're taking Grandpa Anderson to the air show, remember?"

Grandpa Anderson . . . that must be the kids' maternal grandfather, Meg realizes. Clearly, he's still a part of their lives.

The stark reminder that Sam had a wife, a wife he loved and lost, is enough to make her wish she and Cosette had just gone home. They have no business being here with Sam and his family. He has a life, she has her own life.

Why are we even here?

"Then we can have the barbecue on Monday, for Labor Day," Katie goes on excitedly. "Are you around Monday, Meg?"

"I . . . I think I have an appointment." Yes, she realizes, she really does. It's Sophie Flickinger's first voice lesson.

"What time? Because we could do the cookout later, after that."

"I'm not sure . . ." Meg sneaks a peek at Sam, to gauge his reaction to his daughter's enthusiastic invitation. "I have a lot of unpacking to do around the house, too, and I still need to find a handyman who can come sooner than next weekend . . ."

"What do you need done?" Sam asks.

"Basically, everything . . . but the thing I'm really worried about is the wiring. I can't find a good electrician—or any electrician, really. You wouldn't happen to have one, would you?"

"What's wrong with the wiring? Is it knob and tube?"

"I'm not sure . . . it's old. I think there must be a short or something."

"That could be dangerous. I'll take a look at it for you."

"You know about electrical stuff?"

"I've learned, living in that house for the last few years. I bought a good circuit tester, and, believe me, I've put it to good use."

"My dad is really handy around the house," Katie pipes up. "He can be your handyman."

"That's okay," Meg says quickly, not wanting Sam to think she was hinting around. "I've got someone coming."

"But you said not until next weekend," Sam points out. "If you need something done in the meantime, I'll help you out."

"You don't have to do that."

"You didn't have to help me out today, either." He motions his head toward Katie. "I appreciate it. Let me do you a favor in return."

She can't help but smile. "Okay. If you can take a look at the wiring, that would be good."

"Great. As soon as we get back later, then, I'll check it out."

"Oh, we're not going straight home," she finds herself protesting.

"You're not?"

"No, we've got . . . a couple of other stops to make."

Cosette's ears magically tune into the conversation at that. "Where are we going?"

"I've got a few more things to pick up."

"What?"

"Just some things for the house."

"Like what?" Cosette persists.

"Do you need a list?"

"Yes."

Meg gives her a warning look.

To her relief, Cosette heeds it for once, probably reluctant to make a scene in front of Ben. She folds her arms and scowls, grumbling about wanting to go straight home.

Trust me, I'm ready to go home, too, Meg thinks.

She just isn't ready to have Sam in her house at night again. The first time that happened, they wound up kissing.

The second time, she wound up at his place, making love.

There won't be a third time.

Chances are there won't be, if Meg limits her contact with him to broad daylight.

Not that she isn't just as drawn to him by day . . .

But the thought of Sam coming over on a rainy night . . .

Well, something tells her the old wiring wouldn't be the only thing sizzling with electricity.

Chapter
13

Luckily for Sam, the storm on Saturday felled a tremendous maple tree on the end of the street and knocked out electricity for the entire block.

Even better, it wasn't restored until early this morning.

The kids, not used to being unplugged for even a short time, were beside themselves with irritation. No TV, no music, no computer, no PlayStation.

Nothing to do, they complained.

"Enjoy the peace and quiet," Sam instructed them.

The three of them wound up playing board games by candlelight Saturday night. Old board games he found in the attic that used to belong to him and Jack: Sorry, Monopoly, Life. Then on Sunday morning, he picked up his widowed father-in-law as they had planned, and they all drove up to Rhinebeck to see the air show.

A retired pilot, Sheryl's dad was thrilled to see the show, and of course, his grandchildren. He invited them to come back home with him to spend the rest of the weekend.

Ordinarily, the kids don't jump at the chance to hang out with their elderly grandfather, but this time, they welcomed the invitation. Ben wanted to watch the Yankee game, Katie wanted to listen to the new CD she bought at the mall, and they were both eager to check their e-mail.

Ordinarily, Sam doesn't jump at the chance to send the kids away overnight, either. But this time, he welcomed the opportunity for some solitude.

Yes, he enjoyed the uninterrupted time with his kids all weekend due to the power outage. But he was also tired of thinking of ways to entertain them. And there was no telling how long it would be before the power came back on. After swinging home to pick up their clothes and assorted electrical devices the kids wanted to plug in at their grandfather's, he dropped them all off in Larchmont. He would be picking them up first thing Tuesday morning.

He spent last night alone, getting organized for the start of school and reading by candlelight.

A few times, he wondered what Meg was doing next door, in the dark.

But he told himself the outage was, if not a sign that he should stay away from Meg, then at least a godsend. It saved him from facing temptation, once again.

Yes, he has every intention of helping her out with her wiring if she needs him to take a look.

He was just relieved when she told him she wasn't going straight home on Saturday night; he knew that if he found himself alone with her in her house, he might end up making a move he would regret.

Of course, the three kids would likely have been around somewhere . . . or not. They can never be counted on not to get lost when Sam wants—needs—them around.

But with no electricity, there was no way Sam could check the wiring at Meg's Saturday or yesterday.

Now it's Monday afternoon, Labor Day, and the power must have come on again sometime in the night. No more excuses. At least he's had a chance to regroup: there's been enough time and distance between Sam and Meg—in her new jeans—for him to trust his willpower again.

He has to call her anyway; he's trying to reschedule the rained-out soccer practice for his team.

Cosette answers on the first ring, sounding breathless. "Ben?"

Obviously, they have caller ID over there.

"Actually, no, it's Ben's Dad."

Sam can almost picture the disappointment on her face as she says politely but without enthusiasm, "Oh. Hi."

He realizes she's probably been wondering where Ben is and why he hasn't called her.

He debates telling her that they were gone all day yesterday and Ben will be at his grandfather's until tomorrow, but that would be presumptuous of him, wouldn't it?

Anyway, a little space between lustful teenagers is always a good thing.

"Is your mom there?" Sam asks.

"Hang on a second."

The phone clatters and he hears a bellowed "Mom! Phone!"

A few moments later, Meg picks up. "Hello?"

"Hi, Meg. It's Sam."

"Oh!" She sounds surprised. "How are you?"

"I'm good. I'm calling for two reasons. One is to tell you that I'm having a soccer practice tomorrow at one over at the field."

"Okay, Cosette will be there. I might have a friend in town, but he can come with us."

He.

Ignoring a flicker of jealousy—and his hope that the friend will turn out to be her gay friend from last weekend—Sam goes on, "The other reason I called is to tell you that I can come over today to look at your wiring."

"Oh, you don't have to do that."

"Did you find an electrician?" he asks hopefully.

"No, but I will."

"I'll come take a look. You shouldn't take chances with stuff like this. It could cause a fire."

"I know. If there were absolutely anyone else I could even think to ask to take a look, I would, really . . . but there's no one else."

"So I'm really rock bottom on your list then, huh?"

There's a pause.

She says awkwardly, "I don't, um, I mean, I really appreciate—"

"I'm just teasing you," he says with an equally awkward laugh, wishing he would just shut up and hang up.

Instead, he asks, "What time do you want me to come over?"

"Um . . . about three-fifteen, three-thirty would be good."

"No problem."

Then, instead of hanging up, he says, "You know, I'm glad it worked out so that we could have dinner with you and Cosette the other night. I mean . . . I think the kids had a good time."

And so did I.

Despite his initial reservations about going to a restaurant with her—afraid it would feel like a date—it didn't. Not with the kids there.

The conversation flowed, and they laughed a lot. For a while, they played, "Do you remember . . . ?" and "Did you know so-and-so . . . ?" That was particularly fun. It's still amazing to Sam that Meg was on the periphery of his world for years, yet he never knew her.

And it was refreshing to come across somebody other than Bill Dreyfus and a handful of other longtime locals who remember what Glenhaven Park was like in the old days.

Meg remembers. She seemed as wistful as Sam is about lost people and places of their childhood.

Now, she says, "I had a good time, too . . . thank you for dinner."

"You're welcome."

He insisted on picking up the check at Cheesecake Factory, then wondered later if he shouldn't have. Maybe that made it seem like he thought it was a date.

But . . . a date? With three kids on board?

She didn't think that.

The only reason it even entered his mind was that he was so darned attracted to her.

And now you're headed to her house this afternoon.

Is that a good idea?

He doesn't have a choice.

And anyway, Cosette will be home and awake, to put a damper on any romantic rekindling that might occur.

"You're going *where*?"

"To Geoffrey's," Cosette says again, as Meg stands in the bathroom, wrapped in a towel, having just gotten out of the shower. "You have to drive me to the train in fifteen minutes. He's meeting me in Grand Central."

Meg shakes her head. "No."

"Mom, you have to. It was his idea."

"I thought you said he called for me, to make plans for coming up here tomorrow."

"He did, but you were in the shower, and he said it would be great if I took the train down and spent the night with him, and then we could take the train back up together tomorrow morning in time for soccer practice."

"He said it would be great, or you did? And don't lie, because you know I'm going to see him tomorrow and find out the truth."

"Well, I was telling him how boring it is here and how much I miss the city and how I would love to come down just for a night, and he invited me. And now he's on his way to Grand Central and I have to go catch the one-twenty-six because I just told him I'll be on it. I knew I had to catch this train because you're giving your first voice lesson at two, and I already packed my bag. Okay?"

No. This is not okay.

For one thing, she isn't entirely anxious to spend the night solo in the house. Yes, the last few nights have been uneventful, and it isn't as if she's seen that apparition again, but there have been times when she's felt as though someone is in the room with her, only to find it apparently empty.

But she can't really insist that her daughter hang around overnight because she's afraid the house is haunted, can she?

Or because if Cosette leaves, Meg will be here alone with Sam when he shows up . . .

Unless she can convince Olympia Flickinger to stick

around after Sophie's voice lesson to chaperone the inspection of the wiring—and any stray sparks that might erupt.

"Mom . . ." Cosette prods, "*Okay?*"

"Okay," Meg says reluctantly, thinking Sam might show up with his own kids in tow anyway. If he doesn't, he'll have to get back home to them. He's not going to stick around. Nothing is going to happen with him.

And the resident ghost—if it exists—isn't going to act up, either.

"Good. Go get dressed," Cosette says briskly. "Oh, and you should blow-dry your hair and wear makeup, and your new jeans."

"Cosette, I hate to burst your bubble, but there's nothing going on between me and Sam, so I don't have to get all fixed up for him."

"Sam?" Cosette gapes at her. "I meant because the Flickingers are coming over, and you should make sure you look good for your first lesson."

"Oh." Meg's face grows hot.

"There's something going on with you and Sam?"

"No! I said there's nothing going on between me and Sam."

"I know what you *said* . . . but why would you say it unless there was a chance of something happening . . . or you want there to be a chance of something happening?"

"I'd say it because I know how your mind works, and I didn't want you to get the wrong idea."

"I don't have the wrong idea, Mom. Not at all," Cosette says cheerfully.

*   *   *

But he doesn't want to take a shower before bed or

Another half hour to go until it's time to head over to Meg's, and Sam paces the house as restlessly as a doomed patient waiting for test results.

No, he thinks, frowning, pacing. *Not like that at all.*

He feels more like a kid who wakes at dawn on Christmas morning and has to wait a little longer to see what Santa left.

Yes, this is eager anticipation, as opposed to dread.

Dread would be more suitable. He hates that he's excited about seeing Meg again, but for some reason he can't help himself.

For some reason? She's a desirable woman and you're attracted to her. That's the reason.

Well, it's purely physical. Chemical. Biological.

And if he can get turned on, he should also be capable of turning it off. It's that simple.

He's a science teacher, for God's sake. He should understand how these things work.

Yes, but you teach physics. Not chemistry or biology.

He's out of his league when it comes to that stuff. Oh, he's memorized the periodic table of the elements, and he's dissected plenty of frogs, even a pig.

But when it comes to romantic chemistry and biological urges . . .

Well, he's clueless.

And he can't rattle around this house for another thirty minutes thinking about those things, or he'll go crazy.

Physical activity. That's what he needs to take his mind off Meg.

That, or a cold shower.

But he doesn't want to take a shower before heading

over there because then it might seem as though he's trying to look nice and smell nice for her.

No, he'll go just as he is, in sweatpants and a T-shirt and sneakers, unshaven, shaggy-haired.

So . . . physical activity.

Sam strides out the back door and hesitates on the small wooden deck. Now what? Run around the yard?

Or clean it. The perimeter is lined with tall old maples and oaks; a couple of limbs came down in the storm and need to be dragged to the brush pile.

But Sam is feeling too restless for any of that. Spotting Ben's basketball perched on a bin in the open garage, he strides toward it.

After August's last gasp of heat and humidity, this September afternoon is sunny, dry, breezy . . . and welcome.

Sam bounces the basketball a couple of times. He's about to dribble toward the hoop when a sound reaches his ears.

Somewhere, somebody is singing. Beautifully.

So beautifully that it literally stops him in his tracks, the basketball tucked under one arm, balanced against his hip as he listens.

It's probably the radio, he thinks momentarily.

Then he knows that it isn't.

It's Meg.

Her voice is carried through an open window, high and clear and lilting, like nothing Sam has ever heard before.

He knows nothing about music, other than that he likes some of it—mostly classic rock—and dislikes some—mostly rap or whatever it is that kids at school listen to when they blast their car radios, the stuff with the throbbing bass and lewd lyrics.

"I don't know why I'm frightened . . . I know my way around here . . ." Meg sings sweetly, and Sam is mesmerized.

She must have written this song, he realizes as the lyrics unfold.

It's about coming home to rediscover a familiar place, about how she's slowly discovering that everything is as if she never said good-bye.

The melody is lovely, but it's the passion in her voice— and in the lyrics—that captivate Sam so that he can barely breathe. He can only listen, his heart pounding as he grasps the meaning she's fervently conveying in the song.

"I've spent so many evenings . . . just trying to resist you . . . I'm trembling now, just thinking how I've missed you . . ."

She tried to tell me, he realizes. She said she had a crush on him back in high school . . . that she was afraid the other night to be with him, afraid of what might happen . . .

All of this—it's what she was trying to get across to him, but he didn't quite understand how profound her feelings really were. Now, in song, propelled by the soaring passion in her powerful, lyrical voice, her feelings are evident.

Stunned by the heartfelt outpouring of emotion, Sam stands absolutely still, listening, until the song is over, and there's nothing but the chirping of birds and the rustling of leaves in the boughs overhead.

He wonders if Meg suspects that he might be out here, listening. If she was singing to him.

Probably not.

She's simply an artist, expressing herself.

What she's saying, though, is coming straight from her heart, speaking straight to his. And Sam can't ignore it.

He tosses the ball blindly into the open garage and glances toward Meg's house.

He's going over there . . . and not just to inspect the faulty wiring.

There's no reason to keep things strictly platonic today. His kids—especially Katie—aren't around to get ideas about him and Meg hooking up permanently.

Anyway, Sam isn't thinking about the future right now. He's thinking about the past . . . and the present. Just as Meg is in her song.

Sam is tempted to go right to her, but it isn't time. He swiftly strides toward his own house.

He's going to take a shower.

Not a cold one.

A long, steamy shower.

Then he's going to shave and get dressed for what might promise to be a long, steamy night ahead, if Meg's daughter wasn't around.

That's how he knows things won't go too far this time.

If Cosette wasn't there . . . well, there's no telling what might happen.

But with a built-in chaperone, they'll be safe.

All Sam knows is that he can't stay away from Meg or pretend that there's nothing simmering between them. Not after hearing the desire in that song.

Meg is still dumbfounded by the Flickingers' announcement that Glenhaven Park High School will be putting on *Sunset Boulevard* as this year's fall musical production.

"It's an ambitious undertaking for a high school production," Olympia said, seeing the look on Meg's face when she heard the news.

Yes, that . . .

And it's ironic after what happened to Meg in the city.

Talk about a fading star . . .

At least you're not trying to make a comeback, though.

Not onstage, anyway. Her own personal comeback is right here in Glenhaven Park.

And so far, she's faring about as well as the fictional, legendary Norma Desmond did.

Well, at least she knows all the music to that show; she was cast as Norma back in her summer stock days.

Watching the Flickingers drive away after they've extracted a promise to meet with them again midweek—*as Cosette would say: ch-ching!*—she reflects on what just happened.

When Sophie and her mother showed up with all the sheet music from the show, Meg was immediately in her element. She fought the urge to sing her way through the entire Andrew Lloyd Webber score, settling on her own favorite show stopper, the haunting *"As If We've Never Said Good-bye."*

Singing it today, however, she found new meaning in the lyrics about a woman who suddenly finds herself revisiting— and trying to recapture—the past.

She sang it with her soul, with her entire being, the way she used to sing on the stage. She would lose herself in song, and the theater and the audience would disappear.

When you sing something over and over again, it becomes methodical unless you can discover something fresh every time. Great artists do that.

I used to do that.

It's been a long time, though. Too long.

Today the walls of the decrepit old house fell away, and

the Flickingers disappeared, and there was nothing but Meg, and her music, her passion, once again.

When she finished her impromptu performance, both Olympia and Sophie were silent for a change. Even Chita Rivera, who had wandered into the room to listen, sat staring appreciatively at her mistress.

Naturally, there was no applause.

For Meg, giddy days of spotlights and footlights, of curtain calls and standing ovations, are over.

But I don't need any of that anymore.

Really, she just needs the music; it nourishes her soul, just as food does her body.

I almost forgot how much I love it.

So maybe it's not the city and my old friends and my old life that I miss as much as it is the music.

She can still have that here, though.

She just has to start singing again. And she will, now that things are settling down.

Settling down?

Sam Rooney is headed over here any second now.

As far as Meg is concerned, things couldn't be more unsettled.

Walking up the front path toward the door, Sam realizes he's being watched. Sure enough, when he glances up at Meg's house, he sees someone peeking out the second-story window.

It's Meg; it has to be. She's as anxious as he is to see each other again.

Only she doesn't know that I know how she feels . . .

Unless she knew when she was singing that I could hear her, and she wanted me to know . . .

Talk about convoluted.

Really, though, it doesn't matter *what* she knows. What matters now is that Sam knows.

And he's going to act on it.

Right. But how?

I'll figure it out when I see her.

He quickens his pace and mounts the steps to the porch. Lush wisteria has grown rampant across the built-in wooden trellis adjacent to the rail, its sturdy vine snapping and splintering the wooden supports in some spots, bent on taking over the—

"Hi."

A voice startles Sam. It came from somewhere nearby, just beyond the verdant screen.

He turns around and does a swift double take.

Meg is standing on a crate, straining to screw a lightbulb into a high fixture.

But he thought . . .

Oh, well. So it was her daughter, and not her, who was looking out the upstairs window just now.

He wanted to think that it was Meg, waiting for him, as eager to see him as he is to see her.

She's glad he's here, though. He can tell by the look in her eyes.

Her eyes . . .

They look bigger, rounder; her lashes thicker, darker.

It's makeup, he realizes in surprise. She's wearing makeup. She's outlined her celadon eyes in smoky shadow and mascara. Her lips are frosted in a pale pink sheen.

Makeup.

And her hair looks different, too: straighter, silkierlooking, partially pulled back but hanging around her eyes in wisps that beg his touch.

Obviously, she took extra time to make herself look gorgeous.

Was that for his benefit?

It's not as though she's all dressed up, though. She's got on a sleeveless green ribbed turtleneck that matches the shade of her eyes. It's tucked into a pair of jeans.

Those jeans, Sam notes—the ones she was trying on in the store the other day.

Face it: she looks fantastic. And you can't wait to get closer.

"Let me help you with that light," Sam offers, hurrying over to her.

"It's okay, I've got it."

No, she doesn't. Her fingers reach just short of the fixture. For him, it's within easy grasp even standing with his feet flat on the floor.

"Here, let me see it." He takes the bulb from her, conscious of her fingers grazing his in the process. "Did you check the wattage?"

"This is the same as the one that burned out."

"Then it's good." Can she see his hand shaking as he inserts it into the socket and turns it?

All the while, he's conscious that his body is practically encircling hers; that when she's standing on the crate like this, her face is closer to his than it would be otherwise. All she'd have to do is turn her head . . .

And he could kiss her.

He hears himself swallow, then let out an audible shallow breath. He's hoping he can stay just like this, close to her, turning this lightbulb until he works up his nerve . . .

But then suddenly he can thread the metal base no farther. It's time to let go of both the lightbulb and his wayward fantasy about putting his arms around Meg, turning her toward him, and kissing her.

Unless he just goes ahead and does it. Right here and right—

Too late. She's starting to climb down from the crate.

"Need a hand?" He takes a reluctant step back. He doesn't want to move, but she's about to step into the spot where he's standing. Of course, he could seize this golden opportunity to let her descend right into his arms—

But the logistics of pulling it off smoothly might be awkward.

Dammit. Why does he feel like a boy again, uncertain how to act around a girl?

"No," she says.

No?

He realizes she means it in response to his query about whether she needs a hand. That seems like ages ago.

"I'm okay," she says, and the crate promptly wobbles. She laughs. "I mean, maybe I do need a hand."

Holding his breath, he extends one. Still on uneven footing, Meg grabs it.

Wow.

If Sam didn't know better, he'd think he had just somehow been zapped by a short in the light socket: a potent current just ran up the length of his arm.

"Whoa," Meg blurts, jerking a little.

So she felt it too.

The question is, what is she going to do about it?

No . . .

The question is, what are you going to do about it?

She lands lightly on her feet, close to him, still holding on to his hand.

You could kiss her.

The wisteria barrier is nearly opaque; the street is deserted anyway; Cosette is safely upstairs.

Safely, because she won't catch them kissing . . .

And safely, because with her there, he and Meg can't be tempted to take things further than kissing.

Meg's fingers are warm clasped in Sam's hand; he can smell the light, clean herbal scent of her lotion or shampoo or whatever it is that's wafting tantalizingly to his nostrils.

You have to kiss her.

It's now or never.

Kiss her, or let go.

Sam reaches out and rests his other hand on her bare upper arm.

She looks down at it, up at him.

The question in her gaze is fleeting; she must have seen the answer in his.

He bends toward her face. She tilts her head instinctively and he tilts his in the opposite direction.

Their lips meet, glide, meld.

Somewhere in the back of Sam's mind is a fact that is both reassuring and frustrating: that these kisses and caresses are no prelude to lovemaking. Not this time.

Her mouth opens to his delving tongue, and a shower of sparks rain through Sam. He deepens the kiss, swaying her against him, boldly allowing her to know just what she's doing to him.

He's a ravenous guest at a lush banquet, uninvited to stay for the main course. Knowing his fierce hunger isn't meant to be sated with an exquisite feast, he savors this delectable appetizer.

His hands slip up to cup Meg's face gently; he dips his head to taste her luscious mouth over and over again, filled with wonder, filled with need.

But his appetite has been whetted, not appeased, and he craves her more than ever. His willpower is waning; he's intoxicated by the dizzying combination of her ethereal song and her willing flesh. He wants to show her she isn't alone in her desire; that it's okay for her to feel the way she does about him. That he feels something too, something glorious and terrifying and completely unexpected.

She flinches a little, pulls back, and he drags heated lips from her mouth.

He opens his eyes and is walloped by the wanton expression in hers.

"What are we doing, Sam?"

"We don't know," he says raggedly, with a trace of a smile, "but we can't help it."

Then he kisses her again.

Every time Sam's lips collide with hers, Meg is lost all over again.

If he would just stop for a moment, just give her time to think . . .

But he won't stop.

It's like he can't stop.

There's something different about him today; a bold intensity that caught her completely off guard. She never in a million years expected him to show up here, take her in his arms, and kiss her senseless.

If she had thought there was a chance of that, she'd have run away.

Instead, here she is held fast against him, struggling to keep from losing herself in pure sensation.

You can't let that happen.

You have to keep your head.

Her mouth feels bruised and swollen from his kisses; her breasts, crushed against his hard chest, ache with fervent need. With a sigh, she arches her neck, throwing her head back as he nuzzles her throat, her fingers twining in his hair.

"This is crazy," she whispers more to herself than to him.

"What's crazy?" he murmurs against the tender hollow beneath her jaw.

"I told myself I wasn't going to sleep with you ever again."

"I told myself the same thing. And we won't."

"Then what are we doing?"

"Kissing. That's all."

"You really think you can stop at this?" she asks, and hears herself add brazenly, "Because I know I can't."

"Yeah, but nothing's going to happen now, with your daughter up there."

That stops her cold. She pulls back, looks around worriedly. "Up where?"

"Upstairs. In her room."

"She's not up there. She's in Manhattan."

"What? No, she can't be. I just saw her."

Again, she looks around. "Where?"

"In her window, I thought."

"No, she took the train to Grand Central at one-thirty. I

watched her get on myself, and she just called a little while ago and said she'd made it there."

Sam swallows hard. "When is she coming back?"

She can tell he's afraid to ask; that in turn makes her afraid to answer.

"Tomorrow." Her voice is hushed. "Why? Where are Ben and Katie?"

He says nothing for a minute, but he doesn't have to. Something has ignited; she senses that when she looks at him; his expression is more telling than anything he might say.

"My kids are in Larchmont," Sam informs her succinctly when he finally does speak. "Until tomorrow."

Later—hours later, when twilight falls through the uncovered windows of Sam's bedroom to bathe them in its alabaster blue glow—he feels as though he's awakened from a long sleep.

In reality, he should be exhausted, ready for sleep. It's been a long—and acrobatic—afternoon and evening. He and Meg found their way over here from her porch, because it wasn't as though he showed up at her house prepared, condoms in his pocket and sex on his mind.

Well, maybe the last part was true . . . but he never really thought it could happen.

When he realized that it could, and was about to, he at least managed to find the presence of mind to bring her to his place. They've since put quite a dent in the supply of condoms he'd stashed in the bathroom cabinet.

Thank you, little brother. How right you were about being prepared, just in case.

Yes, Sam is pretty worn-out after all that.

But how can he possibly sleep when he's exhilarated?

He can't stop looking at her, touching her—maybe he just needs the tactile evidence that this is real. Or maybe she just feels too good.

He toys with her hair spread on the pillow, skims the curve of her bare hip, strokes her cheekbone with the back of his fingers.

No longer feeling like a shy schoolboy, he isn't afraid to stare into her eyes; nor is she hesitant to return the gaze.

I can lie here forever, he thinks. *Forever, just watching this woman, touching her, treasuring her.*

Never before has Sam experienced intimacy this profound: not in his marriage, certainly not with the girls who came before. This . . . this physically, spiritually, emotionally pure connection . . . this is the intangible, evasive *something* that was missing all those years. This is the source of his marital restlessness; it's what he subconsciously sought all those years. It's what people dream about, talk about, write about, sing about.

Would he, could he, ever have found this completion with his wife?

No. If it wasn't there from the beginning, it never would have been.

He knows that as instinctively now as he sensed, back then, that there should be something more to marriage, more to life.

He was right. How about that.

So what next?

What do I do about this?

Now isn't the time to figure it out.

Coherent reason never led two people to fall tumultuously into each other's arms and tumble into bed. It isn't a part of this interlude, and can't be.

Illogical passion . . . that's what brought him and Meg together, that's all there should be here with them now.

Sam strokes her face, memorizing the tapered arc of her eyebrows, and every faint freckle on her nose, and her lips, their rosy tint, though every hint of gloss has been kissed away, swollen from his mouth against them . . .

Incredibly, impossibly, Sam is beginning to feel the stirring of arousal once more.

Meg laughs when he pulls her close. The laugh trails off as he kisses her deeply. It's the intimate, self-assured kiss of a lover.

"Again? You're insatiable," she whispers as he rolls onto his back and hauls her with him. She bends to nuzzle a silken path from his mouth to his neck to his chest.

"So are y—" His breath catches in his throat and words are lost to him as her mouth finds his nipple.

She coaxes it to rigid attention. He groans at the sensation and at the memory of what she did to him with that moist mouth earlier, when her feather-soft hair was trailing sensually across his thighs as opposed to his pecs.

"Come here." He strains to pull her up, needing to kiss her, but she laughs and resists, moving on to lick and tease his other nipple. Sam closes his eyes and gives in to the seduction, to the feeling of her erotic mouth and warm skin sliding over his body.

Finally, she sits up on her knees, straddling him, and lowers herself onto him.

With a moan of pleasure he reaches up to cup her bare breasts as she rocks in seductive rhythm. Their eyes are locked, bodies joined, and as Sam nears the brink, emotion surges in his soul to threaten laughter, or maybe tears. It's something somewhere in between the two that escapes him as he skyrockets over the edge, clinging to her, taking her with him.

"Meg," he gasps, still shuddering into her quaking flesh. An errant thought spills into his brain, then from his lips. "Oh, my God . . . I—"

No!

Like a dam, a shred of reservation catches the phrase and holds it back.

He can't say *that*.

Even now, with reason all but obliterated, he comprehends that it would be a mistake.

Because it's too soon? Or because it can't possibly be true?

Who knows?

Sam is in no frame of mind to analyze why he can't say those three words to her; he just knows that he can't, shouldn't.

With a sigh, she settles against him, blissfully oblivious to his conclusion.

Her body is stretched out to fit alongside his, her head rests against his still-racing heart, and her fingertips lightly play his chest as if to accompany a silent song.

Maybe that's why he can't say it . . . or believe it.

Maybe the outpouring of emotion he overheard in her song might have triggered in Sam something more profound than raging desire.

It might have triggered something more powerful, something he isn't capable of claiming, or sharing.

Ironic, then, that it came along now, when he wasn't looking for it—not anymore.

Yes, just when he's finally reached a place where his life is humming along, where his kids are functioning, where they've settled into a world in which they all belong . . . this happens to him.

She happens to him.

But you don't mess with stability. Not after the tempest the three of them, Sam and his kids, have endured.

Period.

Still . . . what if there could be something better for us? Something more than just humming along, functioning, settled?

Yeah, what if . . . ?

Get a grip, Sam. There are always going to be what ifs.

As in: what if you take a chance and go for it with Meg, and you turn the world upside down again for all of you?

It's not just about what Sam wants, or needs.

It hasn't been about that since he became a parent. As a single father, he's responsible for three lives. He doesn't dare take on anything—anyone—else. Not with his children's well-being at stake.

Meg lifts her head to look at him, smiling, unaware that he just came *this close* to transporting their relationship into entirely new territory, then backed away.

"Are you hungry?" she asks.

He is, he realizes as he nods. Not just hungry. Ravenous. For food, yes, but also, still . . .

For her.

Physically sated, he's wrestling with a deeper craving unfurling within him now, begging to be nurtured.

He finds himself thinking of the potted rose Katie gave her mother on that long-ago birthday.

If you ignore something, if you starve it, it will eventually wither and die.

"I'm hungry, too. Do you want to go out to eat?" Meg asks, sounding reluctant.

"Do you?"

"I'm starving."

"We don't have to go out," he says, afraid that if they do, they'll go their separate ways when the meal is over.

He isn't ready for that yet. He wants this one night with her; one night to make love to her without reservation and hold her as she sleeps, one morning to wake with her in his arms.

This is all they have; their kids will be back tomorrow, and life will go on.

"I've got stuff in the fridge." He sits up and pulls her with him. "I'll make us something to eat."

She smiles.

She, too, wants this night.

Does she, too, realize it's all they have?

"That would be good," she says, and swings her legs over the edge of the bed, bending to find her hastily discarded clothes.

Watching her, admiring the graceful curve of her spine and the sweep of her hair, he knows that tonight will never be enough.

That, without her, for the rest of his life, he'll be plagued once again not just by restlessness—but by helplessness.

Because now, he won't wonder what it is that's missing.

Now, God help him, he'll know.

Chapter

14

Meg? It's Mom!"

"Mom!" Breaking into a smile, she's glad she just dropped her paint roller and flew through the house to answer the ringing telephone.

Had Cosette been here, Meg would have been inclined to let it ring right into voice mail, thinking it was going to be another prank call she'd pick up to find nobody there.

That's been happening a lot the last few days.

There's no breathing, no hang up, nothing like that. Just . . . dead air. It's unnerving.

Especially because whenever those calls occur, the caller ID window comes up blank.

Why would—how could—that possibly happen?

It could happen if a ghost were making the phone ring, that's how. Meg did some reading on the Internet and learned that some people—experts in so-called paranormal activity—claim that spirits can manipulate energy to affect household devices like radios, televisions . . . and telephones.

Meg doesn't believe it, necessarily. She just wishes the strange calls would stop.

Cosette isn't home on this Wednesday afternoon—she's winding down her first day at her new school—and Meg has been anxious about her all day. Her first thought when the phone rang was that it might be about her daughter, in some kind of trouble again.

"What are you doing?" her mother asks. "Did I catch you in the middle of something?"

"I'm painting Cosette's new room, actually."

"Not black, I hope." Mary Addams is well aware of her granddaughter's recent decent into gothdom—and it troubles her.

"No, Mom, actually, she picked out a nice shade of dark green." She glances down at her paint-smeared hands and hopes it will scrub off before she leaves to pick up Cosette in fifteen minutes.

"Thank goodness. Daddy and I were wondering how you're settling in. We haven't spoken to you since late last week."

"I know, I'm sorry . . . I've just been so busy."

"As long as you're happy, Meg."

"I am," she says, with more conviction than she feels. "I mean, it's been quite an upheaval, but I'm sure we'll get used to all the changes eventually."

"You will. I'm sure you've figured out by now that after any upheaval, things right themselves again eventually. Somehow, life always goes on."

"I know that," Meg murmurs, thinking back over the years to when Calvin abandoned her, eight months pregnant.

"Anyway, Meg, Daddy and I were thinking we'd come

up to visit you and Cosette for Thanksgiving . . . if that would be all right with you."

"That would be more than all right," Meg manages over a lump in her throat.

She had already been dreading that particular holiday. In years past, she and Cosette always spent it with Geoffrey and an assortment of good friends from their neighborhood, one of whom had an apartment that overlooked Central Park West and the Macy's parade route. It was a tradition to kick off the holiday with coffee and bagels, watching enormous balloons drift by at window level.

This year, Meg assumed she and Cosette would either go—and not feel as though they fit in any longer—or stay here in town for a lonesome turkey dinner for two.

"Then we'll buy our plane tickets," her mother says cheerfully.

"I'm glad, Mom."

"Are you sure you're all right, Meg? You don't sound like yourself."

"I'm fine. Really."

"Have you made any new friends? Or found any old ones, other than Krissy?"

Meg hears a familiar, disapproving note in her mother's voice. Her parents never did like Krissy. They thought she was a bad influence.

"Not very many people I used to know live here anymore," Meg tells her mother, wondering if she should prepare her for the drastic changes in their hometown.

"You mean Krissy is the only one?"

"Well . . . there's Sam Rooney. He actually lives next door."

"Sam Rooney . . . Sam Rooney . . . Oh! The Rooneys lived on Boxwood. That's right, I remember them. Great family. Well, it's nice that he's right there next door."

"It is nice." More than *nice*.

Actually, *naughty* would more fittingly describe the recent turn their relationship has taken.

She and her mother chat for a few more minutes, but not about Sam. Meg isn't about to let on that he's anything more to her than a neighbor . . . because technically, that's really all he is.

Finally, she looks at the clock and tells her mother she has to get cleaned up to go pick up Cosette.

"Tell her Grandpa and I said hello, and that we'll call back to see how she likes her new school."

"I will, Mom."

And life goes on.

Funny how that happens, Meg thinks as she drives over to Glenhaven Park High ten minutes later, paint scrubbed off, wearing a fresh pair of jeans and a T-shirt. It happens even after the kind of upheaval she experienced with Sam over the weekend.

That was like taking a terrific vacation and managing to forget, the whole time you're away, that you have to go back home again.

One minute, you're on a strange and exotic new island; the next, it's back to business as usual, as if you never left the real world at all.

Yes.

One minute, she was making love to Sam, experiencing all the things she ever fantasized about with him . . .

The next, she was back home unpacking boxes and

feeding the cat and arguing with Cosette and painting her room.

This is how it has to be, though.

She and Sam never said it when they went their separate ways on Monday morning, but she knew. If he wanted more, he wouldn't have seemed so wistful when they made love that last time.

They lingered in his bed for longer than they should have, before the mood was shattered. The weather was iffy so Sam's phone began to ring nonstop with parents wondering whether he was having soccer practice. Then his kids needed to be picked up from their grandfather's, and the train was coming in from the city . . .

Sam and Meg kissed hastily and dashed in different directions, no backward glances, no promises. Nothing other than Sam's hurried mention that he'd be happy to take a look at her wiring someday this week. That was it.

There wasn't time to discuss what had happened between them, and maybe that was best.

What was there to say?

Soccer practice was on. Geoffrey went with her, and Sam was busy on the field. Katie was there. She spent most of her time tending to a couple of toddlers, but she also sat with Meg for a while, happy to see her. She updated her on everything that happened over the weekend, unaware, of course, that Meg had spent the best part of hers at Katie's house, with Katie's dad.

Meg wore sunglasses despite the overcast day, not wanting Katie or Geoffrey or the Fancy Moms to realize she couldn't stop staring at the coach.

"Somebody's falling in love!" Geoffrey's singsong

declaration startled her at one point, until she realized he was talking about Cosette.

Clearly, something is going on between her and Ben. Even Meg, obsessed with keeping an eye on Sam, couldn't miss the flirtatious glances between her daughter and his son, or the way they gravitated toward each other every chance they got, on and off the field.

Cosette might be falling in love, but Meg is determined not to.

She might ease up on herself if she thought she and Sam stood a chance in hell. But he gave no indication that he wants anything more than what they shared, and she's been down this road before, with other men. She knows the signals, the body language.

Too many times, she was the only one trying to make something work.

She's already vowed not to do that again. Not even with Sam.

Anyway, being infatuated with Sam Rooney is old hat, she tells herself as she slows the car in front of the school, looking for a place to park. So it shouldn't be difficult for her to go on with business as usual. She did just that for years where he was concerned.

And now I'm right back at the scene of the crime, she thinks, climbing out of the car and looking at the familiar redbrick school. In the distance, from one of the open windows, she can hear the last bell ringing.

Seized by nostalgia, she hurries forward.

This morning, when she dropped Cosette off at school, she didn't even park or get out. Cosette wouldn't let her. She barely wanted her to slow the car at the curb, and leapt from the passenger's seat with a brief "see ya."

Now that there's no Cosette here to stop her, Meg can walk right up the sloping sidewalk toward the entrance. She gives a wide berth to a garbage can with loudly buzzing bees hovering above it, then passes the familiar stone bench donated by the Class of '40 in memory of their classmates killed at Normandy, and the spot by the towering flagpole where she used to meet Krissy every morning, and the bike rack where Sam used to park his Schwinn.

Nearing the end of her memory lane, she looks up as students begin to flood from the wide double doors, abuzz with first-day excitement.

She finds herself scanning for familiar faces, and has to remind herself that this is a new generation. She's not going to know anyone in this—

Oh, yes, you do!

To her surprise, she finds herself looking right at Mr. Dreyfus, her old drama teacher, who has emerged and is standing on the steps, talking to a couple of students. He's aged a bit, but she's pleased to see that his wiry, diminutive presence still emanates his trademark dynamic enthusiasm.

Smiling, Meg keeps an eye on him while looking around for Cosette. Her daughter has yet to materialize when Mr. Dreyfus finishes talking to the students and turns to go back inside.

"Mr. Dreyfus?" She hurries toward him.

He turns and his eyes widen with pleasure. "Meg? Meg Addams? Or, wait, I'm sorry, I know it's Astor Hudson now . . . I've been following your career."

"No, it's actually Meg again," she says with a grin, giving him a quick, hard hug.

"And you need to call me Bill, now that you're not a student. You look great. I'd know you anywhere even if I hadn't seen your face in a couple of Playbills since you left here."

"You've come to my shows?"

"Of course."

"And you've never come backstage? But you should have! I would have loved to see you."

"I wish I had, then. It's so good to see you, Meg."

"You, too. And you look exactly the same."

"Oh, come on, I'm gray, and I've gained about thirty pounds."

He's right; he is and he has, but he's got the same smile and the same energy, and she welcomes it. At last, someone familiar here in Glenhaven Park. Someone besides Sam.

Oh, come on, do you always have to think about him?

Yes, apparently, she always does. He flits in and out of her mind like lyrics to an old song that gets stuck in your head after you hear it on the radio.

"You might look the same, but you seem more relaxed," he tells her.

"Really?"

He nods. "Back then, you were consumed by teen angst."

"Well, now it's my daughter's turn for that."

"Oh, right, I heard you have a daughter starting school here. That's great."

"I'd love to introduce you to her if I can find her." Meg looks around.

It takes a moment for her to recognize Cosette. She's still toning down the hair and makeup, and she's wearing regular blue jeans and a polo shirt. Black, but a polo shirt nonetheless.

Seeing Meg, Cosette turns her back, pretending that she has no idea her mother is standing here waving her arms. She's talking to a pair of girls, Meg realizes, narrowing her eyes in the sunlight, watching them, hoping they'll become Cosette's friends.

Please, God, just let her make friends.

"Is that your daughter over there?" Mr. Dreyfus asks her.

"Yes. She's not going to be in any of your sections, though. I checked her schedule when she got it. She's in instrumental appreciation this term; vocal appreciation isn't until next. I was trying to convince her to audition for the musical, though."

"Oh, she should. It's *Sunset Boulevard.* In fact . . . how busy are you these days?"

"That depends. Why?"

"Because I'm in over my head between this musical and the new school year and building an apartment over my garage so that my mother can move in with me."

"You're building it yourself?"

"Do you know how hard it can be to find a trustworthy, available, affordable contractor around here?" He rolls his eyes. "I figure, once you've supervised the building of a couple of high school musical sets, you can figure things out on the home front."

"Wow, really? Maybe I should have been on stage crew instead of just onstage."

"You? No, you had to be onstage. It was your calling. Anyone could see that."

Meg smiles. It's nice to be appreciated, especially now that she's out of the spotlight.

"I heard you've retired from all that now, though," Mr. Dreyfus continues.

"You did? How did you hear that?"

"Small town, remember? News travels fast."

"Wow, I guess so. Who told you? Krissy?"

"No, your new neighbor, Sam. Sam Rooney. He teaches here now . . . you know that, right?"

She nods, her heart quickening at the mention of Sam's name and the realization that he's been talking about her.

Why?

Is Mr. Dreyfus a close confidant? Did Sam tell him that he and his new neighbor got caught up in some kind of romantic—

"I mentioned in the teachers' lounge at lunch today that I need help with the show because I just can't do it all alone. I asked if anyone knew anyone, and Sam spoke up and recommended you."

Oh.

Well, what did you expect? He wasn't rhapsodizing about having a crush on you. This isn't high school.

Not for the teachers, anyway. Grown men don't go around confiding about their love lives to their coworkers.

Or maybe they do, but obviously, Sam didn't.

"What do you say, Meg?" Mr. Dreyfus asks, as she's trying to process her illogical disappointment.

"Hmm?"

"How about helping me out with the show?"

"Sure, why not," she says without a second thought.

"You're kidding. You'll do it?"

Startled, she drags her thoughts away from Sam and realizes that she just made a tremendous commitment, and Mr. Dreyfus is beside himself with excitement.

"Wait until everyone hears that you're involved, Meg. This show is going to be a tremendous hit when everyone hears we've got a Tony-winning actress as our assistant director."

Assistant director?

"I can't thank you enough." Mr. Dreyfus sweeps her into a surprisingly strong hug for one so wee.

"You're welcome," she says lamely, wondering what the heck she just did.

Walking into Tokyo Cafe a few days later, Meg can't help but remember the coffee shop that once occupied this site. It was lined with booths along one wall and a lunch counter on the other—invariably populated by at least a dozen familiar faces at any given moment. There was a chalkboard that listed the daily soups and specials, frequently meat loaf and moussaka. The waitresses were tired single moms who lingered over cigarette breaks in the alleyway between the restaurant and the old warehouse next door.

The brick warehouse has long since been converted to office space and shops, and the alleyway is now lined with entrances to the building's boutiques.

And here in Tokyo Cafe—formerly known as the Glenhaven Park Diner—there's no sign of the booths, lunch counter, or chalkboard.

The minimalist decor features black lacquer, blond wood, and rice paper screens. The lunch counter is now a sushi counter manned by male Japanese chefs with serious expressions and quick hands. The waitresses are gentle young Asian women in kimonos.

Hovering just inside the door, Meg sees that the place is

crowded, but there's nary a familiar face—including Kris's.

"I'm meeting my friend for lunch," she tells the hostess. "But I don't see her yet. She made a reservation, under Holmes."

The woman checks her clipboard, then nods. "Right this way. You're the first to arrive."

Meg follows her through the restaurant, conscious of the glances from strangers and glad she took care with her appearance for a change.

She's wearing a simple black sleeveless turtleneck tucked into trim black pants, with leather flats and silver accessories. Her curls are restrained by a low ponytail.

Stylish, understated, and chic.

I fit in just fine, she thinks, sneaking a peek around her as she settles at the table and accepts the menu the hostess hands her.

Then she realizes she's seated at a table for four.

"Excuse me . . . I'm just meeting one friend. Her name was Kris Holmes. I think I'm at the wrong table. She made a reservation . . ."

"We know Ms. Holmes very well," the hostess says with a smile. "This is the right table. Reservation for four at one o'clock."

Four?

Kris didn't mention that anyone would be joining them when she left a message this morning to confirm their lunch date.

Hmm. Maybe she invited some other old friends along to join them as a surprise.

That would be fun.

So where is everyone?

Checking her watch, Meg sees that it's 1:04.

She sips ice water and studies the menu, glad she's no stranger to sushi. She and Cosette ate it all the time in the city.

Yes, and it was cheaper, most places in Manhattan, than it is here.

She got a couple of twenties from the ATM machine down the block, thinking that would be enough to cover her lunch and the new paint roller she's going to pick up at the hardware store before she heads home.

Doesn't look that way.

"Are you Meg?" a voice asks, and she looks up to see an attractive auburn-haired stranger standing beside the table with the hostess.

"Yes . . . ?"

"I'm Brett, a friend of Kris's. She's running late again, it looks like." The woman slides into the seat opposite Meg's without further explanation.

"It's, uh, nice to meet you."

"You, too." Brett places a napkin on the lap of her own black slacks—which, Meg couldn't help but notice before she sat down, are much more fashionably cut than her own. And Brett's simple black top somehow manages to scream Designer Label, though there's nary an auspicious trademark in sight. Both pieces—pants and top—drape gracefully over her near-skeletal frame. Brett's hair—that smooth, obedient kind of hair Meg has always envied—is also pulled back in a low ponytail. But hers is sleek, as opposed to Meg's waves, and hers is held by an elegant silver clip, as opposed to Meg's coated rubber band—*to think I was so pleased to find a black one in the bathroom drawer.*

"So how do you like it here in our little town?" Brett asks.

Our little town?

It's my *little town, actually,* is what Meg wants to say.

She refrains. She's getting used to being treated as an outsider.

"I grew up here," she informs Brett mildly, "so for me, it's really coming home again."

"You *grew up* here?" Brett couldn't look more surprised if Meg told her she grew up in an African pygmy tribe. "That's so amazing! I mean, hardly anyone did."

"Oh, a lot of people did," Meg can't resist saying airily. "There were hundreds of us."

"Oh, I know there were . . . but nobody who's here *now* grew up here. That's what I meant."

"Kris did." *And Sam did. And me. That makes three.*

"That's right . . . you know, it's funny, but I always forget Kris is a townie."

A townie? So that's what they're calling it now?

"So is that how you know Kris?" Brett asks. "From growing up together?"

"Yes."

"Well, that's just . . . neat."

Yes, isn't it just.

"How do you know Kris?" Meg asks. *And why are you here?* she wants to add.

"My first husband and I bought our first house from her. I've been working with her ever since."

"Working with her? You're a Realtor too?"

"Oh! No," she says, looking taken aback—and amused. "I mean working with her as my Realtor."

She says it the way most people refer to their physicians or their accountants.

My Realtor.

"So you've bought more than one house, then? As, um, rental properties, or . . . ?"

"Rentals! No. We could never be landlords. We live in them."

"How many houses do you live in?"

"One at a time," Brett says with a grin. "Kris is right. You are completely charming. Should we order some sake?"

"We definitely should," mutters Meg, who isn't sure why *completely charming* suddenly sounds completely insulting.

As they sip their sake and make small talk—mostly about the menu, though Meg learns that Brett has a daughter in college, a stepson in high school, and two more sons in elementary school—and notices that Brett doesn't ask more than cursory questions about her own life.

Either Kris filled her in already, or she doesn't really care.

Meg suspects the latter. Brett gives off an air of self-involvement that seems to be as pervasive among privileged suburban moms as it was among the theatrical divas Meg left behind in the city.

Relaying a boring anecdote about her last trip to Japan, Brett interrupts herself to exclaim, "Laurelle! How nice to see you!"

Her gaze is focused on someone—and Meg can guess whom—over Meg's shoulder.

Sure enough, she turns around to see Laurelle Gladstone standing there.

"Hi, Brett. Hi—Meg, is it?"

"Right." As opposed to Maid. "How have you been?"

"Great."

Meg can't help but notice that Laurelle doesn't ask how she's been.

To her dismay, Laurelle takes the chair beside Brett's.

Ah. So their little foursome will be complete when Kris shows.

"Isn't Kris here yet?" Laurelle asks, draping over the back of her chair a purse that undoubtedly cost more than the Blue Book value of Meg's car.

"No, she's late, of course," Brett says. "You know how she is."

Meg, who no longer knows how Kris is, can't help but resent these two women who do. Watching them nod knowingly, she wants to blurt, "I knew Kris before you did!"

But that would be incredibly childish. Right? Of course it would.

Do I really care what they think of me, though?

Yes. You do. You don't want these women to gossip about you behind your back.

Yeah, yeah, whatever.

Why the heck are they here? And why isn't Kris?

"So what have you been up to, Laurelle? Did you find a live-in yet?" Brett asks sympathetically.

Apparently, Laurelle's maid problems are legendary in these parts.

"Oh I did! And he's entirely macrobiotic."

He? A macrobiotic male maid? Meg thinks. *What does that even mean?*

It's hard to tell, even as she listens to Brett and Laurelle conversing back and forth on the topic.

"Sorry I'm late!" a familiar voice announces, none too soon.

They look up to see Kris standing there, cell phone in hand, très chic in a beige pantsuit.

"Meg, I thought it would be good to have you meet some of my friends—and I wasn't even here to do the introductions." Kris delivers air-kisses all around, then dives into her chair, cheeks flushed, expression distracted as she sets her phone on vibrate and tucks it into her pocket. "So what did I miss?"

"Laurelle was just telling us about her new chef," Brett tells her.

She was? Meg can't help but feel as though she missed something—and she's been here the whole time.

"Good for you! Did you get the maid settled into the new room upstairs, then, so the chef could take over her old one?"

"Yes, but now Ludmilla is miffed because she has to share her bathroom, and she isn't speaking to me or Ted."

Who's Ludmilla? Meg wonders. *Must be her teenaged daughter.*

"Well, is she speaking to the kids, at least?" Brett asks.

Oops, guess Ludmilla isn't her daughter.

"Who knows? Beth is always plugged into her iPod and now that Trevor's got his Jag he's never home, so they wouldn't care either way."

From the ensuing conversation, Meg figures out that Laurelle's full-time live-in staff includes not just the maid and macrobiotic male chef, but also a gardener and Ludmilla, the nanny, whose charges are stepsiblings: an iPod-plugged-in, soccer-playing fifteen-year-old and a Jaguar-driving eighteen-year-old.

Laurelle, who refers to herself as a stay-at-home mom, seems primarily involved with hiring and firing household staff and overseeing something called Sharing and Caring, which Meg gathers is a local philanthropical endeavor as opposed to a personal philosophy.

"We're taking donations for our silent auction next month," Laurelle announces. "Can I count on you guys to come up with something spectacular?"

She can. Brett immediately offers a week at her villa in the Virgin Islands, and Kris donates front-row seats and backstage passes to an upcoming U2 concert, courtesy of her husband, an executive at their record label.

Laurelle turns expectantly to Meg. "It's a great cause. Can you donate something?"

"Meg used to be on Broadway," Kris speaks up. "How about prime seats to a sold-out show, or something?"

"I'll see what I can do," she promises lamely, and is relieved when the subject changes to soccer.

But only for a moment, until the conversation zeros in on the soccer coach.

"Beth said all the girls have a crush on Sam's son."

"Really? I have a crush on Sam," Brett says, with a laugh.

So Meg's not the only woman in town who isn't immune to his rugged appeal. That isn't surprising . . . but it is disturbing, for some reason.

Why? You have no claim on him whatsoever.

"I thought you had a crush on your riding instructor," Laurelle tells Brett.

"I thought you were married," Meg hears herself say.

"Oh, that doesn't stop Brett." Kris shakes her head affectionately. "Anyway, Sam isn't married."

"I hate to admit it, but that wouldn't stop me, either," Brett adds with a laugh. "I keep asking Kris to put in a good word for me since she's known him forever, but she won't. You think I'm joking, but I'm serious."

"I know you are." Kris shakes her head as she pulls out her vibrating cell phone. "I don't think Sam would be interested in a married woman."

Kris checks her phone and lets the call go into voice mail with obvious reluctance.

"Anyway, you don't want to get mixed up with Sam," Laurelle puts in. "He's got way too much baggage, between those kids and still being in love with his dead wife. Plus, he doesn't know how to dress. And he's a high school teacher," she adds—clearly the worst stigma of all.

"So? I'm not interested in his résumé or his bank account, let alone being seen with him in public," Brett says. "Just a discreet, steamy little fling. Is that too much to ask?"

The waitress arrives to take their orders, and Meg finds that her appetite has all but disappeared. So much for worrying about paying for lunch. She'll be lucky if she manages to choke it down.

Why didn't Kris speak up and defend Sam?

Why didn't you?

Because she was afraid they might somehow figure out that she and Sam are—no, *were*—involved.

Which is none of their business.

He hasn't even called her, despite what happened between them over the weekend.

Obviously, he's moved on.

So should you, Meg tells herself.

He's got too much baggage, between those kids and still being in love with his dead wife.

Laurelle was right about that, at least. Sam is obviously not ready for a relationship—even these women, who barely know him, are aware of that.

I need to get over him, Meg tells herself firmly. *The sooner the better.*

By Friday afternoon, Sam is ready to welcome the weekend . . . and it's only been a three-day week. But it takes a while after school starts up again for things to resume their regular rhythm so that it feels right to be here day in and day out.

Right now, all Sam wants is to get the hell out of Dodge.

He's on his way, striding toward the door, his thoughts on tomorrow's soccer game—and seeing Meg there—when, incredibly, she pops up right in front of him.

"Hi!" Caught off guard, he stops short and tries not to grin like a big, sappy fool.

"Hi!" She looks just as surprised to see him. Though she shouldn't be. He works here. He belongs here.

"What are you—"

"Doing here?" she finishes for him when he breaks off. "I have a meeting in the auditorium in a few minutes."

The auditorium. Oh. That's right. "You must be helping Bill Dreyfus with the musical, then?"

She nods. "Thanks for suggesting me. I was going to tell you that when I saw you, but . . . I haven't seen you."

"No, I've been insanely busy the last few days." *And avoiding you.*

"Me, too."

Sam finds it impossible to break eye contact with her and wonders if she, too, is remembering what happened between them last weekend.

I should have at least called her, he tells himself. He doesn't want her to think he's the kind of man who has casual flings.

But if what happened with Meg wasn't a casual fling, what was it?

Anyway, she didn't call *him* or come knocking, either. Why not?

For all she knows, he was hoping to take things to another level. She would have no idea that she scared the hell out of him, with her song and her sensitivity and her passion.

"So . . . how's the school year going so far?" she asks, shifting her weight.

"So far, so good," he says unoriginally. "How are things going with the house? Oh, no." He slaps his forehead.

"What?"

"I never did check your wiring for you."

"That's okay. I found an electrician."

"Oh, good. What did he say?"

"He hasn't been there yet. He's coming a week from Tuesday, though."

Sam groans. "That's not good. I'll come take a look."

"You don't have to do that."

"I know, but I was supposed to—" *Before I rolled into bed with you instead*—"And I want to."

"Really, Sam—"

"No . . . I'll be there tonight. What time will you be home?"

"I don't know . . . late," she says somewhat noncommittally.

It suddenly occurs to him that she might have a date or something. That was his first reaction when he spotted her on the soccer field Monday afternoon, looking cozy with a man. It took him a minute to recognize that it was merely the friend who'd helped her move in—but in that minute, he was insanely jealous.

That was a bad sign. It was enough to renew his determination not to let her into his life.

Yet here he is, forcing himself into hers . . .

Only *to check out her wiring, though. Just to make sure her house doesn't go up in flames.*

"Why don't you just call me when you get home, and I'll run over?" he presses.

"No, there's no rush."

"Tomorrow, then."

It's important that he settle this here and now.

Because it's potentially unsafe for her to go any longer with faulty wiring . . .

And because he needs to know that he's going to see her again, and the hell with his resolve.

"We have our first soccer game tomorrow . . . right, Coach?"

Oops.

"Oh. Right. Well, right after that, then. Okay?"

She shrugs. "Okay."

What else is there to say?

"Well . . . see you," he tells her after a minute.

"Right, see you."

He can't help but wonder if she's as glad as he is that they have a definite plan to reconnect tomorrow.

Only in a platonic, neighborly way, though. Your own self-imposed rules, remember, Coach?

Yeah.

Right.

And he still intends to play by them.

Chapter

15

It's a perfect Saturday for Cosette's first soccer game. Blue skies, bright sun, midsixties.

As Meg and a red-uniformed, shin-guarded Cosette approach the field, she looks over to see that Cosette is biting her lower lip, looking pensive.

"Nervous about the game?" she asks.

"No."

"You look like you're a little concerned, though, and it's natural because it's been a while since you—"

"I'm not worried about the game," Cosette says sharply.

No. She's worried about something else, though, Meg realizes with a sinking feeling.

Is she being bullied again?

There's been no indication of that. If anything, Cosette has seemed more grounded these last few days, since school began.

Meg is inclined to chalk that up to the time she's spent with Ben. The two of them have been running together every morning before school, and again at night before sundown. Whenever she's on her way to see him or returns home from being with him, Cosette exudes a muted exhilaration.

Meg recognizes the glow; she's been there herself.

Most recently with Sam.

But that's over.

Cosette and Ben seem to be at the beginning of something.

Several times, Meg attempted to initiate a conversation about her daughter's newfound relationship—whether it's a romance, or mere friendship—only to be promptly shot down.

Having learned in the past that pushing Cosette for personal information only leads to sneaking around and lying, Meg keeps dropping the subject.

Too bad she doesn't feel comfortable trying to get Sam's take on it.

Maybe when he comes over later . . .

No. That's not going to become an opportunity for intimate conversation. Or intimate anything else, for that matter.

If she weren't so genuinely concerned about the wiring, in fact, she'd tell him to forget it. But the lights keep flickering, and not always the same ones, so the problem isn't in the fixtures themselves. Anyway, the appliances seem to be off-kilter as well—and not just the phone, which still rings for no reason. The other day when she was watching television, it turned itself off.

When it happened, Meg couldn't help but remember that night at Sam's house, when the cable was out for no apparent reason. If that hadn't happened, chances are, they would have turned on Conan O'Brien and focused on the TV rather than on each other.

In any case, she doesn't intend to take any chances when it comes to something that can cause a fire. And if it turns out there's nothing wrong with the wiring, she'll just have to fall back on her other theory: that the house is haunted and the ghost is tampering with her appliances.

"Mom?" Cosette asks, stopping abruptly, staring ahead at the field where the players have gathered from their own team, in red, and the opposing team, in blue.

Meg looks over at Cosette. "What's wrong?"

Here we go, she thinks. *She's going to say she doesn't want to play.*

And I might tell her she doesn't have to.

Maybe this isn't for Cosette's own good—this fitting into wholesome small-town life, playing soccer. Maybe it's more about Meg's expectations when she moved here. She thought she wanted to re-create her youth for Cosette, but maybe she just wanted to re-create it for herself.

Right down to getting hooked on Sam Rooney all over again.

"Do I look . . . okay?" Cosette reaches up to pat her dark hair, caught back in a ponytail.

Meg is shocked by the uncharacteristic concern, yet somehow manages to act as though she takes it in stride.

"You look beautiful," she says sincerely. Her daughter's big eyes are rimmed in a soft, carefully smudged liner that looks more brown than black, and she's wearing a natural lip gloss as opposed to her usual thickly applied dark lipstick. Her skin glows, and her cheeks are naturally rosy, the result of a week in the sun and fresh air.

"Thanks." Cosette seems self-conscious, and Meg notices that she's scanning the field anxiously.

She sees what she's looking for, and of course, it's Ben.

Or so Meg thinks at first.

But she sees that Cosette's gaze has shifted to a cluster of blue-clad girls from the opposing team.

Hmm.

Something is definitely up.

Not with Ben, though. Meg sees him see Cosette, light up, and wave to her.

"See you, Mom." Cosette makes a beeline for him.

Relieved, Meg turns toward the bleachers, almost crashing into Sam. He's in full coach mode: shorts and a red uniform shirt, a whistle around his neck and a clipboard in his hand.

"Hi!" He looks happy to see her, though he's obviously distracted.

"Hi, Sam." There go those butterflies flitting around in her stomach, darn it.

You'd think she'd be over that after twenty years.

Twenty years?

No, these aren't the same old butterflies from the old days of her unrequited crush on schoolboy Sam.

These are brand-new butterflies. Glorious, exotic butterflies—released from long-dormant cocoons the first time she kissed grown-up Sam.

"Coach!" a kid yells from across the field, waving him over.

"I guess I'll see you after the game," Sam tells Meg, and is gone.

She makes her way to the bleachers.

Laurelle and Brett are right there in the bottom row, deep in conversation and either pretending not to see her or truly oblivious to her presence.

Which is fine with Meg. She isn't eager to be privy to

more discussion of the coach's finer physical assets—and lack of financial ones.

She makes her way, reluctantly, toward the midsection of the bleachers, where Olympia Flickinger is lying in wait. She's dressed in weekend silk, her gold jewelry glinting in the sun.

"Meg, I was just telling Kirsten and Brooke that you're casting the high school musical this year."

"Oh, I'm not in charge of it," she clarifies hurriedly to the two well-heeled brunettes sitting beside Olympia. "I'm helping out Mr. Dreyfus. He's the director."

"But you do have input, and you're overseeing the auditions?" asks Kirsten or Brooke, with vested interest.

Meg nods reluctantly.

Keeping a judgmental eye on Brad and his camera equipment at the edge of the field, Olympia informs Meg, "Brooke's son Austin is a terrific tenor."

Surprise, surprise.

To Brooke, Olympia says, "Can you just see Austin and Sophie playing romantic leads together? Wouldn't it just be too much?"

Too much, Meg thinks. *Definitely too much.*

"When are the auditions, exactly?" Kirsten asks.

"Tuesday after school."

"Let's squeeze in an extra voice lesson for Sophie on Monday," Olympia tells Meg, and whips out an electronic organizer. She enters it in before Meg can agree.

Then again, who's arguing? She can definitely use the money, and what else has she got to do besides unpack boxes and lust after Sam Rooney?

"I'd love to get Austin in on Monday, too," Brooke pipes up. "Do you have a slot available?"

Meg reaches into her purse and pulls out the freebie calendar she got from the Hallmark store last December. She pretends to check her schedule. "You're in luck. I've got a five o'clock cancellation. Should I pencil you in?"

"That would be terrific."

Kirsten excuses herself to go have a last word with her daughter, in a red uniform on the sidelines.

"That poor thing," Olympia says, and she and Brooke shake their heads sadly.

Meg can't help but ask, "What's wrong?" Maybe Kirsten is suffering from some horrible affliction. She's skin and bones.

Then again, her appearance may be more of a fashion statement than a terminal illness. She's noticed that a number of the Fancy Moms around town are emaciated chic.

Olympia and Brooke exchange a glance.

"I don't want to bias you," Olympia says, "but Kirsten's daughter Victoria is absolutely hopeless."

"In what way?"

"She can't sing, act, or dance, and she has a slight overbite."

Let's just shoot the poor thing and put her out of her misery then, shall we?

Meg manages to keep from saying that, though.

"She's insisting on auditioning," Brooke tells Meg in a conspiratorial whisper, "but I'm not even sure you'll be able to find a place for her in the chorus."

"I'm actually not in charge of casting," Meg reminds her. "So I guess that will be up to—"

"Oh, of course." Olympia gives a brisk smile and nod. "I just wanted to give you a heads up that the level of talent fluctuates wildly when it comes to these things."

"I'm sure it does."

Meg turns her attention to the game, which has just gotten under way. Down on the field, Cosette is running toward the goal in the pack of blue bodies. Meg can't see her expression from here, but she appears to be playing with more enthusiasm than she did at the practices.

"Meg! Hi!"

She looks down to see Katie waving at her from the base of the bleachers, where she's tending to one of the toddlers again.

"Hi, Katie!"

"My dad said he's going over to your house after the game!" Katie announces for all Glenhaven Park to hear.

Even Brett and Laurelle turn their heads, momentarily distracted from their nonstop whispered gossip.

Conscious of her intrigued audience, Meg just smiles and nods.

"Her dad?" Olympia asks. "Isn't that the coach?"

"Right. Sam."

Seeing her brow furrow, Meg wonders how to let her and the others know that there's nothing romantic going on between her and Sam. Well, not anymore. But she isn't about to let on that there ever was.

"Did she say the coach is going over to your house after the game?" asks Kirsten, climbing back up into the bleachers.

Meg nods. "Yes, but he's just . . . checking something for me. He lives next door."

"Well, that's convenient." That comes from Brooke, accompanied by a knowing nod.

"And it explains a lot," Olympia declares.

"What do you mean?" Meg asks, bristling.

"Just that it's obvious he's been coaching your daughter on the side. Look at her."

Meg follows her gesture just in time to see Cosette kicking the ball toward the goal.

She scores, and a cheer goes up from her team and the crowd.

"Way to go, Cosette!" Meg shouts gleefully, standing to get a better look at that action.

Then she feels the stares of Olympia and her friends, and sits down again. "Sam hasn't been coaching Cosette on the side," she says adamantly.

"Oh, come on, Meg, it's all right. We won't tell the rest of the team."

"But he isn't."

The others exchange glances.

Brooke asks, "You're saying she just drastically improved on her own?"

"Well, she used to play in the city. And she was always good. She just wasn't giving it her all when practices first began. But now she's into it."

"Right. Got it. Well, good for her." Olympia is obviously humoring Meg.

She's going to believe what she wants to believe.

Annoyed, Meg sits there, tolerating the vacuous small talk, for another few minutes.

Then she stands, and says, "I'm going down to the snack bar. Does anyone want anything?"

"Not unless they've put in an espresso machine," Brooke tells her, and they all get a kick out of that one.

Meg is grateful for the escape and takes her time walking from the bleachers toward the snack bar. It's the same one that was here when she was a kid. She wonders if they still sell Charleston Chews and Big Buddies. Probably not.

"Hi, Meg." Katie ambles toward her, a towheaded toddler on her hip.

"Hey, Katie. Are you babysitting?"

"Sort of. I'm watching Catalina for her mom. Isn't she cute?"

"Adorable." And her stylish leather baby shoes cost more than everything Meg is wearing, put together. Including her watch.

"Cosette is doing great in the game," Katie says, bouncing Catalina on her hip. "I guess my brother's been helping her."

"Do you think so?"

Katie nods. "He and his old girlfriend used to practice soccer moves sometimes. When they weren't kissing and stuff." She snickers.

"Ben has an old girlfriend? I didn't know that."

"Oh, don't tell my dad, okay? Ben didn't want him to know. He paid me to keep quiet when I caught them together one day."

"What were they . . . ?"

"They were French kissing on the couch. My dad was at a meeting and Ben was supposed to be watching me and he wasn't supposed to have anyone over. But he's good at sneaking around."

Terrific. "Why does he have to sneak around?"

"Because of our dad."

Poor Sam. "He doesn't seem that strict."

"You don't think so? He's always worried about us. Like, always. We don't like to tell him a lot of stuff that happens because he freaks out. Like one time, this girl was being mean to me every day in the girls' room at school and I told my dad and he went to the vice principal and made a huge stink. It just made it worse for me."

"No parent likes to see his child hurt, though, Katie."

"I know, but . . . my dad just worries a lot. So we don't like to give him extra stuff to worry about. Please don't say anything to him, Meg."

"About Ben's old girlfriend?"

"Or anything. That's her out there, actually," Katie says, and gestures her head at the field, her hands busy with little Catalina.

"Where?"

"The girl with the long blond hair on the blue team. She goes to Harvey." That, Meg knows, is a nearby private school. "See her over there? Her name's Ariel."

Meg shades her eyes with her hand and scans the opposing players. She zeros in on an athletic-looking blonde running in the herd.

"I wonder if that's weird for Cosette, seeing Ariel here."

Yup. That must be what she was so distracted by when they first arrived at the field, Meg thinks. But she doesn't want to let on to Katie.

"Oh, I don't think it's weird for Cosette. She really doesn't let many things bother her."

"If I was playing against my boyfriend's old girlfriend, I'd probably let it bother me."

Meg smiles at Katie's candid remark, then asks, with forced nonchalance, "So Cosette and Ben are boyfriend and girlfriend?"

"You didn't know?" Katie's wearing an oops expression. "Please don't say I told you, okay?"

"Ben doesn't want your dad to know?"

"Probably not. Because my dad would think he was going to get a heartbreak, or get her pregnant, or something. Oh, don't worry," she adds hastily, seeing Meg's expression, "I'm sure nothing's going on. They're probably just making out."

Right. And who knows better than Meg that one thing leads to another?

Climbing the steps to Meg's porch, Sam finds himself shooting an expectant glance at the corner beneath the light fixture, where he found her—and kissed her—last weekend.

Today, the spot is empty.

But oddly, as he looks at it, the bulb seems to flicker on, then off again.

Was it just the sun, glinting?

No. The porch is almost completely shaded by the wisteria vine on the trellis.

Okay, then . . . loose connection?

Sam steps closer, watching the light. Nothing.

He reaches up, and gives the bulb a twist. Still nothing. The bulb was already twisted firmly into the socket and the glass is cool to the touch. Then how—?

"Hi, Sam."

He nearly jumps out of his skin, then looks up to see Cosette watching him from inside the house, just beyond the screen door.

"What are you doing?" she asks.

"Just checking this fixture. Your mom said the electricity has been acting up."

"That's not because of the electricity."

"It's not?"

"No. This place is haunted." Cosette steps out onto the porch.

That again. Sam wants to groan. Instead he says, "What's been going on?"

"You know . . . lights going on and off, stuff like that. Mom thinks it's the wiring . . . or so she says. I think she just doesn't want to scare me and admit there's a ghost."

"Have you seen it?"

"No," she admits. "Not since that night we ended up staying at your house. But that was really scary." She shivers at the memory. "If it happens again, you'll know it, because Mom and I will be over there in a heartbeat."

"Anytime," Sam says congenially. He can think of worse things than Meg Addams popping up on his doorstep to spend the night.

"So where's your mom?" he asks Cosette.

"She's upstairs somewhere, putting stuff away. Come on in." Cosette holds the door open for him, then asks hesitantly, "Is, uh, Ben next door?"

"He's around there someplace. On the computer, I think."

"Do you think I could go over? I want to ask him something about school."

"Sure."

"Great, thanks!" She takes off across the porch and down the steps like she's fleeing a burning house.

Watching her go, Sam decides he should have another talk with Ben. He's said he and Cosette are just friends, but you don't look at your friends the way his son looks at Meg's daughter.

"Meg?" he calls, stepping into the dim foyer, the screen door creaking closed behind him.

No answer.

He looks around. It looks better. Not great, but better. There are still random boxes stashed here and there, and no furniture yet, besides a piano visible in the living room beyond the archway. Glancing in that direction, Sam sees a sleeping cat curled in the corner. Then he spies a gleaming statuette on the fireplace mantel.

Overcome by curiosity, he steps into the room to examine it.

He raises his eyebrows when he realizes that it's a Tony Award . . . presented to Astor Hudson.

Meg, in another life.

Impressed, intrigued, he realizes for the first time just what she gave up to move back here to Glenhaven Park. Bill Dreyfus alluded to her having had a big career on Broadway. Only now, though, faced with physical evidence of her stardom, does Sam stop to contemplate the implications.

Why did Meg turn her back on that life? What did she seek here that she couldn't find there?

You came back to Glenhaven Park, too, he reminds himself. Back home.

Yes, because he sensed, when his life was at loose ends, that this was where he was meant to be. That this was where he could find peace.

Maybe the same is true for her.

Maybe, since we're both here . . . we were meant to be here together.

Hearing footsteps, he retreats hastily back to the hall, where he looks up just as Meg appears above.

She looks upset.

"What's wrong?" he asks immediately.

She shakes her head. "I was just . . . where's Cosette?"

"She went over to talk to—"

"Ben. Right. I know," she says flatly, descending the stairs. "That was so well orchestrated they deserve an award."

He resists the urge to glance at hers, on the mantel. "What do you mean?"

"They were online talking to each other just now," she tells him.

"How do you know?"

"Because when Cosette left her room, I went in there to put some of her things away, and I saw that she'd left the computer screen open, and she was signed on. I swear I've never done this before, but . . . I had to look."

"And . . . ?"

"And she and Ben had been instant messaging about seeing each other as soon as you left the house. They had it planned that she would go over there so that they could be alone together."

"Doing what?" he asks, his heart sinking.

"Who knows?"

"Well, they aren't alone. Katie's there."

"Ben pays her to leave him alone when he's with his girlfriends."

Sam frowns. "What are you talking about?"

"Just . . . Katie said you worry about them, and that they try to keep things from you so that you won't."

"She told you this?"

Meg nods. "But please don't say anything to her about it. She told me in confidence."

"My daughter is telling you secrets, and you're keeping them from me?"

"It's not like that, Sam."

He thinks back to the soccer field earlier, when he looked up and saw Katie talking to Meg. That made him feel unsettled, just as it did last week, but he shrugged it off.

Not anymore.

"Listen, my kids are my business," he tells Meg, seething with frustration and irritation. Seeing the dangerous gleam in her eye, he quickly adds, "I know you mean well, being all maternal with Katie, but it's not good for—"

"I'm not being maternal with her!" Meg cuts in. "She talks to me. She's lonely. That's all."

"I realize that. But it's not healthy for her to latch on to you when you're only going to—" He breaks off, shaking his head.

"When I'm only going to what?"

Hurt her. Leave.

"Nothing," he mutters, and shifts gears. "Where's the fuse box?"

"Forget it."

"What?"

"Forget about the wiring. I've got an electrician coming anyway. And we can't just turn a blind eye to whatever's going on between Cosette and Ben."

"I don't intend to."

"Then what are you going to do?"

"Have a talk with him."

"Do you really think he'll open up to you?"

No. But Sam is feeling ornery and argumentative. "He's my son. I think I know him."

"Well, Cosette is my daughter, and I don't think I know her at all."

"Really? That's funny, because you seem to think you know mine."

As soon as the words are out, he wishes he could take them back.

Too late.

Meg's eyes blaze as she says, "You know what? You should go."

"I said I'd help you. I'm going to help you."

"No, really. Just go." She strides to the door, gives it a push, and holds it open with her foot. "And send Cosette home when you get there."

Sam gives a curt nod and strides across the threshold. "Good luck," he says in parting.

As though this is an official parting of ways.

"You, too," she responds crisply.

As though she agrees that it is.

Wondering what the hell just happened, Sam retreats toward home.

He fights the urge to look back, knowing she won't be watching him anyway.

Chapter
16

A lot can happen in two weeks and a couple of days.

A lot, or nothing at all.

It depends on how you look at it.

For Meg, reflecting on the first half of September as she pulls into the Metro-North Station parking lot, it's been a whirlwind of domestic drama, and, well, bona fide drama. As in theatrical drama. She's been busy preparing for today's *Sunset Boulevard* auditions here at school, and with Sophie Flickinger and a couple of her friends who also signed up for private voice lessons. Meanwhile, back at 33 Boxwood, her furniture has arrived and the licensed electrician—who finally showed up—has a complete overhaul under way. He said there was no sign of faulty wiring and couldn't tell her why things were flickering and fizzling, but talked her into updating everything anyway.

Not only that, but she's sure now the house is haunted.

So yes, a lot has happened.

But where Sam Rooney is concerned, nothing at all has happened.

She's seen him only from afar, at the soccer field, in his

yard at home, or in the parking lot at school. Nothing more. No interaction. She's been trying to convince herself she hasn't been looking for him at every turn and that she doesn't care that things ended on a sour note.

That isn't true.

She does care, and she has been looking.

She can't help it.

He worked his way under her skin. That's her own fault; she should have known better. She *did* know better.

Yet she allowed herself to repeat her old pattern of falling for the wrong guy, knowing up front that he isn't in the market for something long-term. That was evident with Sam from the start. All the way through, really.

It should have been no surprise at all when he picked a fight with her, then walked away.

Will she never learn?

Worse yet, Kris confronted her with a phone call, saying she'd heard through "the grapevine" that Meg and Sam were involved.

Meg, who had no doubt that the grapevine consisted of Brett and Laurelle, assured her old friend that there's nothing going on between her and Sam.

Which currently happens to be true.

"Are you sure, Meg?" Kris asked. "Because I don't want you to get hurt. Sam might seem like a great guy—and he is, really—but believe me, he's off-limits."

"Why? Not that I'm interested, because I'm not," she added hastily. "Just curious."

"He and his wife were perfect together. Everyone said it. He was devastated when she was killed, and he isn't looking to replace her. You would only get hurt if you got involved with him, so don't."

"I won't," Meg promised, and added a silent, *ever again.*

Now, as she pulls the Hyundai into a spot, she hears a train whistle and sees that the 5:56 from Grand Central is pulling into the station.

Good timing. Geoffrey should be on it.

They're going to have to hustle if they're going to make it to the Glenhaven Park Auditorium before the six-fifteen auditions get under way.

Much to Bill Dreyfus's delight, Geoffrey has agreed to sit in on the auditions with him and Meg.

"Two seasoned Broadway performers—how did we get so lucky?" the drama teacher exclaimed when he shared the news with the students at the last preaudition meeting.

Among them were both Cosette and Ben.

Meg was only mildly surprised when her daughter announced her intent to try out for the musical—she's made a few friends already, and they're mostly theater kids.

But Ben? That was unexpected. As far as Meg can tell, his circle of friends—aside from Cosette—is made up mostly of jocks and student government types.

If she and Sam were on better terms—speaking terms, even—she'd ask him about Ben's motivation.

But they're not. And when she asked Cosette, she just shrugged and scowled.

That's nothing new. She's shrugged and scowled her way through adolescence; why should things change now?

Maybe Meg expects more of her because she's changed outwardly. No, she hasn't conformed entirely to prepdom—and Meg doesn't particularly want her to—but her extreme appearance has gradually given way to a more mainstream style.

Not, Meg senses, out of conscious effort to fit in among her peers, thank goodness. Rather, Cosette seems to have reached a point where she no longer has something to prove.

Ben probably has something to do with that.

As far as Meg can tell, her daughter and Sam's son are a romantic item. Cosette steadfastly refuses to confirm that, though.

Meg didn't tell her that she read her IM log that day in her room, and she hasn't resorted to snooping ever since. But she's done her best to keep tabs on her daughter and to keep the lines of communication open.

Cosette and Ben continue to jog together most mornings and nights, and to talk on the phone, and, presumably, online. There's no reason to put a stop to any of it. Meg can only cross her fingers that her daughter doesn't wind up getting hurt somehow.

Like I did.

Spotting Geoffrey descending the steps from the platform, she honks the horn.

He makes a beeline over, toting a Bloomingdale's shopping bag and an overnight bag. He's finally agreed to spend the night in suburbia so he can oversee the auditions and attend Cosette's soccer game tomorrow.

"Hello, honey." He gives Meg a bear hug as he slips into the passenger seat.

"How was your trip?"

"See that guy over there? I shared a seat with him."

Meg follows his gaze toward a good-looking businessman wearing a suit and toting a briefcase, climbing into a parked black BMW.

"I hate to break it to you, Geoffrey, but he's probably going home to his wife and kids."

"I know, but he's still a hottie. And that commuter train is full of them at this time of day." Geoffrey settles back. "You know, I'm going to take the train up from now on. It definitely beats driving."

He spent three hours last weekend stuck in traffic on the Henry Hudson. He arrived in a foul mood, demanding to know when Meg was going to give up this suburban charade and move back to the city.

"I have to give it a chance," she told him.

"You have. And it's over. Come home, Astor."

"I did come home. And it's Meg."

She only wished she felt that strongly about Glenhaven Park being home. Yes, she's settling in. But she still hasn't found many—all right, any—new friends.

Yes, Kris is here—but Meg isn't particularly eager to join her circle of friends. Anyway, her real estate career is hectic. When they parted ways after lunch at Tokyo Cafe, she promised they'd get together again soon, but so far, hasn't been able to fit Meg into her schedule.

Meg just received a telephone invitation to an upcoming party at Olympia Flickinger's house, and she's going. But she suspects it will be populated by former female professionals who run their families' lives like precision corporate teams with enormous budgets.

Not that there's anything wrong with that. Meg just can't relate.

Now, as she pulls out of the parking lot and heads toward the school, Geoffrey fills her in on his week, and she realizes with a pang that she can no longer relate to his world, either. He's immersed in his usual social whirlwind and in urban cultural pursuits, auditions, show openings, travel plans.

"Oh, I almost forgot to tell you!" he exclaims. "I met Deeanna Drennan at Lorrie's cast party the other night. She was there as somebody's date."

"And . . . ?"

"Do you want the truth, or do you want me to make you feel better?"

"I'll take the truth."

"I really wanted to hate her. I wanted her to be a vapid, uncharismatic bobblehead. But she isn't. She's definitely got something. Don't get me wrong, she's no Astor Hudson—you're one of a kind—but she's got that glow. And she was a sweetheart, on top of it, very friendly and nice. Oh, and there's already been some buzz about the show, and she's supposedly terrific in it. Sorry, Astor."

"It's Meg," she murmurs.

I really am Meg, now, she realizes. She must be, because what Geoffrey just said about her rival didn't sting.

Her envy of the actress who usurped her, her pain over not being cast—all of that seems as though it happened to someone else. Much fresher is her ongoing stress with the rattletrap house, and her worries about Cosette, and, yes, her heartache over Sam.

I live here now. This is my life.

Yet Glenhaven Park still doesn't feel like home. And New York no longer is.

"So now you know what I've been up to," Geoffrey concludes. "How about you? What's new?"

"Nothing, really."

I'm just caught in between two worlds, and I'm lonely. That's all.

"How can that be when you've lived here for only a month? Technically, everything is new."

"I know, but . . ." She trails off, wishing she could unburden herself, wondering if he'd possibly understand.

"I'm all ears."

She hesitates, trying to figure out how to begin, bringing the car to a stop at an intersection as the light turns from yellow to red.

The car driving behind her honks loudly.

"It's red!" Geoffrey shouts out his window. To Meg, he says, "Do they want you to go through a red light?"

"Probably. Nobody here has much patience."

"And I thought New York was bad." He shakes his head. "So what's doing, honey? You said you had to talk to me about something."

"Do you remember my New Year's resolution?"

Wait a minute. What is she doing? What is she saying? This wasn't supposed to be about that.

"Do I remember the insanely impossible vow you made about not getting involved with men? Oh, yeah."

"I broke it."

"Good for you!" he crows, and holds up a hand in an attempted high five.

Meg ignores it. "It's not good, Geoffrey. I'm a mess."

"You don't look like a mess."

"But I am."

"Well, you were a more obvious mess when your career went down the toilet and your daughter got expelled. So what happened now? Did our young Annie Oakley bring a rifle to her new school?"

"Nothing like that."

"So you fell in love."

"No, I didn't!" she protests. "I never said anything about love."

"Well, it's obvious. You said yourself you're falling apart."

"I didn't say that, either."

"No, you said you're a mess."

"Right. That's not the same thing as falling apart. *Falling apart* means you're hopeless. And I'm not."

"Semantics," he says with a shrug.

The horn honks behind her again.

Frustrated, she sticks her head out to shout at the impatient driver.

Geoffrey stops her. "Um, honey? The light is green. You're supposed to go."

Oh. Oops.

She drives on, aware of the tailgating road rage candidate behind her, wishing she had never opened this conversational door with Geoffrey.

"You know," he says thoughtfully, "I only met him briefly, I know, but I really didn't expect Sam to turn out to be an ass like the rest of the guys you've dated. Pardon my French."

"It's not that he's an—" She breaks off, looking over at him in disbelief. "Did you just say *Sam*?"

He nods.

"But I never told you who I was talking about."

"You didn't have to. The vibes between you two were obvious when I met him the night you moved in. And that day at the soccer practice, the way you were looking at each other from afar . . . I'd have had to be blind not to notice that you were in love."

"We're not in love!" Meg protests. "We're not even speaking."

"You broke up?"

"We were never even a couple."

"What happened, then? And don't tell me nothing, because clearly, it was something."

"It was something . . . but I'm not sure what. I guess it's the same old story. Sam obviously doesn't want to get involved, and God knows I don't need another failed relationship in my life."

"No," Geoffrey agrees, "you don't." He covers her hand on the steering wheel with his own, gently. "Honey, you need to forget that Sam exists and move on."

"He lives next door to me. How can I forget he exists?"

"You can't, as long as you live there. Maybe you really should move back to New York."

"But Cosette is happy here. Finally, she's making friends, fitting in . . . she's even auditioning for the musical."

"I know. So can we cast her in the lead?"

"Are you kidding? The other parents would grab torches, form a mob, and run me out of town."

"I've met them. You're probably right."

"Here we are," she says as they pull up in front of the redbrick school, relieved to be able to drop the subject of Sam.

He reads the signboard out front. "Glenhaven Park High. Look at this place. How small-town charming."

That's a nice switch. Small-town charming wouldn't have sounded like a compliment coming from him a few weeks ago.

"So Mr. Wonderful teaches here?" he asks.

"I didn't tell you that."

"That he was wonderful? I just assumed."

"No, that he teaches here."

"You didn't?"

"No," she says, turning off the ignition and narrowing her eyes at Geoffrey, "I didn't. So how did you know?"

Geoffrey merely shrugs guiltily.

"You know I'm going to find out. So spill it. Who have you been talking to?"

"Who do you think?"

"Cosette."

He nods.

"About my love life?"

"About hers, really. I don't think she's aware that you have an active one."

"Had," Meg amends. "And what did she tell you about her love life?"

"I can't break her confidence. I promised I wouldn't."

"She's my daughter."

"Sometimes kids don't want to share things like this with their parents."

"Things like what?"

"Let's just drop it," he says maddeningly.

"Let's just not. Don't you think I have a right to know what's going on with her?" No response. "I know she told you about her and Ben . . . right?"

"Ben? Who's—"

"Don't play dumb, Geoffrey. I know she's involved with Ben. I just don't know how involved. They're not . . . she's not . . . in any kind of trouble, is she?"

"Trouble? No."

"Well are they . . . physically involved?"

He shrugs.

"How involved?"

Geoffrey mutely indicates that his lips are sealed.

Exasperated—and, yes, jealous—Meg jerks the car door open and is climbing out when it occurs to her that this is how Sam must have felt when he found out Katie had confided in Meg and not in him.

All right, so maybe he didn't deliberately pick a fight. Maybe he had a right to feel betrayed by his daughter.

And, yes, by Meg.

But it's too late to fix it now. And what good would it do for her to tell him she understands?

Nothing will change the fact that she and Sam have no future together.

The trees that dot the school property cast long shadows across the sweeping lawn in the early-evening light. Meg heads toward the building with Geoffrey meandering along a few steps behind her. She glances toward the bike rack, remembering how she used to watch for Sam to park there every morning of her high school life.

Meg glimpses something—or someone—standing there.

A woman.

She's got long hair, and she's tall and thin, and she's . . .

Filmy, Meg realizes with a gasp, and stops short.

Crashing into her, Geoffrey grabs her by the shoulders. "What? What's wrong? Did you step on something?"

"No, I . . ." She starts to point at the nearly transparent figure of a woman, but realizes it's no longer there . . .

If it was at all.

Of course it wasn't there. You're stressed, and you're seeing things.

Does stress cause people to see things?

It must, Meg decides grimly. *Because I am.*

"What happened?" Geoffrey prods her.

She blinks. "I stepped on a rock or something. Come on. Let's go."

"Calling it a night?" Bob Callicott asks, sticking his head into Sam's office and seeing him stacking the tests he just finished correcting.

"Yeah, I'm done." He had to stay after school for a staff meeting, then returned to bring Ben to musical auditions and stuck around for an hour to catch up on a few things.

"You want to come out for a beer? I'm meeting some people down at the Grill."

The Glenhaven Grill used to be Sam's favorite watering hole when he came home on college vacations. Now, like everything else in town, it's been transformed into a more upscale place. There arc tables instead of booths, a bar instead of a soda fountain, and the pool table and dartboard have been replaced with a lounge area of couches and flickering votive candles.

"No, thanks," Sam tells Bob.

"Oh, come on. Just one beer. I told Ellen I'd get you to come. She'll be there with some people from her school."

Ellen is Bob's wife; she's an art teacher in a neighboring district. The Callicotts are younger than Sam by at least a decade, a fun-loving couple who are always trying to get him involved in their busy social life. Sometimes he accepts—like when they invite him and the kids to a barbecue or pool party.

Tonight, he's exhausted and not in the mood to socialize. He has to pick up Katie at Kelsey's house, then swing back over to school at nine to get Ben after musical auditions.

"Tell Ellen I'll take a rain check."

"Are you sure? Just one beer, c'mon . . ."

"All right, Bob, what's up?"

"What do you mean?"

"Why are you trying to talk me into this?" He has a feeling he knows.

"Ellen's friend Samantha is going to be there."

Bingo. Just as Sam suspected. Bob's wife has been trying to fix him up with various women ever since she found out he was eligible.

"She's great, Sam, you'd like her a lot," Bob says as he shakes his head adamantly. "Beautiful, fun, smart, sexy . . ."

"Not interested."

"Why not?"

Because I already know somebody who's beautiful, fun, smart, and sexy . . . and if I were going to go out with anyone, it would be her.

But he isn't, so . . .

"I don't have time to get involved with anyone, Bob. Between my kids and work and the house and coaching—"

"That's a copout."

Sam shrugs.

"Come on . . . think of this: you're both named Sam. Maybe it's a sign that it's meant to be."

"And maybe you've been hanging out with your wife and her friends a little too much."

Bob grins a little sheepishly. "Point taken. But listen, if you change your mind, we'll be there until around midnight."

"By then, I'll be having sweet dreams."

Yes, probably about Meg. She's popped up in his dreams a few times.

Even more vividly—and disconcertingly—so has Sheryl. But not in an erotic way, like Meg.

No, whenever he dreams about Sheryl, he's running, and she's behind him, calling his name, trying to catch up to him. She keeps shouting something at him, some kind of message, but her voice is always too faint for the words to reach his ears. Oddly, he keeps straining to hear what she's saying, yet he doesn't stop running.

It makes no sense.

Nor does the fact that Meg keeps popping up when all he wants is to ignore the fact that she exists.

At least Katie hasn't been hanging around her these last few weeks. Sam has managed to keep her busy with activities, and has even given her a little more freedom to do things with her friends. Yes, she's still prone to latching on to people, but better her friends and their families than someone she might see as a potential stepmother.

After Bob leaves his office, Sam puts together some paperwork and text materials to take home over the weekend. Then he flicks off the light and walks through the empty corridors, his footsteps echoing.

Another Friday; another week coming to a close.

He can hear piano music coming from the auditorium and wonders how Ben is doing with his auditions.

His son's decision to go out for the musical surprised him. Not that Ben doesn't have a decent singing voice. He inherited that from his mother; Sheryl and Ben were always singing around the house or in the car.

Ben stopped after Sheryl died. Now, he listens to music

avidly, but Sam hasn't heard a melodic peep out of him in years.

There's a break in the piano music. Sam can hear Bill Dreyfus speaking from the stage.

Curious, he slows his steps as he approaches the auditorium, wondering if he dares to spy or even just eavesdrop. Chances are, he won't catch Ben's audition, but he's interested in seeing the competition . . .

And, all right, Meg, too. He knows she'll be here; Bill is thrilled with her input on the production. He seems to assume that Sam and Meg are neighborly pals.

We probably should be.

Or even still could be . . .

If only Sam had never made that first move to kiss her that night in her house. Whatever possessed him to do that?

And what possesses him, now, to slip into the back of the darkened auditorium?

He spots Meg immediately. She's down in the front. Her hair is caught back in a jaunty high ponytail. She's wearing a pair of clingy jersey sweatpants that ride low on her hips, and a T-shirt that rides high, leaving an exposed stretch of skin.

Sam can feel his lower body immediately growing taut at the sight of it, of her. Dammit. Why is he here?

To see and hear Ben, he reminds himself.

But he can only focus on Meg, captivated by her despite his resolve.

Suddenly, he can't remember why it was so important that he stay away from her. All he wants is to be with her . . . to talk to her, to laugh with her, to hold her, to make love to her.

This is crazy, he tells himself. He spent all those years

longing to feel something this powerful. And what did he do when he finally experienced that ever-elusive depth of emotion?

You ran away.

Maybe he should stop running. Maybe it's time that he took a chance.

But what about the kids? What about Katie? What if she gets her hopes up, gets hurt?

What if she doesn't get hurt? What if something wonderful happens?

The voice in his head sounds like Sheryl's, not his own. Something wonderful? Like what?

You know what, Sam. You heard her singing that day; you heard her express her feelings. And you didn't have the guts to respond.

But the kids . . . if he tried to make things work with Meg, and it didn't work out . . . then what?

You can't protect them from every possible wound forever. Pain is a part of life; it's inevitable. Anyway, Katie and Ben have already survived the worst thing that can happen to a child. They're strong. They'll be okay, no matter what.

What about you, Sam? Are you strong?

He swallows hard. Strong people don't turn their backs on opportunity, no matter how risky.

So what does that mean?

That he should see if Meg is willing to give him—give them—a real chance?

I'll talk to her as soon as this is over, he decides, slipping into a seat in the back row. His heart is beating in elation, which is ridiculous. Nothing promising has happened. There's a possibility that Meg will tell him to get lost.

But there's also a possibility that she won't.

Bill is calling the next student onto the stage. Meryl Goldman is in one of his sections this year. A quiet, studious girl with striking dark hair and eyes, she doesn't seem like the type to seek the spotlight.

As she crosses the stage, sheet music in hand, she seems so hesitant that Sam's heart goes out to her.

"All right, Meryl," Bill calls, "you're auditioning for Norma, right?"

She nods shyly, fumbling with the microphone.

Meg confers with the pianist, then whispers something to Bill.

"Okay, then, let's go to act two, where Norma's just arrived on the set. I'll feed you the lines leading into the musical number."

Meryl bites her lip and turns the pages of her script.

Meg strides up the aisle for a better vantage on the stage. Halfway to Sam, she spots him.

Her eyebrows rise.

He dares to hold her gaze, to offer her a conciliatory smile.

Up front, Meryl announces that she's ready.

In the instant before she turns back toward the stage, Meg returns Sam's smile, tentatively.

His heart soars.

"*Up here, Miss Desmond,*" Bill says, sounding like an elderly man. "*It's Hog-eye!*"

"Hog-eye!" Meryl replies, somehow transforming herself into an elegant diva with booming vocal inflection and the sweep of an arm. "Well, hello!"

"Let's get a look at you."

The pianist begins the accompaniment.

Sam frowns. The music seems familiar. Why?

Meryl begins to sing, her voice hushed, reverent. *"I don't know why I'm frightened . . . I know my way around here . . ."*

It's that song, Sam realizes with a start.

Meg's song. The one she wrote—no, the one he *thought* she wrote—about him.

It's not about him, and she didn't write it. Andrew Lloyd Webber did. It's obviously part of the *Sunset Boulevard* score. It meant nothing.

How could he have been so stupid?

His face flaming, Sam slinks out of the auditorium, caught up in his own private humiliation . . .

And anguish.

Just when he thought there was a chance . . .

But how do you know there still isn't?

She did smile back at him.

Yeah, so what? She's not made of stone. If someone smiles at her, she returns it. A casual smile should mean nothing more to him than the lyrics of the song Meryl is singing right now.

As he heads out into the night, Sam is just thankful he didn't follow through on his ridiculous impulse.

Lying in bed—a real bed, no longer just a mattress on the floor—Meg can't sleep.

She keeps remembering how Sam caught her eye earlier in the auditorium. She was so sure, the way he was looking at her, that he wanted to make some kind of connection with her again.

She couldn't have been more wrong about that.

Not only did he disappear a few minutes later, but when

he came back to pick up Ben an hour later, he did his best to avoid her.

He had to go out of his way to do it, too, because she was actually standing out in front of the school talking to Ben when she saw Sam park his Trailblazer down at the curb and step out. He looked around, saw her with Ben, and loitered by the car until their conversation was interrupted by Olympia Flickinger, who wanted to know how Sophie did in the auditions.

As Meg tried tactfully to prepare Olympia for the probability that her diva daughter wouldn't be cast in a lead role, she watched Sam out of the corner of her eye.

He walked up, chatted with a few of the other students and their parents, then left with Ben, all without giving Meg a second glance.

She must have imagined that anything significant passed between them back in the auditorium. Wishful thinking, that's all.

Anyway, she has other things to worry about now.

Not only did Sophie Flickinger not nail the audition, but her mother didn't seem to understand that she'll be lucky if she's relegated to even a small background role. Same goes for her friend Kirsten's son Austin and her friend Brooke's supposedly hideously untalented daughter Victoria, who is actually a hair more gifted than Sophie Flickinger, and much more likeable.

Meryl Goldman is the hands-down choice to play Norma Desmond.

Meanwhile, both Geoffrey and Bill Dreyfus are pushing to give the second lead to Cosette.

Mingling with Meg's pride in her daughter's flawless audition is reluctance to cast her as Betty. Not only because she'll be accused of nepotism, but because Ben will be playing Joe, the male lead and Betty's—as well as Norma's—love interest.

Haunted by Geoffrey's noncomment on Cosette's physical relationship with Ben, Meg isn't thrilled at the prospect of their spending even more time together. That can't be healthy.

Yet who is she to stand in the way of Bill Dreyfus's casting, and for purely personal reasons?

Meg rolls over, punching her pillow, staring into the near darkness. Moonlight spills through the partially lifted shade at the window.

Oh, well. What can she do about any of this? When the list goes up on Monday after school, she'll just have to be prepared for the fallout. And until then—

Suddenly, Meg sees a flicker of movement in the corner of the room, just beyond the wedge of moonlight.

Her breath catches in her throat as she watches something—no, someone—emerge from the shadows.

It's a human form, the figure of a woman; Meg can distinctly see her lithe body, her long hair . . .

And, in a flash, her face, as she drifts into the silver glow at the window.

She seems to smile at Meg and gives a nod.

Then, all at once, she's gone.

But she was definitely there. Meg didn't imagine it, and she isn't dreaming.

The room is still.

Meg can't breathe, can't move, can't scream.

Not, she realizes, that she's inclined to.

Why not? You just saw a ghost.

There's not a doubt in her mind that she's wide-awake; that the vision was real.

Yet, strangely, she isn't afraid.

Quite the contrary.

Gradually, a strange sense of calm seems to settle over her body. Her clenched muscles begin to relax, and the whirlwind of worries has spun itself out.

As drowsiness finally drifts in at last to claim her, her last waking thought is of Sam.

Chapter
17

North Street is lined with cars on Tuesday evening; Meg has to park her Hyundai way down at the end of the block.

It's strange to walk the familiar stretch of sidewalk beneath the canopy of trees. She finds herself looking for the familiar network of cracks in the concrete squares beneath her feet, remembering how she used to avoid them in an effort to spare her mother's back.

The cracks are gone, though; the old sidewalk long since replaced with a well-tended new one. She passes familiar homes that once belonged to old neighbors and friends who are obviously long gone.

There's a Porsche in the driveway where the blue-collar Steger family once lived; the Carters' tiny ranch has a full second story and a spacious side addition now; in the Zemanskis' side yard, where their three sons and the neighborhood boys played baseball from dawn till dusk every summer, the worn dirt patches have been replaced with lush lawn.

The house where Meg grew up is ablaze with light; Olympia Flickinger's party is obviously in full swing.

Meg is late, having lingered at school with Bill after the first cast meeting for *Sunset Boulevard*.

Sophie Flickinger was there, and sullen. Meg half expected her to turn down her tiny part in the chorus, but she grudgingly accepted her script.

When Brad came to pick up his daughter, he studiously avoided eye contact with Meg, hustling his daughter away to whatever is next on her crammed daily agenda. Obviously, Brad isn't thrilled that his daughter was bypassed for a lead.

Meg isn't looking forward to coming face-to-face with Olympia for the first time since the cast list was announced yesterday. But it would have been even more awkward to try and make an excuse to avoid the party after saying she would come.

Anyway, Olympia is a grown woman. She's not going to raise a fuss.

Or so Meg has been trying to convince herself all day.

Well, if she brings up the casting decisions, Meg will just point out that none of the freshmen were cast in lead roles. That should take care of it.

With anyone else, maybe. But Olympia Flickinger has proven herself a force to be reckoned with.

Meg drags her feet as she gets closer to the house, wishing she were anywhere else.

Even at home, where the electricians have made a dusty mess of the walls and ceilings . . . and where a ghost also happens to be lurking.

She hasn't seen the apparition since the other night. Nor has she mentioned it to anyone. Not even to Geoffrey, who complained the next morning of lights flickering on and off in the guest room and a draft that seemed to come and go.

Meg has no idea why she isn't inclined to flee a haunted house. Maybe it's because the spirit's presence seemed more comforting than menacing.

She's felt more at peace these last few days—even with Sam's ongoing diligence in avoiding her.

Holding a cold beer, Sam steps out onto the porch with Rover trotting at his feet, leaving Katie inside watching one of those reality television shows she enjoys. He just spent a tense hour helping her with her English homework, wishing Sheryl were here. English was her thing; science was Sam's. Katie struggles in both subjects.

Maybe I'll hire her a tutor this year, Sam thinks, settling on a wicker chair and sipping his beer. *Someone who has more patience than I do.*

For some reason, Meg flits into his head.

For some reason?

Hasn't she been drifting around there ever since she moved in and made her presence known? Try as he might, Sam hasn't been able to shake her. She might as well be a ghost, haunting him in his waking hours and in his sleep.

Sheryl is still haunting his dreams, as well. He's had that recurring one almost every night, to the point where he dreads going to bed.

When he confided in Jack about it, his brother suggested that his wife might be trying to send him some kind of message from beyond the grave.

"A lot of help you are," Sam grumbled. "Hey, why don't you move into the old Duckworth Place next?"

"Why? Are the people who live there moving out already?" Jack asked, aware of Ben's budding romance with the girl next door but not of Sam's erstwhile one with her mom.

"Not yet, but I'm sure they'll leave sooner or later," Sam said darkly. "I'll keep you posted."

Does he really think Meg is going to move out of the house as everyone else has?

Is that what's keeping him from letting her back into his life?

Or is he actually more afraid that she'll be there for good?

Admit it. That thought scares you. If she's there to stay, you can't pretend she doesn't exist.

Sam moodily sips his beer, brooding, absently petting Rover's head.

Sooner or later, you'll have to have some kind of contact with her again. You can't go out of your way to avoid her forever.

All right, that's true.

Rover's ears perk up, and he turns his head expectantly toward the street.

But Sam doesn't have to fall in love with Meg just because she's there, under his nose, in his life.

He can control himself . . .

Unlike Ben, Sam thinks, as his son and Cosette appear down the block, returning from their evening run.

Their supposed evening run, that is. They're both dressed in athletic clothing, but they aren't running. They're strolling . . . and stopping every couple of yards to embrace and kiss.

Sam watches, wondering if he should alert them to his presence on the porch, knowing that would probably embarrass them. Or maybe it wouldn't.

Because really, do a couple of infatuated teenagers have a care in the world?

I missed the boat, Sam thinks wistfully.

If only he had known Meg back when she had a crush on him. If only he had gone out with her back then . . . and either gotten her out of his system, or into his life, permanently.

No . . . if that had happened, he wouldn't have met Sheryl. He wouldn't have his children.

Ben and Katie were meant to be his.

Meg wasn't.

It's as simple as that.

How strange it is for Meg to ring the doorbell of what was once her own house.

Olympia opens the door with a warm, expectant smile that chills slightly when she sees Meg. All right. So she's not thrilled about *Sunset Boulevard.*

"Oh, hello. So glad you could make it. I wanted to thank you for working with Sophie to prepare her for the musical."

"Oh . . . well, I didn't—"

"At first she was upset she didn't get a lead. But Brad and I told her to take the part you gave her and make it her own. We told her to bring something fresh to it, something no other actress has ever brought."

"I'm sure she will."

Yeah, right. I'm sure she'll play the role of Girl like no one has ever played it before.

"I need to talk to you about those voice lessons. I think Brad and I are going to go in a different direction after all. But thank you so much."

"You're, uh, welcome." Meg blinks, wondering if she's just been fired.

"Come on in," Olympia says graciously nonetheless.

Meg fervently wishes she hadn't come, and she suspects Olympia feels the same. But she can hardly turn around and walk away now.

The house looks elegant, with flickering candlelight, fresh flowers, and platters of sumptuous hors d'oeuvres everywhere.

But it's not supposed to be this way. It's supposed to be comfortable and cozy and my home, not theirs.

Her anxiety building, Meg drifts into the crowded living room, looking for a familiar face, and finds none. But there's the corner where the Addams's Christmas tree always stood, and there's the nook where the flowering hibiscus plant she gave her mom one Mother's Day eventually grew into a tree. The hibiscus is still alive in her parents' new house down South.

But it belongs here.

Swallowing a lump in her throat, Meg moves on into the dining room, where she shared so many meals with her mother and father.

Tonight, a chattering female crowd of strangers is gathered around an elegant table, which seems to be covered in beauty products of some sort.

A uniformed caterer hands Meg a glass of wine, and she tries to find an unobtrusive place to stand and sip and reflect.

She spots Brooke nearby. Seeing her, Brooke gives a polite nod, but she doesn't look particularly friendly.

If Austin were playing Joe Gillis, she'd probably be falling all over me, Meg thinks grimly.

But she strives for a casual tone when she greets Brooke.

"Hi, Meg." Brooke doesn't sound casual, or friendly. Nonetheless, she politely introduces her to Sidney and Allison, with whom she was deep in conversation. It ground to a self-conscious halt when Meg arrived.

The women aren't unfriendly. They just aren't ... friendly.

Trying to think of something to say, Meg asks Brooke, "What is all that?"

"All what?"

"Why is all that lotion and makeup spread out on the table?"

"So that we can sample it. Did you pick up your order form when you got here?"

"Order form?"

Brooke just points at a stack of papers on a nearby table. Meg picks one up and glances over it.

Uh-oh.

Apparently, she's stumbled unwittingly into a modern-day version of a Tupperware party. Only instead of plastic food storage containers—which she can actually use—Olympia is offering an exotic array of cosmetics and creams. The least expensive item—a tube of facial scrub—is fifty dollars.

And thanks to the pricey electrical work that will claim her voice lesson income—if there is one—for the next few weeks, Meg is pretty much broke. Calvin's next check won't arrive until the beginning of October—not that she would be inclined to spend a penny of that on face scrub that must be made of gold particles or something.

Okay, so now what?

Brooke, Sidney, and Allison have resumed their conversation. Meg looks around at the other women. They're chatting, laughing, sampling, and filling out their forms without a financial care in the world.

One woman, standing slightly apart from the rest, meets her gaze. She has a friendly-looking, vaguely familiar face.

"What are you getting?" she asks Meg, stepping closer.

"Oh . . . I'm not sure yet. How about you?"

"Same here. I'm not usually big on this kind of stuff." The woman's pretty features are unenhanced by makeup. Meg also notices that she's not exactly skeletal, unlike most of the women here, and that her jeans and sweater promote casual comfort more than a fashion statement.

Talk about a breath of fresh air.

"Have we met?" she asks.

"I don't think so."

"I don't either, but you seem familiar for some reason. I'm Meg Addams." She extends a hand.

"Jenny Keller. Nice to meet you."

"Are you a friend of Olympia's?" she asks, finding that hard to believe.

"I live next door."

"Really? In the Dutch Colonial or the brick cape?"

"The cape." Jenny looks pleased. "You know the house?"

She nods. "I grew up here."

"In town?"

"Yes, but, actually . . . here. On North Street. In this house."

"Oh, how funny! Does Olympia know?"

Meg nods. "That's really how we met."

"Wow. You're the first person I've even met who's from Glenhaven Park and still lives here."

"Actually, I just moved back."

"It must be strange for you to be here."

"In town, or in the house?"

"Both."

"It is," she admits. "Especially in the house."

"The Flickingers are making a lot of changes," Jenny tells her. "Right now, they're redoing the kitchen. Olympia said the whole thing will be gutted later this week. She wanted to get the party out of the way before the dust starts flying."

As if summoned by the mention of her name, Olympia appears. "Oh, good, you've met. I was planning to introduce you. You've both got something in common now that Meryl is the lead in Meg's show."

"It's not *my* show," Meg protests, wondering what Meryl has to do with this.

"I thought you were the casting director."

"No . . ." Awkward pause. "I'm just helping Bill Dreyfus."

So go ahead and blame him for not casting Sophie in the lead, Olympia.

Not that Meg would have done that, had she been given the option.

"Anyway," Olympia goes on, "Jenny's daughter is playing Norma Desmond, so you'll be seeing a lot of each other."

Somebody calls Olympia from across the room, and she swoops away as quickly as she showed up.

"So you and Meryl are related? Actually, I should have

picked up on that," Meg comments. "She looks a lot like you."

"She's my daughter. I kept my maiden name; that's why you didn't figure it out. Meryl's is Goldman, like my husband's. And I know you said you weren't the one who cast her, but Gary and I are so grateful to whoever made that choice. She's always been shy, and we're hoping this will help bring her out of her shell."

"I'm sure it will. And there's a great bunch of kids in the show."

"Oh, believe me, I've heard all about it. Meryl has had such a crush for the past few years on the boy playing Joe."

"Ben Rooney?"

"Right. She's always said he doesn't know she's alive, but I told her that he will now." Jenny smiles.

Meg's heart sinks. In part because she knows how Meryl feels, infatuated with someone oblivious to her existence. That was her, with Sam, back in high school.

Even more disturbing is the realization that Meryl is hoping to win the heart of Cosette's boyfriend . . . and that Cosette is playing the "other woman" to Meryl's Norma in the show.

Talk about a love triangle.

She has a feeling the onstage drama of *Sunset Boulevard* might just be rivaled by backstage drama.

Sam is still sitting on the front porch, alone in the dark, when he sees Meg's car pull into her driveway long after his son—with Rover—and her daughter have retreated into their respective homes.

He hears her turn off the engine, open the car door, close

it. Then he hears her footsteps crossing the gravel drive toward the door.

You can let her go inside, or you can talk to her.

And you've got two seconds to decide.

He stands abruptly and crosses the porch to lean over the railing. "Meg?"

Decision made.

It's what a responsible parent would do. Set aside his own reservations to put his son's well-being first.

The footsteps stop. He can see her standing there in the shadows beneath a tall maple, poised, her back to him.

Then she turns. "Hi, Sam."

He wishes he could see her face.

You can . . . if you go closer.

He finds himself leaving his porch, crossing his yard, then hers.

Arriving a few feet in front of her, he can see her face—but he still can't tell how she's feeling. Her expression betrays no emotion . . . no apparent interest, whatsoever, in him.

"I wanted to talk to you for a second," he says uncomfortably, wishing he hadn't started this after all.

She nods. Waits.

"I just wondered what you thought about Ben and Cosette spending so much time together . . . whether she's said anything to you about it."

Meg shakes her head. "Just that they're friends."

"That's what Ben says, too. But I think they're more than that. Actually, I *know* they are."

"How do you know?"

"I saw them earlier. Kissing."

"Where?" she sounds concerned.

"Right out in the open, actually. Which is probably a good thing. Right?"

"I guess so. They're just . . . young."

"Not that young. They're juniors in high school. Ben will be sixteen in a few weeks. At that age, I was . . . well, kissing girls. And more."

She visibly stiffens, and he instantly regrets having said that. She doesn't need to know the details of his teenaged love life. Especially since she wasn't a part of it—and admitted that she wanted to be.

"It's not the kissing I'm worried about," she tells him. "It's the 'and more' part."

"Have you had a talk with Cosette?"

"You mean, 'the' talk? The general one about the birds and the bees? Of course, a long time ago."

"Me, too, with Ben, but . . ." He takes a deep breath and a step closer. "Look, Meg, I'm sorry about getting upset with you about Katie that night. It was just hard for me to swallow that my kids might be willing to open up to someone other than me. But obviously, I haven't nailed this single dad thing even after all these years. I know they keep things from me. So I shouldn't be surprised that Ben isn't telling me he has a girlfriend."

"Cosette isn't telling me she has a boyfriend, either. And I don't think it's necessarily because I haven't nailed the single mom thing . . . which has been the way things are in our family since she was born. So you'd think I'd have it down by now." She gives a rueful laugh. "Anyway, did you tell your parents everything when you were their age? Or much of anything, even?"

"No," he admits, "not the important stuff."

"Neither did I."

"At this point, I wish you'd tell me that Ben had confided in you the way Katie did."

"Sorry. He hasn't. I don't suppose Cosette . . . ?"

"Nope. They're in their own little world."

"I just don't want them in it over their heads. But every time I try to talk to Cosette about what's going on with Ben, she shuts down. I suppose I could give her less freedom . . ."

"I could do the same with Ben, but he doesn't have that much. Not compared to his friends."

"She doesn't, either. She'll be the first to tell you that."

There's a pause.

Sam can hear crickets, and the distant sound of cars on the main road, and Meg's quiet breathing, and his own.

Oh, Lord, I'm still crazy about her.

If she would just give me some sign that she's open to me . . . anything at all . . . I'd cross that line again. I'd take a chance and to hell with worrying about the future fallout.

He studies her face. Her expression remains guarded.

"So what do you think we should do, Sam?"

About the kids.

That's what she's asking, he reminds himself.

"I guess we should just keep an eye on them and make sure they're not alone together very much."

"That's a good idea," she agrees. "I mean, if you're never really alone together, you can't get carried away and do something you might regret."

"Right."

That's true for adults as well as teenagers.

As long as Sam continues to keep his distance from Meg, he won't be tempted to cross that line.

"Well . . . I guess that's it, then," Meg says with a shrug. "Right?"

"Right," Sam says again. "That's all we can do."

"Okay. Good night, then."

"Good night."

He forces himself to turn back toward his house, as she heads toward hers.

Don't let her walk away.

Don't let her go inside.

Don't let this opportunity pass without at least trying to—

He turns back impulsively, not certain what he's going to say or do, only knowing he doesn't want to let go yet.

He's just in time to see her porch lights go dark abruptly.

Too late.

She's already inside.

Oh, well.

It was a bad idea anyway.

What the heck?

Unexpectedly plunged into blackness just as she was about to descend the porch steps again to go after Sam— without even knowing why, or what she would even say— Meg goes still, wondering what happened.

Silence.

Then, next door, she hears the distant sound of Sam's front door opening and closing. He's in for the night. Too late to stop him.

Meg frowns and looks up at the darkened fixtures.

The electrician assured her that there had never been a problem with shorts in the wiring.

"It must have been your lightbulbs," he told her when she asked how the lights could always be going on and off.

She doubted it then . . .

And she doubts it now.

Because she knows what she saw the other night in her room.

There's a ghost in the house, and she's responsible for the strange things that have happened around here since Meg moved in. Including the lights going out just now, stopping her from calling out to Sam.

She looks around, half-expecting to see the figure of a woman, but she's alone out here in the dark.

"Why did you do that?" she whispers, and waits for a disembodied voice to answer her question.

Because it isn't time yet.

The answer drifts into her head as if of its own accord, propelled not by her own thought process, but by some other force.

What do you mean, it isn't time yet? she asks silently in return. *Time for what?*

Time for you and Sam. When it's time, you'll know.

"Oh my God . . . what am I doing?" Suddenly coming to her senses, Meg fumbles in her bag for her keys, needing to get inside, away from . . .

Well, from the voice in her head.

This is what happens to crazy people. They hear voices. They talk to themselves.

"Great. So now I'm crazy," she mutters, unlocking the front door.

Right. She must be anyway, if she's thinking she and Sam have any kind of chance together, now, or ever.

When it's time, you'll know . . .

What kind of absurdity is that?

Wishful thinking. That's what it is.

Who knows? Maybe the ghost's existence is wishful thinking, too.

Maybe she really didn't see what she thought she saw that night in her room. She was tired, it was late . . .

Her mind was playing tricks on her.

It is now, too.

But you need to get a grip.

You almost did something you would have regretted.

So it doesn't matter why the lights went out when they did.

What matters is that it happened . . . and that it stopped her from making a fool out of herself.

Just like years ago, when she wrote that heartfelt love letter to Sam on a whim. She'd have sent it if it hadn't fallen down the crack between the kitchen cupboards.

Thank God she didn't send it.

By now, it must be in the Dumpster she saw parked on the Flickingers' driveway, part of the construction rubble.

Just as well.

The letter was a bad idea back then, and going after Sam was a bad idea now.

No, she isn't over him yet.

Yes, she still has butterflies in her stomach whenever she locks eyes with him.

But maybe they aren't butterflies after all.

Maybe they're bumblebees buzzing around in there, waiting to pierce her heart with a thousand stingers.

All I have to do is remember that whenever I look at Sam, and I'll be okay.

Chapter

18

With twenty-four hours until opening night and Bill Dreyfus hung up in a late staff meeting, Meg claps her hands loudly to get the attention of the cast. Clad in their Old-Hollywood-era costumes, they had predictably dissolved into chatter when she paused to resolve a lighting problem with the stage crew.

"All right, guys, we've got it under control now." She strides across the auditorium. "So let's take that last scene again from the top. Max, Norma, Joe. The rest of you, find seats and quiet down."

Meryl Goodman, Ben Rooney, and Evan Stein, the senior playing Max, take their places onstage. This is an emotional scene, the one that leads up to Norma Desmond's desperate New Year's suicide attempt after Joe rejects her. There's a romantic song and dance—expertly choreographed by Meg herself—before Norma reveals her feelings for Joe, then kisses him passionately.

The kiss has been a problem from the start. Meryl, who gives a stellar performance throughout the show, has a predictable lapse whenever it's time for the romantic clinch boldly initiated by Norma.

That kiss has been awkward every time, as opposed to Ben's passionate scene with Cosette in Act Two. Watching her daughter kiss Ben's son was strange for Meg at first, but gradually, theatrical magic took over. Now when they perform that scene they aren't high school sweethearts Cosette and Ben. They're star-crossed lovers Betty and Joe.

She only wishes Meryl and Ben could be as convincing as Norma and Joe.

It isn't just Meryl who's holding back self-consciously— poor thing, nursing a secret crush on her costar.

Ben is holding back, too.

And Meg knows why. Because Cosette is watching him like a hawk from the wings.

No boyfriend wants to share a passionate kiss with somebody else as his girlfriend looks on.

But what is she supposed to do about it?

You'd better do something. This is dress rehearsal. It's your last chance to fix this problem.

Onstage, the action has begun.

Meg glances over at Cosette, who's wearing a full-skirted yellow vintage dress and pumps. She's intently watching the actors.

"Cosette," she calls quietly, seized by sudden inspiration, "can you come here for a minute?"

Her daughter approaches expectantly as Meg wildly tries to come up with a plan.

"I need you to do me a favor," she whispers. "Can you please go out to my car and bring me the box on the backseat?"

"What box?" asks Cosette, grudgingly accepting the car keys Meg hands her. She's less prone to protest commands from Meg the Assistant Director than from Meg the Mom.

"The box that has the, uh, rest of the props for the next scene."

"I didn't see anything back there when we drove over."

"Actually, maybe it's in the trunk. Just find it and bring it in. Thanks." She says it loudly enough so that Ben and Meryl can hear from the stage. She sees them pause briefly and glance over to see Cosette leaving.

Meg turns guiltily back to the action onstage, the scene under way once again. It will take Cosette a few minutes to reach her car in the far parking lot . . . then to conduct a fruitless search for a box that doesn't exist.

That should be long enough for Ben and Meryl to finish the scene without his jealous girlfriend looking on.

It's not a foolproof plan, but it's all Meg's got.

And it actually seems to be working. The interaction between Norma and Joe is quickly picking up romantic steam. They sing and dance "The Perfect Year" in flawless harmony. In Ben's arms, Meryl has come alive, convincingly playing a woman wistfully in love with a man who's out of her grasp.

By the time they've reached the pivotal moment, Meg senses that everyone in the auditorium is captivated by what's to come—and so are both the actors on stage.

She holds her breath as Meryl leans in to kiss Ben.

She's supposed to initiate it, yet from where Meg sits, it looks pretty mutual. And breathtakingly real.

They slowly part, and Meryl utters her next line. "*I'm in love with you, Ben. Surely you know that.*"

It's so convincing that Meg doesn't even realize

something is amiss until she hears the rustling and whispers and muffled giggles from the kids around her.

Oh, no.

Poor Meryl.

It takes another moment for her to pick up on the mishap. Then, suddenly comprehending what she just said, Meryl gasps and covers her mouth, clearly humiliated.

Ben shuffles his feet uncomfortably and looks around, probably checking to see if Cosette is back, if she heard.

"Okay, cut," Meg calls, realizing the scene has just hopelessly disintegrated.

The line was supposed to be, *I'm in love with you, Joe.*

She said *Ben.*

Because she is, Meg realizes. *She's head over heels for him.*

Anyone can see that, including Ben.

Including Cosette.

"He's Joe," a familiar voice calls icily from the back of the auditorium, interrupting the scene. "Not Ben. You said Ben."

Meg turns and is dismayed to see her daughter striding down the aisle.

"I know. I'm really sorry." Meryl tries to laugh it off, beet red. She ducks her head, refusing to look at Ben.

Cosette comes to a stop beside Meg and thrusts the keys at her. "There was no box in the car."

"There wasn't? Oh . . . I must've left it at home."

"Yeah, you must have." Cosette flops into a seat and glowers at the stage.

Ben refuses to look her way.

Actually, he suddenly seems to be focused on Meryl. He

leans toward her and whispers something in her ear. She looks up shyly, smiling. Whispers something back.

Maybe there's hope, Meg thinks. Hope for the scene. And hope for Meryl's crush.

I'm not supposed to be rooting for her, she reminds herself. *She isn't me, twenty years ago, and Ben isn't Sam.*

Sometimes, though, it's like watching history repeat itself . . . with potential for a much happier ending.

So where does that leave Cosette?

Teenaged relationships crash and burn, Meg reminds herself. *It happens all the time. You survive, you move on, you find someone new. That's a part of growing up.*

That would have happened to her and Sam, too. Maybe it's better that they never got together back then, as kids.

But that doesn't stop her from wistfully wondering what would happen if they gave it another chance now.

Finding the door ajar, Sam pokes his head into Ben's room and sees him standing in front of the mirror.

"Ben?"

He looks up. "Yeah?"

"I just wanted to tell you to break a leg tonight."

"Thanks," Ben says without enthusiasm.

"Do you know all your lines?"

Ben nods.

"Well, I'll be sitting in the second row on the left. If you get a case of stage fright, look at me, and I'll do this." Sam makes a hideous face.

Ben doesn't laugh.

"I'm kidding, of course." No response. "What's wrong, Ben? Opening night jitters?"

"Cosette and I just broke up."

Thud.

Sam wonders whether to acknowledge the fact that Ben never even told him they were in a relationship to begin with.

No. Better to just go with it.

"What happened?" he asks, knowing Ben isn't about to tell him.

"You know Meryl Goodman?"

Hmm. Maybe he is about to tell me.

"The girl playing the lead in the musical? Yes. She's a sweetheart."

"Yeah. She is. I noticed that, and I kind of . . ."

"Like her?" Sam supplies gently, trying not to jar Ben out of the conversational flow.

Ben nods. "It's not that I don't like Cosette, too. But I want to ask Meryl out. I can't help it."

"You're not supposed to be able to help it. You shouldn't be settled down with one girl at your age. You're supposed to play the field. You're fifteen."

"I'm sixteen, Dad."

That's right. Ben just had a birthday. Sixteen. He went down to Motor Vehicles to get his learner's permit that afternoon.

It seems like only yesterday that he was playing with his Matchbox cars on the floor. Now he's sitting behind the steering wheel of a real one as Sam coaches him on parallel parking and four-way stops.

How it's flown by, Ben's childhood.

Any second now, he'll have a driver's license. Any second after that, he'll drive away. Off to college. And Katie will be next.

And I'll be alone, Sam thinks glumly.

"What do you think I should do, Dad?" Ben is asking . . . remarkably. Ben wants his advice.

"You should listen to your heart, Ben."

And so, Sam realizes with unexpected clarity, *should I.*

"Meg?"

She looks up to see Olympia Flickinger standing in the corridor outside the music room, where she's making last-minute notes on her script.

"I know you're busy. Opening night."

"Right. Is Sophie excited?"

"She is. She'd be more excited if she were playing a lead, but . . ."

She just had to get that little dig in there, didn't she.

"Anyway," Olympia says, "I just wanted to give you something."

Meg waits expectantly for her to cross the room in her sophisticated heels. Until Olympia showed up, impeccably dressed as always, Meg was feeling pretty good about the way she herself looks tonight.

She's wearing a figure-skimming red dress she bought last year for a wedding in the city. It's not new, but nobody here has ever seen it, and it's flattering on her. She put her hair up on top of her head in a tousled knot—her sex kitten 'do, as Geoffrey always likes to call it. And she's wearing makeup. Not heavy stage makeup like she just put on Cosette, but enough to accentuate her features and make her look attractive.

Or so she thought until Olympia swept into the room in her swanky black pantsuit, heels, and professionally styled hair.

Oh, well. Meg isn't trying to outdo anyone. She's

comfortable enough in her own skin that she's stopped feeling so self-conscious whenever the Fancy Moms are afoot. She's even managed to make a new friend, sort of.

She ran into Meryl's mother, Jenny, at the florist's shop this morning. Meg was picking up the arrangements needed for the set, and Jenny was buying a bouquet of roses for her daughter.

She confided to Meg that Meryl was a nervous wreck. Meg assured her that she was doing a great job.

She neglected, of course, to say anything about the kiss that blossomed between the two leads at last night's dress rehearsal.

She and Jenny wound up grabbing a quick cup of coffee together at the cafe next door and made plans to have lunch someday next week.

So things are looking up on the friendship front.

At least, they were, until Olympia Flickinger burst onto the scene.

"This is yours, I think." She extends a hand and drops something into Meg's.

She looks down. It's an envelope.

She must be paying me for that last voice lesson she had scheduled before she canceled, Meg thinks. Well, this will come in handy.

"Thanks."

"The contractor found it yesterday when he ripped out the old cabinets, and he gave it to Brad."

What?

Meg turns the envelope over with hands that are suddenly shaking.

"We recognized your handwriting from the notes you

sent home with Sophie," Olympia goes on, oblivious to Meg's emotional state.

Sam Rooney, 31 Boxwood Lane, Glenhaven Park, New York 10535

It's the letter. The love letter she wrote to Sam.

Who knows what would have happened if she had gone ahead and mailed it all those years ago?

Maybe you and Sam would have gotten together.

Then you would have eventually broken up.

Look at Cosette, licking her wounds over the argument she had on the phone with Ben after school. Meg couldn't help but overhear Cosette's end of the conversation. Nor could she help feeling guilty, as Meryl Goodman seems to be the source of the trouble between Cosette and Ben.

Thanks to me.

But if it hadn't been Meryl Goodman, it would have been something else, sooner or later. The timing wasn't right for Cosette and Ben.

"So you knew Sam Rooney, then, when you lived here?"

Startled back to the present, Meg nods numbly at Olympia.

"I wonder what's in the envelope. Do you remember what it could possibly be?"

Meg shrugs. "I'm not sure."

"Aren't you going to open it and see?"

"Not now," she says, tucking it into her tote bag. "I've got to get ready for the show."

Obviously disappointed, Olympia looks poised to protest. But then Bill pokes his head into the room.

"Meg? Minor emergency in the girls' dressing room. Nobody can find the hair spray."

"I've got some in here." She hurriedly grabs her tote bag and slings it over her shoulder, relishing the frustrated curiosity on Olympia Flickinger's face.

Seated in the second row of the auditorium, waiting for the lights to go down and the show to begin, Sam feels conspicuously alone.

Katie is here somewhere, but she insisted on sitting with her friends. Both Jack and Sam's father-in-law have tickets to come to tomorrow night's performance. There are plenty of familiar faces in the crowd—students, parents, faculty members—but no one Sam would feel comfortable joining.

That's okay. He's used to going places solo. He'll just sit here and reread the program until—

"Mr. Rooney?"

"Yes?" Sam looks up to see Julia Kiger, one of his sophomore physics students, standing in the aisle.

"I just found this on the floor in the hallway. You must have dropped it."

"What is it?"

"I have no idea, but it's addressed to you."

He takes the envelope from her and turns it over. She's right. It is.

But he didn't drop it. Somebody else must have.

"Thanks, Julia."

"No problem. You must be psyched to see Ben in the show. I heard he's really good."

He smiles. "I hope so."

As Julia scurries off to join her waiting friends, Sam turns the envelope over, looking for some clue to what it might contain. There's no return address, and no stamp.

Clearly, it's something somebody intended to mail to him, though . . . it has his name and address on it. So he might as well open it, right?

Right, he tells himself firmly, already sliding a finger beneath the flap.

The applause in the theater is deafening.

Standing in the wings, watching her cast take a second bow to a standing ovation, Meg is elated.

"They did it!" she exclaims to Bill Dreyfus, who's standing beside her, flushed with exhilaration.

"So did we!" Bill replies.

Then a couple of kids from the chorus grab his arm and Meg's and coax them both onstage.

Beaming, self-conscious, she takes a bow with Bill, holding hands.

How strange it is to be back in the spotlight after all this time.

Yet, unlike poor, doomed Norma Desmond, she finds that she doesn't crave it. What a relief it is to be behind the scenes now.

Blinded by the lights, she gazes out into the dark, crowded auditorium, knowing Sam is out there somewhere.

Part of her wishes she could see his face; part of her is glad she can't.

A thousand bumblebees, remember? Just waiting to sting your heart.

She cringes.

And the curtain falls on opening night.

* * *

Sam awakens to sun streaming in the window and a strange aura of expectancy streaming in his blood.

Why?

What's today?

Saturday, he remembers. Soccer game this afternoon, and—

Oh. That's right.

His mouth curls into a smile and he turns to look at the folded sheets of stationery on his nightstand.

Meg.

He grabs the letter to reread it once more. Not that he hasn't read it dozens of times already.

Dear Sam,

First of all, I don't usually go around writing letters to people when I can just go right up and talk to them. But in this case, I feel like a letter is the best way for me to say what I need to say. Actually, it's the only way. I'm afraid if I try to do it in person, I'll lose my nerve or make a fool of myself.

Okay, here goes:

I love you.

I know it sounds crazy. I know you must be wondering who this crazy person is, popping up out of nowhere to crash into your life and tell you something like that, something that doesn't make the least bit of sense. And of course I know you can't possibly love me back, so don't think that I want you to say it, or feel it. You probably never will.

But I had to tell you, just in case there's a chance.

I just can't help feeling like you and I are meant to be together. Whenever I see you, I feel like I can't even breathe, or think straight, and my heart starts beating like crazy.

So I was thinking maybe we could at least talk. It's a start, right? I'll look for you tomorrow morning at eight, in the school auditorium. Nobody else should be in there at that hour. If you show up, we can talk. If you don't, I'll know that it means I should just drop this whole thing and get over you.

I hope I see you there, Sam. I'll be waiting.

Sincerely,

Meg Addams

Funny, Sam thinks, that she signed it so formally, with her last name. As if there could be any other Meg in his life.

Strange, too, that she wants him to meet her in the auditorium at school. Why not here? Or at her place?

Privacy, he realizes. And she's right about nobody else being in the auditorium at that hour on a Saturday. Even on weekday mornings when school is in session, nobody ever uses that room until afternoon assemblies. It's always been that way.

Sam carefully folds the papers together again and slips them back into the envelope, then glances at the clock.

It's past seven now. He swings his legs over the edge of the bed. There's no way he isn't going to show.

Meg knocks on Cosette's door.

No response.

She knocks louder.

Still no response.

She opens the door and sticks her head in. Sure enough, her daughter is still in bed, the covers pulled over her head.

"Cosette?" she calls, wishing she didn't have to wake her. She had a late night, and it was full of ups and downs.

There was a cast party after the show at Evan Stein's house. Ben was there, of course, and so was Meryl. They spent a lot of time together—furtively, though, as if they were both aware of Cosette's feelings. She, however, alternated between glowering at them and flirting with Evan, who's cute and funny and artistic. Not a bad way to get over Ben, Meg wanted to point out to her daughter— but that would surely send her running in the opposite direction.

"What do you want?" Cosette grumbles, as Meg shakes her a little.

"Have you seen my tote bag?"

"Huh?"

"My tote bag. I remember sticking it into the car after the show, but I can't find it anywhere."

"It's probably still in the car."

"It's not. I checked. And I could swear I remember carrying it into the house when we got home from the party."

"That was the middle of the night. You were probably half-asleep. You must have stuck it somewhere and forgotten."

"I've looked everywhere."

"Well, I don't know where it is." Cosette pulls the covers over her head again.

Meg is stumped.

She must have left it at school, then.

But I distinctly remember bringing it into the house.

She does, because she was thinking she wanted to open that letter she had written to Sam all those years ago.

Then, too exhausted even to see straight, she decided it could wait until morning. She hung the bag on her bedpost and went to sleep.

The letter was the first thing she went for this morning when she rolled out of bed. Now it—and the bag it was in—are nowhere to be found.

"I'm going over to the school to look for it," she tells Cosette, who mumbles a muffled reply.

Outside, she hurries down the front steps toward the car, her mind on the zillion things she has to do today.

She's giving two voice lessons later this morning, then Cosette has a soccer game, then the show . . .

"Meg! That was great, last night!"

She looks up to see Katie waving at her from the steps of Sam's house next door.

"I'm glad you liked it," she calls back. "Ben did a good job, didn't he?"

"He did. C'm'ere, I have to show you something."

Meg crosses the lawn hurriedly, glad Sam's car isn't in the driveway. At least she won't run the risk of seeing him unexpectedly.

"What is it?" she asks Katie, who's got an open book on her lap. Rover is curled up at her side.

"It's a scrapbook, see? I've been keeping it for years. I just put the program from the show in it, and I'm going to cut out the write-up that's going to be in the paper about it and put that in, too."

"That's great, Katie. Maybe when you're older you'll want to be in a musical."

"Maybe just a play. I'm not a good singer. That was my mom's thing. And Ben's. I have Dad's voice." She makes a face.

Meg can't help but laugh.

"I'm serious. When I was little and we used to go Christmas caroling, Ben said he and Mom used to try and sing really loud to drown us out. Want to see a picture?" She quickly flips the album pages backward, then settles on a page back at the beginning and tilts it for Meg to see.

She finds herself looking at a group shot of people bundled in coats and scarves, standing against a snowy backdrop. Scanning the smiling, cold-nipped faces, she picks out a much younger Sam with an adorable little girl in his arms . . .

"Is that you?" she asks Katie.

"That's me. And here's Ben, and here's my mom." She points.

Meg leans in to get a better look . . . and gasps in shock.

She recognizes Ben's little-boy face. She'd know it anywhere.

But she also recognizes the woman holding his hand, smiling into the camera.

It's the same woman Meg saw in her bedroom in the middle of the night.

Sam sits anxiously on the edge of the stage, his legs dangling over, swinging back and forth.

It's ten after eight. How long is he supposed to wait here for Meg?

The longer he waits, the more nervous he gets.

What is he going to do when she gets here? What is he going to say?

I'll let her do the talking, he decides, standing to pace the stage again. *After all, this was her idea.*

Yeah, and you're glad she came up with it.

If she hadn't written that letter, spilling her true feelings to him . . .

Well, this silly charade probably would have gone on indefinitely.

But she made the bold first move to end it, and he's grateful. Her feelings are out in the open, and his will be, too . . .

If she would just hurry up and get here.

Sam continues to pace, then sit and dangle, then pace again.

What if she doesn't show up?

Of course she'll show up. This was her idea.

Well, what if she changed her mind?

Finally, just when he's reluctantly wondering if he should start thinking about leaving, the auditorium door swings open.

His breath catches in his throat. Meg stands framed in the doorway.

For a moment, it's as if she doesn't see him at all. She seems to be looking around for something. Then she steps into the room, letting the door close behind her, and starts down the aisle.

"Sam?" She stops short.

She's surprised to see me, he realizes. *She thought I wasn't going to show. She thought I didn't feel the same way.*

He hurries up the aisle to where she stands, and before she can say another word, he takes her into his arms and kisses her.

When at last they break apart, Meg looks up at him in wonder . . . and shock.

"I love you," he tells her in a rush, sensing her vulnerability, needing to know that her feelings are mutual.

"You . . . do?"

He nods ardently. "It scares the hell out of me to admit it, but it's true. I love you."

"Sam . . ." Her eyes are glistening with tears. "My God, I can't believe you're standing here saying this to me."

"That's how I felt when I read your letter."

There's a pause.

She looks confused. "My letter?"

"Somebody found it and gave it to me . . . you must have dropped it and thought you'd mailed it, or something . . ." He trails off, realizing she looks horrified.

"You read that letter?"

He nods slowly. "You did write it . . . didn't you?"

"I definitely wrote it. But I never meant for you to see it."

"I'm glad I did," he says gently. "If I hadn't— Anyway . . . you're here. Just like you said you'd be. And so am I. Because I don't want to just drop this and forget it. I want to give it a chance."

"You . . . do?"

He nods. "Don't you?"

She hesitates.

He holds his breath.

Looking into Sam's eyes, Meg is torn. She should tell him the truth about the letter that somehow found its way into his hands.

And she will tell him. Someday.

But not right yet.

Nor will she tell him that they seem to have an otherworldly matchmaker.

Not now, maybe not ever.

Sam, after all, doesn't believe in ghosts.

But Meg does. There isn't a doubt in her mind that the spirit of his late wife has been hanging around her house, scaring people away so that Meg could move in, manipulating her destiny, and Sam's. Meg will never question whether she has Sheryl's blessing to love the man—and the children—she left behind.

She knows.

"Meg," Sam says, his voice strained, "you've got to tell me if you still want to give us a chance."

"Yes. I do."

"So you meant what you said in the letter, then?"

She nods. "I guess I just . . . forgot for a minute there. But now I remember. And I meant every word of it."

"Even the three most important ones?"

"Especially those." She takes a deep breath. "I love you, Sam."

"That's four words."

"I've never been very good at math."

"That's what you said about science."

He's right, I did say that, she realizes, remembering that she said it the first day they met, back in August.

Remembering how the strange sound upstairs and the disembodied footsteps downstairs propelled them into each other's arms that night.

Remembering that afterward, she promised herself she wouldn't let him break her heart.

And now, here she is, in his arms, looking into his eyes.

"Butterflies," she murmurs.

"What?"

She smiles. "Nothing. I was just thinking about butter-flies . . . and bees."

"Isn't it birds and bees?"

"That, too," she says with a laugh.

Then he kisses her, and she feels that familiar flutter.

Butterflies, she thinks contentedly. *Definitely butterflies.*

Epilogue

"Whose brilliant idea was an August wedding, anyway?" Geoffrey grumbles, wiping a stream of sweat from his brow.

"It was either this, or wait until Christmas, remember?" Meg tells him, picking up her bouquet. "Otherwise, Cosette and Ben wouldn't be able to be here. And the weather is too iffy at that time of year."

In a few days, her daughter will be starting her freshman year at Berkeley, a continent away. A few days after that, Sam's son will be headed to Duke.

After their brief romantic fling when they first met, the two of them quickly morphed into a sibling relationship, as did Cosette and Katie.

One big happy family, Meg thinks whenever she looks at the three of them together—Cosette no longer an only child. No longer fatherless. Sam stepped as easily into the role as Meg's ex stepped out of it, treating Cosette just as he does his own daughter.

"Listen," Geoffrey says, still stuck on the weather, "I'll take a blizzard over this heat and humidity any day."

Okay, so it is a little warm here in the kitchen of Sam's house—*my house, too, now,* Meg reminds herself.

Yesterday, she officially signed over the home next door—the old Duckworth place—to the Shaws, a young couple from the city. He's a bond trader. She's a corporate vice president—and pregnant. Someday, she'll be a working mom, a stay-at-home mom—or a Fancy Mom who runs her children's lives like she runs her company.

One thing is certain: the Shaws won't be driven out of their new house by things that go bump in the night.

Meg's last contact with the resident ghost was the morning her tote bag inexplicably disappeared, sending her back to the school on a fruitless search for it.

Of course, it was hanging on her bedpost at home when she got back, just where she could have sworn she'd left it. Just where she'd looked for it repeatedly.

But if she hadn't had a reason to go back to the school, she wouldn't have found Sam there, waiting to tell her that he loved her. If she hadn't shown up, he probably would have assumed she had changed her mind, and left.

So it was fate.

Fate, Meg believes, helped along by something supernatural.

Katie is the only one who knows about that. She confessed one night not long after Meg and Sam got engaged that she had occasionally seen her mother sitting on her bed in the middle of the night, as if watching over her.

"Please don't tell my dad, though. He might get upset, or he won't believe me. Nobody does."

"I do." Meg told her then that she, too, had seen Katie's mother.

"She was trying to tell you she wanted you and Dad to be together. That's what I think."

That's what Meg thinks, too.

And here we are, on our wedding day.

"I just wish you had let me throw you a fancy wedding somewhere in the city," says Geoffrey, newly wealthy thanks to his unexpected success as a regular in a sitcom that became a smash hit last fall. "Someplace *air-conditioned,*" he adds pointedly, mopping his brow.

"That's sweet of you, but we wanted to get married right here at home, in the garden." Meg glances at the backyard setting, beyond the blooming geraniums on the windowsill. She spots Chita Rivera walking along a branch in the maple tree as if bent on getting a prime vantage point for the proceedings. Beneath the tree, Rover—dashingly dressed by his master in a black bow tie for the occasion— dozes in a patch of shade.

On the lawn, rows of white-draped chairs wait expectantly on either side of a grassy aisle. A flower-and-ivy-decked arch has been set up beneath the maple tree. The first guests have begun to arrive. There's Olympia Flickinger, with Brad and Sophie, sailing into a prime seat in the front row. They've grown on Meg and while they'll never be her closest friends, they're an intrinsic part of the community—and her new life here.

Meg smiles, watching Sam's brother Jack, the head usher, lean in to tell Olympia those seats are reserved for Meg's parents.

Displaying her personal trademark blend of pique tempered by impeccable breeding, Olympia allows herself to be steered into the second row, where Jenny and Gary already have the seats closest to the aisle there. Amused,

Meg watches Olympia attempt to convince them to move in and let her have the aisle.

To their credit, Jenny and Gary hold their ground, and the Flickingers move somewhat huffily on down the row.

All right, so some things never change.

Luckily, some things do.

Fifteen minutes later, Meg is on her father's arm, stepping out the back door into the hot August sunshine.

Katie and Cosette are in front of her in their pastel bridesmaid's dresses, slowly making their way, single file, down the aisle.

Sam is up there somewhere, Meg knows, flanked by his son and his brother, waiting for her.

Ben's girlfriend Meryl, the soloist, begins to sing an a capella rendition of "As If We've Never Said Good-bye."

As she and her father walk down the lush green aisle, Meg takes in the familiar faces beaming at her. A few are old friends from the city, most are new friends—oh, and a couple of old friends, like Bill Dreyfus, and Kris—from right here in town.

In these past two years, Glenhaven Park has become familiar once again. She's grown accustomed to the traffic and new stores and restaurants; even to the Fancy Moms. She'll never be one of them, teaching voice and married to a schoolteacher, and she wouldn't want to be. But she's met plenty of other down-to-earth moms. She's not lonely anymore.

A telltale buzzing sound becomes audible above the singing. Meg's bouquet of white roses trembles in her hand when she looks down to see a fat August bumblebee lazily hovering above the sweet-smelling blooms.

Still walking, her smile frozen on her face, Meg watches it with trepidation.

Please go away. Shoo. Get out of here.

But she doesn't dare drop the bouquet and run away in hysterics, the way she ordinarily would. Not with all these people looking at her. Not on this day she's been waiting for all her life.

Ignoring her silent plea, the bee sniffs around the flowers. Then it flies on without incident.

Meg relaxes.

It didn't sting her.

Everything is okay. She's okay.

She looks up and catches a glimpse of Sam at the end of the aisle, waiting for her, about to become her husband.

Everything is going to be better than okay, from now on.

Sam smiles, and she wants to run into his arms.

She forces herself to walk, though. To savor this moment, being Sam's bride, on the verge of building a new life together.

It's going to be wonderful, Sam. Just the way I always knew it would be, all those years ago.

Joy ripples through her and her pace quickens. She can't help it. She's been waiting so long for this; too long.

When she reaches his side at last, her father places her hand in his, and Sam gives it a squeeze.

"Are you ready?" he whispers, for her ears alone.

"Are you kidding? Yes."

Looking into his eyes as they laugh softly together, Meg knows she's come home at last.

About the Author

"Wendy Markham" is a pseudonym for *New York Times* bestselling author Wendy Corsi Staub, who has won several awards, including RWA's "Rita," and published more than sixty novels under her own name and various pseudonyms. A happily married mother of two, she lives in an old house in a picturesque New York City suburb very much like the fictional Glenhaven Park. There, she is surrounded by Soccer Moms, Yoga moms, yes, a couple of Fancy Moms, and perhaps even a resident ghost or two—but most importantly, a wonderful network of cherished friends and neighbors. Wendy loves to hear from readers, so be sure to sign her Web site guestbook at www.wendymarkham.com or write to her at corsistaub@aol.com!

THE DISH

Where authors give you the inside scoop!

♥ ♥ ♥ ♥ ♥ ♥ ♥ ♥ ♥ ♥ ♥ ♥ ♥ ♥

From the desk of Michelle Rowen

Dear Reader,

I have a confession to make.

Sarah Dearly, the main character from my novels BITTEN & SMITTEN and FANGED & FABULOUS (on sale now), thinks she's in control, and she is!

When I first conceived of my book about an "everygal" who becomes a vampire after a blind date from hell, Sarah was just a bookworm introvert who longed for a more exciting life. But as soon as I started writing, she let me know that she was no bookworm. More of a DVD aficionado with a love of fashion who uses sarcasm as her greatest weapon. And, she liked her life just fine the way it was.

She had two guys to choose from in the first book *Bitten & Smitten*. I said, "Hey, Sarah, you're going to end up with Cute Guy #1." And she said, "No, I want Cute Guy #2." I told her I was planning to kill him at the end. She then kicked up a huge fuss claiming that "she loved him," so I let him live because he was just too hot to die.

Then I got the chance to continue her story in

Fanged & Fabulous. Sarah still wants to do things differently than I had planned. And she still has a very specific idea of who she wants to end up with. She thinks that since I put her through so much stress, life-threatening situations, and the fact that as a vampire she has to drink blood (which is a totally gross concept), that I "owe her."

Stubborn characters. Sheesh.

Now if you'll excuse me, the men in white coats have arrived to take me away.

Happy Reading!

Michelle Rowen

www.michellerowen.com

♥ ♥ ♥ ♥ ♥ ♥ ♥ ♥ ♥ ♥ ♥ ♥ ♥ ♥ ♥ ♥

From the desk of Wendy Markham

It's just an hour from New York, but for newly transplanted Manhattanite Meg Addams from LOVE, SUBURBAN STYLE (on sale now), suburban Glenhaven Park feels as challenging—and remote—as the northern Adirondacks. So our heroine adapted the following handy resource:

~~Wilderness~~ Suburban Survival Guide

Even the most savvy ~~hiker~~ single mom can wind up stranded in the middle of nowhere. Be prepared to combat any of these commonly found ~~wilderness~~ suburban threats:

Predators

You never know what creatures might lurk in ~~the forest~~ Starbucks or ~~stream~~ in the soccer field bleachers: venomous ~~snakes~~ snobs, cunning ~~coyote~~ yoga moms, or maybe even a ferocious ~~bear~~ PMS victim. Just remember, if you don't bother it, it won't bother you. But if all else fails, ~~run!~~ offer chocolate, preferably Godiva.

Hunger and Thirst

Foraging may yield ~~mushrooms~~ decent pizza or ~~berries~~ a diner that serves cheeseburgers (just make sure they're not ~~poisonous~~ made of soy). Remember, ~~insects~~ tofu burgers and even ~~grubs~~ low-fat veggie-sprout sandwich wraps may be unappetizing, but they are edible. With luck, you'll find a ~~stream~~ friendly local pub nearby, where you can indulge in plenty of life-sustaining ~~water~~ frozen margaritas.

Loneliness and Isolation

Being alone in ~~the wilderness~~ a rundown fixer-upper with only ~~wildlife~~ a moody teenager for company can drive anyone crazy. It's crucial to ~~keep your mind and body active~~ turn to your nearest neighbor for adult companionship, even if he is your unrequited high school crush.

Cold

Perhaps ~~exposure~~ a broken heart is the most dangerous threat of all. Before embarking on a ~~wilderness adventure~~ new romance, always learn how to create a spark, and gradually, without smothering the flames, build a fire that will burn indefinitely.

If you follow this guide, not only will you survive ~~the wilderness~~ suburbia; you might even ~~thrive~~ fall in love with the dad next door!

Happy Reading!

[signature]

www.wendycorsistaub.com

♥ ♥ ♥ ♥ ♥ ♥ ♥ ♥ ♥ ♥ ♥ ♥ ♥ ♥ ♥

From the desk of Jane Graves

Dear Reader,

Maybe I shouldn't admit this, but I love torturing my characters. That sounds sadistic, but let's face it. Watching polite people in ordinary situations be sweetie-nice to each other is a bore. Watching strong people face challenges and overcoming them—now, *that's* entertaining. After all, would we watch all that reality TV if everybody got along?

Here's another truth: My characters don't think what's happening to them is funny, but trust me, it is. Did Lucy Ricardo think it was funny when she was trying to make candy, but the conveyor belt went so fast she couldn't keep up? No! Did Bill Murray's character in *Groundhog Day* think it was funny when every day was *not* a new day? No! But, we laughed, didn't we?

Darcy McDaniel, the heroine of HOT WHEELS AND HIGH HEELS (on sale now), is facing the biggest challenge of her life. Her wealthy husband sends her on a vacation with a friend and, in her absence, cleans out their bank accounts, sells their house, and disappears.

Darcy is terrified of being destitute, but tough times call for tough measures. When ex-cop turned repo man John Stark repossesses her beloved Mercedes, she starts working for her sexy adversary with the goal of moving from receptionist to repo agent so she can make some decent money. Though, John refuses to turn a spoiled ex-trophy wife loose to legally steal cars, and soon, their battle of wits and sexual one-upsmanship burn hotter than a bonfire out of control.

I require all my characters to have one quality: No matter how hard they're hit, they get back up again. And, the results will leave you laughing. Pick up a copy of HOT WHEELS AND HIGH HEELS, and ride along with John and Darcy on their rocky road to happily ever after!

Enjoy!

Jane Graves

www.janegraves.com